CLOUDS
LIKE
BLACK DOGS

To my parents
Peter and Lyn
and to
Jean Parker,
for Langebaan

CLOUDS LIKE BLACK DOGS

GRAHAM LANG

JONATHAN BALL PUBLISHERS
JOHANNESBURG & CAPE TOWN

The author would like to gratefully acknowledge the support of the Research Management Committee of the University of Newcastle, Australia. Sincere thanks are also due to the following individuals: Doctor Moosa Motara from Rhodes University for his memories of campus politics, and Barry Feinberg and Robin Malan for their belief in this novel and their invaluable advice.

Although this story takes place within a recognisable historical context, all of its characters are products of the author's imagination and are not intended to resemble any living person. Any such resemblance, therefore, is coincidental.

Extract from *The Flowers that I Left in the Ground*, by Leonard Cohen
From: *Poems 1956-1968*,
Published by Jonathan Cape
Reprinted by permission of The Random House Group Ltd

Published in 2003 in trade paperback by
JONATHAN BALL PUBLISHERS (PTY) LTD
P O Box 33977
Jeppestown
2043

ISBN 1 86842 164 3

Design by Michael Barnett
Cover photograph by Graham Lang
Digital manipulation of cover image and
reproduction and typesetting of cover
by Triple M Design & Advertising, Johannesburg
Typesetting and reproduction of text by Alinea Studio, Cape Town
Printed and bound by CTP Book Printers, Cape

CONTENTS

The flowers that I left in the ground,
That I did not gather for you,
Today I bring them all back,
To let them grow forever,
Not in poems or marble,
But where they fell and rotted.

Leonard Cohen

QUESTIONS

1 THE QUESTION OF ORIGIN

We have travelled far to come to this cottage which lies along the upper reaches of the windswept lagoon. Helen slept for most of the journey, lying curled up on the back seat of the car, her head resting on John's lap. She awoke only when I turned onto the rough overgrown road that leads down to the water. I watched her sit up and stare wide-eyed at the bleak wilderness around her.

Zelda stared too. But without the wonder.

We arrived in the evening, almost a month ago. Short, cold gusts were blowing across the lagoon, bringing with them a clinging drizzle and the faint smell of guano from the islands, Meeuw and Schaapen. As I stopped the car outside the cottage John got out and limped off into the veld. Zelda told me he can't stand being cooped up for too long. Much to my annoyance Helen has rather taken to him and she called out, John … John? He hesitated and looked back with his flat impenetrable stare, then went on. So we followed him in the clinging drizzle up the hill. Helen quickly tired of pushing her way through the wet brush so I lifted her up on my shoulders. We plodded on after John, our boots releasing a pungent odour from the wet earth. Above, the clouds were dark and heavy, about to burst.

From the crest of the hill we gazed across the lagoon. We could see the ghostly forms of sandsharks drifting slowly through the green shallows. The deep water was dark and flurried and far off the lights of Churchhaven twinkled in the gathering darkness. The village of Langebaan lay a few miles north. There were gulls wheeling and soaring above the grey houses, their sharp cries audible to us through the wind.

I stood with Helen on my shoulders, arms outstretched, silhouetted against the sky. Helen waved her arms and laughed and yelled, her small teeth and fat cheeks glowing. Together, against the sky, we were a shouting, ragged scarecrow. I breathed in gusts of cold air into my lungs, bellowing madly as

I exhaled. I snorted and crowed. Ja, for a precious instant I was free, a ragged, dancing scarecrow clicking its heels, the air aloud with berserk squawks. Zelda and John stood and watched. Helen giggled helplessly as I squawked and leapt. She screamed and gripped my hair with her hands. And then Zelda began to laugh too, her round spectacles reflecting the breaking sky. I took her in my arms and we danced around in circles. I embraced her. I kissed her. Helen's eyes were wide with wonder at this special moment. A special moment indeed, for we held each other with an elusive tenderness. Zelda has been sorely tested over the years, but she has a weakness for my crazy side.

Zelda reached out an arm for John. Join us, her eyes implored. Savour the moment with us. But he shook his head and looked away, hiding the edges of a strange, bitter smile. Her brother, her twin. So different, so distant. It was a small victory for me, but the strangeness in his smile left me uneasy and I stopped playing the fool. Then, without a word, he turned and started back down the hill towards the cottage. My euphoria dried up like water on a hot stone.

Zelda raised her arms and dropped them, as she so often does: 'I don't know if we've done the right thing, coming here.'

'It was your idea,' I replied.

'I know. I thought it'd be good to get away from everything. What else could we do?'

I followed her gaze past the cottage towards the Groothuis, just visible behind a row of gum trees. 'Is that the old man's house?' she asked.

'Ja, that's Tak's place.'

'Will he mind us being here?'

'I don't know.'

'I thought he was like a father to you.'

'Not really. The line between master and servant was always there. He paid for my education, that's all.'

Zelda sighed. 'Everything's so bloody complex.'

'Especially with John around.'

Zelda gave me a hard look. 'John needs me, Manas. Please don't cause trouble, okay?'

Such has been the state of things since we arrived.

Adversaries forced upon each other by our love for Zelda. By saying we've travelled far, I mean in ourselves. John, probably, has come the furthest, if I'm to gauge personal distances. At first I thought it sacrilege for him to come here, to the place of my childhood, but I was in no shape to argue. And on the surface he's been no trouble really. Each day he works from dawn to dusk on the old Cape rowing boat that belonged to my grandfather. Already he's knocked out the rotted timbers and replaced them, to what purpose God only knows. One can only surmise why he labours thus, for John doesn't talk much. I watch him, knowing the struggle within him and sometimes I see wings protrude through the bars of his prejudice. Sometimes he even takes off, shakily, only to crash down again, brought to earth by an inability to transcend his skin ... God, everything reverts to skin. John's sweat and toil is surely a purgation; it's his way of coming to terms with the bleak consequences of duty. I pity him (and I fear him) as silently he gets on with his task, his flat brown stare concealing a bitter hatred of me, and more than a brotherly love for Zelda.

Zelda, too, has come a long way. From her distant Eastern Cape farm, she saw beyond her horizons, beyond herself. The lover of a coloured man. The mother of our child, Helen.

Zelda nurses us all through our phases of immaturity ...

This tip of Africa is immersed in winter. It has rained for most of the time, confining Zelda, Helen and me to the cottage. Only John braves the outdoors as he works on the boat, killing time. Today it's colder than usual. It must be snowing on the mountains inland. A weak green light breaks through the clouds in the east. Zelda and Helen are sleeping in the room nearby. Zelda loathes the rainy southern winter. I know she longs for warmer climes. I know she longs for the farm, but now she's stuck with us and each day she learns another lesson in futility. So she sleeps away the winter, her snores rasping in a dark room filled with my ghosts. Of course, Helen follows her mother's example. Sometimes I hear their wings flutter and their cages clang against the walls.

Having spoken of personal journeys, I should say a real one awaits us also. In a few weeks we (Zelda, Helen and I) are supposed to be leaving for Australia. That's the plan. Every-thing is in order; our fares have been paid, our papers are ready. Everything, that is, except ourselves. Zelda says she wants to be with John during this crucial period of waiting. She knows the thought of us (I should say, her) leaving does not sit well with him. She's scared he might retreat further into himself. Until yesterday I'd been sure of her commitment to leaving. But now I sense she's deciding between the two of us, and my drunken binge last night won't have helped my case.

Zelda and I have become less obsessive about South Africa's descent into anarchy, but at seven every evening, after Helen has been put to bed, we listen to the news on the radio. John listens too, looking indifferent enough as he sits next to the fire. The unrest is much in the news, but beyond the cagey announcements of the SABC there's nothing to suggest an end to the violence that has wracked the country and cost so many lives. Nothing except the increasingly desperate security meas-ures that are always the sign of impending collapse.

Last night, aside from the usual biased reports on the machi-nations of the Tricameral Parliament and slurs on people like Desmond Tutu, we heard about investigations into 'alleged' police death squads, more bombs in Johannesburg and Durban, the death toll rising in the townships around Pietermaritzburg, an off-duty policeman and his girlfriend beaten and burned to death in Tembisa. The country drags itself along like a dying beast.

Not realising she would fan the flames of a closer struggle, Zelda said, 'Oh God, this country's such a mess. Sometimes I'm glad we're leaving. It'd be nice to hear news that's not about people hacking each other to death for a change.'

'You won't have to in Australia,' I said.

Zelda shook her head. 'I really despair, you know. It's so bloody hopeless … so endless. And the damn government blames everyone else, don't they? Communists, terrorists, jour-nalists, interfering foreigners. Couldn't be our beloved National Party now, could it?'

Ordinarily I know the futility of talking politics, but with John present I couldn't restrain myself. 'You can't only blame the Nats,' I argued. 'They're just the voice of their people. You whites voted them into power.'

John just looked at me and sighed, as if bored.

'What whites are you talking about?' Zelda went on. 'You whites – come on! They're not the voice of all whites, Manas. They certainly don't speak for me.'

'Just making a point. You can't always blame the government. Don't forget, the Nats have increased their majority, which means it's not only die-hard Afrikaners voting for them. Ja, it's you English as well – in your droves! So what does that say to black South Africans, hey?'

'That's what scares me most. It's got to the point where it doesn't matter what the hell your beliefs are. In the end we'll be judged by our skin. It's so bloody stupid. What do you make of it, John?'

'Make of what, Zed?'

Getting anything out of him is like drawing blood from a stone. Zelda threw up her hands. 'Why can't you just answer? You know what I mean.'

'Ask Manas. He's got all the answers.'

'I'm asking your opinion.'

'You know we shouldn't talk politics, Zed.'

'I just want an opinion.'

'I don't want to argue with you.'

'Oh, for Christ sake … we don't have to argue!'

'You know we always do.'

'John … I won't argue, damn it!'

John assumed a patient air. 'Okay, if you really want to know. I think it's our colonial destiny. We were always minority occupiers among a dispossessed majority. So we're ending up where we were destined to end. Flat on our arses, with our teeth kicked in. Beaten and powerless. It could never have been any different.'

'Of course it could've been different.'

'That's my opinion, Zed. You said you wouldn't argue.'

'Okay, but it could've been different if only we'd been more giving. If the whites had shared more in the past, things wouldn't have got so bad.'

13

'Sharing was never an option. It's always been us or them. The conflict's about power and possession. You don't just walk into someone's house and take it over as your own, then ask him to share it with you.'

'God, you see things in such absolute terms! It's not only about power, you know.'

'Of course it is.'

'Don't be so blind, John. It's not just a question of us and them. It's about being human ... about good prevailing.'

John laughed bitterly. 'Good prevailing, hey? You're the one who's bitching about the violence. You're the one who's leaving the bloody country because you reckon the kaffirs can't see past the colour of our skins.'

'Don't twist what I say.'

'Then why are you leaving, Zed? When there's so much good prevailing?'

Zelda raised her voice. 'The vast majority of people in this country are tolerant and humane. They just want a say ...'

'Oh, is that why South Africa's so peaceful and secure?'

I interjected. 'No, John, we're leaving because it's not the tolerant and humane majority calling the shots in this country. It's the violent ones who cause all the shit, like the ones in the police and army who shoot innocent civilians, who torture and murder, who turn people against their own. They're the ones destroying the future for everyone else. You should know that, John. Better than most.'

John gave me a level stare, then shrugged. 'You asked my opinion, Zed. Told you Manas knows it all.'

I smiled. 'I'm surprised you're still so defiant, John. It's hard to let go, hey?'

'Let go of what, you smug prick?'

'The paranoid, power-obsessed beliefs of white South Africans, that's what. A group separate and superior to others.'

'Don't get too smart, Manas. I'm not hanging onto anything.'

'Then why are you so frightened?'

Zelda raised her arms and dropped them. 'Oh please, Manas! We were having a general discussion, for God's sake! I didn't ask you to get personal.'

14

'He makes it personal, Zelda.'

John cut in. 'Frightened? Who said I'm frightened? Sick, yes. Sick of watching you fuck up my sister's life. Sick of you, yes.'

'Admit it, John, you're frightened. Everything you believed in has fallen apart.'

'Fuck off, Manas.'

'You're frightened, John. Shit-scared of what's coming.'

I saw the hatred leap into his eyes and knew I'd gone too far. He leaned towards me and for a few seconds I thought he was going to hit me. I felt a surge of fear. I still bear the scar across my nose from the last time he struck me. But, to my relief, he sat back again, knowing who the frightened one was. There was a long silence. I could see Zelda was furious. Then he got up and went to his room, shutting the door behind him.

'You like to rub it in, don't you?' Zelda said.

I didn't answer.

'I wish you'd lay off, Manas. I hate it when you do that.'

'He asked for it, Zelda. What right's he got to question you for leaving?'

'You know it goes deeper than that. I hate it when you bait him. I see the worst side of you when you do it. Worse than when you drink. It's deliberate. It makes me question whether I'm doing the right thing going to Australia with you.'

'Looking for any excuse not to go, aren't you?'

'What?'

'You always take his side, Zelda!'

'He's got a lot to deal with, you know. And you don't help by rubbing it in.'

'Okay, I'm sorry.'

'Sorry doesn't help. Think before you open your big mouth. He's not stupid, Manas. Just remember that.'

I just nodded. With Zelda I always admit defeat.

She got up and went to bed. I sat alone and smoked a few cigarettes, angry with them and myself. And when the anger wouldn't subside, I, who'd solemnly promised not to, walked out through the rainy night to the village, found a bar in the coloured township and got blind drunk. I did it knowing how much was at stake. Such is my nature. I vaguely remember vomiting when I got home. Kneeling before the lavatory. Wild, uncontrolled retching. Ja, worshipping before my altar, singing psalms ...

That was last night. Today there will be repercussions, for sure. From where I sit next to the window I can see John down below on the slipway, working on the boat. Dressed in an army raincoat he scrapes and hammers at the old hulk. Every so often he sits back on a bench to assess his progress and rest his leg. It never ceases to amaze me that he lay side by side with Zelda in his mother's womb. They are so different in their ways, their beliefs, even in their looks. Zelda's eyes have the blueness of horizons; his have the sullen darkness of tombs. And yet they are bound together by a love I cannot fathom. They need each other. They will always need each other.

I wonder what occupies his thoughts. Surely not just the mundane imperfections of the boat, although, admittedly, his workmanship shows no evidence of a wayward mind. No, surely from time to time his mind strays from the dull monotony of the physical task at hand and he is besieged by the terrible thing that turned his life upside down. There are many in this country who have stories of violence to tell. Some, like John, more than others. But John doesn't talk much. He just broods, mostly. And, no doubt, the night of death visits him in his unguarded moments. That long, loud night in the township where, as a young army lieutenant, filled with the conviction that he was there to protect and preserve the last precious pocket of civilisation in barbaric Africa, he presided over the killing of civilians. Where he, injured and frightened, ordered his men to open fire on a crowd of people, and where he, when he beheld the ensuing carnage, screamed at his men to stop, but to no avail. The madness had taken hold. A final body count of thirty-two. An impressive night's work, even by South African standards. And the next day he was the centre of outrage and condemnation. God knows what effect it had on him. As I say, he hides his feelings and one can only surmise. Fucking Neanderthal. See how his silence poisons me!

*

16

My mother loved the spring flowers that formed such a contrast to the desolate land. Their colours were like moisture to a parched mind, was the way she put it. Forever in my mind are the pink and white weeskindertjies and yellow vygies that she arranged on the window ledges. She could also not resist the occasional pieces of driftwood that washed up on the beaches, flotsam white from sun and salt. She found their eroded shapes very beautiful. As the months went by these pieces would collect in the corner next to the hearth until the winter when they'd be used as firewood. When I think of my father I'm tempted to say she was drawn to things that drifted. She liked to provide a home for flotsam. Ja, I remember her face so well. That look of resigned regret as she surrendered each piece to the flames, as though it were a sad waste. And I saw things differently then. I saw the hope in her sacrifice. Staring into the flames I saw beautiful patterns and colours, different from those given off by the ordinary wood we burned, such as gum or rooikrans. Enraptured, I dared to dream of perfect worlds.

The darkness of my home was lit by the strange blues and oranges of salt and sun-drenched wood. The face of Jesus was also lit by these colours. He existed in a cheap picture that hung on the wall above the kitchen table. The fleeting impression I have so often when I think of her: eyes closed as she whispers her prayers beneath the face of Jesus, her small, calloused hands clasped together. Appearing on the window ledge behind her, spring flowers in worn and faded rum bottles that once belonged to sailors of old. And God's sculptures, eroded and imperfect, burning on the hearth. Special patterns and colours, providing the cottage with its small share of beauty. The snatch of a song as she sweeps up the crumbs from under the table. Above her, Jesus looks down like a blue-eyed pop musician, a product of the hippy era.

And later: a withered remnant, eyes disturbed by a growing darkness as she meets the stare of Jesus, her heart ransacked …

But these arbitrary thoughts mean nothing, attached as they are to mere whim. For the sake of clarity let me construct my history, piece by piece. Let me put things in their correct order. First, my name is Manas Smith. I inherited the common English surname from my father. He claimed to be the descendant of an English gentleman, but you could never believe a word he said. I'd have preferred to be called Roux, after my mother's people, for they are my true family. But such is my name, such is my life.

My mother's people were fisherfolk, the descendants of Cochoquas (the Khoi tribe around Langebaan) and footloose sailors who were washed up on these barren shores two centuries ago. No one knows exactly when this cottage was built. Before the time of farms and fences, my grandfather used to say. The building adheres to a rustic style seen in most old fishing villages in South Africa – a simple rectangular structure with an end chimney and buttresses on the walls. The rear and end walls are of stone; in the front a framework of wall posts was constructed and filled in with reeds and mud from the marshes.

For convenience, a few changes were made over the years. My grandfather knocked out a part of the front wall and added an enclosed stoep. He fitted new windows into the thick walls. After my father died of stupidity Tak had pipes laid from a spring to provide the home with running water. Before that my mother would carry water from the spring in a bucket each day. Tak also installed a wood stove in place of the old hearth and bakoond, and a new toilet with a septic tank. Such were my mother's terms.

It's been my wish to preserve the character of the place. I've re-thatched the roof with reeds from the marshes and whitewashed the walls. I've kept the brush and weeds from the door. I fulfilled this commitment out of a frail sense of honour, a respect for the humble history of my folk. I believed that one day I would own this place not only with my heart, for I was the first to be educated, the first with a chance to earn a living with my head, not my hands.

I believed beyond the realities of my country. Suffice it to say only the bones of dinosaurs and mammoths lie safely buried beneath me.

The open sandy ground on which the cottage stands belongs to a farm, Nooitgedacht, the most recent heir of which is Oubaas Tak Scheepers. Tak is the last in line of an old Afrikaner family, one which, in order of importance, boasted a Springbok rugby player and a National Party MP. The Scheepers', who already owned a wheat farm near Vredenburg, bought this land in 1909 as extra grazing for their sheep. Increasingly the family preferred Langebaan's tranquil shores to the bland wheat hills around Vredenburg, and eventually they built an imposing house in the traditional Cape Dutch style, with a curved front gable as the dominant architectural feature. The photographs that grace the passage walls of the Groothuis, as we coloureds called it, show a succession of dour family groupings on the steps beneath the Cape Dutch gable. Everyone in their Sunday best, the men in black suits and white ties, the women in ankle-length dresses and Voortrekker kappies. The children all look obedient and half-frozen. The boys' heads are cropped like sheep. No one smiles.

Ja, a respected God-fearing family that filled the front pew of the Dutch Reformed Church every Sunday. They all listened attentively as the dominee bellowed fire and brimstone from the pulpit and they all sang the hymns in solemn unison. Tak's uncle, the Springbok centre who was famed for his sidestep and fearless tackling, died of alcoholism in Johannesburg, a pathetic, tearful barfly, unable to face life on the grandstand. Tak's father, the politician, was imprisoned during the Second World War for acts of sabotage against the Smuts government. An ardent Nazi sympathiser, he blew up two bridges before being caught red-handed planting dynamite under a railway line outside Pietermaritzburg. His trial and internment later proved politically expedient, judging by the speed with which he rose through the National Party ranks. Even after a heart attack forced him into early retirement, he remained unrepentant about his wartime activities. Publicly, his fondness for racial doctrine was cleverly couched in policies that alluded to the 'spiritual and social upliftment' of the darker races. He became a remarkably persuasive architect of apartheid. Privately, the mask of upliftment was removed to reveal the surly contempt in which he held the mud people, as he referred to us. I never knew him, fortunately. He died before I was born and now resides, no doubt, in the Great White Homeland in the sky. But my mother used to tell me what he was like, how he always carried a sjambok and didn't hesitate to use it on any of our people who displeased him – man, woman or child.

Tak's parents married late and bore only one child, blessed, ironically, with a dark birthmark that covered the left side of his face. Rumour has it that his father covered his eyes and wept at first sight of the disfigurement, while his mother lapsed into a depression lasting several weeks. Both were at a loss to imagine what on earth they had done in God's eyes to incur such wrath. But in time they recovered and stoically accepted God's mysterious ways, while the local white community expressed their sympathy by never mentioning the issue. But poor Tak felt the silent stares and from early childhood was shy and reclusive. He had few friends and wasn't an exceptional scholar or athlete at school. To add to his woes his hair started going grey during his teens and by the time he was thirty it was completely white. This resulted in his nickname, Oubaas. Tak's Christian names were Tertius Adolph Koenraad – Tak for short – hence, everyone, white or coloured, addressed him as Oubaas Tak.

From Tak's reclusiveness there developed a fragile sensitivity that plagued all his social encounters. He wasn't one to mix easily, especially with females. Out of a desperate inferiority complex he was frequently rude and hostile towards those who tried to befriend him and eventually he was ostracised. Consequently, he never married and his parents died in sorrow, not knowing whether the final seed would multiply. Their concern, I suspect, was rooted not so much in Tak's wellbeing but in the fate of the farms. To the Afrikaner, land is more than wealth – it's a symbol of belonging, his right to Africa.

Jan Van Riebeek once said of Langebaan: 'There is no land in the whole world so barren and unblessed by the Lord

God.' A morose exaggeration, no doubt; more the biased criticism of a man used to the lush meadows of northern Europe. Nevertheless, Nooitgedacht had but limited farming potential. With a low winter rainfall and the vegetation consisting mostly of fynbos and dwarf succulents, the most it could sustain was sheep. Still, with their main income stemming from the wheat production of the other farm near Vredenburg, the Scheepers' were fairly prosperous. Always a tidy sum in the bank and not owing anything either. But when Tak took over times had changed. To meet the demands of the modern world farmers were urged to maximise their land's potential. Big business began to set the pace, encouraging farmers to spend money to make money. As a young man Tak was headstrong, eager to overcome his social ineptnesses by being successful. So he foolishly spent the family savings and even took out several Land Bank loans to finance the expansion of his wheat fields and the importation of feed for his burgeoning sheep flocks. All it took was a few years of drought and low wool and meat prices for Tak to find himself in serious debt. In the end, he was forced to sell the Vredenburg farm to pay off his creditors and only just managed to keep Nooitgedacht, which was never much of a going concern itself.

Up on the main road leading to the village there's a graveyard, one that commands a view of the whole expanse of the lagoon, from Saldanha to Churchhaven. A spectacular spot to be laid to rest, you might think. But despite the view it's a sad, bare place where countless tears haven't made the slightest impression on the stony ground. Exposed to the elements, the inscriptions on some of the gravestones are no longer legible but I know they belong to foreign sailors of long ago – men lying forgotten, thousands of miles from their homes in Europe. There's always a wind blowing up there, sounding like a crowd cheering as it filters through the leaves of the huge solitary gum tree beneath which lie the graves of my family.

Grouped together are the ones closest to me – my grandparents, my mother, my father ... lonely graves painfully

21

symbolic of our tenuous right to exist. I don't remember much about my grandparents. My grandmother, Hettie Roux, is just a faint image in the recesses of my mind, seated in a creaking rocking chair against the light of the window, shelling gooseberries, toothless and half blind. I remember she promised me wonderful things, when her ship came in. Her ship never came in. She died before my grandfather. I vaguely remember her funeral. It was the only time I ever saw tears in my grandfather's eyes.

I have a clearer image of my grandfather. Solomon Roux was a thickset man with fierce black eyebrows and hands that were hard and gnarled. From hearsay Oupa was robust and wise, set in the old ways and respected by all the lagoon folk. Certainly he was the most prominent member of the family that anyone could remember. He was one of the last of the old fishermen and his proudest possession was the twenty-foot boat in which he and a crew rowed out to harvest the cold Atlantic waters. I recall waiting with my mother on the beach as the men lugged Oupa's boat up above the high water mark after the day's fishing. The men grunted, hheeeup! as they lifted in unison, transporting the vessel a few feet at a time. Among them, my grandfather, the veins in his neck bulging with effort. He was not a man who was afraid of hard work.

He and my grandmother had three children, two sons and a daughter. I never knew the sons, my uncles. Neither had any desire to be fishermen. They knew that the big fishing fleets would soon monopolise the industry, leaving no place for people like my grandfather. And as neither had any inclination to work on the farm, both moved off before I was born. One went to Johannesburg where he died in an accident on the mines. The other went to Durban where he worked for a few years as a bus driver. He, too, met a premature end, stabbed to death by a thief as he walked home from night shift. As a result of their tragic misfortunes (which effectively emasculated the Roux family) my mother always harboured a terrible fear of the outside world, especially the cities. To her they were treacherous places, infested by cutthroats and thieves.

Oupa had just got over his sons' deaths when my father came into the picture. My father was a drifter, one foot on the road, the other in jail. A man with no history, no background. Oh, there was the boast of his English ancestry but you had to take that with a pinch of salt. He lied so much no one knew what to believe. Josiah Smith was his name (he pronounced the surname with just a touch of hot potato, insisting on pronouncing the *th*, while everyone else called us Smit) but somewhere down the track he picked up the nickname Bokkie, probably due to the thin goatee beard he sported. My mother, Sannie, was plump and pretty and fate decreed that they should meet. God only knows what she saw in him. He was not particularly handsome, nor did he possess any outstanding qualities, except maybe that incurable restlessness that is fatally attractive to women and which they strive, futilely, to cure.

Oupa saw the scoundrel in him immediately but his obvious contempt had little effect on my mother. She was under the reprobate's spell. And the contempt was mutual. Despite the fact that he was a no-good drifter, leeching off others, my father had all of life's answers, naturally. He scoffed at the old man, so steeped in the old ways. My father was for change, for any new scheme that made life easier, for any way to make a quick buck. And in my grandfather's presence he never allowed an opportunity to pass where he could niggle and scorn the old man.

When my mother became pregnant with me there were scenes of fearsome argument and wrath. Oupa swore he'd kill the swine with his bare hands. There was much weeping and imploring by my mother. Like countless smitten women her intelligence had deserted her, but somehow she got Oupa to simmer down and an uneasy truce was made. They managed to talk it over and my father vowed he would find a job, and that he would honour and care for my mother. Oupa snorted and waved him away.

And you could say my father did make an effort. He renovated a small cottage in the coloured township outside Saldanha and scrounged some old bits of furniture. He even found a job painting boats. They were married and he collected his new wife and her belongings by donkey cart. I can just picture it all. Bokkie and Sannie in holy wedlock. Slowly, heavily, she climbs onto the cart. She sniffs and weeps because the thought of leaving her parents forever has saddened her. She seats herself next to her man. He grins his bandit grin, whistles, cracks the whip and off they go. He turns and winks at my grandparents. No need to worry, old people. Ek sal sorg. Ja, I shall provide. The cart pulls off up the road. My grandmother dabs at her eyes with a handkerchief and waves. Oupa glowers fiercely beneath his black eyebrows.

Of course, Oupa was no fool. It was not long before my father went back to being his old self, a shameless drunkard and womaniser. More and more, he left my mother alone and went about his aimless ways. All night long, talking nonsense and lies in the bar. Soon the stories of his escapades became the talk of Saldanha and even reached the ears of people in Langebaan. Stories of drunken cavorting with loose women, stories of scrapes with the police. It became a regular chore for my mother to fetch him from the jail where he'd spent the night, usually for being drunk and disorderly. And he'd emerge from the cells begging her forgiveness, or protesting his innocence. Together they'd walk down the road to their empty home, he gesticulating and chattering incessantly, she breathing heavily beneath her many burdens, including me.

Their marital bliss lasted only six months before he lost his job and they were back scrounging off Oupa. The scrounging lasted another six months (during which I was born) when, out of the blue, the city beckoned. My father drifted off to the bright lights of Cape Town, and my mother returned, weeping and disillusioned, to her parents who took her in and shut the door.

And to think my mother had his skeleton buried among the bones of fisherfolk! She, herself, lay down beside him in the end. Two skeletons grinning at each other through the sand …

I was eight years old when Oupa died. His burial and the wake afterwards have remained with me in all their vividness and sadness. Being the respected man he was, folk came from all around. Tak, himself, was there, dressed in his black suit. I stood next to my mother beneath the solitary gum tree as the dominee spoke about Jesus having a place in his heart for fishermen. The leaves overhead clapped in the wind. There were tears from the mourners as the men, including my father, filled in the grave. My father shovelled with unusual energy. With a flick and flourish of the wrist he sent sand cascading down onto the coffin. You would never have guessed he was a wastrel, the way he handled that spade.

And afterwards, the maudlin drunkenness of the wake …

The food and drink that everyone had contributed was arranged on trestle tables on the shore of the lagoon. The wind had dropped and it was pleasant and warm on the sand. And what a wake it was! Fresh loaves of bread, smoked harders, steenbras, red roman and kabeljou. Perlemoen, ribbetjies and broodkluitjies. Soetkoekies and fizzy cold drinks for the kids. There was wine by the gallon and some good bottles of brandy, which Tak donated. We children ate and then played games in the sand. But although some of us screamed and yelled, we were not too far removed to hear the older people who soon became noisy themselves.

Loudest of all (I feel the hot flush of shame overcome me) was my father. He was dancing with a sweet, embarrassed girl to the music of a konsertina. The girl, the daughter of a man who had crewed for Oupa, was not a patch on my mother in terms of looks and was clearly a most unwilling partner. But my father was too far gone for looks to be any consideration. The air rang with his drunken, insistent voice. Ho ho ho! Where's your spirit, meisie? Where's your sense of fun? I glowed with shame as the other kids laughed at him. The more he danced the more ridiculous his movements became. A drunken scavenger, he hurtled to and fro, knocking the other dancers flying. Soon it was just the two of them dancing, the others having retired to watch the spectacle. My father rose to the occasion. He began to gyrate, thrusting his pelvis provocatively. Ja, he'd show these damn peasants how they did it in the city! If he'd possessed feathers he might have wagged his tail and inflated his crop. But he had no special attributes. He was just a drunken man in shabby clothes, still covered with grave soil.

He went on and on, silencing the girl's protestations with guffaws and kisses. And most of the adult folk were drunk enough to think it was all a big joke. Bokkie the dronklap. Especially when the seat of his trousers began to slip lower and lower, eventually exposing his backside. His left buttock showed a few ragged scars, an ugly reminder of one encounter with a police dog. I burned with embarrassment at the sight as the children howled with laughter. The young girl was on the brink of tears, when my father put his mouth to her ear and said in a voice that everyone could hear, 'Don't be afraid, sweet thing. I am the hero of a dozen fishing harbours!'

I looked across and saw my mother sitting among the women. She was watching him with the saddest expression I've ever seen. There was no anger in it, no hate, just sadness and loneliness and longing. She shivered in the creeping shadows.

Tak was also there, sitting apart, a bottle of brandy in the sand between his feet. He watched my father dance. Even now, with the advantage of hindsight, his eyes tell me nothing of what he was thinking. Then he got up suddenly, dusted the sand from his clothes and ambled off down the lagoon, bottle in hand.

Ja, the gulls high in the summer sky, swooping down and taking off with the leftovers, children throwing lumps of squashed bread which they snatched in mid-air. The sun raising such a glare off the white sand that even its memory makes me shield my eyes. And the colours blazed in the sky when the sun began to set, and the long shadows crept towards us from the hills across the water, and the konsertina music continued to play. Ja, this vivid background to a man dead and buried, and the scarred backside of my father. And the saddest face in the world.

*

On a finger of land that hides the cottage from the village stands the ghost of an old shell-crushing factory. I recall, dimly from the past, green-painted boats dredging up fossilised oyster shells from the lagoon to be processed by the factory as a supplement for poultry food. The discovery of this potentially rich harvest caused quite a stir at the time. Everyone thought Langebaan was heading for a boom of sorts. Of course, this fanned the all-consuming flames of my father's imagination, not that it made the slightest difference whether he was able to benefit from this wealth or not. It was simply the idea of unlimited wealth that consumed him that was his sickness. My father, the hero of a dozen fishing harbours ... even now I can see him sitting at the kitchen table, his eroding face lit by hearth fire and wine. Yet another abandoned pencil sketch of my mother lying at his elbow – how many portraits were never finished because of wine! (How many unfinished portraits found their way into my mother's cupboard because she could not bear to discard them.) With his usual expansive gestures he is explaining to my weary mother the dimensions of wealth that lie on the lagoon floor. 'Jesus, Sannie,' he says, 'fifty million tons of the fucking stuff, the scientists reckon. Just lying there in the fucking lagoon, just waiting! Fifty million tons!' The word 'million' holds a special power over my father. He is entranced by it, made reverent by it. To my mother it means nothing. For her it's an empty word, like the others that spill from his lips. Her tired expression doesn't change as his drunken voice drones on and on.

And a few years later the shell-crushing business fell through. The factory closed down; the dredgers were left to sink and rust in the lagoon. The wrecks are still there, cables hanging limply from the decaying superstructure, symbols of defeat.

I mention the collapse of this enterprise because it always reminds me of my father. It's a sad irony, though, that I should criticise him for exuding futility. He and I are not so distant. I often overlook the fact that my artistic bent stems from him, from his own natural abilities which in moments of sobriety he saw and nurtured in me. How to draw with an expressive line, how to apply watercolour washes, how to use perspective to show depth. He claimed to have learned these skills long ago while working as a factotum for a visiting German wildlife artist in the Kalahari. True or not, I should thank him for them because they have given me what purpose I have in life.

But the other parallels hurt. While I have no great physical resemblance to him, the growing void caused by my persistent drinking fills me with a fear that one day I might share his fate. He is a weight that I bear. He stumbles without warning into my thoughts and leans against me, his breath foul with rotgut brandy. And I lean against him to keep my balance. Two drunken men, leaning against each other, killing each other with rotgut curses. While, outside, the ghost of the shell-crushing factory billows and flaps as it gulps the winds. I can almost hear the sounds of forlorn machinery grinding, ranting at the winds ...

There was a time when my father's dreams of wealth actually gained some substance. He started stealing cars for a living in Cape Town and did pretty well for himself out of it. He worked for a crime syndicate that specialised in dismantling luxury cars and reassembling them again at a secret location in the Transkei, for sale to white businessmen with fewer assets than they would care to admit.

But whenever things got too hot in the city he'd seek refuge with us here – sometimes a week, sometimes a month – just until it was safe to go back. He'd appear at the door, a shifty expression in his eye, and greet me with apparent gusto. 'Hey, Manas! Shake my hand, man!' he'd yell, squeezing my hand too hard. Sometimes there was something between his hand and mine and once the idiotic handshake was over I'd find some money in my palm. Or he'd reach in his pocket and fish out an expensive brush or box of watercolours.

He arrived one day in a silver-grey Alfa Romeo with fancy white fluff on the dashboard. Mag tyres, the works. Wearing dark glasses and a red American baseball cap. Floral shirt and white trousers, white shoes. When he smiled he really looked a sight, especially since he had no front teeth. Mr Success himself. Of course, we had to go for a spin, with him roaring with laughter at our expressions of peasant terror as we tore around the roads.

The way he marched into the cottage as though he owned it. The way he ignored my mother's efforts to keep the place clean and nice. And she always greeted him with more warmth than I thought appropriate. He brought her money and gifts, such as the mini skirt she never wore publicly (such attire, she thought, would immediately brand her a woman of easy virtue) and the transistor radio which filled our peaceful home with such banal fare as 'Squad Cars' (my father's favourite), 'Pick a Box' and 'The Pip Freedman Show'. (My father delighted in hearing this white man ape African and coloured accents.) My mother chose not to think too much of his activities in the city. To her the outside world was evil and bewildering, and people had out of necessity to become a bit evil themselves in order to cope. She accepted the money he gave her gratefully and my father always made a big show of presenting his ill-gotten gains, as though he was doing her a favour she could never repay. Allowing him access to her body was the least she could do.

So at night I listened to his grunts and her moans. The clink of his bottle as he set it down on the floor. Bed springs creaking late into the night. Once I heard them arguing, my father's voice distorted and ugly with drunkenness. Something about us going with him to the city. 'No!' my mother cried. This was her home, she would never leave Langebaan. 'Why the hell not?' he shouted. 'Why live like pigs on a fucking farm?' The thought of going to the city caused her to weep hysterically. My father started swearing and shouting. Silently I cursed him. He was a sick animal, the way he treated her. His ugly raving was frightening in the darkness. I was too scared to rise from my bed to help her. The slap of his hand as he struck her. I gripped my blankets in torment. Slaps and obscenities. Shuffling and crashing. Glass breaking. 'You can lie here and rot, for all I care!' he brayed. 'You and your son!'

The door banged shut. The stolen car started up and wheelspun its way up the road. Gradually it faded from earshot. I prayed he would kill himself and never return. Silence, broken only by a gentle wind through the bushes outside and my mother's soft weeping. I crept through the darkness to her room. I climbed into her bed, I put my arms around her. She kissed my hands. They were wet with tears and mucous. Sometimes a glimpse of something else broke through my hate ... an awful realisation that I did not know her truly, that she did not share my hate. But that's all it was – a glimpse.

I prayed he would leave us alone but he always came back, like a bad dream. And not even his sober moments, the moments of contrition when he begged my mother for forgiveness or when he took me sketching along the shore, could ever make up for the pain he caused. No one could shit on their own doorstep like he could. It was an embarrassment to go into the village with him. The mere sight of him evoked sniggers and whispers. There goes Bokkie, the jailbird, the dronklap, I would imagine people saying behind our backs. And for some strange reason this attention pleased my father. Somehow he saw himself as a heroic figure, someone who had done things his way, who bucked the system. The hero of a dozen fishing harbours. I can't count how many times I went down to the bar to bring him home. There he'd be, flattering himself in the presence of skollies or draping his arms over whores. 'Ma wants you,' I'd call from the door. He'd look at me in mock-puzzlement and glance behind him, as though I were talking to the wrong person. Such a card, my father. And after finishing his drink, he'd swagger out – ag, the chores of married life – and everyone would shake their heads and laugh as I escorted him away.

This is what I know of my father. This is what I want to know of him. How then do I reconcile this with the memory of the two of them on the beach in front of the cottage, that rare moment of real togetherness? Try as I might, I cannot eradicate the inconsistency.

The dusk was gathering and the shell-crushing factory

hovered like a mosquito above my father's lips. My eyes were playing tricks on me. The factory would not assume its correct perspective. It buzzed about my father's head, sewing up his flimsy aura. My mother sat quietly next to him. Her eyes scanned the world serenely. She was relaxed and content. Little did I know then that the cigarette my father passed to her every so often was, in fact, a dagga joint. They talked quietly as the evening changed slowly to night. Then they began to laugh softly, as though the whole of life was one big joke. I was playing in the sand next to them, my interest in them rather than the dams I was building that, perhaps, would contain interesting creatures the next morning at low tide. Despite my hatred and jealousy I glowed with pleasure because she was happy. I even allowed him to reach over and ruffle my hair. Ja, this memory is so clear and special. My father voicing his dreams. One by one he planted the sterile seeds of escape in her head. And my mother swayed her head to the sound, the presence of his voice, as though she were listening to music from a reed pipe.

Strange clouds were bounding across the sky. I pointed to them and said, 'Look! Clouds like black dogs!'

My mother pulled me to her and kissed me. 'You have a wandering mind, Manas,' she laughed. 'Just like your father.'

This is difficult for me. I still cannot accept that she loved him. I still cannot accept I am like him. I stand in the winds of fact, my turned-out pockets flapping.

*

And then my forlorn prayers were answered, though it gave me no great joy. I discovered one of death's anomalies. People do not simply leave. They remain as presences, guilt mongers, to be more precise. So it was with my father.

Let me reconstruct (bearing in mind the inventions of resentment): Late one night in the city the police caught him stealing a BMW outside the Heerengracht Hotel near the foreshore. There ensued a wild car chase down Adderley Street to the docks during which he sideswiped a motorcycle, sending it and its hapless rider into a fountain, drove through red traffic lights, rammed through a customs boom and drove through a warehouse, sending boxes of export fruit flying. The cops lost him when they were cut off by a train near the Harbour Café. When the train cleared the track, my father had disappeared. They searched everywhere to no avail. He'd given them the slip it seemed.

One week later, a worker sitting on the quayside eating his lunch noticed something glinting in the water below. On closer inspection he made out the grill of a car. The authorities were alerted and that afternoon they pulled the stolen BMW out, with my father still inside. Naturally, by the time they'd got the crane ready and the divers had fastened the cables to the car, the press was there, along with all those good citizens who have a taste for the macabre. The police and the harbour officials had a tough time keeping the growing mob away from the quayside. A reporter was pushed backwards into the slimy water. He emerged with a wild expression in his eyes and struck out furiously for the side, as though a thousand demons lurked beneath him. Spewing watery curses, he was helped out and stood looking ruefully at the sodden notebook in his shirt pocket. Roars of laughter. A temporary diversion from the main feature, you might say.

The car was hoisted from the sea and hung, spurting jets of water, while the crane operator waited for the crowd to make way. There were some squabbles among the photographers but at last a space was made and the car was set down.

Cries of horror.

My father, the hero of a dozen fishing harbours, was sitting casually in the driver's seat, grinning that bandit grin at the assembled crowd. The cameras started clicking, absorbing the images that would become the subject of debates on tastelessness in the media for weeks to come. Always the showman, my father, now nothing could ever daunt that gap-toothed smile. A rose in his teeth would have been perfect for the swooning women, but the waving feeler did well enough. Ja, bristling through his bones were a multitude of long, twitching antennae, for his rotting carcass was infested

32

by an insatiable horde of kreef. (It was rumoured later that for a while the city restaurants experienced a decline in interest in crayfish dishes, after people had read about my father.) Yes, there my father hung grinning inside his fancy stolen car, rotten and writhing with squeaking crustaceans – the centre of attention, even in death.

The inventions of resentment. Often this hideous image, gleaned from hearsay and press reports, has inflamed my imagination. It may even have been embellished in the countless unwary moments it has invaded my thoughts. It was indeed unfortunate that they discovered and liberated his remains from their watery grave. I might have grown to subdue my hatred for him had he stayed among his crustacean companions at the bottom of the sea. But when all was said and done, my mother, bless her soul, had these same bones brought back to Langebaan in a cheap pine coffin which she had buried next to my grandparents. He had returned to her at last, our hero of the harbour. Hers forever.

My mind's eye wavers. I cannot stay with this.

*

The Scheepers' jokingly referred to our menfolk as their resident itinerants. They knew that my family had lived here for as long as anyone could remember, certainly longer than they had themselves, but this did not mean we could remain on the farm without putting in our pound of flesh. No, the Scheepers' would not abide unproductive mud people. So all of our menfolk worked for them during the harvesting and shearing months, more for the right to remain on Nooitgedacht than the poor wages paid to them. During the harvesting they were transported to the farm near Vredenburg and it was sometimes many weeks before they returned. In addition, one quarter of our fishing catch went to the farm as a sort of rental. Under this arrangement everyone's interests were served, more or less. But we all did our bit to retain the right to stay. Most of the women worked in the Groothuis as servants at one time or another, and as a child even I had my chores – I herded sheep, fed the chickens and tidied the sheds.

After Oupa died there was talk of moving us off the farm because there were no able-bodied men left – you could hardly consider my father to be in that category. My mother's worst fears were being realised. We were to be cast out into the evil world of cutthroats and thieves. I can remember the panic in her eyes as she begged Tak to let us stay. 'We have no place to go,' she said. 'No people to go to.'

Tak's blue eyes scanned her face. Unlike his father there was something resembling a heart in him. 'How can you make yourself useful?' he asked her.

'I shall work as a man in the fields, master,' she replied.

Touched by her fear and earnestness, Tak smiled and shook his head. 'No,' he said, 'you shall work for me in my house.'

My mother got down on her knees to thank him.

And so she worked for Tak in the Groothuis. Each day, except for Sundays, she left the cottage at daybreak only to return after dark. She cooked his meals, washed his clothes and swept the floors. For this she received a meagre salary which together with the pittance I earned from my chores enabled us to subsist. From my mother's perspective, things must have seemed dismal. Sure, she had a husband who visited her every now and then, and she had a devoted son, but they were not enough to keep her safe in a world that was hard and cold. Still, things could have been worse and each night she prayed to Jesus on the kitchen wall and received some solace from his cool stare. By now the picture of Jesus was not unaccompanied. My fledgling artistic talent had developed through my father's sporadic interest and alongside Jesus hung all my little creative efforts – crude watercolour sketches of the lagoon and my own portraits of my mother. I remember how patiently she sat for those modest attempts, a strained smile on her face as though she was being photographed.

It was after my father died that our lives changed completely. When she heard the news my mother sank into a desolate despair. I suppose she always saw in him a prodigal son, someone who would return home one day for good, suitably chastened and repentant. Now, like a caged bird, she gave up hope. She became ill and was bedridden for many days. I remember how much she wept and that she would not let me out of her sight. She seemed to be shrivelling up in her grief and nothing anyone said about it being just as well made the slightest impression on her.

Now Tak began appearing frequently at our door. He sat at her bedside and spoke cheerfully to her, the way a father would speak to a favourite child. He paid for a doctor to come and see her. The doctor diagnosed her illness as psychosomatic and prescribed some tranquillisers, which Tak also paid for.

Tak went out of his way to be helpful to my mother, and I saw nothing more to it then. And so when he laid pipes from the spring to provide us with running water and supplied us with meat and vegetables and milk, and assured my mother there was no need to worry about staying in the cottage – she could remain for as long as she wished – I was surprised when, this time, she didn't go down on her knees.

Despite his kindness, my mother was uncomfortable with Tak around so much. She hardly even thanked him for making things easier for us. She seemed more concerned with what the other coloured families on the farm would think. But as she began to recover, Tak's visits began to linger. He seemed to bask in the sparse warmth that was left in our home. Often he'd sit and drink coffee at the table and talk about the everyday things on the farm. And I realised then that he hated being alone, he hated his empty house, his empty life. He seemed to be between everyone, neither part of one group nor another. He had no real friends among the white community, only the increasingly retiring remnants of his parents' loyal throng. And, of course, to us, the coloureds, he was the master, the baas. My mother listened with an empty heart as he spoke.

But Tak was persistent. Ja, the numbing flash of discovery as I came to the door of the cottage one day, school books under my arm, unsuspecting. Tak and my mother were sitting at the kitchen table. Tak was talking quietly. My mother's hands were on the table, beneath his. They were looking into each other's eyes – hardly master and servant. And as my shadow appeared at the doorway, my mother wrenched her hands from beneath his. Tak did not move. He just stared at me, steadily …

Even now, when all is said and done, I struggle with this. It is difficult to suppress a malignant cynicism. When it comes to sexual relationships between Afrikaners and the people they deem inferior by virtue of their darkness of skin, there are countless examples of hypocrisy – indeed, if Afrikaners had simply to trace their origins, many would be in for a surprise, for they would discover ancestors of not exactly pristine European stock. But I try to think the relationship between Tak and my mother was different, that the sordid hypocrisy did not apply to them. I try to think that because of Tak's alienation from his own community, he suddenly rejected the code by which his people and his church had taught him to live and was drawn to us by a desire for simplicity and human warmth, neither of which he got in abundance from my mother anyway. I try to think it was something deeper than sexual desire; a lonely yearning to make contact with others before life passed him by, perhaps. Ja, I try to think this way, but I struggle to rationalise it, even now with so much water under the bridge. From the beginning it was difficult for me to accept Tak as anything more than our benefactor – the white baas helping his faithful servants to find their feet again. As my mother's lover, no. Why could my mother not see that I was enough for her? I would look after her. There was no need to complicate her life with difficult men. Men who were out to take advantage of her.

Naturally Tak's attentions did not go unnoticed by the coloured folk on the farm. There were two other families on Nooitgedacht, the Arendses and the Witboois. They had always been good friends and had stood by us in the hard times, but now there were all sorts of nasty rumours going around that eventually spread to the white community. This was exactly what my mother had dreaded. Perhaps it was a sign of the Scheepers' previous social standing that Tak and my mother were not prosecuted under the *Immorality Act*. I suppose they saw Tak as a harmless crank, the degenerate remnant of a once-respected family. But we were punished in other ways. The Witboois, our closest friends – Abram Witbooi had even been a pallbearer at Oupa's funeral – would hardly speak to us, and the Arendses encouraged their children to bully me. At the small farm school I went to on the Donkergat road I became the target of playground taunts. The other kids took my books and trampled them in the dust. They said that soon I'd have brothers and sisters with birthmarks on their faces. They said my mother and I were assuming airs, that we thought ourselves too good for the common folk.

My response to this spite by my own kind was curious, as warped and confused as its cause. I remember the time my mother and I were walking to the village, when a passing farmer slowed his truck and called out in mock-familiarity, 'Hello, Mevrou Scheepers! Tell me, what's it like to naai the Oubaas? Like doing mouth-to-mouth resuscitation, hey?' My mother just glanced at him and continued walking. The farmer guffawed, displaying a fine array of gold fillings in his teeth. The coloured workers on the back of the truck killed themselves laughing too, as the farmer accelerated away, spinning dust and grit into our faces. I felt my face flush with anger and hate. But my hatred was not for the farmer. No, we coloured folk are used to being talked to by whites as though we are shit. My hatred was for the workers. Who were they to laugh at us? The one thing I have in common with the Afrikaner is his language, rich and earthy, and in the heat of the moment I screamed after the truck, 'Fuck off, you bunch of arsecreepers!' My mother looked at me with an amazed expression. Eleven years old and carrying on like a skollie. Her hand lashed out and my ear stung. She shook me until tears came into my eyes. She was more concerned with my bad language than the humiliation she'd just suffered. 'I have tried to bring you up decently,' she scolded. 'Where on earth did you learn such filth?'

But I can now see my blindness at that age to the larger system that created this strange inverted spite, that system born in our colonial history and coming of age in our Afrikaner masters. Ja, I was blind to an artificial, stratified society where a person's worth was determined by the colour of skin. Where even the very people who suffered the consequences of colour were conditioned to accept their place in society and frowned on those who strayed beyond.

I walked three kilometres to school and back each day. Usually I went with the other kids from the farm but when they ostracised me I began taking the longer way back home, past the marshes and along the beach. I came to relish this time alone near the lagoon. As I walked I watched the terns plunge into the water from high and the flamingoes standing out on the sandbanks. Often I lay back in the sand and listened to the small waves splash on the shore, and to the buzzing of bees among the flowers on the dunes, the smell of the sea in my nostrils.

One day I fell asleep on the beach and wakened only as the sun was going down. I hurried back to the cottage only to find that my mother was not home yet. Assuming she was still finishing her chores over at the Groothuis, I made myself some supper and did my homework in front of the fire in the hearth. I waited for what seemed like hours and still she didn't come home, so I put on a jacket and walked over to the Groothuis. The place was in darkness except for a light in the lounge. Tak's dogs, two aging retrievers, were asleep on the front stoep and hardly stirred as I climbed the front steps. Through a crack in the curtains I saw her and Tak sitting together on a couch, talking. I watched, fascinated. It was blowing and I couldn't hear what they were saying, their mouths just moved amid the sounds of wind and water. They talked very seriously, it seemed, and for a long time. Then my mother got up and went down the passage. Tak sat for a while, deep in thought. Then he gulped back his glass of brandy and followed her.

I ran back to the cottage and went straight to bed. I lay awake until the early hours, when I heard her come in. She stood at my door for a long time and watched me. She called my name softly. I pretended to be asleep.

That night I dreamed I was searching through the Groothuis for her. It was dark as I made my way along the passage from one door to the next, hardly breathing in my fear. Silence, silence, except for the soft creak of the floorboards beneath my feet. I walked, carefully placing one foot in front of the other, my hands outstretched before me like a sleepwalker. There was a gentle movement of air and ahead of me a door groaned and clicked shut. And I was immersed in complete darkness. I couldn't see my hand in front of my face. I couldn't hear anything save my wild breathing and thundering heart. The darkness was too much. I panicked. I lay curled up, my head in my hands, screaming and crying.

A light. Footsteps. A paraffin lamp is placed down next to my bed. My mother appears in the circle of light, clutching her heart. 'What is it, Manas?' she cries fearfully. 'What's the matter, child?'

Some things will not assume their place in the past. They drag me into fear, the thin bones of my fingers ploughing the earth, my toes clenched between their teeth ...

*

The terms of my mother's intimacy soon became clear. One day Tak drove down to the cottage and told me to come with him. Thinking that he needed me to open and close the farm gates (the only time I ever got a ride) I jumped on the back of the bakkie. But Tak didn't want me for the gates. This time he drove around the lagoon, past Churchhaven, past Preekstoel, to the beaches on the other side.

He parked the bakkie and gave me a small canvas rucksack to carry. We walked a short distance along the sand. Tak began talking about the old tribes that once lived here, Strandlopers, the Khoi and Bushmen – nomads held to one place by its plenitude. He showed me the remains of their middens and we scratched around and found some old pieces of pottery. I have this one cherished memory of Tak seated among these heaps of shells, talking so knowledgeably about these extinct people, rubbing his hard fingers over the objects we had found. His white hair was windswept and he looked at me with blue eyes so soft against the hardness of his face. A hardness caused by squinting at the hot summer glare, and a resigned indifference to the stares his birthmark attracted.

With a broad sweep of his hand, Tak gestured at the land. 'Truly this place belongs to the nomads. Although, to them, the idea of the earth belonging to anyone was completely foreign. We, the white men, drove the nomads away or we killed them, so the land belonged to us. Owning the land is the white man's way. Owning things, especially land, is important to us. Sometimes more important than our own children. Do you understand what I'm saying, Manas?'

I shook my head.

He smiled. 'Ag, ja, what would you know about such things? It's better you don't. How old are you, seun?'

'Eleven, Oubaas. Standard Four.'

He picked up the canvas rucksack and we walked back along a narrow beach flanked by some low cliffs until we came to the solitary anvil-shaped rock called Preekstoel. Tak sat in the shade of an overhang and, to my surprise, took a sketchbook and some pencils from the rucksack. He also took out a thermos flask and two plastic mugs which he filled with sweet tea. He handed me one and we drank for a while in silence. Then he said, 'Your mother tells me you have a gift. I've seen your drawings and paintings she puts up on the wall, and I think maybe she's right. But I want you to show me by drawing this thing.'

He pointed at Preekstoel. I looked at the weathered monolith.

'It's hard to draw, Oubaas,' I said.

'That's why I chose it, Manas. I want to see how good you are because I don't want to waste my money on you.'

'Waste your money, Oubaas?'

Tak eyes grew serious. 'Ja. Your mother has asked me to pay for your education. She wants you to finish school and go to university – to be like a white man. She says you are special, you have the talent to make a living with your head, not your hands. But first, you must show me by drawing this rock. I want to see how you do it. I want to know why I should spend money on you. If it's too hard we can go back.'

'I can do it, Oubaas.'

In a slight daze I took the sketchbook and pencils and began to draw, aware of Tak's eyes on me. Knowing what was at stake, I summoned all my accumulated abilities, along with the infrequent advice of my father. I roughly positioned Preekstoel so it would fit the page. I threw it into prominence by sketching a low horizon in the background of the distant shore and hills. Then I began to apply detail to the rock's surface – first the shadows and then, with a sharp pencil, its tapering contours and cracks. All the while Tak sat there and watched, occasionally pursing his lips.

Finally, after what seemed an eternity but was probably only an hour or so, it was finished. Just to be sure I performed the simple trick my father had taught me: I turned the drawing upside down on a rock and got up to stretch my legs.

'Is it finished?' Tak asked.

'I think so, Oubaas. But I must wait a few minutes. Then, when I look at it again I'll see if there are mistakes.'

After a while I turned the drawing over. As far as my eleven-year-old eyes could see there were no mistakes. Nervously, I handed the sketchbook to Tak to pronounce judgement. He held the drawing at arm's length and shifted his gaze half a dozen times from it to the rock, nodding his head. Then he asked abruptly, 'Can I keep it?'

'Of course, Oubaas,' I replied timidly.

He carefully placed the sketchbook back in the rucksack.

'Okay, Manas. I will agree to your mother's wishes. I don't know if it's the right thing. I'm just a simple farmer – I don't know how anyone can make a living by being an artist – but that is your mother's wish and I will see to it that you are educated properly. On one condition: white boys in this country are forced to go to the army when they have finished school. I think the experience does them good, it teaches them some discipline. I'm not saying you must go to the army, Manas. What I am saying is you must work for me on the farm for the same period as the white boys go to the army. You must prove to me that you are disciplined and responsible. Then you can go to university if you're good enough. I shall provide the money, you must provide the results. Do you understand?'

'Ja, Oubaas.'

'I want to see results, Manas, because I haven't got money to throw away. Verstaan?'

'I shall work hard, Oubaas Tak.'

'You better.'

As we drove back to the farm I was elated. The sun was warm and the beetles and birds in the bushes beside the road sounded especially sweet to my ears. I was old enough to understand that my change of fortune amounted to a transaction of sorts but that did not dampen my spirits. I was also old enough to have often felt despair at the hopelessness of the future. What would I become? Like all the other coloured kids on Nooitgedacht, a labourer condemned to a lifetime of monotonous toil? Suddenly hopelessness had given way to hope. Yes, there was a future ahead of me that I, Manas, would determine. Now everything was possible. It was all a question of perspective. I could adjust the world to whatever size I wished by simply moving my hand further away or closer to my eye. I could fit valleys and plains on a fingernail. Mountains could be climbed by moving thumb to forefinger. My eye was the limit to which even the universe conformed.

*

Working within its scant means, the Department of Coloured Affairs was at the time of my schooling able to insist on a few 'privileges', such as compulsory education to Standard Two for farm kids within a four-kilometre radius of a school. This meant the primary school in Langebaan opposite the old coloured graveyard (both since removed without a trace to make way for the rezoned white area along the foreshore) was out of my reach. Instead, the school I went to was on a farm called Jacobsvlei, along the Donkergat road. The farm was named after Jacob Van Zyl, the long-deceased patriarch of an old Langebaan family.

Jacob Van Zyl was an emotionally-scarred survivor of the Boer War, during which his mother and two sisters died in British concentration camps. For this, he would never forgive the British. But he was a church-going man and he feared his hatred kept him at odds with God, so he devised a means to compensate. Believing it was God's will to educate the heathen, he built a school for the local coloured farm children. By all accounts Jacob Van Zyl was a zealous benefactor, insisting on Bible studies and often checking the children's punctuality, sjambok in hand. Until he died, he took his revenge on the British by refusing to allow English to be taught in his school. That was long ago, before the Second World War. In my time school policy was dictated by the Department of Coloured Affairs, where both Afrikaans and English were compulsory subjects. A more relaxed atmosphere prevailed, though Jacob Van Zyl's heirs showed little interest in the school's upkeep and it consequently fell into disrepair. In recent years the Van Zyls closed it down and now use it to house their farm machinery.

There were two long rectangular brick classrooms separated by a cement courtyard. The corrugated iron roofs leaked and the walls were cracked. The few drab cypresses scattered around the buildings offered little shade in the hot dry months. A bare playground ran down to the fence bordering the road to Donkergat. In summer the dust from passing vehicles found its way through the broken windows into the classrooms and covered everything, including the framed photograph of Prime Minister Hendrik Verwoerd. Still, it was our school and better than nothing, as we were so often reminded.

The school catered for about fifty children ranging from

kindergarten to Standard Five. The younger kids occupied the larger of the two classrooms which was the domain of Mrs 'Frikkadel' Fourie, a three-hundred-pound colossus whose nickname (which we dared not whisper in her presence) was derived from the apparently endless supply of cold meat patties which she crammed into her mouth at any time of day. Her husband, Mr 'Stok' Fourie (as scrawny as she was obese) taught Standards Four and Five, the easier load since a fair number of kids left once they became barely literate.

The Fouries were an odd white couple, to be sure, united more through ennui it seemed than the education of children. They had met as teachers in Beaufort West. Mr Fourie was a high school teacher, Mrs Fourie taught at a junior school. Rumour had it that Mr Fourie got in some trouble with the Cape Education Department and had been ejected from the lofty realm of white education. There were lots of stories going around but no one really knew what his transgression was. However circumstances were such that he and Mrs Fourie felt it wise to leave Beaufort West. Being a distant relative, Mrs Fourie appealed to the Van Zyls for help. Not that the Van Zyls exactly approved of either of them, but, ja, blood is thicker than water, and so the Fouries ended up at Jacobsvlei. In every sense a demotion, but despite the indignity they no doubt suffered in teaching us coloured kids, this remote farm school suited them perfectly. They had cheap accommodation in a cottage on the farm and the school was seldom visited by pesky departmental inspectors. The Van Zyls themselves could not have cared less about whether educational standards were being met or not; they often expressed the view that the school was a waste of their property and were it not for the frantic pleas from the coloured community, they would have closed it down long ago.

Under the ponderous care of the Fouries, each school year seemed an eternity. I doubt there was ever a strict adherence to any prescribed curriculum. Being none the wiser we took each day as it came. Some were good (especially those when the Fouries did not turn up, which was not infrequent), the rest not so good. Both junior and senior classes ended at noon, for by that time the Fouries' eyelids had drooped and the lessons were punctuated by cavernous yawns. Naturally they were the victims of naughty pranks. As he slumbered at his desk Mr Fourie's shoelaces would be carefully tied together, causing him to trip when he got up, and Mrs Fourie once displayed unusually quick reflexes when she rushed off to find a tap after swallowing a frikkadel laden with peri peri. Ja, there was always some stupid kid willing to lay himself on the line for a few laughs, but I was never among the jokers or the troublemakers because when Mr Fourie started wielding his cane I found myself trembling in terror. But even when we were well behaved the children were a constant source of irritation to them, judging by their frequent outbursts of irrational anger.

The school day began and ended with prayers, with all the kids congregated in Mrs Fourie's classroom. Beneath the photograph of Hendrik Verwoerd on the wall next to the South African flag, we prayed to God to lift us out of ignorance and sin, so that we might serve our country in humility and obedience. When I first went to school, I thought Verwoerd was God – everyone seemed to incline their heads towards his fish-eyed visage when we prayed. Mrs Fourie pounded away on an ancient piano as we sang the national anthem over and over again, until she was satisfied. She had big wads of fat under her arms that wobbled as she struck the keys. One day, the Fouries looked more gloomy than usual as we assembled in the morning. Mrs Fourie kept dabbing her eyes and blowing her nose with foghorn blasts. We were told that Verwoerd had been assassinated by a lunatic and there would be no school as it was a day of mourning. We all tried very hard to affect expressions of sorrow, not that we knew very much about Verwoerd and how his grand schemes affected us – it was simply an unexpected holiday. We all took off down the road, laughing and cheering, much to the Fouries' disgust. Some time later, they took Verwoerd's photograph down and replaced it with one of his successor, BJ Vorster.

As hewers of wood and drawers of water, coloured kids

were not entitled to the same education enjoyed by whites, yet were better off than black children. I recall accepting that almost without question. Not that there were many black people around Langebaan to compare ourselves with, the Western Cape having been designated a 'white and coloured preferential area'. In fact, up until this stage, I'd met only one black man, a Xhosa named Moses who Tak took on as a shepherd. For about two years he stayed alone in a small stone cottage on top of a granite hill on the farm's northern boundary, a bleak, bare place, battered by relentless winds. God knows how he survived the loneliness, being separated from his family in the Transkei, but I remember Moses as a gentle, polite man, always in good spirits. He used to carve small wooden animals, cattle or donkeys, for the farm kids, which we prized highly. But then one day a government inspector arrived and had some terse words with Tak. And Moses left, never to be seen again. The stone cottage on top of the hill is now derelict, a roosting place for seagulls.

I suspect black people were an abstraction to most of us, and I now acknowledge with some guilt the meagre comfort many coloureds took from their slightly elevated status. Such is the conditioning of racial privilege. As peasants on the land no one in my family rocked the boat; they yearned only for the privilege of a decent life. Only once do I remember my father cursing the inequality of the system – schools for kids whose shit doesn't stink was the quaint sarcasm he used to describe white education.

So we made do, being none the wiser. We wrote on black slates and only used exercise books if we could afford them. New textbooks were few and far between. Most of the kids shared the torn, outdated copies that the school had accumulated over the years. We attended school barefoot and in ragged clothes, the poorer ones among us often hungry. Somehow most of us learned the basics. Somehow our knowledge crept beyond our horizons. We learned how the white men defeated the Zulus and the Xhosas, how the Voortrekkers tamed the vast interior, and how unfairly the Boers were treated by the British. And we learned the exact location of the world's most beautiful and civilised country. It was situated at the bottom of Africa, and it had been given to the Dutch settlers by God. At thy will to live or perish, Oh South Africa, dear land.

But when my mother made her deal with Tak, my status at school changed. I alone became the exception to the rule. Tak began paying close attention to my progress and I was supplied with everything I needed to succeed – new text books, new exercise books, geometry sets, pens and pencils, a slide rule – even new clothes and shoes. The other kids looked on with undisguised envy. And if they could have seen my room at the cottage their envy might have turned to despair for their own bleak future as poor peasants on the land. My room had been transformed. Now there was a new desk and chair and a kerosene lamp so I could study at night. There were shelves containing my growing library of books, and my collections of birds' eggs and shells. On the wall next to my bed there was a huge map of the world and, alongside, prints of my favourite paintings and extracts from poems that I used to memorise before going to sleep. My most prized possession was the set of encyclopaedias Tak had bought me for my birthday, arranged always in careful alphabetical order on a shelf above the desk. How proud I was of my room, and what pleasure it gave me to see my mother's simple awe as she peered through the door.

But I was not the most popular fellow around. No one seemed interested in stealing a glimpse of my sacred room. At the time I was hurt and puzzled by it. Life seemed full of ironies. When my father was around, making life hell for us, I had lots of friends. Everyone felt sorry for me, I guess. But when Tak came along, suddenly there were no friends. My new status irked them. It was unfair that I alone should have the chance to make something of my life, while their parents simply could not afford to keep children in school who were old enough to be earning their daily bread. My new status placed me beyond their league. At school they used to call me Mister. Mister Big Stuff. More than once the buttons were ripped from my new shirts and I was given a bloody nose.

The Fouries did nothing about the bullying; they also thought I was getting too big for my boots.

When I passed Standard Five we were faced with the problem of where I would attend high school. The options were to go to boarding school in Malmesbury or Paarl. There was talk of a new high school being built in Louwville Township in Vredenburg which was closer to home, but construction was not yet underway. Tak and my mother considered the options and came up with a third. Rather than send me away, Tak came to a private agreement with the Van Zyls and the Department of Coloured Affairs that Mr Fourie, being qualified to teach a number of secondary school subjects at the level required in coloured education, would coach me through high school. Tak also hired the services of Mrs Grace Cook, formerly an English teacher at Bishops, an elite boys' school in Cape Town, who'd retired in Langebaan on a meagre pension that required her to advertise private lessons. Tak was obligated to pay Mr Fourie and Mrs Cook for their services and to purchase all necessary books and equipment. This arrangement lasted three years, until Standard Eight. I think Tak figured that two white teachers providing individual tuition were a better deal than boarding school in Malmesbury or Paarl. He was wrong about Mr Fourie.

So I was timetabled to attend classes with Mr Fourie four afternoons a week. Mrs Cook (who insisted on me calling her Grace) used to visit me at the cottage three mornings a week, arriving in her old Morris Minor. She was an elderly widow whose only husband was killed long ago in a car accident. Always prim and proper in her tartan skirt and white hair tied back in a bun. Clear blue eyes and a delicately wrinkled skin that smelled of Oil of Olay. And, as I soon discovered, Grace was a liberal, one of the original Black Sash members, in fact. Ja, a gentle soul with a heart of gold.

Grace had her ways. You could hear her coming from miles off, such was her love of the Morris Minor's hooter. Anything that moved on or near the road – man, bird or beast – received a deafening blast. As she made her way down to the cottage, Tak's sheep would scatter wild-eyed into the veld. She would give a final blast as she pulled up in front of the cottage to alert me unnecessarily to her arrival. I would carry her baskets inside, which aside from books usually contained some homemade rusks or shortbread that she allowed me to consume during a strictly observed tea break between lessons. If my mother was there she would give her a peck on the cheek by way of greeting, much to my mother's complete astonishment.

Grace taught me English and Geography. She also enthusiastically encouraged my painting, being something of an amateur watercolourist herself. For my birthdays and for Christmas I could be sure to get some good-quality watercolour paper, some paints or a coffee-table art book from Grace. I looked forward to her visits, which were quite unlike my depressing encounters with Mr Fourie. We would sit in my room and go over literature and grammar, or learn which crops people grew along the Nile or the Ganges. We would go on nature rambles during which she would tirelessly correct my poor English. 'Hills, Manas – not yills,' she would say. Or (funnelling her lips), 'Road … road – not rrroat!' She was strict and fussy when it came to pronunciation and grammar; in the beginning she used to shake her head and mutter anciently, 'Heavens! what on earth have those Fouries been teaching you all these years? You're practically illiterate, boy!' But while she was strict, she would also occasionally reach over and pat my hand gently, saying, 'You're a good boy, Manas. I've taught spoilt white boys most of my life, over-privileged boys who think that money and social class makes them better than others. But they're no better than you, Manas. So be proud. I know you'll make something of your life. I know you will.' She encouraged me to speak my mind, not to be afraid of white people. 'White people are just people – never stoop to anyone just because they're white,' she said. For a while I believed her. Ja, I loved and believed Grace, my elderly angel. Scarer of sheep.

Not quite the same story with Mr Fourie. While not averse to the extra pay, Mr Fourie was singularly unimpressed by the extra time he had to put in to help me through to matric.

49

From the very beginning, he made it apparent that he was doing me a big favour. My weak subjects were Maths and Science. For the life of me, my wandering mind would simply not conform to the tyranny of numbers and equations. And so, the long afternoons with Mr Fourie, going over algebraic theorems and so and so's law of something or other. Maths and Science were Mr Fourie's forte but he shared his knowledge with a sullen resentment, his chameleon eyelids closed to mere slits. Often he cuffed my head in anger, not so much through my inability to think convergently as through his struggle to accept my airs and graces. After all, coloureds were labourers, servants – not scholars. It was their lot to hoe and harvest, not to think (my dismal mathematical ability must surely have been a confirmation of this belief). Ja, it was tough going in more ways than one. Alone with me he farted and yawned ceaselessly, and so it's not without reason that I associate Maths and Science with bad breath and surreptitious emissions of wind.

When I got to Standard Eight two things happened which brought this phase of my schooling to an end. First, Grace died, alone in her small house in Langebaan. Suddenly the mornings were bereft of her noisy Morris Minor, the sweet rusks and Oil of Olay, the kind words of encouragement. I was heartbroken; I knew she was old but she'd always seemed so wonderfully sprightly and alive. How could angels die? They just stop breathing in their sleep, that's all. But even in death, Grace's kindness reached out to pat me gently on the hand. In her will, a small sum of money was left to me along with a note, which read: 'This money is for university, Manas. I expect you to do well.'

The second thing was Mr Fourie assaulted me.

We were alone in his classroom one afternoon, struggling as usual through some Maths exercises. It was a hot day and Mr Fourie seemed especially resentful and gaseous. Twice he got up from his chair and stalked around the room. Then he leaned with his arse on the window sill, stroking his short black moustache with his fingers, watching me. He grunted. Then it started.

'My little brown Einstein. 'n Regte klein genius, nè?'

I wasn't sure I was hearing right. 'Pardon, Meneer?'

He laughed dryly. 'I said you're a genius, Smit. Much too clever for the rest of us, hey?'

'Meneer?'

'Ja, definitely a brown Einstein. What do the other kids call you, Smit?'

'I'm sorry, Meneer …'

He spoke slowly, as though to an idiot. 'I said what do the other kids call you? What's your nickname, Smit?'

Bewildered, I replied, 'They call me Mister.'

Mr Fourie laughed, shaking his head.

'Why do they call you that, Smit?'

'I don't know why, Meneer.'

'Of course you know. It's because you're kop toe. Full of yourself, hey?'

I didn't reply.

'Answer me, Smit.' He assumed a ridiculous posh English accent. 'Or maybe I should be calling you Smith. Ja, Mister Smith. You think the sun shines out your backside, don't you, Mister Smith?'

'No, Meneer …'

'Yes you do, Mister Smith. You think you're a cut above the rest, don't you? Better than the rest.'

'No, Meneer …'

There was an expression on his face that scared me.

'What are you trying to do, Mister Smith? Become a white man?'

'Please, Meneer, I don't understand …'

'You don't understand? Of course you don't understand, Mister Smith. You don't understand you're more kaffir than white. More baboon than human being. Not so, Mister Smith?'

I didn't answer. Mr Fourie smiled. 'Ja, Mister bloody Smith … all this learning, and I suppose at home you shit behind a bush.'

When incensed, there is a stupid, defiant side to me. It came out there and then, all my pent-up resentment surfaced in one blind reaction: 'Ja, just like the poor white trash who teaches me!'

A wave of terror went through me as I saw Mr Fourie's face go livid. He advanced on me, shouting, 'Fuck! Say that again, you little bastard! Come on, say that again!'

But he wasn't going to give me the chance. He grabbed me by the hair and pulled me out of my chair, slapping my head with all his might. He rammed my head into the wall, once, twice, three times, splitting the skin on my forehead. He kicked me as I lay on the floor. All the time, screaming, 'Say that again, you little shit! You little black shit! Come on, say it again!'

Then he grabbed his cane from his desk and began thrashing me all over my body. Shocked and bleeding, my body on fire, I staggered up and ran. My head still ringing from being hit against the wall, I ran out of the classroom. It felt like I had a knife in my side. He chased after me down the road, flogging my back. At the gate to Jacobsvlei he stopped and screamed, 'Come back and I'll break your bloody neck, you hear!' Halfway home I hid in the sand dunes and bawled my eyes out. I had never been more terrified in my life.

When I got home my mother went straight to Tak. Tak came over to the cottage and inspected my injuries, a grave, furious expression on his face. He took me in the bakkie to the clinic for a checkup. I had concussion and a broken rib. I was treated and kept overnight for observation. Tak and my mother drove straight to Jacobsvlei and confronted Mr Fourie at home. According to my mother, quite an argument ensued, with Mrs Fourie getting involved. Threats and counter-threats flew thick and fast. Tak threatening to report Mr Fourie to the police and Mr and Mrs Fourie reminding Tak that the law would not look kindly upon his present relationship with my mother. Tak finished the argument by lifting Mr Fourie by the throat until his toes barely touched the ground. 'Manas was right,' he said. 'You're white trash, Fourie, an insult to Afrikaners. An insult to the human race.'

A heroic gesture from Tak? Ja, except to say a few days later he came to me as I lay recovering in bed at home and pointed his finger in my face. 'Never talk to a white man like that again,' he warned me. 'Never! I don't care what he calls you. If you do, then don't come running to me. I won't be there to help you, you hear? Know your place in this country, seun. Know your place!'

The incident cost me a year, since it happened just before my Standard Eight exams. I was taken out of Jacobsvlei and booked into boarding school in Malmesbury the following year. But a few weeks prior to leaving for Malmesbury Tak read an advertisement in the newspaper for Deakin College, an international correspondence school. Knowing my mother dreaded the idea of boarding school, he telephoned the college for details and found it satisfied all the requirements I needed to gain university entrance. And unlike other correspondence schools, it also offered art as a subject. So I was given the option of learning from home, which I accepted with some relief, considering I also didn't exactly relish the prospect of three years in boarding school.

Though I missed my lessons with dear old Grace (who'd just begun to make progress with my dreadful English) Deakin College proved a more than satisfactory alternative to Jacobsvlei. The course I took provided me with comprehensive study guides that were preferable to those demeaning afternoon sessions with Mr Fourie. To my distant supervisors I was just a faceless name and perhaps because facelessness is difficult to discriminate against, their own faceless correspondence was always polite and helpful.

Like a recluse I retreated to the quiet confines of my room with my assignments and worked. For three years, I worked each day. Tak and my mother were impressed by my self-discipline. I plodded away at the hard subjects, like English and Maths. Sometimes Tak helped me, since Maths was the only subject he'd been moderately good at, and his English wasn't too bad for an Afrikaner. With the subjects I enjoyed I was like a starved man who suddenly finds himself in fields of ripened fruit; I filled myself to bursting with things I knew so little about. I discovered the world of art, which Grace had only occasionally given me a glimpse of. It came to me in the shape of the Parthenon, of Michelangelo and Leonardo, of the Impressionists and Picasso. And my spirits were lifted to the clouds when I saw that mud people could be famous artists too. My faceless art supervisor never got to see me personally, though, of course, he had some insight into my background through the regular portfolio of paintings and drawings I was obliged to send him that usually consisted of portraits of my mother and studies of the local landscape. Thinking I might not relate fully to the Eurocentric art history syllabus, he sent me some magazines containing pictures by black artists.

And so I was introduced to the likes of Gerard Sekoto, Ephraim Ngatane and Julian Motau whose works reflected a reality closer to mine. They taught me that there was a way, through art, to make sense of our lives and that images can have wings that all artists can use for their freedom. Beauty no longer remained confined to sunsets and flowers and bits of driftwood washed up on the shore. Alone in my small room, with just the sound of the lagoon breathing in and out, beauty could be constructed and new worlds discovered. Such was my innocent euphoria.

A youthful vision of purity. God, where did it all go?

2 THE QUESTION OF TRANSGRESSION

Shortly after we arrived I went to pay my respects to Tak at the Groothuis. I undergo this formality each time I return to the cottage. I found him sitting on the stoep gazing at the lagoon, looking very old and thin. Apparently his interest in the farm has waned since my mother died; it's said that Abram Witbooi, his foreman, practically runs the place now. I confess to an uncertain sense of triumph; it pleases me to think that he longs for her. But with Tak you can never be too sure of anything. Perhaps it has nothing to do with my mother. Perhaps he's just grown old and sick of life.

I greeted him formally, as usual. He gestured to a chair and asked me to sit but I shook my head and told him I couldn't talk for long, though, of course, I had all the time in the world. Across a barrier of space we spoke uncomfortably about the weather and other irrelevant matters. Then I told him I had friends staying with me at the cottage. Once again I couldn't bring myself to explain my circumstances with Zelda and Helen, let alone mention anything about Australia; Tak and I had only my mother in common, really (or that is how I justified my deceit). What business was it of his, anyway? Tak's blue eyes scanned my puffy face as I talked. They tried to hold my slippery eyes, but failed.

'You've been drinking too much, Manas,' he said. 'You must straighten yourself out.'

I just nodded and took my leave, burning with humiliation.

Since then we've seen him only once or twice on the ridge looking down at the cottage, and I allowed myself to forget about him. Ja, I allowed myself to forget that Tak is not a character from the past, that he could walk into our lives at any moment. Which is precisely what he did this morning.

We were sitting around the table after breakfast. John sat leaning against the wall, as usual, warming his hands around a

55

mug of coffee. Zelda was dressed in a blue anorak and jeans, the ends of which were stuffed into woollen socks. There was a thick blanket over her lap. Despite the ample warmth in the kitchen she was taking no chances – cold is a serious business with Zelda. With her legs stretched out towards the stove she brushed and plaited Helen's hair. Helen looked very fetching in her red corduroy dungarees and blue jersey.

Zelda was going on at me.

'Doesn't the resultant void ever deter you?' she asked.

She was referring, of course, to my binge last night. I didn't answer her. I had nothing to say, really, and I didn't relish the idea of being hauled over the coals in front of John. I just watched her doing Helen's hair.

'Stove's hot, mustn't touch the stove,' Helen said, turning to Zelda.

'Keep still, my girl,' Zelda said.

'Stove's very hot!'

Zelda smiled. 'Yes, you mustn't touch the stove. It'll burn you.'

'It'll burn me sore!'

'That's right, my darling. Come, stand still. I'm not finished yet.'

I lit a cigarette and coughed as I inhaled.

'Daddy feeling sick?' Helen asked, wide-eyed.

'A little bit sick, my love,' I replied, smiling wanly.

'Daddy must have muti.'

'My sweet, Daddy needs much more than muti,' Zelda sighed, shaking her head. 'You promised not to drink, Manas. I thought you were going to prove to me we have a future together. You can forget about me going to Australia with you in this state.'

'Why's Daddy feeling sick?' Helen persisted.

'At least you used to talk about it,' Zelda went on. 'About what makes you drink. You gave some indication that you were willing and able to stop. Now you seem resigned to it – you seem to have resigned us to it too.'

'Why's Daddy feeling sick, Mommy?'

'Shush. Keep your head still.'

'Was Daddy drunk?'

*John looked at me with his flat dark gaze. They were all look-
ing at me.*

'You see,' Zelda said. 'She's not too young to notice any more.'

'Especially when you talk in front of her,' I replied.

'Don't shift the blame, Manas.'

*I laughed plaintively. 'Christ, Zelda, what is this? Okay, so I
tied one on last night. So what? You never used to bitch at me.
Remember the Grahamstown days. It was a big joke then, wasn't
it? Now all of a sudden I can't put a foot right.'*

*'You know it's not the same as in Grahamstown. You know
it's gone way past that. I hate it when you start ducking the
issue. You know it's a problem but you won't face it.'*

'Zelda ...'

*'Take a good hard look at yourself, Manas. Do something,
damn it! I can't bear this pathetic surrender! If you can't do it
for yourself, then do it for Helen and me – aren't we worth it?'*

I had no answer to that.

'Talk to me, Manas! Aren't we worth it?'

'Of course you are ...'

'Then why don't you do something?'

*I shrugged, resentful of the way she scolded me like a child,
especially in front of John.*

*'I'm frightened for you, Manas. Do you realise what's at
stake?'*

'Yes.'

'Is that all you have to say? Yes?'

'Yes, madam.'

*She rolled her eyes. 'God, you can infuriate me sometimes.
You're so bloody hopeless! I wish you could've heard yourself
vomiting last night. I don't know why you can't at least do it
quietly.'*

*Let it not be said that I am unashamed of my drinking. To
counter my embarrassment I produced my usual defensive
flippancy. 'Was I too loud, missus? I'm sorry, next time I'll fit a
silencer or something. A gizmo to vomit quietly in – a diving
helmet with an extractor fan, maybe. John's a practical bloke,
I'm sure he could knock something together for me.'*

'Is Daddy talking rubbish, Mommy?'

Zelda sighed. 'Be serious, Manas. Listen to what I'm saying for once!'

'Yes, madam.'

'And please don't give me that bloody mock-subservience shit. You know it irritates me.'

Helen gasped with delight. 'Mommy said shit! Mommy said shit!'

'And bloody,' I colluded.

'Shit and bloody! Oh, Mommy!'

'You're evading the issue again, Manas.'

'Sorry, missus.'

'You're impossible, you know.'

'Impossible? Nothing's impossible, madam, if you believe in the Lord ...'

Zelda gave me a mirthless look. 'That's right. Make a joke of it.'

'Trust in the Lord and anything's possible. Even me not being impossible.'

'Daddy's being silly!' Helen giggled.

Zelda gave Helen a pat on the leg. 'Okay, my girl. All finished.'

'Can I go play outside?'

'No, it's too cold and rainy. We must wait for Mr Sun to come out first. Go and find one of your books.'

'Don't want to read.'

'Well, you're not going outside, miss. You must either read or play with your toys. Or what about doing a nice drawing for Mommy?'

'Okay.'

Zelda pinched her cheek. 'Go along then.'

As Helen ran past John, he whisked her up and kissed her on the cheek. 'One for nothing,' he teased.

Helen squealed with delight. 'One for nothing! One for nothing!' she sang as she scampered off to the bedroom.

'She's a real little character,' John laughed.

I felt a sapping pain.

Zelda rubbed her thighs beneath the blanket. 'She's trying to be brave. That's what tears me up – she knows everything's falling apart.'

'Ag, Zelda, please don't start that again,' I said.

'You don't seem to realise, Manas. I'm not going to Australia with you like this. I've told you before.'

'You're just looking for excuses to stay. One mistake and you're at my throat.' I gestured at John. 'It's about him, isn't it?'

'Manas, you have an absolute genius for saying the wrong thing.'

'But it's true! You're just looking for an excuse ...'

John held up his hand. 'Whoa, I don't want to listen to this bullshit. Just leave me out of it, okay?' He got up and rinsed his mug out in the sink. But as he reached for his raincoat on the rack next to the stove there was a knock on the door. We looked at each other in surprise, then I got up and opened the door. Tak was standing there in the rain, his hat and raincoat dripping. He doffed his hat when he saw Zelda and nodded at John.

'How about a cup of coffee for an old man?' he said.

I hesitated for a second before showing him in.

'Hell, my old bones can't take this damn cold anymore,' he said, dumping a sack of potatoes on the floor next to the stove. 'You better eat these soon. Some of them are growing shoots.'

'Thanks, Oubaas,' I said.

'Don't mention it,' he replied, hanging his raincoat and hat next to John's.

We were speaking in Afrikaans and I knew Zelda and John could not speak it very well, so I introduced them to Tak in English. He and John shook hands. Then I offered him a chair and poured him some coffee.

'They always made a good cup of coffee in this house,' Tak said jovially in his thickly accented English. 'I'm sorry, I've got a bad memory for names. It's John and Zelda, isn't it?'

'That's right,' Zelda said. 'John and Zelda Sutton.'

'Ag, ja, you're the couple from the Eastern Cape. Manas mentioned you the other day.'

Zelda smiled. 'Not a couple, as such. John's my brother. Actually we're twins.'

'Ja? You'd never guess. You don't look the same.'

'I'll take that as a compliment,' Zelda said.

Tak laughed. 'I suppose you're artists too. Like Manas.'

'Zelda is,' I said. 'John's a farmer.'

''n Boer? Oh, then John and I have something in common, thank God. I know nothing about art so we better leave that subject alone. How do you come to know Manas?'

Zelda looked at me, a hint of confused anger in her eyes. 'We met in Grahamstown.'

'At university?'

'Yes. But I thought Manas would've told you...'

'I forgot,' I interjected. This sounded so lame, Zelda gave a plaintive laugh. She turned to me, eyebrows raised in an expectant manner, as if to say, what next? I glanced at John. He was nodding to himself as though nothing I did ever surprised him.

Tak smiled and shook his head. 'Ag, we all forget these days, don't we? Who am I to criticise? But, still, it's nice to meet your friends, Manas – it's good to see you have friends!'

I laughed weakly. 'Ja, one must be grateful for the Lord's blessings, Oubaas.'

Zelda glowered at me.

Tak turned to John. 'So where do you farm, John?'

'On the Fish River,' John replied. 'Mainly cattle but we grow a bit of chicory and some pineapples too. My Dad's always trying out something new. He's been running a few Angora goats lately.'

'Well, I wish I had the choice. All I can do on this place is graze sheep. After a while you get sick of the sight of them! So you're down on holiday?'

'Sort of.'

Tak laughed. 'Hell of a time to come on holiday! Didn't Manas tell you it rains the whole time here in winter?'

'These rooinekke like the rain, Oubaas,' I said.

Tak nodded and sipped his coffee. 'Ja, die Oos Kaap ... Fish River, you say. I've been up there once or twice. Nice part of the world, as I remember it. But that was years ago.' He turned to me. 'So, Manas, what are your prospects these days?'

'Prospects?'

'Ja, what are your plans? What are you going to do?'

'I don't know, Oubaas.'

'I thought you had plans, Manas,' Zelda said, eyes wide with feigned innocence. 'Big plans for the future.'

'Ag, not really...'

'Oh, I must've misunderstood you then. I thought you said something about going overseas.'

I glared at her frantically. All I got back was that same expectant look. Only her quickness of breath betrayed her anger. I lamented not having told Tak about her. It seemed crazy that I hadn't.

For his part, Tak seemed unaware of the tension. 'Overseas!' he scoffed. 'What's there to do overseas? You need to earn a living, Manas. You can't live off fresh air.'

'Ja, ek weet, Oubaas. I need time to think.'

Tak found my eyes and stared right through me. 'Sometimes it's better not to think too much, Manas,' he said. 'Sometimes it's better to let hard work occupy your time.'

Tak swigged back the last of his coffee.

'More coffee, Oubaas?' I asked, dutifully.

'No thanks. I must be going.'

Then, what I'd been dreading ... As Tak got up, there was a high-pitched call from the room.

'Daddy!'

Helen's voice cut the air like a knife.

'Daddy!' she called again.

'Ja!' I answered, looking at Tak.

'Daddy, I can't find my crayons.'

Helen appeared in the bedroom doorway. Dear, sweet little Helen. When she saw Tak's face with the strange birthmark, she cried out and ran to Zelda.

'Don't be frightened, my baby,' Zelda said.

'Oubaas Tak's not going to eat you, my sweetness,' I said.

Tak stood there uncomfortably, looking at Helen's troubled face. He seemed dumbfounded by her sudden appearance. I could almost hear his brain ticking over, tying up all the loose ends. Then he got down on his haunches and stretched out his hand. 'Come here, kleintjie,' he said gently.

Helen clung to Zelda.

'Go on, my girl,' Zelda said. 'Oubaas Tak's a nice man.'

61

Reluctantly, Helen went over to Tak. He took her little hand in his and placed her on his knee. 'What's your name, kleintjie?' he asked.

She told him in a tiny voice.

'Ag, liewe Vader, that's a pretty name for such a beautiful girl. How old are you?'

Helen held up three fingers. 'Nearly three,' she said.

'So you're a big beautiful girl, aren't you?'

Helen nodded solemnly.

'With big fat cheeks to collect all the nuts for winter. Just like a squirrel!'

'No!' Helen laughed scornfully.

'I can see you have your grandmother's eyes,' Tak said, 'and your mother's smile.'

He reached into his pocket and took out a small piece of biltong.

'Here, kleintjie, chew on this. It's good for your teeth.'

Then Tak took her off his knee and stood up. He took his raincoat and hat off the wall and bade Zelda and John goodbye. As I followed him outside, I saw Zelda was close to tears. I cursed life for being so damn complicated.

'Why didn't you tell me about the child?' Tak demanded when we were out of earshot.

I shrugged.

'Why, Manas?'

'I didn't think you would approve, Oubaas.'

Tak looked into my eyes and shook his head. 'My God, you've acquired all that knowledge you once thirsted for, but you haven't learned a thing – damn it! Why would you think I'd be angry?'

Again, I shrugged.

'You must open your eyes, Manas. I worry for your future, you know. I care for you.'

I didn't reply. I was sick to death of guilt.

'Knowledge should fill you, not empty you, Manas. Do you know why I came here today?'

It was raining and I was getting wet, and I couldn't have cared less why he came. Or so I thought.

'I came here because your mother died on this day.'

And he left me standing in the rain with the memory of her, of her warmth and sweetness, and the pain I felt when it was gone.

And so, we continue to wait, only there's a new dimension to the waiting, for Tak is part of our tangle now. John continues with his confounded hammering and scraping down on the slipway, the only one who doesn't complain about the cold. Zelda has taken Helen for a drive. She said she wants to clear her head, to get things into perspective. I'm filled with a sense of foreboding. I know important things are being deliberated. I know our future hangs in the balance.

I've built up the fire as a meagre defence against the cold and now I resign myself again to my table next to the window. Ja, the cold plays its part too. Langebaan is a place of extremes, a place of the emotions. In summer the land lies brown and dry under the hot sun; only the winds off the Atlantic make it tolerable. And in winter one cold front after another sweeps over the Cape. This year the rain has been very heavy. The farmers inland are concerned that the roots of their vines will rot, should the deluge continue. As we travelled here from Cape Town, we could see the mountains near Stellenbosch and Paarl white with snow.

And here, the winds from the Antarctic have chased away the land birds. The last to go were two pied crows that used to perch on the telephone poles up on the main road. And now the new arrivals are here. Avocets in their hundreds, nimbly negotiating the receding tide on their spindly legs, their upturned bills probing the sand. And there's been the rare sight of an albatross tilting and soaring above the lagoon, then sweeping up over the far hills back towards the sea. I took that as a good omen for some reason.

A messenger of change ...

*

The thought of our future hanging in the balance evokes a painful nostalgia for the place that brought us together. I long for lost awakenings. For the discovery of myself in my love for Zelda. For the sense of purpose that was once a shining path.

If I close my eyes I can see Grahamstown nestling among the Eastern Cape hills. I see the Settlers Monument, modern and incongruous, poised like Sisyphus's rock above the town that, by contrast, looks almost medieval with its old buildings and spires poking the sky. A place famous for its churches and as a place of learning. There are the grand schools, places of privilege and excellence, and, of course, Rhodes University cradled below Gunfire Hill, surrounded by its immaculate lawns and gardens. A town with a proud sense of its history. Stone Georgian homes painted white with slate roofs. Quaint places built by those stoic British migrants who sought a better life in Africa, who braved the untamed land and marauding Xhosa warriors. Oak trees. Fungus. Bells. A poignant glimpse into a bygone time. Settler country, settler spirit …

Then my mind's eye blinks and I'm looking across at the sprawling shanty townships stretching up to the tree-lined knoll called Makana's Kop and beyond, among the poorest and most squalid in South Africa. A haze of smoke hangs over the cluttered hovels of Fingo Village. Ragged children play soccer on the dirt streets in the wake of yellow police casspirs. Thin dogs bark at the presence of troop carriers that line the main road to the north. Dust. Plastic bags impaled on bushes and barbed-wire fences …

Ja, the warm venom of nostalgia. Often I ask myself why I yearn for that wretched place that blessed and damned me and left me washed up on this shore, an opdrifsel, searching for some meaning to what I've become. Searching for a lost enchantment …

But, wait, I'm running ahead of myself again. Such sentiment must be filtered through fact before it assumes any meaning. Let me sift once more through the chaos of fact for what makes sense. Let me go back to my agreement with Tak.

Because I had to work for Tak after finishing matric, I endured a frustrating wait of two years before going to university – two years was the time white boys spent doing their national service. Frankly, I considered this obligation (as did many of my white counterparts, no doubt) a complete waste of time. But Tak, in his unfathomable wisdom, saw it as a test of character; through labour and drudgery I would learn discipline and prove my mettle – some still believe in such nonsense.

Labour and drudgery, that's all it was to me. Along with the Arendses and Witboois I tended sheep and fixed fences. I spread gravel on the roads and whitewashed the walls of the Groothuis and sheds. I acquired a heavy-duty driver's license and carted sheep to the abattoir in Vredenburg. I also acquired a love for solitary drinking. Nooitgedacht conformed to an old tradition on Cape farms where at the end of the day each adult worker received a dop of crude wine to quench their thirst. The amount varied from a half-pint to a pint, depending on seniority. While the Arendses and Witboois liked to sit around talking of mundane day-to-day things as they drank, I preferred my own company on the dunes. I'd take my half-bottle down to the shore and sit watching the sun go down, happy to escape the tedium of farm labour and the veiled hostility which the Arendses and Witboois still had towards me. The wine was not enough to get drunk on but it gave birth to a yearning for the lonely comfort it gave me.

All the while Tak observed me without comment. He allowed me the weekends off to practise my drawing and painting; no doubt he sensed my frustrations. I tried to read at night but was usually too tired. I had the cottage practically to myself then, as my mother had moved into the Groothuis with Tak. That and the pure waste of time working on Nooitgedact fostered a growing resentment in me. I struggled to remember I was fortunate.

But, at last, there came the time when Tak felt I'd paid my dues. He finally gave his consent for me to apply to the universities he considered appropriate. If I was going to university I might as well go to a proper one, he said. It was enlightening to hear this inadvertent acknowledgment from an Afrikaner that the system functioned poorly for us 'nie-blankes'. Ja, he said he wasn't going to waste his money on the autonomous or homeland universities that were full of betogers and troublemakers. Tak had read enough in the newspapers to know that places like the University of the Western Cape and Fort Hare were constantly plagued by violent protest – such places were the playgrounds of skollies, he muttered, insisting that I emerge from university with a degree and not a criminal record. So it was Tak who insisted I attend an English-medium university, given that the Afrikaans-medium institutions would not sully their premises with non-whites, other than the likes of gardeners and cleaners.

I soon found that places in 'proper' universities were scarce. English universities had the right to admit only limited numbers of non-white students; consequently my application to the University of Cape Town (my preference) was unsuccessful but I managed eventually to get a place at Rhodes University. The thought of Grahamstown made me apprehensive. The Eastern Cape was a long way from home but, as Tak succinctly put it, beggars could not be choosers and maybe the distance would do me good. It would make me more independent – I could not hold onto my mother's apron strings forever. Since the campus residences were full Tak organised accommodation for me by placing an advertisement in Grahamstown's local newspaper, *Grocott's Mail*. He received a reply from a coloured builder, Manie Brand, and they settled on a reasonable monthly figure for board and lodging.

My mother saw me off on the bus to Cape Town. She'd been suffering from prolonged headaches for a few weeks, which Tak and I attributed to her fussing over my pending departure. I like to remember the way she looked as she waved goodbye, her smiling face filled with pride and hope, my departure to university the fruition of her dreams. Barely a trace of the withered look she had begun to assume. From Cape Town I took the train to Grahamstown and arrived at my destination two days later, late in the afternoon. I stood on the platform in the new clothes Tak had bought me, the conservative blazer and tie and shiny black shoes, suitcase in hand. And my meagre courage just shrivelled inside me. I felt like crying. Ja, twenty years old and frightened as a child. The stationmaster shouted at me to move along, so I went outside to the car park where I waited for Manie Brand to fetch me, as had been arranged. It was hot and there was a storm brewing over Gunfire Hill towards Port Elizabeth. A group of black children approached me and asked for money. These beggars, some of them mere infants, were brazen and streetwise and they made me feel uneasy. I gave them a few coins and they went on their way without a word of thanks.

At last, just as it began to rain, Manie Brand arrived. Manie drove a battered Toyota bakkie into which he had crammed his wife, Hester, and seven children. My first impression of Manie was of a big-bellied man with no arse. He looked like an elephant from the back as he grabbed my case and threw it on the bakkie. I was introduced to the children in order from eldest to youngest: Paulus, David (whom the others called Stompie, because of his stocky frame), Piet, Marie, Fanie, Willem and Annetjie. Willem and Annetjie were twins. They were all so excited. I guessed tenants were not an everyday thing in their lives.

It started to pour as we drove to their place. The kids on the back threw a tarpaulin over my suitcase to keep it from getting wet. Hester sat squashed between Manie and me up front, her legs astride the gear lever. She was a slight, pale-skinned woman, whose short dress was not designed for straddling gear levers. Each time Manie changed gear there was a silly moment of embarrassment in which Manie looked matter-of-fact, Hester stared fixedly ahead, and I inspected my fingernails.

But it was only a few minutes' drive from the station to their place and we arrived with the kids not too drenched and Hester's dignity somewhat ruffled but intact. The Brands lived along Currie Street in Grahamstown's semi-industrial area which acted as a sort of buffer zone between the white areas and the black township. Their house was situated across the road from a panel beater. Attached to the gate was a sign that read: MANIE BRAND – QUALITY BUILDER & PAINTER. Manie's place hardly bore testimony to these proffered skills. The house was run down with gutters sagging and in sore need of a coat of paint. There were half a dozen rusted cars lying around in the yard in various stages of disintegration, all old wrecks Manie had failed to resurrect. A black mongrel jumped all over Piet as he opened the gate and chased after us as we drove in.

We skirted the minefield of dog shit on the lawn and I was ushered inside and shown to my study, a tiny room that Manie had sectioned off the enclosed back veranda with masonite boards and a makeshift door – just big enough to accommodate the small school desk that faced the window and the cupboard and bed against the wall. Water was dripping through the corrugated iron roof in the corner. I guessed that in summer I would bake in this room and freeze in winter. Outside, the black dog was standing up at the window, watching us with a ludicrous grin on its face.

While Hester made supper and the children got ready for bed, Manie fixed the leak in my room with a bit of Pratley's Putty. Then he walked me up Currie Street to the crest of Fitzroy Street where we could get a good view of the town. It had stopped raining and the air was fresh and clean. Manie pointed out the dark spire of the Cathedral and the university buildings, and showed me which roads to take to reach the campus. We stood for a while in silence, looking down at the small town that had not changed much in a hundred years. I asked Manie how long he'd lived in Grahamstown.

Manie pursed his lips. 'About fifteen years, or so. I come from East London originally.'

'Do you like it here?'

'Ag, Manas, you know how it is. We've had our ups and downs. But in this country you can't pick and choose. At least we're better off than those poor bastards across the spruit.'

I could see the township hovels across the Kowie stream shrouded in the blue smoke of cooking fires. Then we walked back. After the rain the sounds were sharp and clear. I could hear dogs barking and people shouting from Fingo Village. I could hear trains shunting down at the station. There was a strange blue light coming from some of the houses, which Manie told me was the glow from television sets. Such a novice was I to the real world!

Supper with the Brands was a noisy affair. They were a Christian family; everyone bowed their heads solemnly and shut their eyes as Manie said grace. After that, the children chattered like monkeys, hardly pausing to swallow their food. Manie talked nonstop, too, about the problems he was having with some building job. Hester and I couldn't get a word in edgeways, not that I had much to contribute.

After supper Manie put the children to bed. I offered to help Hester with the washing up but she wouldn't hear of it. So I stood awkwardly in the kitchen and talked with her. She asked me all about my background and how I'd managed to afford university. I told her that Tak was paying, without divulging too many details.

Then Manie came in and made some coffee and the three of us sat around the table and talked some more. Manie couldn't stifle his yawns and Hester and I were awarded a fine view of his tonsils and uvula behind an array of crooked teeth. At last, he finished his coffee and bade us good night. Hester shook her head as he went off to bed. He works too hard, she said.

I turned in too. I lay in my bed thinking of my mother and Tak and the peaceful lagoon. I thought of the way the station-master had shouted at me as I stood on the platform, as though I were a dog, and I wondered if this was all worth it. Mostly I thought of my mother.

The next day I woke early to the sound of Manie's bakkie starting up outside. Manie went off to work at 5.30 each morning when he had work on the go. I was soon to discover that the Brands lived a precarious existence. Manie managed to keep his business ticking over only by undercutting the white builders. After costs, he made next to nothing.

I got dressed and went to the kitchen where I found Hester ironing some clothes.

'You're up bright and early,' she said.

'I thought I'd get going before the children get up.'

'You mustn't mind them,' Hester said. 'There's some porridge on the stove. Help yourself.'

69

I dished up a bowl of porridge for myself and sat down to eat. Hester looked at my blazer and tie.

'You look very smart,' she said.

'I have to register at the university today.'

'What will you be studying?'

'Fine Art.'

'Fine Art? What's Fine Art?'

'You know, art. Painting and sculpture, stuff like that.'

'What can you do with that?'

'I don't know. Become an artist. Teach maybe.'

'You're very lucky, you know.'

'I know.'

'The white man who pays for you must be very kind. You don't get many like him.'

'He's a good man.'

Hester sighed. 'I wish my children could have a decent education. Piet and Marie, especially. They're bright kids.' There was a quick flash of anger in her eyes. 'But there's no hope for them. They will have to learn to struggle, like Manie and me.'

She was about to say something else, then didn't.

After breakfast I walked into town, down past the station towards the Cathedral. There was plenty of time so I paused to browse through the books in Grocott's store. Then I ambled slowly down High Street, looking at all the shops. Again, the little beggars swarmed around me asking for money. I gave them the few coins I had in my pocket. Then, suddenly, there was the sound of sirens as a police motor-cade came tearing down the road, turning in at the Law Courts. From one of the prison vans came the sound of men singing and the beggars waved at them as they passed. I asked them who the men were and they looked at me as though I was completely stupid. They are the comrades, they said. African National Congress, ANC, fighters for our free-dom. They are being tried for treason. One of the kids laughed and held up his fist. 'Viva treason!' he shouted.

I went on and came to the university where I was directed to the Union. There I stood in a long queue to register for my course, feeling ridiculous in my blazer and tie. Jeans and T-shirts seemed to be the general uniform – hardly what I'd expected in the hallowed halls of learning. Ja, I cringe when I think of myself there, the naive, conservative boy from the distant West Coast, amid all those bright, articulate white kids, all so casual and sophisticated, taking everything in their stride. I wondered if I would ever bridge the gap.

After a couple of hours of standing in line and filling in forms I finished registering and wandered back into town. As the beggars began to gather again, I vowed to get rid of my blazer and tie. Any sign of affluence was like the scent of carrion to flies.

I was beset by a sudden compulsion. I withdrew some money from the building society where Tak deposited a monthly allowance and bought a cheap bottle of Paarl Perlé at a hotel off-sales. Then I walked up into the pine forests above the town, where I sat down and drank the wine. It was a wonderful warmth that overcame me, as I sat there with my thoughts. It was the first time I got drunk. The wind through the trees was sweet to my ears, and my fear was gone …

Ja, the first time. Sitting there gazing over the strange new town – fearless, filled with brave thoughts. Filled with a belief that only good things lay ahead. I would become a famous artist, admired and envied across South Africa. My achievements would fill my mother with pride. I would make Tak envious – I would make the ghost of my father envious. And then the encroaching sickness, falling on my hands and knees as my insides erupted. The nagging bewilderment I felt as I made my way back to the Brands once I'd sobered up.

*

My first year at Rhodes was a time of frustration and ineptness where I found it a constant struggle to cope. My sense of inadequacy was, no doubt, caused in part by my unfamiliarity with university culture and in part by my circumstances at the Brands, which brings my own social shortcomings into question. But my poor English proved the biggest stumbling block. Aside from the compulsory first-year Fine Art subjects I'd chosen English as a minor in the belief that a better grasp of it would help me through the course. It soon became apparent that although Grace Cook's kindly tutelage and Deakin College's faceless correspondence courses had begun to repair Jacobvlei's prior neglect, I was nevertheless ill-prepared for university-level English. Now my poor grammar and limited vocabulary made my written assignments pedestrian at best and tied my tongue in knots in studio discussions or tutorials. While my fellow students were friendly and helpful enough, I felt an outsider, embarrassed by my many limitations and by my fractured English delivered in a pronounced Cape Coloured accent.

I managed reasonably well in the studios; fortunately in art one can be articulate without words, despite what the conceptualists may say. First-year Basic Art comprised Cast Drawing, Object Drawing and General Composition. I looked forward to these studio sessions where the language of mark was mostly all one needed to communicate. But in the academic subjects – History of Art and English – the level to which I now aspired seemed insurmountable. I could hardly understand what my lecturers were saying, let alone respond intelligibly.

I soon realised that as far as History of Art and English were concerned, drastic measures needed to be taken if I was to survive. So, outside of studio sessions, I began to spend most of my time in the library. Each day I secluded myself in its quiet confines and worked until it closed at night. My room at the Brands became merely a place to sleep; I left early and returned late at night, often after they'd all gone to bed. In the beginning Manie and Hester seemed taken aback by my absence, especially when I didn't turn up for dinner in the evenings. I didn't want to seem unsociable, so I went to church with them every Sunday, and sometimes I went with them down to Port Alfred for a day on the beach. Those were pleasant outings. While Manie fished and Hester slept under an umbrella, and the kids slid down the great white dunes in cardboard boxes, I walked along the water's edge, dreaming of impossible things.

The social life of the university passed me by. I missed all the festivities that began the year – Rag, the dances and wild, drunken parties. It was all too new and strange. By all accounts my fellow first-year students were having a riotous time, but I preferred to keep my nose in my books, and if I did get drunk it was on my own.

The world of politics was also new to me. As South Africa's internal conflict worsened in the early 1980s, the liberal universities experienced their fair share of campus unrest, and Rhodes was no exception. My reluctant initiation into politics came courtesy of the radical Black Students Movement. The BSM had been born in what the University referred to as its 'decommissioned' residences. These were segregated de facto residences claimed to be outside the general residence structure, an elaborate ploy by the Rhodes administration to get around government legislation against accommodating non-white students on campus. During their existence these residences became hotbeds of BSM activism and, not surprisingly, they were raided regularly by the Department of Community Development and the security police. More than once I thanked my lucky stars I'd not been able to get into a residence.

Because of our advantaged position (compared to other non-whites), black, Indian and coloured students, including those outside the residences, were expected to fall in line with whatever the BSM dictated. For a while I was badgered into attending meetings and did so half-heartedly, bewildered by all the abbreviated names of anti-apartheid organisations and what they stood for – AZAZO, AZAZM, AZAPO – amoeboid groups secretly affiliated to the banned African National Congress or Pan Africanist Congress, constantly changing shape to confuse the security police. I disliked the fierce rhetoric I heard at these meetings and one day simply stopped going. I watched warily from a distance, my instincts telling me to avoid those who hacked so furiously at

73

the Achilles tendon of white society. Naive and reticent, I just wanted to get on with my studies and not waste Tak's money by getting into trouble with the police.

While there were, of course, many liberal white students sympathetic to the struggle, some with deep passion and willingness to sacrifice, most seemed politically apathetic. Benign and conservative (though espousing liberal views) they read newspapers and fretted about the growing unrest. They shook their heads at the state of the country. They voted for the Progressive Federal Party. They even signed petitions against such things as the Internal Security Act or conscription. But they were also secretly irritated by the hostile behaviour of groups like the BSM. For them, there was a time and place for everything, and university wasn't the time or place to be fooling around with subversive politics. They were at Rhodes to become qualified so they could get on in a world that was becoming increasingly harder to get on in, even for whites. Besides, the English universities were the only relatively free institutions in South Africa – what possible purpose would be served by subverting them? I felt an uneasy affinity with these apathetic ones: those who felt that violence was not the way to achieve political ends, those who had not borne the brunt of the system.

Problems of language and politics aside, this time was not without its rewards. I spoke of the solace I found in the studios. It was in the studio classes that my faltering confidence was restored sufficiently for me to persevere. There I found that when it came to ability I measured up well against the other students. I revelled in the discipline imposed by our lecturers, the only discipline that's ever been attractive to me. Always first in the studio and last to leave, I slaved at my assignments, always doing more than was expected.

I realised that inadvertently Tak had made the right choice in sending me to Rhodes. It appealed to my conservative bent, an admission I now make with a strange mix of gratitude and reserve. As emphatically regional as any art centre could be, Rhodes Art School prided itself in an earthy philosophical attachment to its locale. Seemingly indifferent to outside trends in contemporary art, it advocated a hybrid romanticism in which a sense of place ruled supreme. The 'Rhodes style' in painting was well known around the country – sublime pastoral scenes of the Eastern Cape, the timeless appeal of windswept trees against turbulent skies, thick impasto surfaces you'd expect to find in a Constable or Van Gogh. While other South African art schools contemptuously dismissed Rhodes's cherished pantheism as retrograde academicism they could not ignore the fact that all art schools were in the same boat, more or less. They all conformed to a peculiar introspective tendency during the 1980s where the ability to focus outwards, beyond South Africa, was rare. True, this introspection was partly the result of South Africa's ostracism from the world; the Cultural Boycott had denied South African art an international voice. But it also stemmed from the massive political revolution that was unfolding, where real matters of life and death made embracing the facile artistic trends of a hostile outside world seem a little strange and futile. So not for South African art schools the call of New York, London or Cologne. And certainly not for Rhodes the flimsy pluralism of postmodernism, the boutique intellectualism of French theory or the clumsy excesses of American and German neo-expressionism. No, Rhodes dug itself deep into the layers of its own soil and attempted to grow from itself.

And I felt safe and secure in this soil. I worked tirelessly at my studio assignments and looked forward to the weekends when I could walk up into the hills above the town and sketch the surrounding countryside. I'd always had an affinity with landscape, I suppose because landscapes don't stare back the way people do. The subject of people made me nervous, mostly because I had to confront myself through them. The only figure studies we did in first year were drawings from plaster casts of old Renaissance and classical statues, a practice more akin to still-life drawing; real people didn't exist in those statues, only aesthetic rules. That suited me fine for a while, but I soon recognised a need in myself to go beyond such safe confines. I felt that if I really wanted to explain the world through art it must be through people. So I hunted through the library for artists who had confronted themselves through people. I discovered men like Goya and Giacometti and emulated them. I filled sketchbooks with figure drawings, perhaps too consciously imitating Giacometti's linear style. Giacometti's fear of the world was something I was immediately drawn to. My lecturers complimented me on my commitment. Ja, when it came to learning my craft I would leave nothing undone, no stone unturned.

Around May each year the Fine Art Department would host an exhibition called *Milestones*. Held in conjunction with art schools in Port Elizabeth, Alice and East London, the exhibition was open to lecturers and students alike and was intended to survey art trends in the Eastern Cape. I submitted a small oil landscape, a scene looking down the Kowie River near Bathurst. Quite detailed but already demonstrating I'd acquired the trademark Rhodes impasto. I attended the opening, arriving a little late because I'd felt the need to fortify myself in the forest with a few beers first, and was astonished to find a red sticker next to my painting. A fellow student congratulated me and told me it was Professor Strachan, my History of Art lecturer, who'd bought it. I celebrated by consuming enough wine to make me quite vocal for a change, enough also (when it reacted with the beer) to make me vomit on the way home to the Brands.

The following week I received a message to see Professor Strachan. I viewed this with some trepidation because as far as lecturers went he was the most intimidating, so much so I cowered at the back of my Art History tutorials, avoiding making eye contact with him. Professor Roland Strachan was one of the university's eccentric figures, a familiar sight around campus, a lanky man in his late fifties, striding along beneath a wide-brimmed straw sombrero which he wore to protect his prominent Gaelic nose from the African sun. Short-cropped grey hair, salt-and-pepper beard, and merry blue eyes. According to what my fellow students said, he'd once been a prominent landscape artist but for some reason had given up painting and devoted his time to teaching and writing (what his detractors called coffee-table) biographies of artists he fancied. He also occasionally wrote reviews for Port Elizabeth's *Herald* newspaper. As with any conspicuous figure, he had his supporters and detractors. Among his supporters, some respected his erstwhile abilities as a painter, some respected the critical insight he delivered in his teaching and writing, while others admired his forthright (if cantankerous) manner and his ability to drink anyone under the table. His detractors, particularly those in the university's senior management, thought he was a pretentious, arty-farty troublemaker. They gained this impression because Professor Strachan was a tireless crusader for the arts, especially when the question of funding equity arose.

The first thing that greeted me as I walked into his office was a wooden African carving of a man with an enormous erect phallus, which acted as a doorstop. Then I noticed my painting on the wall next to the window. Professor Strachan motioned at me to sit and reached for a folder that lay on his desk. He hummed tunelessly as he paged through it. At last he removed a recent essay on Greek sculpture from the folder and placed it on the desk in front of him. He placed a hand on it, looked at me with an astonished expression and burst out laughing. I sat there uncomfortably, unused to his peculiarities.

His laughter stopped abruptly.

'How do you pronounce your name? Manas or Munnus?'

'Munnus, Professor.'

'Ah, the Afrikaans way. That explains your essay. With a surname like Smith I was a little confused as to your origins, Manas.' He turned to eye my landscape on the wall. 'I take it you've noticed I approve of your painting. That's a nice little piece. A few compositional faults, but I like the mood.'

'Thank you, Professor.'

He swivelled his gaze to me and sighed.

'Of course, moody, romantic landscapes could not be more out of touch with what's happening overseas in the real world, but since when have we here at Rhodes ever worried about contemporary discourse? Ha! Since when have we had our finger on the international pulse? Don't be silly, dear boy – bugger the world, we have our finger on our *own* pulse!'

He burst out laughing again, and stopped. 'I'm sorry, I shouldn't denigrate my own institution, but sometimes I can't help it. In time, Manas, you will understand what I mean. But I didn't ask you here to sample my sarcasm. I asked you here to tell you I like your painting. It shows the dedication that might well make you an artist one day – that's clear enough. And that might be enough in itself, but will it be enough to earn a degree? I'm afraid not. Not in this institution at any rate. That's what I really want to talk to you about.'

'You failed my essay. Again.'

'No, Manas. *You* failed your essay.'

I sighed. 'It's hopeless. My English is hopeless.'

He smiled. 'Let's not get too despondent. I really have just one thing to say: Don't give up. Your English is weak, yes, but it's not an insurmountable problem – it's just something you'll have to overcome. I never lose sight of what we're here to do, and that is turn talented people into artists. Professionals, not amateurs. And, of course, if you want to be a professional a sound knowledge of art history is undeniably important but whether you can write glib academic tomes about it is really not what we're after. Good ideas made tangible through good technique is more important, not so, Manas?'

He held up my essay. 'But of course to get your degree you're going to have to do something about your English. Let me make myself clear; this is bad but it isn't hopeless – there's some substance and originality in what you're trying to say. The trouble is, your language lets you down. So what you're trying to say is not your problem. It's how you're saying it that is. In other words, your basic grammar is up to shit.'

Professor Strachan laughed again. 'Fortunately for you, Manas, your problem is easily remedied through simple practical application. Hard work. Increase your vocabulary. Learn your basic grammar. Read as much as you can. Speak as much as you can, even if it is embarrassing. From now on I want to hear more of you in your tutorials. If you're tenacious and dedicated enough you'll soon acquire the necessary skills to pull through. It'll take hard work but look on it as a means to an end. If it were creativity you lacked there would be no purpose to this interview.'

I sat mute, scared to open my mouth, lest I say something stupid.

Absently, Professor Strachan picked up a loose piece of paper and began folding it into a paper jet.

'But you must remember,' he went on, 'first and foremost, you're here to become an artist. That's your main responsibility.' He glanced again at my essay. 'I took the liberty of finding out how you were doing in English. Your lecturer tells me you're failing there too, but only marginally. That means you can pull through providing you work hard. I hope this provides an incentive to continue with the course, Manas.'

Professor Strachan finished folding the paper jet and threw it into the air. He watched, amazed, as it glided across the room.

'You know, I once wanted to be a pilot,' he said, 'but I was – am – colour-blind, so I didn't pass the eyesight tests. You might find that astonishing, coming from a person who used to paint pictures.' He shook his head. 'Too bad, I think I'd have loved flying. But that's irrelevant. Get to work, Manas. I'll be watching your progress.'

I got up.

'Thank you, Professor,' I said.

He grunted impatiently and waved me away.

*

My illiterate grandfather had never placed much importance on my mother's education. While her brothers, my dead uncles, reached the lofty heights of Standard Three, she only went as far as half of Standard One before Oupa took her out to do, as he saw it, more useful things around the home, the result being she was virtually illiterate. So the correspondence that passed between us went through Tak. One day, I got a letter from Tak asking me to phone the farm, reverse charges. I made the call in the evening from a public phone outside the post office. Tak answered and we engaged in our usual formal pleasantries before my mother came on the line.

'Hello, Manas,' she said. 'How are you, my seun?'

'I'm well, Ma. And you?'

There was a short silence, then she said, 'Oubaas Tak is looking after me, my child. Tell me, how are the Brands treating you? Are they feeding you properly?'

'Ja, Ma. They're treating me well.'

'And how is it going at the university?'

'Very well,' I lied.

'That's good,' she sighed.

There was another silence before she asked, 'Are you safe, my son? They tell me the universities are full of trouble-makers. Betogers. Is that true, Manas?'

I laughed. 'That's nonsense, Ma! Don't listen to Oubaas! He thinks there's a betoger behind every bush.'

My mother laughed too, but there was pain in it.

'I miss you, Manas,' she said.

'I miss you too, Ma. Very much.'

'You must look after yourself, see?'

Then she started crying.

'What's wrong, Ma? Wat makeer?'

'Nothing, my child. I just miss you and wanted to hear your voice. It means so much to hear you.'

'Don't worry about me. I'll be fine.'

'I know. I just wanted to hear your voice again.'

'One day I'll make you happy and provide for you, Ma. One day I'll make you proud and buy nice things for you. Wait and see.'

That started her crying again. 'I'm already proud of you, my child. I must go now, Manas.'

'Goodbye, Ma.'

'Totsiens, Manas. Look after yourself, see?'

As I walked home to the Brands that night I knew something was wrong with my mother, but I could not have dared imagine how serious it was. Then, in the days that followed, I allowed myself to forget her, so engrossed was I in my studies and in the growing body of drawings and paintings I was producing. Works that seemed to hold all the answers.

And then my mother died, and there were no answers to that.

She and Tak had decided not to tell me about the inoperable tumour that had begun growing in her brain. In her naive selflessness, my mother was concerned it would divert me from my studies. In the beginning she was given a fifty/fifty chance but even when the odds shifted to the point where her doctor advised her of the probability of death, neither she nor Tak anticipated the cancer would finish her so quickly; she'd been undergoing chemotherapy for some weeks when suddenly her condition deteriorated rapidly and she died in a coma.

The pain and shock of it was like nothing I'd known. It made the days ahead seem meaningless and futile. Life seemed gutted, devoid of warmth and sweetness. I was filled with grief and despair. My mother had always been precious to me, but in recent years I'd become concerned only with what I was to be, with what I would mean to her. Now I realised, too late, she was all I had in the world.

It was approaching winter when I made the long, cold journey home to attend her funeral. Tak fetched me at the bus stop in Langebaan. As we drove to the farm, he said, gently and simply, 'Your mother has been saved from her suffering, Manas. You must try to think of it like that. She has found peace at last.'

I tried not to weep, but I did.

My mother's burial was a lonely affair. Aside from the dominee who implored God to open the doors of heaven for the travel-weary soul who knocked, there were just Tak and me standing there, heads bared in the rain, looking down at her grave between my grandfather's and my father's. We listened to the dominee's words. He spoke of the endless love and mercy of God and I felt thankful it was just the three of us at the graveside, that the Arendses and Witboois had not seen fit to brave the rain to pay their respects – perhaps they had no respects to pay. And when the sermon was over Tak and I took spades and filled in the grave. Tak offered the dominee a dop afterwards but he declined. He was in a hurry to be on his way.

Later, as the evening came over, Tak and I sat on the stoep of the Groothuis. There was a cold wind blowing off the silver water and I couldn't stop shivering, not even when Tak poured me a stiff dop of brandy. We sat drinking quietly, then I said, 'What happens now, Oubaas Tak?'

Tak just stared at the lagoon.

'What happens now, Oubaas?' I repeated.

Tak looked at me. 'We carry on, Manas. That's what we do. We carry on.'

'But now that she's dead, Oubaas, what happens to me?'

Tak smiled sadly. 'You don't give me much credit, do you?'

'Oubaas?'

'I pay my debts, Manas. I fulfil my promises, if that's what you're getting at. I shall continue to pay for your studies, and you may use the cottage as your home.'

'Thank you, Oubaas.'

'You don't need to thank me, Manas. There was more to this than a business transaction, you know.'

I spent the next few days alone in the cottage, alone with the memories of childhood conversations and of the colours of burning driftwood, and flowers on the window sill. I slithered beneath the warmth of the aura she had left behind. With just my eyes protruding, I probed the shadows …

*

I went back to Grahamstown and lost myself in my studies, determined to honour my mother's memory by fulfilling her expectations of me. I knew I had to do this if there was to be any future ahead of me. I lived with the frail hope that someone like her would enter my life one day and fill the void she had left. I passed the mid-year studio exams with good grades but marginally failed the written subjects, as expected. Because of my personal circumstances I was given a condoned pass for those.

The July holidays came and I couldn't bear the thought of going home to Langebaan, so I stayed and worked. And when I wasn't working, I slept or drank to pass the time. On two occasions I passed out up in the forests above the town from too much wine, causing Manie and Hester Brand some concern because I didn't arrive home to sleep. When Hester smelled the alcohol on my breath she rebuked me, accusing me of falling in with bad company. She might have been even more concerned had she known the bad company I was keeping was my own.

I never got used to living with the Brands. For this I must accept most of the blame, since I had chosen to remain a stranger to them. The Brands were decent folk, salt-of-the-earth types, but I found it hard to fit in with them, especially after my mother died. It got to a point where my presence seemed to create a tension in the home. When I appeared conversations would stop, the children's infectious laughter would fade and everyone would stand around, ill at ease, making polite comments about stupid things like the weather or Currie Cup rugby. So while I liked Manie and appreciated his struggle to make ends meet, I never overcame the little we had in common. And while I had a soft spot for the twins, Willem and Annetjie, who were so cute and funny, and for quiet Marie, who took life so seriously for her tender years, I was unable to show this affection and, of course, it wasn't returned.

But there was also Hester's constant prying into my background. She rarely missed a chance to remind me of my good fortune in having Tak pay for my education. And her tactless comments about my mother angered me. I realised Hester's envy had its roots in despair. Privilege in South Africa, from the perspective of the poor, is a dirty thing. It is preordained, selective – the preserve of whites, not people like me. Hester's envy was embedded also in resentment; why should some have chances while the rest suffer? She and her children faced a future shackled by poverty. There was no light at the end of the tunnel for them. Why should I be different? But I too felt a resentment. I hated the sense of guilt privilege imposed upon me.

And also, quite simply, I found I hated living cheek by jowl with others. For most of my life I'd lived with just my mother in our remote cottage at Langebaan. I'd been fortunate to have taken privacy for granted. With some shame I acknowledge my absurd fastidiousness; circumstances at the Brands were hardly what others might call overcrowded. (Spare a thought for those in the townships, not a stone's throw from the Brands.) Still, the Brands' home always seemed bursting at the seams. Everything was so different from the quiet cottage at Langebaan. All so cluttered, so noisy. I wasn't used to being unable to find a moment's peace on my own. Even in my study I'd look up from my books to find a couple of the kids, usually Piet and Fanie, watching me through the door, giggling at whatever they found amusing about someone reading books. I'd taken privacy for granted before; now I realised I couldn't live without it.

Try as I might, I couldn't get used to living with the Brands. My bleak study, slapped together by Manie in an attempt to meet Tak's minimum requirements, was damp and inhospitable. There were no shelves for my books and the single ceiling light made it difficult to read at night. The wall above my bed was festooned with bathroom plumbing that squawked and shuddered the moment a tap was turned. Also, there was a lavatory at the other end of the veranda that seemed to be in constant use. And to cap it all, each cold winter's night the poor black dog whined outside and scratched on the window. Once, I took pity on it and let it sleep in the study. This caused remonstrations from both Manie and Hester. The dog is there to guard the house, nothing else, Manie said firmly.

Noise, always noise. Manie liked to listen to the radio in the lounge and when he wasn't around the older kids would tune in to a pop music station and turn up the volume full-blast. Hester fussed endlessly with the pots and pans in the kitchen. And during the day there was a fearsome racket from the panel beaters across the road, to say nothing of the din kicked up by the twins (who were not yet at school) as they ran around the yard outside. Ja, if I think back to the Brands in Grahamstown, one thing comes to mind immediately – noise.

I noticed the arrival of spring and summer almost absently, a disinterested recognition that flowers were blooming and the leaves were changing colour and that I no longer needed a jacket when I went drawing outdoors. With exams looming, though, there was not much time to savour the outdoors. Most of the time I was shut away in the library, working on written assignments. My confidence grew as my command over English improved. I was pleased with my new ability to contribute to the lively discussions during tutorial sessions, especially in History of Art where Professor Strachan made sure I got involved. My lecturers complimented me on the progress I was making.

I returned to Langebaan after the end-of-year exams. The lagoon was as beautiful as ever, surrounded by the brown sun-baked hills whose craggy ridges across the water seemed like a wall against the world. But it was a painful homecoming, as I expected. My mother was everywhere. In the smell of kelp and dune flowers, in the gentle lapping of waves on the shore. At night, as I stoked up the wood stove, I almost expected her to emerge from the darkness, to put her arms around me, as she used to, and say, 'Ag, Manas, you're a good boy. What can I do to stop you growing up, to make you stay the same forever?' Ja, it was painful, but I wanted to be near her, in whatever form.

So I carried out my chores as I used to. I cleared the weeds and brush from around the cottage. I swept and dusted the interior. I whitewashed the outside walls and painted the doors and window frames. Tak came by a few times to see how I was getting on. He seemed impressed by my devotion to keeping the place spick and span. Once he took me fishing with him. I think he was trying to get through to me, but couldn't find a way through himself, or me. We cast our lines in beyond the shallows and stood together on the beach without talking. Neither of us was much good at breaking the ice.

I spent days at this table next to the window painting the same scene of the water and the hills beyond in all their hazy transformations, one day calm and hot, the next blowing a gale. I did those small, repetitive watercolours (were they akin to prayers?) feeling as though my mother was watching over my shoulder. That's why I buried them one night at the foot of her grave. I had in mind the notion that the paper and images would dissolve beneath the soil and filter down to her. To be frank, I'd drunk a bottle of wine to get into that frame of mind.

My exam results arrived just before Christmas. I'd passed everything. Oddly enough I gained more satisfaction from scraping through the written exams than from the high grades I received in the studio subjects. For me it was a huge personal victory. I'd prevailed against the odds. For the first time since my mother died I felt a jubilant belief in the future. Once more my eye was the limit to which the universe conformed. Tak seemed impressed, even mildly surprised, when I showed him the results. He scrutinised the transcript for a long while, slowly nodding his head. Then he smiled and said, 'You have worked hard, Manas. I expected nothing less.' Ja, a promising ending for a year that had not been the best.

Tak asked me over to the Groothuis on Christmas Day. It was a fine summer's day with not too much wind and I went for a leisurely swim in the morning before going over. Tak had given all the farm workers, including the house servants, the week off so we had the place to ourselves, with no prying eyes to worry about. We had a few dops and did some fish outside on the braai. Tak presented me with an expensive fountain pen as a gift. The alcohol and the sun melted the ice and for the first and only time we chatted amicably, as friends and adults. We even got a bit silly as the afternoon wore on, laughing uproariously at amusing events from the past, such as when Abram Witbooi's hefty wife, Tiekie, slipped and fell while feeding the pigs, dislodging the posts and collapsing the sty in a chaotic heap.

But then the sun went down and I put a question to Tak that I shouldn't have. I asked him if, when I'd finished my studies and was earning a decent living, he would let me buy the cottage. There were reasons why this had become something of a fixation with me. I wanted the cottage to honour my mother's belief and pride in me – the first of the family to earn a living with his head, not his hands. I believed her soul would rest easy if it were mine. But, more, I wanted to return one day, a man of means, to the place of my ancestors knowing it belonged to me, that my history was not just a figment of my imagination, that my roots had substance. I had no wish to drift, as my father had done, from one place to another.

So I started explaining how we could get around the *Group Areas Act*. Manie Brand had given me the idea one day when he explained how he happened to be building a house for an Indian client in a white area. It was simple, I told Tak. I would find a white person to act as a front. Officially, the property would be drawn up in the front's name, while, of course, I would be the true purchaser. I also pointed out that the land on which the cottage stood was mostly sand, and no good for farming. Too late did I notice Tak's discomfort, the fading of humour from his face. As I've said, to the Afrikaner land is more than wealth; it's a symbol of his right to Africa. Even though he had no heir to it, Tak wasn't about to sell his land to me. Something he still clung to in his Afrikaner upbringing forbade it.

'What do they teach you in university these days?' he asked me irritably. 'To break the law?'

Of course, I wasn't blind to the hypocrisy. It was convenient for him to use the law as an excuse. When it suits the Afrikaner, the law is everything.

'Oubaas, the laws of this country are unjust …'

'I don't care what you think of the laws, Manas. You're forgetting they exist! And if you break them you go to jail!'

'I'm prepared to take the chance.'

'Well, I'm not. Don't ask me to break the law.'

'There's no way the authorities can find out, Oubaas.'

Tak shook his head. 'Don't ask me to break the law.'

'It's more than that, isn't it, Oubaas? It's more than just the law. You were happy to break the law when it came to my mother, but now you can't bear the thought of me owning your ground, can you? Me, a coloured man. One of your plaasvolk.'

Tak looked away. 'And even if I was prepared to break the law, what makes you think you'll ever be able to afford to buy the land? Do you know what prices they're asking these days?'

'You're evading the issue, Oubaas. Go on, admit it. You can't accept seeing your land in my hands, that's all.'

'You're annoying me, Manas. You're abusing my hospitality. It seems that university has made you too big for your boots. If it wasn't for your mother I'd tell you to go away.'

I smiled bitterly. 'Ja, you could share your life, your bed, with my mother, but you can't give me a tiny piece of your land. Land that always belonged to my family anyway.'

'Watch what you say, Manas. Don't push it too far.'

I shook my head, fighting back tears.

'Don't ask me to break the law, Manas. I've said you can stay in the cottage whenever you please. Why's that not enough for you?'

'Because it's not the same as owning it.'

'Ja, but it's better than nothing. And if I were you I'd count my blessings. It's not everyone who gets the chances you've had.'

'That's easy for you to say. A white man who's never known what it's like to be without.'

Tak sighed irritably. 'How dare you presume such a thing? I don't dwell on my problems like you, Manas, but I know what it's like to be without. You know, my father was the poorest man in the world. You know why? Because all he could give me were things. Land, possessions – things. That's all he could give me. Nothing else, because he had nothing else. He had no love. No kindness. He is the only man I've ever hated for being poor. And my mother was not much better. Believe it or not, I used to look with envy at the love your mother gave you. Even your wastrel father gave you more love than my parents combined. So don't talk to me about being without! Count your blessings, Manas. Accept what I offer from the kindness of my heart, and don't come to me with this nonsense again!'

And that was that. The dream of substance, just a dream. Tak grew silent. The ice froze over again and that unique moment of togetherness was gone.

I woke the next morning, cursing myself.

*

It was almost with a sense of belonging that I returned to Grahamstown the next year, to the clutter and noise of the Brands' home, to the now familiar art school studios and to my silent studies in the library. The Brands seemed pleased to see me again. They were in altogether better spirits, as Manie had secured a couple of good building contracts, so for the time being they didn't have to worry about the wolf at the door. Manie confided in me that he had almost gone bust the previous year. It had been touch and go, he said. Now, with a show of new confidence, he offered to pay me to help Piet and Marie with their English. He dismissed my reservations as to my suitability (passing first-year English at Rhodes was good enough for him) so I told him I'd do it for nothing. He insisted, but I stood firm. He found a compromise by buying a cask of wine every so often (a practice frowned upon by Hester as neither she nor Manie were big drinkers) which we consumed in the evening during meals, the effects of which sometimes made me uncharacteristically effusive. So twice a week I sat with talkative Piet and quiet, serious Marie, teaching them the basics of sentence structure and spelling. It gave me pleasure watching them improve. As Hester had said, Piet and Marie were bright kids and deserved better than the second-rate education they were getting at school.

Once again I immersed myself in my studies. Having leapt the first hurdle I faced my second year with dedication. I continued with English as a minor and embraced my new subjects, Still-life Painting and Anatomy, with enthusiasm. Again, the festive social atmosphere that began the academic year passed me by. Occasionally, I resorted to my ritual of drinking alone up in the forests, but not to the extent where it caused me concern.

The Eastern Cape summer changed and the autumn days were cool and fresh. They say that Grahamstown can get all the seasons in one day; this is because the region catches the edges of various weather systems – the Karoo's dry westerly winds, the cold southern fronts and warm subtropical weather from Natal. But that autumn the weather was settled and pleasant, and at the university the students at last gained a sense of purpose after the heady celebrations of March and April.

One night I looked up from my work in the library to see Professor Strachan standing there, watching me. From the bleary look in his eye I could see that more than one drink had passed his lips that night.

'They tell me this is your new address,' he announced, slurring slightly, 'Christ, might as well move your bloody bed in here.' He laughed out loud, causing a frown on the librarian's brow. He picked up the essay I was working on. 'What the hell's this? *A Question of Status: the Rise of Sir Joshua Reynolds and the Royal Academy.* What rubbish is this?'

'The essay you set last week, Professor,' I answered.

'My God, I think I've created a monster! A boring bloody wordsmith!' He laughed again. His breath reeked like an old vat. Then he leaned forward and whispered, 'Fuck Sir Joshua – for now, at any rate. It's time you got some fresh air, boy. Too much time in the stale atmosphere of books destroys brain cells, you know. Just look at that old battle axe over there behind the counter. That's how you'll get if you're not bloody careful.'

The librarian, a grumpy tyrant with thick glasses, glared back at him.

He plonked my essay down on the table. 'Reynolds can wait, pompous fart that he was. Come with me, Manas. There's something I want to show you.'

'What about my essay? I've still got a lot to do.'

He eyed me sourly. 'Just move your arse, will you? You're so bloody conscientious it's pathetic.'

As I packed up my books Professor Strachan browsed through the nearby shelves and as we went out he informed the librarian that there weren't enough books on aviation. She muttered disapprovingly and waved him away with a hefty paw that looked as though it had boxed a few ears in its time.

The night air was chilly as I followed him off the campus. As we walked, he spoke nostalgically about when as a young man he'd worked as a postman in Kitwe in Northern Rhodesia. He told me about the days spent alone in the bush as he trekked about the outlying districts, delivering post on horseback. That was the only time he'd ever felt free, he said. I tried to think of a time when I felt free, really free. When Tak had told me he'd pay for my education was the closest I could come.

We came to a double-storey building directly opposite the police station in New Street. The lights of the building were on and music came from inside. The place seemed somewhat in disrepair; the walls were cracked, the gutters were sagging and there was a pile of junk on the front veranda that not even the beggars had been tempted to remove.

'What is this place?' I asked.

'Master's degree studios.' Professor Strachan replied. 'Your Anatomy lecturer showed me some of your drawings. Seems you've got a feel for the figure. A bit mannered for my liking, but I thought you might be interested in what's going on in here.'

We went inside and were immediately assailed by the familiar reek of oil paints and turpentine. Typically, the place looked a mess. Canvases and easels strewn everywhere and floors that hadn't seen a broom in months.

'Anybody home?' Professor Strachan yelled. He gave an unexpected bark of laughter.

91

'Hey, Prof!' came a male voice from upstairs. 'Is that you?'

'It is I!' Professor Strachan bellowed back. 'And I've brought a visitor!'

'Come on up!'

We went upstairs to what appeared to be a communal coffee room, complete with a dirty sink, a quarrelsome fridge, some old chairs and a dilapidated sofa. There we found two students lounging on the sofa, a Neil Young tape playing in the background. The male student was dressed in a khaki shirt and jeans. His fair hair was long and tied at the back in a pony tail. He leapt to his feet as we appeared and brandished a demijohn of red wine. He was pretty inebriated too.

'Some wine, Prof?' he asked.

'Just a drop, then, if you insist,' Professor Strachan consented, reaching for a large coffee mug in the sink to facilitate the 'drop'. The other student, a bespectacled, dark-haired girl in a leopard print sarong, smiled as her friend filled the mug. I found her fine (though slightly bookish) features and slim body attractive, not that I thought much beyond that.

'By the way,' Professor Strachan said, 'this is Manas.'

The male student thrust out his hand. 'David Harris,' he said and shook my hand, grabbing my thumb, African style.

'And this wild animal,' Professor Strachan said, indicating the girl, 'is Zelda Sutton – my God, Zelda, when are you going to do something about your clothes? Those leopard spots make you look ever so … lethal, for God's sake.'

Zelda ignored him and rather imperiously held up a thin hand that had dry white stuff all over it. 'Excuse the plaster,' she said. 'I've been making moulds all day.' I shook hands and she smiled coolly.

David meanwhile had unearthed another mug and was cleaning it out with a dubious looking rag. 'Some wine, Manas?' he asked.

'Yes, thank you. If you have some to spare.'

David eyed me for a second, the three-quarters full demijohn poised. Then he shook his head and laughed. 'Don't be so fucking formal, Manas – excuse the French.'

'Fuck the French,' Professor Strachan growled.

David handed me a full mug. 'Relax, Manas. Manners maketh me morose.'

I took a deep swig.

'David thinks he's a poet,' Professor Strachan informed me, sotto voce. 'Final year BA.' He looked at me wide-eyed, as though that explained everything.

'I heard you, Prof,' David said.

'Just telling Manas to beware of would-be poets. They talk shit when they drink too much.'

'What about has-been painters?' David retorted.

Professor Strachan laughed, also impervious to insult. Then he moved over to the window and stared out at the police station across the road. 'So, how are the boys in blue? Up to their usual tricks, are they?'

'Not so much in blue these days,' Zelda replied. 'You mostly see them in riot gear. They've been arresting a lot of people lately. Even kids. We can see everything from here. I can't stand it when they lay into them with sjamboks. I mean, kids!'

'Whitney says the townships are ungovernable,' David added.

'Whitney says so, hey?'

'Ja, Prof. She says big shit's about to hit the fan. Right across the country.'

Professor Strachan looked at me. 'Whitney is David and Zelda's so-called friend. Calls herself a revolutionary. A walking funny farm, more like it.'

'Don't be facetious, Prof,' Zelda said. 'At least she's doing something. Not just sitting on her arse, like the rest of us.'

Professor Strachan shook his head. 'When are you two going to realise Whitney Skewes is an idiot? A bloody moron! Nothing but trouble waiting to happen.'

David seemed peeved. 'If there were more people like her around, Prof, this country wouldn't be in the mess it's in!'

'Quite right, David – it'd be in a bigger mess! But I'm not here to allow perfectly good wine to be spoiled by stupid Whitney or the horrors of apartheid ...'

'That's the trouble with your generation, Prof.' Zelda said. 'You turn a blind eye to everything.'

'But I am blind, dear girl. I hate to concede anything to nitwit art students but you're absolutely right. I am blind – colour-blind.'

'Oh, no!' Zelda groaned. 'Not the colour-blind story again.'

Professor Strachan affected a hurt expression. 'But it's true! I am colour-blind. That's the reason – one of the reasons – I stopped painting. You can imagine how bloody frustrating it got. Did I tell you I once wanted to be a pilot?'

'Yes!' Zelda and David shouted in unison.

'Did I tell you I once wanted to be a ship's navigator?'

'Yes!'

Professor Strachan seemed stumped. He sipped his wine.

'Did I tell you I once wanted to be a house paint colour consultant?'

We all laughed. I took another deep swig of wine and felt a welcome warmth spreading through my veins.

Professor Strachan assumed a businesslike air. 'But, look, Manas and I aren't here to fool around arguing the toss with you two layabouts. I'm here to show Manas your work, Zelda.'

'Give me a break, Prof. Not tonight.'

'Please don't posture, Zelda.'

'Posture … posture!' Zelda exclaimed.

'If it's inconvenient …' I ventured.

Professor Strachan dismissed my concern with a wave of his hand. 'Absolute bullshit, Manas. Zelda's dying to be noticed. Her gargantuan ego feeds off our humble opinions. You artists are all the same, you know – bitch like hell when you're not taken notice of, and bitch like hell when you are.' He drained his mug. 'Bloody misers too, when it comes to wine.'

David got up and did the honours, topping up my mug while he was about it.

Zelda gave Professor Strachan a level stare. 'I wish you wouldn't presume too much about me, Prof. I didn't come to art school to be noticed – *noticed*, for Christ sake!'

'Oh, come on, Zelda! None of us were born yesterday. If you didn't come here to be noticed, then what did you come here for?'

'To *learn*, Prof. To learn how to be an artist. Does that sound a little weird to you? Coming to university to learn?'

Professor Strachan laughed. 'Ah yes, to learn. And I suppose my or Manas's opinion of your sculpture is of absolutely no interest to you in this learning process?'

'Absolutely none. Especially your opinion.'

'See what I mean, Manas. A bloody prima donna. And a sarcastic one at that. But, sadly, her little gestures of protest fall on deaf ears. By the powers vested in me, I must insist. So let us equip ourselves with wine and make haste to your studio at once! Come on, Zelda, get a move on! You're like an old woman!'

'Come on, give me a break, Prof. You know I hate people dissecting me.'

'No one's going to dissect you, Zelda. I just want to show Manas your work, for God's sake!'

'If she doesn't want to …'

'Utter nonsense, boy! Of course she wants you to see her work. Besides, I'm not interested in what she wants. I'm interested in what you need to see. I'm here to open your eyes, Manas.'

'Wonderful! How bloody philanthropic!' Zelda muttered.

So we took the wine and ourselves downstairs (with much lurching and laughing by Professor Strachan and David). We followed Zelda to a room at the back of the building and waited as she fumbled in her bag for a key to the door. At last, we were shown into her studio.

I beheld a shabby room filled with at least a dozen still people. Emaciated, lonely souls, cast in plaster or Ciment Fondu, slightly smaller than life-size, they stood isolated from each other by the silent space that enveloped them. The gaunt faces that stared back at me were the eerily serene faces of war and famine, of Auschwitz and Africa. Heads inclined, eyes closed or staring resignedly into space, eternally waiting for an uncertain salvation. I marvelled at the precise realism and the expressive touch that had given life to such real presences. Art had never moved me as much before.

After Professor Strachan and I had inspected each figure we sat down on the rough brick floor with David and Zelda, who were talking rather seriously about the person called Whitney.

'Christ, there's a time and place for everything,' Professor Strachan complained. 'And this is not the time nor place to be talking about Whitney bloody Skewes, thank you very much!'

'You know David's got the hots for her, Prof,' Zelda said.

'Yes, and I also know David needs psychiatric help. I can't see why he doesn't direct his attention to more worthy causes. Like dispensing wine, for God's sake!'

David smiled a bit sheepishly and replenished our wine. He offered me a cigarette, which I took though I hadn't smoked before. No one seemed to notice as I puffed away like a fool, coughing only when I tried to inhale.

'Well, Manas,' Professor Strachan said. 'What do you think?'

Zelda drew herself up defensively. 'I thought you were just going to show Manas my work. I'm not in the mood for a critique right now, Prof.'

'Don't be so bloody touchy, Zelda. I'm just asking Manas his opinion. Speak up, Manas. What do you think?'

I silently cursed him for putting me on the spot like this. 'I don't know what to say, Prof,' I said.

'Come on, Manas! I didn't bring you here to be struck dumb.'

I shrugged. 'They're very nice ...'

'Nice!' Zelda cried, rolling her eyes.

Professor Strachan burst into laughter. 'Don't be so bloody polite, Manas! Speak your mind, boy. Zelda's not going to bite!'

Of that, I was not too sure. A little humiliated, I took a deep swig of wine and again felt that welcome warmth spreading through my veins. 'I don't mean nice. I mean beautiful. They seem so real.'

Professor Strachan looked perplexed. 'Beautiful? What the hell is beauty, for God's sake? I'd venture Zelda hasn't the faintest idea what beauty is.' With creaking limbs he got up unsteadily and made a great show of running his hands over one of the heads. 'Beautiful, eh, Manas? Why do you find them beautiful?'

I shrugged. 'Why? I don't know. Because they're so real?'

'But are we talking about beauty here, Manas? Aren't we talking about something else? Beauty implies decoration, outdated aesthetics, superficiality. When I look at Zelda's work I'm reminded of Edmund Burke's ideas about the sublime ...'

'Oh come on, Prof!' Zelda interrupted. 'Spare us the lecture, please! If Manas wants to call my sculpture beautiful, let him!' She added as a peevish afterthought, 'He can call it anything he bloody likes as far as I'm concerned.'

'Yes, but you wouldn't call your sculpture beautiful, would you now?'

'I might.'

'Ha! Told you she has a gargantuan ego, Manas!'

Zelda's eyes flashed angrily. 'Look, right now I'm not interested in calling my sculpture anything, okay? I didn't ask everyone to come sticking their noses in my studio, did I? I didn't ask everyone to start pulling my damn work to pieces.'

'Dear girl, who's pulling your work to pieces? Manas called it beautiful. You did too, a moment ago.'

'I said I might.'

'Well, that's what I want to know. Why would you call it such a superficial thing?'

Zelda became exasperated. 'Because I might just understand beauty to be something more than decoration, Prof. Beauty can be profound. Sublime, if you like. It depends on your definition.'

David nodded. 'I agree. Manas was right to call it beautiful. I think Zelda searches through pain for beauty ... the purest beauty.'

Professor Strachan gave an inappropriate bellow of laughter and took a mighty swig of wine. 'Ha! Pain and beauty! Imagine if Botticelli had painted Venus disembowelled! We live in a warped world, Manas! Warped!'

'It's not warped,' Zelda said. 'It's the way it's always been. Things exist only through their opposites. Can't you see, Prof? Hope through hopelessness? Light through darkness?'

'The psychologists have got names for you people who find beauty in pain.'

'I said *through* pain,' David said. 'Not in pain.'

'Okay, but the big question remains: Why make these things, Zelda? What use are these scrawny-looking bastards to the world?'

Zelda raised her hands and dropped them, exasperated. 'Scrawny-looking bastards! Shit!'

'Perhaps I should rephrase ...'

'What *use* is trying to understand the world, Prof? What *use* is explaining the world? What *use* is finding meaning? You tell us, Prof.'

'Stuffed if I know.'

'Then what are you doing teaching art?'

'Stuffed if I know.'

David rallied to the cause. 'Prof, are you telling us you don't believe in what art does? In art's purpose?'

'I don't know what art does. You tell me what it does.'

'Like Zelda said, it explains the world. It explains people.'

'To who?'

'To *people*, for Christ sake!'

'What for?'

'Jesus, Prof!' David shouted. 'So we can learn! Learn from ourselves!'

'Yes, but what use is learning if it doesn't change people?'

'It does change people, Prof!'

'You're saying art can change the world, then?'

'I said it changes people!'

'If it changes people then it can change the world, surely?'

'Are you saying it can't?'

Gleefully, Professor Strachan rubbed his hands in anticipation of the demolition job he was about to complete. 'That's exactly what I'm saying!' he scoffed. 'Art changes nothing. Fuck all! Ask yourself, who reads poetry? Who looks at art? Who *makes* art? A tiny bunch of useless, over-educated, indulgent ponces, a drop in the ocean of humanity! What effect can art possibly have on the world?'

David bristled. 'I presume you're including yourself in the ponce category, Prof.'

Zelda was also incensed. She looked skyward, as if imploring the heavens for light to dispel the darkness from the professor's soul. All that glowed above her, though, was a dim 60-watt globe in the ceiling. 'Of course art changes the world,' she argued irritably. 'Everything we do changes the world in some way. At least with art there's some bloody meaning to it. Shit, why create art if it's not to communicate, to change the way people think? To open their minds? Why teach art, Prof, if you don't believe in it?'

'Because it's my mission in life to open your eyes to the real reason why artists make art. Despite all your lofty protestations to the contrary, you bloody arty farts are really after one thing only, aren't you?'

'And what might that be?'

'Money, dear girl! Filthy lucre!'

I noticed the good professor was standing wide-legged, like a sailor on a heaving deck. *'Money!'* Zelda and David exclaimed in unison.

'Yes, you starry-eyed idiots, money! All this talk about changing the world is pure bullshit. The truth is, when you cut the crap, that you artists – and wanker poets – are just lackeys to the wealthy elite. A bunch of pathetic egotistical hypocrites, sucking on the tit of capitalism, who just want to be rich and famous!'

'Rich and famous! Jesus!'

'Face it, that's all you greedy self-centred ponces are after! Ha! Tell me I'm wrong!'

Zelda and David seemed stunned by this slurred barrage. Some silent, ominous seconds ticked by. Then a great dentally problematic smile spread slowly across Professor Strachan's face. 'Jesus, naive! Talk about lambs to the slaughter. Babes in the wood! When are you two ever going to learn when someone's messing with your minds?'

David shook his head ruefully. 'You're a bloody old

shit-stirrer, Prof. Let's run him naked through town, Zelda. Flogging's too kind.'

Zelda laughed. 'He'd probably enjoy that, knowing him!'

Professor Strachan held up his hands. 'Ah, so young and so much to learn. So many disappointments ahead. Yet, is there anything so sweet as the sound of angry young voices?'

David glowered. 'Don't patronise us.'

Professor Strachan drained his mug. 'Just keeping you sensitive artists on your toes.' He glanced at his watch. 'Alas, since we all know now what we do art for, I must be off. My wife awaits my company, no doubt clad in a black see-through negligee, surrounded by bunches of grapes, cream, Bolero and all that other bullshit. I'm afraid beauty and art must now step aside for something much more formidable – lust!'

We laughed, the thought of the good professor doing anything more strenuous than collapsing into a drunken slumber, plainly absurd. 'That's what you call wishful thinking, Prof,' David commented.

'Call it what you like, you snide little upstart. But I depart secure in the knowledge that you're in good company, Manas. I trust tonight has been educational.'

'Sorry, Manas, but I must split too,' Zelda said. 'Can I drive you home, Prof?'

'I'd appreciate that, dear girl. The old legs seem a little unsteady tonight. I can't imagine why. Must be old age. By the way, I actually find your sculpture a little too theatrical – a bit mawkish, in fact.'

'One more word about my bloody sculpture and you can walk.'

He winked at her. 'You're very attractive when you're angry.'

'Move it, old man,' she snapped.

Zelda steered us out of her studio. While she was locking up Professor Strachan took a final swig straight from the demijohn David was holding. Then he bade us an effusive farewell and he and Zelda left. We heard Zelda's car start up outside. The silencer was broken and we could hear their progress clear across town to Henry Street where Professor Strachan lived. David and I went back upstairs.

'Bloody old reprobate!' David laughed. 'He knows how to get us revved up, all right. He can be a pretentious old prick sometimes. You never quite know where he stands. I really don't know if he likes Zelda's work or not.'

'I don't think he'd have brought me here if he didn't,' I said.

'I know he doesn't like my poetry. Too political, he reckons.'

'I suppose I should be going too.'

'Stick around,' David said. 'We've got all this wine to finish, and I hate drinking on my own.'

I was relieved. I wanted to stay. The wine had produced an ecstatic glow within me. And so I sat there until we finished the wine. I can't remember much of what David and I spoke about. I suppose we just established the foundations of a friendship based on the unconscious knowledge that we were both irretrievably lost to the devices of false escape.

And when the wine was finished, David took me home in his dented Volkswagen Beetle, a trip I vaguely remember as hair raising. He hooted and shouted something unintelligible as he drove off. I watched his car go down the road, feeling unbearably happy. I stepped in a pile of dog shit as I crossed the lawn to the Brands' house. That didn't deter me from giving the black dog a break from guard duty that night. Hester really got worked up the next morning when she found the flea-ridden thing asleep on my bed.

*

I became a regular visitor to the studios in New Street. I'd drop in after classes and more often than not find David or Zelda there. There were two other Masters students whom you hardly ever saw, one a part-timer, a teacher at the Carinus Art Centre who drifted in maybe once or twice a fortnight when she could find the time, the other a somewhat eccentric fellow from Zimbabwe who spent most of his time painting outdoors, pushing his paints around in an old pram. So David and Zelda had the place pretty much to themselves. Although not an MFA student, there was no one else around

CLOUDS LIKE BLACK DOGS

to object to David having more or less taken over the upstairs
coffee room. When he wasn't attending lectures you could
find him up there, seated at his typewriter near the window,
knocking out poetry (or late literature assignments) or nursing a hangover to the sound of Leonard Cohen.

David and Zelda shared digs in a farmhouse a few kilometres out on the Port Alfred road and usually came into
town separately. David was something of a night owl, pre-
ferring to arrive late morning and stay until late. He said his
brain only kicked into gear at night. Quite often, though, if
he'd been out drinking the night before, he'd only appear in
the afternoon, feeling wretched, bleary-eyed, unable to con-
centrate. Zelda lived to a pretty tight routine. She arrived
early and usually worked all day, breaking only for a stroll
down to the tearoom for lunch. Sometimes she attended
campus meetings, or she drove out into the countryside to
clear her head. But mostly she just worked, a slave to her
mind and hands.

At first I got on better with David, thanks to the juice of the
grape. I think Zelda tolerated me because of him; she looked
on David as a wayward brother. To be honest, I didn't know
what to make of her. She seemed so damned arrogant and
superior sometimes. The way she smiled disdainfully when
she spoke, and that quizzical look in her eye that indicated
she wasn't one to readily suffer fools.

The New Street studios became a kind of sanctuary for me.
Not to the point where it interfered with my studies; I still
shut myself up in the library when there were written assignments to complete, I still laboured at my studio work. I
nevertheless began spending most of my spare time with
David and Zelda. I also began to enjoy university life at last.
The three of us went to parties and concerts. We attended
most of the Fine Art jols. I immersed myself completely in the
swing of things. I'd long since got rid of the smart clothes
Tak had bought me and replaced them with the artist's uniform – jeans and a hand-woven shirt and a few obligatory
beads and bangles. I wore an old frayed jacket bought at a
flea market. I grew my hair long and wild. Ja, no longer

Manas of the blazer-and-tie brigade. No sir, with David and Zelda, I was one and the same.

Often David and I got drunk together. Sometimes wildly, boisterously drunk. This was the cause of increasing strain in my relationship with the Brands who objected to my unruly homecomings late at night. But I didn't care. I was having a good time. When it came to drinking Zelda never got out of hand like David and me. She was the controlled one, always doing things in moderation, but never judgemental of others. She and David took the occasional puff of dagga, but I didn't care for the stuff. I preferred getting drunk. The few times I did smoke a joint it felt as though time had stopped and I was stuck forever in a horrible limbo. Once we took a long drive in David's Volkswagen deep into the Karoo and camped out under the stars. David wanted us to experience a true Karoo sunset, away from any sign of humanity. He and I spent most of the time in a state of glorious intoxication, with David waxing lyrical about the mysterious Whitney Skewes who, I learned, shared digs with them. Neither of us remembered any sunset afterwards. Zelda did most of the driving, thank God.

None of this impinged on my work yet. I was still making good progress with my subjects; my English and History of Art grades improved and my commitment to my studio work remained undiminished. No doubt this commitment was due in part to my fascination with Zelda's sculpture. Her work had been a revelation, a way forward to finding my own form of expression through the human figure. Though I frequently complimented her, she brushed aside my praise irritably. It seemed the esteem of a naive second-year under-ling wasn't enough to bolster what I eventually discovered, beneath the facade of arrogance, to be a frail self-confidence.

But then my relationship with her took a more positive turn. One day she was asked to stand in for our Anatomy lecturer who was away sick. Arriving unexpectedly at the studio, she dispensed with the usual skeleton and casts of flayed Greek gods and brought in a live model, an old beg-gar woman who sat in her rags with her meagre belongings in a plastic OK Bazaars bag next to her chair, patiently picking at her broken nails as we drew her. Zelda's approach was simple. She told us to 'feel our way' into the subject. Normally life drawing was the preserve of third-year students, something you 'earn' after two years of hard slog drawing casts, skeletons and bowls of fruit. So it was like a breath of fresh air for those of us who'd begun to tire of labelling bones and muscles. And it was the first time Zelda saw what I was capable of. As I sketched the woman, probing for the remnants of dignity left in her sagging posture, I was vaguely conscious of Zelda moving around the studio, vaguely aware of her voice as she spoke to other students. She seemed to avoid me, as though embarrassed to approach me in the role of teacher. Time passed without my noticing, so engrossed was I. Then Zelda called a break for the model. As I continued to work at my drawing, applying sharper detail with pencils and *Conté*, trying to evoke the resigned forbearance in the old woman's eyes, I felt a hand on my shoulder. I turned to see Zelda behind me. Her eyes were focused intently on my drawing. She shook her head and said, 'You're one for surprises, Manas. I didn't know you could draw like that. And here I've always thought you were just David's drinking buddy!'

'With David, there's not much time for anything else.'

'He's a worry, I know! I shouldn't let him corrupt you.'

'I like being corrupted.'

'So I've noticed. That's a good drawing, Manas. Seriously.'

I sat there at a loss for words.

She laughed. 'Oh shit, don't tell me compliments embarrass you!'

I shrugged stupidly. 'You can have it if you want.'

She shook her head. 'Don't part with your work lightly, Manas. Thanks anyway.'

That afternoon I took the drawing to her studio and pushed it under her door. The next day she kissed me on the cheek and thanked me. She always treasured that drawing of the beggar woman more than anything else I produced.

After that she seemed more comfortable with me around,

as though I'd proved myself worthy of the company of artists and poets. And I felt comfortable enough to try a few portrait studies, first of David, then of her. Quick, gestural drawings, not formal sittings. I experimented with charcoal and pastel, and graphite and turpentine washes. I also worked with diluted oils on primed paper; the translucent effects of this provided an elusive vitality quite unlike the laboured, disguising effect of impasto.

When David wasn't around I'd sometimes sit with Zelda in her studio, drinking coffee and talking. Sometimes we talked about ourselves. She told me about her private-school upbringing and the farm down on the Fish River, and I told her about Langebaan. But mostly we talked art, and I suppose it was then that we sensed an affinity in each other.

She talked about what inspired her. At the time, the Eastern Cape was suffering its worst drought on record. The images of desolation so close at hand and their symbolic associations with South Africa's political situation weren't lost on her. The townships all over the country had erupted into violence, a prelude to the catastrophic situation in 1985 and 1986. The Grahamstown townships were among the worst. Day and night we could hear the rioting. There was the constant drone of police vehicles through the town. We witnessed awful scenes at the police station across the road. Bloodied people being hauled from vans, being kicked and beaten. Mothers and fathers pleading for their detained children. The haunting sound of prisoners singing in their cells at night. We felt the weight of fear descend upon us. At times it was almost surreal. The bizarre music of sirens. The harsh white beam of the searchlight they mounted on Gunfire Hill that raked across the townships like a frightened eye. The distant sound of mortar explosions and rifle fire as the army held manoeuvres near the town – the growling of a beast about to be set loose.

Out of this Zelda modelled a series of angels in clay – broken, forlorn creatures waiting, she said, for 'moral rain'. Zelda had a magical way with clay. With a touch of her hand she could give it life. Moments of extraordinary realism – a face, a hand, an emaciated torso – that appeared miraculously from nothing. Sometimes she let me help with the mould-making or the casting, technical processes she found tedious. I witnessed her relief as she removed the cast safely from the mould and the care with which she'd patinate and polish the finished piece. Ja, she inspired me. No question about that. I began to understand her belief that nothing exists without its opposite. No beauty without ugliness, no joy without tears.

I was also inspired by David. By all accounts he was a poor student, barely having scraped through to his final year. But, of course, the thing that inspired me wasn't his academic record but his passion for poetry. Despite his careless ways, David believed emphatically in what he wrote about. The symbolic associations of drought weren't lost on him either; his poetry was riddled with references to aridity and desolation, to moral thirst. But unlike Zelda's sculpture, his poetry was frequently steeped in a brutal absolute. Zelda once confided in me that she found the futility in his verse depressing. I think he's talking about himself most of the time, she said.

It took me some time to realise the truth in that. In the beginning I was captivated by David's tough, often grotesque metaphors. Like the parable of two men condemned to a pathetic journey together. A black man with no head, and a white man with no limbs. The black man was forced to carry the white man because the white man was the only one capable of issuing directions. But they kept running into obstacles and falling over. It's what we've become, David said. A fuck-up going nowhere.

Of course, David had another futile passion. Occasionally I saw the object of this passion at the studios. Whitney Skewes, a Sociology student, would drop by every so often, usually to cadge a lift back to their digs. Pale, hawk-nosed, always a little self-conscious in her hippy garb. A chain-smoker. I'd come to learn that she was a big noise in student politics, renowned for tirelessly organising protests and being brazenly outspoken in her support for the armed struggle. Many considered it the luck of the devil she was not in jail.

I first met her in Zelda's studio. For days Zelda had been stuck on the pose of one of the angels. Whitney had offered to model for some small clay maquettes Zelda was doing to fix the problem. When I was introduced Whitney greeted me (being what she affectionately called a 'darkie') effusively, shaking my hand African style. And Zelda, quite spontaneously, asked Whitney whether she minded my drawing her. An embarrassing moment for me, since I was uncomfortable with the idea of drawing a naked white lady, even if she was an activist. I needn't have worried because Whitney refused. Sorry, she said, I won't pose for a male. It's a power thing, you know.

David was besotted with her, and I guess in her wan, freckled face and darting green eyes there was a certain attractiveness. But according to Zelda, she never responded to his advances. Whitney had more important things on her mind.

*

Things continued to change for the better. I began renting my own studio at St Aidan's, a short walk from New Street. Formerly a Roman Catholic boys' college, it closed in 1973 and had been deserted since. Once it was praised as the best example of Gothic Revival architecture in South Africa; left neglected, it quickly became derelict and prone to vandalism. It had been up for sale for years but with the economic situation being what it was, no buyers were willing to commit themselves. Professor Strachan was one of the town's most ardent campaigners to have it restored. He came up with various initiatives, including lobbying Rhodes to rent it as Fine Art studio space, to no avail. Eventually the trustees offered to rent out space privately to students. Professor Strachan suggested I take advantage of the offer, since the rent was so cheap. This was where Grace Cook's money came in handy. My inheritance (which until then had remained untouched) enabled me to rent a former junior dormitory.

David and Zelda helped me move in. The dormitory was

a shambles. The roof leaked, windows were broken, there was pigeon shit everywhere and vandals had burned holes in the wooden floors. David and Zelda were amused by the tiny Royal Doulton basins and toilets in the adjoining bathroom. It brought back their boarding school days, they said. I was glad I didn't have boarding school days to reminisce about. With a bit of work we got the place looking spick and span. We fixed the roof leak as best we could, we replaced the window panes and nailed some planks over the holes in the floor. We scraped off the pigeon shit, brushed away spider webs and persuaded an owl who lived in the attic to seek alternative accommodation. When we'd finished my solitary easel and few pieces of furniture looked rather insignificant in the huge space.

Of course, the new studio made a big difference. Previously, I'd had no real base to work from or to store my gear, aside from the small room at the Brands. Now my productivity increased. Filled with a new sense of purpose, I churned out drawings and paintings, mostly figure studies though I still did the odd landscape. Also, instead of being largely confined to small portable studies, I could now entertain working on a large scale.

A creature of habit, I revelled in my simple daily routine. After lectures or studio classes, I'd drop in at the New Street studios for coffee and a chat. Then I'd amble off to St Aidan's where I'd work, sometimes until the early hours. This would only change when I needed to go to the library, or when David came around looking for a drinking partner. Occasionally Professor Strachan stopped by. He'd muse over my work, mostly nodding in approval. He liked the translucent technique I'd developed and felt my figure studies were coming along fine. The portrait of David I submitted for *Milestones* that year was highly commended by the judge, a gallery owner from Johannesburg. But the person whose praise I valued most was Zelda. A good word from her had me brimming with confidence and purpose.

I passed the mid-year exams well, getting top grades for my studio subjects. To celebrate and to get away from the

Arts Festival crowds David and I went camping in the Karoo for a few days, up in the mountains near Graaff Reinet. We'd planned a longer sojourn but the winter nights were so cold we nearly froze. Not even our plentiful supply of booze was any defence against the cold. Forgetting for a moment the miserable, sleepless nights and frosty mornings, I remember with fondness the two of us seated around a small fire, shivering as we sipped wine, talking … talking about life's stupidities, life's realities. I remember David's infectious laughter as he told me about his boarding school days in Pietermaritzburg, how he'd fallen from grace, expelled for bunking out and getting drunk. I don't fit anywhere, he said. A square peg. Kindred spirits … ja, he and I had some things in common. It was good to get away together. This time we did see a sunset or two.

We returned to Grahamstown, and to South Africa's dismal realities. Political tensions across the country had worsened with the introduction of the new tricameral system. In a referendum the previous year white South Africans had voted overwhelmingly to include Indians and coloureds in government. This grand plan, where ostensibly all South Africans – white and non-white – would get the vote, was held up to the world as a show of radical reform. The only problem was that the black population, the huge angry majority, was excluded. The National Party argued its case with its usual oafish logic: Let's be reasonable. The blacks are not South Africans per se. They belong to their own countries, the independent homelands, the Bantustans, like the Transkei and the Ciskei, like Bophuthatswana. Are these not separate countries? Free sovereign states?

Of course, the majority was not blind to such crafty manoeuvres. They saw the new system for what it was – an attempt to pull Indians and coloureds into the white laager. They knew the independent homelands were puppet dictatorships. Apartheid's garbage dumps. So the angry majority reacted accordingly and violence quickly escalated across the nation. In the short time David and I were away there had been a sudden convulsion of unrest in the Eastern Cape, and when we got back to Grahamstown the local townships had become virtually ungovernable. And whereas most towns and cities in South Africa have their townships hidden away out of sight (and out of mind), Grahamstown's strife was never too far away for anyone to ignore. We could all see and hear what was going on.

It had always been my policy to steer clear of student politics. I saw such involvement as the business of brave fools, such as Whitney Skewes. Unfortunately my friendship with David and Zelda meant I no longer had much say in the matter. So it was against my better judgement that I joined the newly-formed United Democratic Front, at the instigation of Whitney, of course. Not that I disagreed with what the UDF stood for. On the contrary, if I was going to join any political group the UDF was the only legal organisation that gave me a sense of genuine political belonging. Formed to unite the thousands of anti-apartheid organisations around the country to defy the tricameral system, it was characterised by inclusiveness. It's objective was to unite all South Africans against apartheid. At the first meeting I attended the rhetoric I heard was pleasantly different to what I'd encountered before from groups like the BSM, which seemed only interested in a future belonging to black South Africans where, at best, other races might be tolerated. Such exclusiveness had sounded too much like the present system to me. No, my reluctance to join the UDF was not based on any lack of its credibility; it stemmed from my own lack of moral courage. I was afraid of the police. I was afraid of what solidarity might bring. As I intimated before, I'm no revolutionary, no hero.

So it was with some misgivings that I attended a UDF protest gathering organised by Whitney, out on the campus lawns near the Drostdy Arch. There were about seventy of us, clutching placards and chanting slogans. All brave fools, except me – I was just a fool, minus any redeeming adjective. Standing there with David and Zelda, trying to look brave and casual but feeling shit-scared. Zelda held a placard that read, NO APARTHEID VIOLENCE – STOP THE KILLING!

David was holding up a small makeshift gallows on which a sign read, FREE ALL DETAINEES! Whitney, cigarette protruding through yellow fingers, marched up and down in front of us, yelling through a loudhailer, exhorting us to stand fast. At one point she broke into a tuneless rendition of *Nkosi Sikelel' iAfrika*, the oppressed's anthem.

We all listened to her, but our eyes were glued to the policemen who'd appeared at the Arch. About twenty in number, they stood around casually, talking and laughing, as though they were on a Sunday picnic. Some of them flicked at the grass with their long red sjamboks. Ja, we were small fry to them. Behind them some journalists were lining up their cameras and snapping pictures.

In an effort to bolster our sagging resolve, Whitney turned to the policemen and hurled a torrent of denunciations and demands at them through the loudhailer, sprinkled with some choice socialist slogans – just the sort of thing to get any red-blooded South African constable into top gear. We were all, no doubt, impressed by her brazen courage, but, by God, our resolve might have been stiffened by a more circumspect choice of words. Among shrill demands for an independent inquiry into police brutality, she called them bastards, murderers, pigs and cowards. We looked askance at one another. Even the most foolish among us realised this would be no ordinary day.

As she ranted on the policemen suddenly fanned out and faced us. One of them stepped forward and announced, 'This is an illegal gathering! You are all breaking the law! You have exactly one minute to disperse, or face prosecution!'

I thought the announcement was made with ample clarity, but no one moved. Whitney turned to us. 'Don't listen to that crap!' she shouted. 'We're entitled to protest on university property! It's our right! It's our duty!'

If indeed it was our inviolable right to protest on university property, the boys in blue over at the Arch had not been timeously informed. As soon as the minute was up, they charged. Fortunately there was a limit to Whitney's hold on us. As the policemen ran towards us, brandishing their sjamboks, we broke and scattered. It was chaotic. We just dropped everything and bolted. People were falling over discarded placards. Shoes and hats fell off and were left lying everywhere, abandoned. Fear has a strange effect on the vocal chords. Some people scream, some laugh. It was crazy, almost funny, seeing seventy backsides scooting across the lawn in all directions. People one usually associated with quiet intellectual pursuits were now the very embodiment of violent physical action. Athletes, one and all, knees pumping, hair flying. There were shouts and screams as the police caught up and sjamboks began flailing. I caught a glimpse of Whitney being dragged off, fighting like a wildcat – the only one who stood her ground.

I saw one of the cops, a black constable, thrashing someone on the ground. It was Zelda. She was screaming and holding up her arms to protect herself. Caution deserted me. I caught the sjambok straight in the face as I yanked her up by the scruff of the neck, and we ran like hell with the cop after us, across the lawn to the car park. I caught a good few clouts across the shoulders for my troubles. There was an absurd scene as we ran in circles around cars trying to evade the same cop, a big goon with tribal scars on his face. Then we took off again towards the Administration building, thinking he wouldn't follow us there. Being generally unfit and a little overweight, I've never regarded myself as much of a sprinter, but on this day I ran like a Springbok. I pulled Zelda along through flower beds with the cop after us; like a wild predator he'd fixed his quarry, come what may.

As we ran up the stairs into the Administration building, I caught a glimpse of Professor Strachan and his straw hat watching the scene helplessly from Artillery Road, a hundred metres away. We hurtled into the building, past the marble busts of Cecil John Rhodes and Alfred Beit, down the main corridor past closed doors. Up the stairs and down again. On the way down, the cop slipped and fell heavily, whacking his head against the wall. That gave us a precious few seconds' grace and we ran out the building, this time heading down Artillery Road towards town. The next thing we knew, there was Professor Strachan running alongside us, minus his sombrero. 'Follow me!' he yelled, and took off in front of us, knees pumping. I remember being vaguely surprised by his agility. Summoning our last reserves of strength, we chased after him, with the cop gaining on us behind. At Somerset Street we tore left into the Journalism and Media Studies building. 'Hurry up!' Professor Strachan yelled as he held open the glass-door entrance to Journalism. We burst through the doorway and collapsed on the floor, breathless. Professor Strachan slammed the door shut and bolted it. The big goon skidded to a halt outside. He rapped on the glass with his sjambok. There was a large shiny lump on his forehead where he'd hit the wall falling down the stairs.

'Open!' he shouted.

'Go on, fuck off!' Professor Strachan shouted back.

'Open, now!'

'Do you possess a warrant, or is that too much to ask?'

Rivulets of sweat were pouring down the cop's face. Wild-eyed, he lashed at the door. The glass was reinforced, but still the force of the blow caused a long vertical crack.

'Open!'

'Fuck off, you bloody fool!' Professor Strachan shouted. 'Go away or I'll call the police! Hamba!'

This seemed to provide the cop with food for thought. Police? Did that name ring a bell somewhere? Professor Strachan turned to us, incredulous. 'Christ, that bastard's so worked up he can't even remember he is the police! Goes to show, doesn't it?' He rolled his eyes and gave a bark of laughter.

We waited until the cop simmered down. Eventually he shuffled off, dragging his sjambok on the ground after him, muttering oaths in Zulu. We thanked the Professor for saving our hides, literally, then we ran out the back to the car park and sped off in Zelda's mini. We stopped at a bottle store for some wine before driving up into the forests.

There's a place in the hills above Grahamstown where, if

you look south on a clear day, you can see Port Alfred and the sea, sixty kilometres away. It wasn't a clear day when Zelda and I went up there; there were swift, dark clouds obscuring the horizon and shafts of sunlight were fingering the farmlands below. We drank the wine and laughed hysterically. Ja, we laughed out of fear. With angry weals across our faces we laughed about the arses scooting across the lawn, and how the big cop slipped on the stairs. God, how we laughed! Then we got drunk and threw caution to the winds. I kissed Zelda, and it started.

As the evening came over it grew cold and dark up on the hill, and Zelda suggested we go to their digs. So we laughed all the way to the farmhouse called Stoneleigh on the Port Alfred road. We were wild and careless – life was wild and careless! There was no one home. Whitney was in jail, and, as it turned out, so was David. After the protest had been broken up he'd gone along to the police station to demand Whitney's release and ended up in a cell himself.

And so, it began. The transgression …

I can see her now as she walks across the room to the bed. Her buttocks and the fine muscles along her spine flex and relax. The smoothness of her white skin broken by weals. Her body is slim and graceful. Naked, she is unashamed. Her whiteness is no barrier. She looks back and sees me observing her. She smiles and removes her glasses.

I'm new to this. I have no experience in the postures of lovemaking. But I'm drunk, so it doesn't matter. I embrace her clumsily. Zelda laughs gently and shows me the way. I kiss her, gently at first, then deeper and harder. Blindly I enter her narrow hips and we rock and heave, we taunt our bodies, we writhe with the exquisite pain of the approaching orgasm. We linger as long as we can over this sweet pain, and then I erupt.

I lie with her as she sleeps, too frightened to close my eyes lest I wake to find her gone. I caress and kiss her body. I breathe in its sweet and bitter fragrances. I touch and knead her flesh. I watch the complex pulsations beneath her skin. Her body gleams with a sheen of perspiration. I smooth the fine hairs on her arms flat against her skin. Softly, I kiss her sleeping face. I love her … God, how I love her. Within her all my torments are melted into nothing. She sleeps …

*

When it came to important decisions in the Brands' house Hester wore the pants. As soon as I stepped in the door, she confronted me. Manie hovered around in the background, looking ill at ease.

Hester jabbed her finger at the front page of *Grocott's Mail*. On it was a photograph of a group of protesters. It was a good shot of Whitney: mouth open, eyes wild … above her head, as though festooned to it, David's gallows. And just behind her, as clear as day, Zelda and myself. Under the photograph was a headline saying, STUDENTS PROTEST TRICAMERAL SYSTEM. And that was not all, as Hester ably demonstrated by opening the paper to a double spread of action shots, showing Whitney being carted off, kicking and screaming, and glimpses of myself amidst the pandemonium.

'How do you think we feel when our children see you all over the front page, breaking the law? Carrying on like a township skollie?'

I shook my head.

'It's not a good example to set, you know.'

I nodded my head.

'And look at your face!'

Guiltily, I rubbed the weal across my cheek.

'I mean, what kind of influence are you going to have on my kids? We're a law-abiding family, you know.'

Manie and I nodded.

'Instead of wasting your time breaking the law, you should be concentrating on your studies. You're lucky enough to be at university in the first place. Others don't have that privilege, you know. Others have to work their fingers to the bone just to stay alive. But I see you just take it all for granted. You just want to throw away your chances, fooling around with troublemakers and getting drunk! It's not a good example, you know. Just look at your hair! Like a mop! And your clothes! Once you wore good clothes, you were presentable. Ordentlik. Now you walk around in rags!'

'Ag, Hester ...' Manie began.

'No, Manie,' Hester insisted, jabbing at the photograph on the front page again. 'This is serious. This is the final straw. I'm fed up with Manas coming in late at night, drunk and making a noise. Ja, Manas, don't think I haven't heard you stumbling around. Ag, and that time you were sick all over the bathroom ... I mean, don't you have any consideration? God knows, we've opened our home to you, Manas, but we're obviously not good enough for you. And now this. I don't want you giving my children stupid ideas, Manas.'

'Ag, Hestertjie ...' Manie tried again, smiling weakly. 'What about Piet and Marie? They've been doing so well at school since Manas started extra lessons with them.'

'Manas is not the only one who can teach English in this town. We'll find someone else.'

'Ag, Hestertjie ...'

'No, Manie. My mind is made up. I think Manas must go. I don't want the police banging on my door in the middle of the night. I'm sorry, but I can't have this sort of thing in my house.'

So I packed my things and left the Brands' house. It was not without a sense of relief that I took my last look at the small study and the black dog grinning through the window. Manie walked with me to the front gate. We shook hands.

'I'm sorry, Manas,' he said. 'But once Hester gets something in her head ...'

'Hester's right,' I said. 'It's my fault. I've behaved very badly.'

Actually, it'd been my intention to tell them I was leaving anyway. Zelda had asked me to move in with her.

*

A few weeks before he went to jail, David wrote this poem. It's the only one I can still bear to read, the only one that wasn't corrupted by phoney political hype. One of the few tangible things left that still fills me with a sense of that time, when Zelda and I were lovers.

The sun rises again, again
With sagged shoulders the town wakes
    to its dried legends
    flayed to bone
We stretch our paralysed tongues
We scratch the dust of our minds
    for words
We stand naked, confused by damp dreams
    searching our eyes in mirrors
    for clouds. None.
Chimes, chimes …
Last night, we could hear men
    breaking hills
    for the sake of fear
A fitful darkness, split by explosions
    & twitching searchlights
We listened to silent, burning cadenzas
    the gasp of peeling skin
We wept, as our dreams were shot down
    one by one
    wings aflame

The sun rises again, again
By the simple arithmetic of days
    we are diminished
    our hearts withered
The hills bear a brown sky
The heavens have come to dust
Streams of air
    the breath of rainless hatreds
    of bartered sorrows
The country burns again

Wood, garbage, flesh – things that turn to ash
The ashes of farms, ashes of dreams
    legends
    ashes of hope
    Chimes, chimes …
Last night, men with clenched fists
    were buried in flags
The children of drought were given
    to the burdened earth
Salutes, songs for freedom
    the pollen of dust & decay
    on swollen tongues

The sun rises again, again
The town wakes to its barren aftermath
    we patrol our divisions
    our fences of skin
The dams are drying, the birds are dying …
Amidst this I live
I search for that which must exist beyond
My words grow thinner, more fragile, I know
But where else do I go but to hope?
What else, to survive our frail hearts
    our frail flesh
    & blood?
And how else, to cherish this moment of living?
Chimes, chimes …
The music of bells
Beneath the sun, this black and white town
    fades to grey
And the referees of love and hate
    shift
    into the shade of lecture rooms
Or the dappled, holy colours of churches
where they listen
to clocks

Ja, David, the stricken sage … a brief glimpse of sincerity that soon would be lost, suffocated under the bitter artifice that came after he was released. I wonder what might have become of David had his demons spared him. God knows.

But I shouldn't criticise. He wasn't the only one who did things to please others. He wasn't the only who got lost in his search for that which must exist beyond.

*

Zelda and I tried every possible means to secure David and Whitney's release, to no avail. We asked high-profile academics, including Professor Strachan, to intercede. They did their best, meeting with senior police officers and petitioning the Minister of Law and Order, but without success. Zelda even swallowed her pride and approached the local National Party member who, predictably, just shrugged and raised his hands as though helpless before the divine laws of state. He ended by giving her a sermon on the trials and tribulations of policemen on duty in the townships. We contacted David's father, a wealthy Durban businessman, who travelled down to Grahamstown immediately. Aubrey Harris was a persistent man, but neither his perseverance nor financial clout was able to penetrate the stony silence of police bureaucracy. He was not even able to visit his son, or know of his state of health or whereabouts – all they would tell him was that David was not being held in Grahamstown. Under the prevailing legislation, David could be held indefinitely without access to any legal representation. Such was the predicament of thousands.

But after a month David was released and he came back into our lives, looking pale and bitter. They'd given him a rough time; the yellowing bruises all over his body were proof of that. He had no idea where he'd been held. All he knew was that after a few days in Grahamstown's cells they put him in a closed van and drove for what seemed like hours through the night. When they finally stopped he was escorted, handcuffed and blindfolded, to a cold cell with no

119

windows. Must have been upcountry, he said, because it was so cold at night. They'd beaten him regularly. They used a cattle prodder on his genitals and rectum. They kept him incommunicado. No one to talk to except his interrogators, who found his anguish amusing. No idea of time, no idea when his torment would end.

It seemed incredible that the security police would mete out such treatment to a relative nobody like David. We wondered what purpose might have been served by such cruelty. It didn't make sense. But then the business of the security police never made much sense anyway. We still hadn't heard a thing about Whitney.

Aubrey Harris stayed with us for a few days after his release. David spent most of the time morosely drunk. I felt sorry for his father, a quiet, intelligent man who was sincerely concerned for his son's welfare. He urged David to go back with him to Durban, to get away from Grahamstown, but David refused. There was a gulf between them that Aubrey was trying to bridge, but was unable to. Eventually he left and the tension eased. Later, David told me he hated Aubrey for having left his mother, who (according to David) eventually drank herself to death out of loneliness.

So consumed was he by his recent experience that he affected only mild surprise when he noticed Zelda and I were lovers. Ja, he took it in his stride, and one night drunkenly asserted his sorrow that he and Whitney weren't 'one' too. His eyes grew soft and sentimental at the thought. He forced himself to believe that she'd soon be freed and pressed Zelda for ways to win her over. He could never understand Whitney's continual rejections. Zelda told him to forget about her. She's in love with the struggle, nothing else, Zelda said.

David was very physical in his anger. He chopped wood for hours on end. When he lined up the axe to split a log you got the impression he was aiming at one of his torturer's skull. He went on long walks down near the river. He cut his hair so short that just a blond stubble remained. He got drunk. And he wrote. His poems became steeped in an

uneasy blend of hopelessness and hype; thorns began to protrude through the flesh of words, lines exfoliated to reveal an
inner emptiness.

Things weren't easy for Zelda and me either. Though there
had been talk from the Minister of Internal Affairs about
repealing the *Immorality Act* and the *Mixed Marriages Act*
(as another gesture of 'radical' reform) cross-racial relationships were still illegal and unacceptable to most whites,
including Zelda's family and, no doubt, Stoneleigh's landlord. Also, even with the softening attitudes in government,
the Group Areas laws were still in place, which meant cou-
ples like Zelda and me couldn't simply live where we
pleased. So we had to be careful not to flaunt my presence.
Fortunately we were protected by Stoneleigh's isolation,
situated as it was in a sheltered valley away from the town.
Our landlord, a jovial man by the name of Gaites, seldom
bothered us. He was a farmer who found it more convenient
to live in town. We paid our rent into his bank account and
hardly ever saw him, except sometimes when he drove past
on his way out to the lands. Mr Gaites never seemed to concern himself over my presence; perhaps he thought I was a
servant, the house boy, there to sweep the floors and wash
the dishes.

I can't escape the irony. South Africans were entering perhaps the most brutal period of their history and yet those
days were the happiest of my life. A gentle, private world
unknown to me before had opened up like a flower. What
words can I say that might encapsulate the closeness of heart
and skin? We lived in a strange eternity doomed by the limits of time, immortal within the darkness of mortality. The
magical contradictions of the flesh. Ag, forgive this eroded
sentimentality. These are forlorn tributes, I know …

During this time neither of us did much work despite going
off to our studios each day. We went through the motions of
keeping busy, knowing there needed to be another purpose
to life, but were too distracted to create anything of substance. Besieged by time and mortality, we evoked our
muses, but only halfheartedly – do people pray in heaven?

But, alas, time and mortality are jealous realities that resent being ignored for too long. And so after a while I sensed a change in Zelda. Sometimes, after we made love, she grew silent and distant. And I became anxious because she wouldn't talk about it. Then one day she did.

'It's not you, Manas,' she said. 'It's just ... oh, shit, it's this whole bloody situation! Us having to scuttle into hiding like mice each time we want to make love. It gets to me some-times, you know. Sometimes, I just want to get up and go. To the other side of the world, I swear!'

'Why don't we?' I replied.

'Because that's not all there is to it. There's something else that screws me up. My family. They'll never accept this!'

I shrugged. 'You don't have to tell them.'

'Sooner or later, I'll have to, Manas, if we're to carry on together. I can't hide it from them.'

'Then tell them. What can they do?'

'You don't understand. I love them. I don't want to hurt them. They mean too much to me. I really don't know what to do.'

'If they really love you they'll accept whatever makes you happy.'

'Life's not that simple, Manas. Christ, it's never that bloody easy! I know them better than you do.'

Zelda closed her eyes and laid her head on my chest. She ran her long fingers over my skin. I didn't push the matter. For the time being I was happy and I didn't want anything to change that.

Perhaps a word or two about Zelda's family might put her anxiety into perspective. The Suttons are a respected and well-established Eastern Cape farming family with long-standing traditions and, hence, high expectations of its members. Original settler stock. Indeed, Zelda's ancestors on her father's side, William and Edith Sutton, arrived from England in 1820 and carved their farm out of virgin bush along the Great Fish River. The farm was called Haslemere, after their home town in Surrey. They survived the diseases and the marauding Xhosa warriors. They began the generations whose sons fought and died in the Boer War and both World Wars. They began the successions of sons and daughters who went to private schools in Grahamstown. A cut above the rest. Through good farming and good marriages the farm prospered in size when two adjoining farms were annexed. As the family expanded they bought other farms and businesses in the region (though Zelda's immediate family considered it a privilege to own the original farm). They all married well, the Suttons did, usually into wealthy or at least influential families. They knew a thing or two about intelligent breeding – their children were all tall and straight-nosed, superior in both brain and limb. Likewise, their prime beef cattle, remarkable hybrids of British and local breeds, were regular prizewinners at agricultural shows. Unfortunately, with Zelda and me, their meticulous husbandry was about to be shot to hell.

Zelda's fear of impending rejection worked on her mind and one day she decided to bring matters to a head. With that look of grim resolution (which I'd get to know so well) she climbed into her mini and drove down to the farm. She was away for a week, during which the previously peaceful homestead of Haslemere was thrown into uproar. As she predicted, her parents, Charles and Catherine, would not accept our relationship. Nor would brother John. This is putting it mildly. Her parents, in particular her father, condemned it. They forbade it. They threatened banishment if she persisted. I got a taste of this reaction sooner than I expected.

John witnessed the angry outbursts on Haslemere. Being a man of few words, he watched and listened in stony silence, while the anger built up inside him. Those intricate emotions that bind him to Zelda welled up from deep within, and, being a man of few words, he decided that action was needed to save his sister, his twin, to win her back into the fold. And so while Zelda and her parents argued and shouted and wept, he took matters into his own hands.

I was alone at Stoneleigh when he knocked. It was late afternoon and David was still in town. I opened the door and there he stood, lean and hard-faced, in the background a dusty Landcruiser. I had no idea who he was.

'Can I help you?' I asked.

His flat brown eyes met mine. A look of arrogance and contempt. So sure of himself.

'I'm looking for Manas?' he announced.

'I'm Manas,' I replied.

I hardly saw the punch that caught me between the eyes and sent me reeling back into the house. I floundered around on the floor, dazed and bleeding. John pulled me up by the shirt collar. I stared stupidly into his merciless eyes. Then he gave me another one, this time in the mouth. I fell heavily to the floor.

'Lay a finger on Zelda again and I'll kill you!' he shouted, standing over me, his fists balled. 'You hear me, you bastard? It's finished, okay? Go near my sister and I'll kill you!'

He gave me a kick in the stomach, then turned and left. David found me later in the bathroom, still trying to stem the flow of blood from a cut across the bridge of my nose. He took me to the hospital. John's first blow had broken my nose, which added the sorry effect of two black eyes to my battered countenance. The cut required seven stitches. His second blow chipped one of my front teeth.

I was shaken by the attack, and soberly aware there was nothing I could do about it. Despite my pleas for him not to, David, as helpless to his anger as ever, phoned Zelda at Haslemere and told her what had happened. Apparently, there was a fearsome shouting match between Zelda and John, ending with Zelda storming out of her home, vowing never to talk to her family again. She arrived back at Stoneleigh, took one look at my face and burst into tears. I kissed her.

'Has your mother started making the wedding cake yet?'

Zelda looked at me, almost angrily. 'Oh, you crazy damn fool!'

We walked down to a grove of poplar trees along the river. The trees were beautiful with their bright spring buds and the sunshine was warm and pleasant. Zelda told me about the arguments she'd had with her folks and the mutual sense of betrayal they now harboured. Her father would probably cut her off, she said. That's what he threatened anyway.

She would need to get a job. Maybe she could get an academic assistantship through the Fine Art Department. Not much pay but anything to make ends meet while she finished her course. She hated her folks, she said. She hated John – especially John. She could *kill* John, honestly she could. She said lots of things she didn't mean.

I put it to her. 'I'll leave if you want me to, Zelda. I'm just trouble to you.'

To my relief, she replied, 'That's exactly what I *don't* want you to do. It's not us who're wrong, you know.'

In the days that followed Zelda tried to divert her mind from her troubles by putting on a brave face. She worked hard at her sculpture. And she loved me as though it were the measure of her morality. But I sensed the hurt underneath it all. Everything for her was tempered by the pain of rejection and there was nothing I could do to make it easier. Except get out of her life, but she didn't want that and nor did I. Worst of all was the pain she felt in tearing herself from John. While I gained a profound insight into the depth and intensity of love between twins, only those who've shared a womb could truly understand what Zelda was going through. She told me how close they had been, especially during their childhood. How they had grown to love their differences. It was their differences, Zelda said, that completed them – made them whole. And they'd always believed that nothing, except death, could destroy their wholeness. Not even prolonged absences, like when John went away to do his national service at Upington or when he did an agricultural course at Cedara College near Pietermaritzburg; Zelda had never felt a sense of parting. But they hadn't reckoned on an interloper like me (and the fact that I was a black interloper compounded and aggravated John's sense of betrayal). While Zelda admitted to several boyfriends before me, she hadn't seriously loved any of them. Likewise, John had never found a contender serious enough to wean him from Zelda. For days I was guilt-ridden at having caused such a rift. I felt claustrophobic in the intensity of their strange love.

One night I woke to see her standing at the window, staring outside. I got up and went over to her. 'Are you okay?' I asked. 'What's the matter?'

'He's out there.'

'John?'

She nodded. I peered out into the darkness and saw him standing near the gate, about fifty metres away.

'Oh Christ,' I said. 'The Prince of Darkness.'

'Please don't joke, Manas.'

We watched him in silence, then I said, 'This is crazy, Zelda. What time is it?'

Zelda didn't reply. She continued to stare at John's lonely form outside until it got too excruciating for me to bear. With a sense of loss I said, 'Go to him, Zelda. Come on, you can't stand here all night.'

Tears were running down her face. I was completely out of my depth.

'For God's sake, Zelda! I can't stand this. Please go to him!'

She sighed and kissed my cheek. 'I love you,' she said.

Then she went outside. I heard her footsteps on the veranda. I heard her call out his name. And I saw him flinch at the sound of her voice. He hesitated, then turned and ran off into the night. I heard a vehicle start up and drive off. Its sound was still receding when Zelda came back into the room.

And time was no healer. Time made it harder for her. Time is the soil in which the roots of kinship grow. But Zelda had forsaken her kin for my tumbleweed love.

My father winks …

*

We expected things to happen. Zelda's allowance to be cut off, angry phone calls, even angry visits. But nothing did happen. Only a letter from Zelda's mother, in which she expressed her sadness at what had come to pass, but she hoped the 'terrible insanity' of it would soon be something of the past and the family would be united once more.

And so Zelda and I were left with an embittered David

126

who paced around like a caged animal, brooding over poor imprisoned Whitney. The spring seemed to drag the tenacious remnants of winter along with it. The nights were cold with occasional frosts. As far as our university studies were concerned, our sense of commitment and purpose had returned. Zelda was motivated, no doubt, by the thought of being cast adrift. My studio at St Aidan's was beginning to fill up with work. I was happy with my progress. Professor Strachan and my painting lecturer said the large canvases I was producing were a big step forward. I gained confidence when I thought of the long way I'd come since leaving Langebaan almost two years ago. While my paintings wouldn't have been her cup of tea, my mother would still have been proud of me.

But then David started coming around, usually a bit under the weather. He'd stand in my studio and read his poems out aloud, spouting words like some pompous Thespian. His poems were now laced with images of violence. Police and prisons. Oppression and revolt. Hopelessness. And, of course, Woman with a capital W entered his vocabulary. Woman as victim, Woman as martyr. David said that Woman could be read, in a wider sense, as the embodiment of Africa, tormented and violated – a pseudo-feminist bit of bullshit outside his usual repertoire. But it was clear to me who Woman was. And although I sometimes found these interruptions to my work routine irritating, I listened out of loyalty. I didn't see where it might lead.

David said he liked my new paintings but would prefer more 'struggle stuff' in them. Why just paint figures or landscapes when there was so much shit going on in the country? And I was stupid enough to respond with a series of pen-and-ink drawings. Hard, cruel visions of torture and suffering. Dogs and whips. Slaves and masters, along the lines of David's poetry. David approved of my change in direction. And I received encouragement from Zelda too. She liked the drawings. Politics is a legitimate thing in art, she said. It gives your work substance. Relevance. I believed her.

The book was David's idea. It occurred to him that our

work was compatible, since my drawings were, to all intents and purposes, illustrations of his poems. The idea excited him. He was filled with purpose. It was something he could do to strike back at the source of his bitterness. I was dubious at first. I'd never considered the possibility of those drawings going any further than our closed circle. I felt uneasy about offering them to the world. It was asking for trouble and the possible consequences scared me. In fact, I was amazed that David was prepared to take the risk, considering his recent experiences with the police. But David was persistent and persuasive. He assured me the authorities had far too much on their hands to concern themselves with a little book of poetry. He argued that art was not the property of state, it was the rightful province of artists. It belonged not to power, but to people (the most fallacious of delusions). In the end I was convinced of the morality of our endeavour. I suppressed my qualms. Fear had no place alongside truth, so I believed.

When I completed what we thought were enough drawings – in all, about thirty – I took them and David's poems to Professor Strachan. He took a week to go through them, then he called me to his office. He was dead against the whole idea.

'What the hell's happened to you, Manas?' he said, holding up my drawings. 'This isn't you. What's got into you? All this hick protest crap. Your stuff's not honest anymore – it's propaganda. You're bashing out slogans, Manas.'

'It's how I feel, Prof,' I said.

Professor Strachan laughed dryly. 'Bullshit. This ...' he waved the drawings at me again 'is not you, Manas. It's not how you feel. Political slogans, Manas. Hype. That's all it is. You're jumping on a bandwagon, doing stuff like this. You're completely under the spell of that jackass David.'

'You're saying that the country can burn but art must somehow remain untouched, unsullied. That's a bourgeois notion, Prof. It's an artist's *duty* to attack the system.'

Professor Strachan sighed irritably. 'Oh Christ, Manas, you talk as if you were born yesterday. Look, when it comes to politics I'm the biggest cynic alive. I can tolerate the idealistic indulgences of a few gullible students, people like Zelda and David for example, because they're young and naive. But because I tolerate them doesn't mean I agree with them. While I resent the present system in this country, I honestly don't believe a Utopia will take its place. Christ, I've seen too many political systems come and go in my time, especially in Africa. Power corrupts, and nowhere more so than in Africa. I thought you had more upstairs. All this revolutionary stuff under the name of freedom ... no, politics is not something you want to lay your art on the line for. It's too corrupt, too impure. Too full of bullshit and lies. Stay true to your heart, Manas. Don't let others sway you so much.'

'Nobody swayed me, Prof. Maybe I'm just too full of bullshit and lies.'

'Don't get sarcastic, Manas. Just face facts, okay? I have my sincere doubts whether any publisher in his right mind will even look at this stuff. It's crap, for God's sake! Dangerous crap. Both the poems and the drawings. Too transparent, too obvious. Come on, be honest. Do you really believe in these drawings?'

I nodded.

Professor Strachan held up his hands in a helpless gesture. 'That's my opinion, Manas. Take it or leave it.'

Hurt and angry, I took my leave. As I walked out of his office, past the African sculpture with the erect phallus, I thought how drab and ordinary Professor Strachan really was, beneath the sombrero and other flamboyant jazz. Ja, he'd shown his true colours. He was an old conservative white man, afraid of change, no different from the rest.

David dismissed Professor Strachan's views. 'Take no notice,' he told me. 'Prof's typical of most white liberals. He pays lip service to political change, but backs off when the boat gets rocked. Useless old fart!'

Once David got a bee in his bonnet there was no stopping him. He sent copies of the manuscript off to publishers in Cape Town and Johannesburg – publishers with a taste for left-wing literature, who he thought would cast an admiring eye upon our efforts. Impatiently we awaited positive news. And soon the rejection slips began rolling in. Those horribly polite regret-to-inform-you notes. To the point, with nothing to glean between the lines. Doggedly, we tried two literary agents with the same result.

The long tentacles of doubt began to squeeze. Professor Strachan had been right. No one in their right mind would take us on. David reacted defiantly by doctoring the poems with obscenities. The police became 'fuckheads', the government became a snake with its head up its arse. Mr Heroic Pen, himself. Thinking the extra vitriol would do the trick, David dispatched the manuscript off again to the same publishers. Within a few days, the same response as before. I began to dread those telltale parcels in the post; the manuscript along with a note curtly asking us to refrain from submitting it again.

But David was never one to take a hint. 'There's only one thing to do,' he said. 'We'll publish it ourselves.'

'We'll what?' I laughed, incredulous.

'To hell with all these tight-arse publishers. We'll do it ourselves.'

'But how? It costs money, David.'

'Look, the reason why no one wants to touch this thing is because they're too shit-scared. It's got fuck all to do with how good it is. So we'll publish it privately – overseas. There're plenty of self-pay publishers advertising in the newspapers, begging for business. We'll do it through one of them.'

'Still, that costs money, David.'

'I've got money, Manas. My father showers me with fucking money. It's all in the bank somewhere. I never had a use for it until now.' David's eyes got that faraway look. 'Actually, I really like the idea of doing it ourselves. A small edition we could distribute locally. Straight and simple, no fancy marketing bullshit. It's more in keeping with the whole idea, don't you think? Has a sort of subversive feel to it, eh, Manas? Sort of underground.'

But I wasn't so sure. 'I don't know. Do you really think it's worth it? Do you think it's good enough?'

'Manas, have some bloody faith in yourself. We've got to see this thing through. We can't back out now.'

David's impulsive determination never quite fully restored my faith. Still, the idea of a modest publication made me feel slightly better. It sounded more discreet. I was like a cat wanting to scratch sand over its shit.

So after a bit of newspaper hunting and a few long-distance phone calls David sent the manuscript off to a self-pay publisher in London called, ironically, Patriotic Press. They agreed to produce an edition of two hundred copies in paperback. There was some haggling over costs but eventually David signed the contract and the deal was done. Afterwards, we climbed into David's Volkswagen and sped off to Port Alfred. We bought some beer and drove to a lonely spot in the dunes. It was cold and the sea was wild and windswept. We sat shivering in the sand and drank the beer. There in the dunes above the heaving sea, we were overcome by a maudlin solidarity. Anaesthetised with alcohol, David took out a knife and cut his hand. Then he handed the knife to me and I did the same. And we clasped our hands together, brothers …

*

And then Whitney came back. She wafted into our lives again like a garrulous breeze, looking none the worse for wear after her ordeal. Her integrity intact, her credibility unassailable. We were all glad she'd come out of it okay, though, according to Whitney, the reason the police had held her for so long was to recover from the beatings she received when she was first taken into custody – a black and blue white lady wouldn't do their public image any good, she said. She had lots of gruesome stories about what they did to her – electric shocks, being half-drowned, relentless hours of interrogation. Of course, David hung onto her every word and followed her around like a besotted spaniel, at her beck and call. He gave her a copy of our manuscript to read and practically wagged his tail with delight when she responded so enthusiastically. She crowed with anarchic glee at David's obscene invective and my scenes of police brutality. She wagged her finger at us, her green eyes darting – ja, what have you been up to, you naughty boys!

I was less enchanted by Whitney than David and Zelda were. Her presence changed everything in the house. I felt a sense of foreboding. She spelt trouble. I knew the time of trust and innocence was over.

Naturally Whitney was undaunted in her mission. If anything, her detention now spurred her on to greater efforts. She immediately re-established her presence on the campus. More militant than ever, she harangued her followers at the numerous meetings she organised (to which I was dragged along) with tales of government duplicity and institutionalised terror. 'Witness the number of children in prisons!' she cried. She told us that sacrifices had to be made to destroy apartheid, that passive protest was not enough. We should put our lives at stake for the struggle, she said. We should fight fire with fire. And people listened. She had a prison ordeal to back up her words. Her courage was an example to us all. And not only her flock on campus listened. To her visible delight, she'd gained esteem in the eyes of the township activists. The real thing. Soon, she was as thick as thieves with every ragtag troublemaker straight off the dusty streets of Fingo Village. She called them the 'glorious proletariat'. They called her 'the leopard'; I was never quite sure whether they were alluding to her courage or her freckles. Forgive my facetiousness. It emerges from what I have come to be; I don't trust those whose spirits soar with violence.

Now there were new visitors to the house. The activists became part of the scene, scarred, defiant young men and women who had the angriest and bravest eyes I've ever seen. Hardened by desperate lives of poverty and neglect, they exuded an unnerving carelessness about life. The only thing of meaning for them was the struggle.

As they say, the leopard never changes its spots. Every Friday night Whitney held a gathering at the house. The activists would appear out of the darkness and greet us with

132

raised fists, and we'd sit around the fire in the lounge and talk. Sometimes if there had been trouble in the townships the talk would be serious and the mood sombre; a circle of grave faces spitting doom for a fated country. Only Whitney seemed to enjoy these moments. Once she said to me, gesturing at her new friends, 'These are the real warriors, Manas, not starry-eyed little white-arse students!'

But often the mood was lighter. We all got drunk and happy and sometimes we danced and sang, and in the morning there were glorious proletarians with sore heads lying all over the house. On one such occasion I went outside to take a leak and overheard David and Whitney talking in the shadows of the veranda. As usual, with David the wine was doing most of the talking.

'Are you queer or something, Whitney?'

'What?'

'I mean, do you find men attractive? You aren't lesbian or something weird, are you?'

'Fuck off, David.'

'Well, I need to know. It would explain things.'

'Shit, you're so bloody full of yourself, aren't you? The fact that I don't respond to your pathetic advances could surely have nothing to do with you, Mr Perfect? It must be me, hey? Well, for your information, David, no, I'm not queer. I'm perfectly fucking normal.'

Whitney – normal? I nearly burst out laughing.

'What must I do, Whitney?' David was pleading.

'I'm not asking you to do anything. Except leave me alone!'

'I love you, Whitney.'

'Please don't say that! You're wasting your time!'

'I love you. I'll do anything to prove it! Anything!'

'David, read my lips: I. Don't. Bloody. Love. You! Get that into your thick skull, okay? I don't want you to prove anything!'

'I'll take whatever comes. I don't care what happens.'

'You really don't get it, do you? For your own bloody good, David, fuck off! Leave me alone!'

'Please, Whitney, give me a chance …'

I went back inside, feeling sick at the way David was begging.

And so our lives were changed with the return of Whitney. Zelda and I were surrounded by a motley band of revolutionaries. But we were hardly in the same boat. We knew little (and still know little) of the strategies of political subversion. We were just illegal lovers, defying the laws that forbade our love. That's why Whitney and her glorious proletariat liked us. We were a sort of symbol to them; our togetherness, our intimacy – this was what the struggle was all about, this was the South Africa they were fighting for. Or this is how Zelda and I chose to see it at the time. Also, when I was drunk they found me funny. Ja, I was becoming quite a clown with my weird behaviour. It was at this time that I first started having blackouts, those awful, frightening blanks in my memory where I didn't know what on earth I'd said or done in my drunkenness. But, no, Zelda and I were not in the same league as these new visitors. We were glad that our hearts had not turned hard and cruel, as revolutionaries' hearts must to achieve their ends. And we were glad we weren't included in the secret meetings, those nights when they'd gather around the table in the dining room and Whitney would shut the door.

The township activists weren't the only visitors now that Whitney was back. There were others she attracted (or so I thought), who were not so welcome. One day I was alone in the house – Zelda, David and Whitney had gone off to town, leaving me to nurse a worse than usual hangover – when I heard a car pulling up at the gate. I looked out the window and saw a yellow Ford sedan, the kind plain-clothes cops often use, drive around to the front of the house. It stopped and two men and a big black dog, an Alsation, climbed out.

I quickly locked the front door and sneaked out of the house through the kitchen. As calmly as I could, I walked down the road towards the gate, not looking back. My footsteps on the gravel sounded deafening to my ears, even my breathing seemed too loud as I restrained myself from breaking into a run. Then I heard a voice call, 'Hey, you!' I continued walking, as though I hadn't heard, then the voice shouted, 'Ssa!' and I turned to see the Alsation running towards me. I stood dead still. One of the men called, 'Skelm!' and the dog skidded to a halt. It looked at the man, then it looked at me, a sorrowful expression on its face.

I waited as the two men sauntered over. Both were wearing safari suits, both carried revolvers hidden unconvincingly beneath their shirts. The older of the two was in his fifties, greying and thickset, with hard blue eyes that were fixed on mine. He gave a loud belch, which made the younger man laugh. The younger man was thin and dark-haired. He sported a weedy moustache, and carried a sjambok. With a flick of his wrist, he demonstrated its use by cutting a sapling clean in two. It was a good demonstration; he had my undivided attention. I knew the subservience routine would be my best chance of survival.

They stopped in front of me. The dog shuffled closer and sat at my feet, panting in my face. The men laughed at my discomfort. The game started.

'What are you doing here?' the older man asked.

'Looking for work, baas.'

'Don't lie to me! We've been getting reports of lots of strange people coming onto this property. Township kaffirs. Mixing with students who live here.'

'Students? No baas! I'm looking for work, my baas!'

'Looking for work with long hair like that?' the younger man said. 'What chance has he got with hair like that, eh, Jan? Fuck all.'

'You're right, Boetie,' the older man, Jan, agreed. 'Doesn't look like he's done a day's work in his life. I think he's one of the rubbish mixing with the students.'

'No, baas! Just a poor coloured boy looking for work!'

Jan assumed a ludicrous expression of deep thought. 'Didn't we hear something about some filthy goffel actually living here with the students? In the same house?'

'No, my baas!'

'Where're you from, jong?'

'Langebaan, baas.'

'Langebaan? Where the fuck's that?'

'West Coast, baas.'

'What you doing this side of the country, then?'

'Looking for work, my baas.'

'Ja, and my name's Desmond Tutu!'

Jan laughed at his own superlative wit. Boetie laughed too, guffawing loudly. Even the dog seemed to laugh, panting its foul breath in my face. So I joined in too, not wanting them to think I was bereft of a sense of humour.

One after the other they stopped laughing. First Jan, then Boetie, then the dog.

'Hey! What the fuck are you laughing at, jong?' Jan demanded.

I wiped the smile off my face.

'I said, what are you laughing at? What's so bloody funny?'

'I'm not laughing, my baas.'

'Boetie, the goffel's laughing at us.'

'No, baas!'

'I'll teach him,' Boetie said.

He made to strike me with the sjambok. I cowered beneath my hands. I adopted the posture of a beggar, shoulders hunched, eyes pleading. 'No, baas! Please, my baas!

'I'll teach you, vuilgoed!'

Jan held up his hand and Boetie lowered the sjambok. Clearly Jan was the boss. He advanced on me and stood with his nose an inch from mine. His eyes tried to hold mine but mine were too slippery. His breath was worse than the dog's. I noticed that liquor was one of its components.

'Who told you to laugh?' he asked.

'Nobody, baas! Sorry, baas!'

Jan thrust a stubby finger in my face. He pushed in the tip of my nose. 'Don't try me, jong. Just don't try me, ek sê.'

'No, baas! I beg of you!'

He gave my cheek a couple of soft slaps.

'You laugh only if I tell you. You shit only if I tell you. Understand?'

'Ja, baas!'

136

'I'll kill you if you try me, jong. I'm not joking.'

'Ja, baas. Sorry, baas!'

He lowered his hand and straightened up, satisfied.

'You people are all the same. No fucking manners.'

'Ja, baas.'

'No manners and no brains,' Brain Surgeon Boetie added.

I moved back a few steps but the dog moved with me, crouching at my feet, its throat rattling.

'Hey! Stand still!' Jan commanded. 'You move only when I tell you, you hear?'

'Ja, baas.'

'So you're looking for work, hey?'

'Ja, baas.'

'You don't live here?'

'No, baas.'

'Work, hey?'

'Ja, baas. Work.'

'What the hell do you know about work? Look at your hands. Soft, like a girl. And hair like a girl.'

'I can work hard, baas.'

'Bullshit.'

'Ja, baas. I work hard.'

'Well, there's no work here. Go back to Langebaan.'

'No work, baas?'

'Wash your ears out, man! I said there's no work!'

'Ja, baas.'

Jan and Boetie began to laugh again, this time at my plaintive expression. This time I did not laugh.

'Well, what are you waiting for, goffel? There's no work for you here, understand?'

'I understand, baas.'

'Then fuck off. Don't let us catch you here again.'

'Ja, baas.'

But I did not move. I could not move. We all stood looking at each other. Jan farted. Boetie giggled at the sound. Jan cleared his throat and spat at the ground.

'You want me to wash your ears out for you?' he said. 'I told you to fuck off!'

'Okay, baas, I'm going.'

But still I did not move. I was too frightened to move. Boetie lashed out and the tip of the sjambok nipped my thigh. I yelled in pain and leapt into the air. The dog followed my ascent and descent, open-mouthed, an amazed look in its eye. I rubbed my thigh furiously.

'Go on, fuck off! I'm sick of your face. Go! Voetsek!' Boetie shouted.

I turned and walked away, my legs shaking with fear. The dog moved after me but Jan commanded it to stay. I got to the gate and when I made to fasten it behind me, Jan told me to leave it open. I walked on, my shoulders twitching, expecting the inevitable. I didn't turn around when I heard the swift footsteps behind me, and when the sjambok whacked the back of my legs I gave a thin shriek and leapt again into the air. Behind me, Boetie howled with laughter. I could hear Jan saying, 'Stay, Skelm! Stil!'

I walked down the road, feeling my legs burning and the sweat prickle under my armpits. Expecting the inevitable, I scanned the land for suitable trees. They gave me a hundred metres' start before setting the dog on me. I looked back to see it streaking towards me, ears flattened, grunting with each bound. And I took flight. Ja, I thudded across the earth like a fugitive scarecrow, my knees brushing my chin. Above the rushing air, I could hear their crazy laughter. With the sudden expertise of a cat I clawed my way up a tree. My legs shaking, I perched on a branch as the dog jumped up at me, vainly, its jaws snapping. For the time being I was safe. I was beyond reach. I wept with my head against the tree trunk, my arms around its thickness.

I could hear Jan and Boetie roaring with laughter, slapping their sides. Then, eventually, Jan gave a sharp whistle and the dog slunk off back to them. Every ten paces or so it looked back at me and growled. Then they climbed into the yellow Ford and drove off. As they came past the tree, Boetie grinned and snapped his fingers together at me, which I took to signify an uncontrolled anus.

3 THE QUESTION OF CONSEQUENCE

I am mildly surprised. The rain still intrigues me with its beauty as it sways and swirls across the water. The tide has risen and the wind has become a gale. The boats moored out beyond the promontory where the ruins of the shell-crushing factory stand, rock and heave on flurried, pewter swells. I'd forgotten how wild and uncertain Langebaan can be in winter. So much is hidden behind clouds and rain. And, perversely, I find comfort in this. Ja, the man who has lost everything finds succour in a place that hides itself behind veils of rain.

Zelda has gone. She returned from her drive, her mind made up. Tearfully, she packed her things and got into the car and left, along with Helen and John. But not before the worst of our confrontations.

I knew what was coming when I saw her outside talking earnestly with John, no doubt informing him of her decision. With an aching despair I saw John lean over and kiss her, the expression of relief on his face almost too much to bear. The rain had abated so Zelda left Helen with him and came inside to confront me. She stood in front of the fire next to my table and came straight to the point.

'I'm leaving, Manas. I think we should separate. I'm not going to Australia. The way things are with you, that'd be a disaster. I'm sorry, but that's the way it is. I need to pick up the pieces and make something of my life.'

I said nothing.

Zelda sighed. 'I'm sorry but I can't handle this anymore. I feel I'm suffocating. Really, there's no future in it, for myself or for Helen.'

She spoke as though the words were hurting her throat. Her lips trembled and her chin puckered. Out of nervousness, I began to drum my fingers on the table.

'I hate doing this, Manas. It's not something I've taken lightly.'

139

Zelda's gaze settled on my fingers drumming on the table. I could see the sound was irritating her, so I stopped.

'Say something, Manas.'

'What can I say? I'm sorry.'

'You're always sorry.'

'Well, what can I say, then? You've been looking for some excuse not to go to Australia.'

'Please don't make it worse by blaming me. I just want to talk it over, so you know where I stand. I don't want to fight with you.'

'I know where you stand. I just can't believe you're doing this to me now.'

'You've got no idea, hey? No idea what it's like when you drink. I don't want to be around to see you fall apart completely. I don't want Helen to see it either.'

'Ag, Zelda, why give up now? Things will come right in Australia. I know they will.'

'How do you think we'd survive in Australia with you going on like this? What must I look forward to in Australia? The rest of my life with a hopeless drunk? No, Manas, I've had enough of hopelessness. More than enough.'

I searched for excuses. 'Last night was an exception.'

'You promised you wouldn't drink.'

'It's been hard with John here.'

'Oh, please! Don't blame John. He's got a lot more to deal with than you. And I don't see him falling to pieces.' She looked through the window and shivered. 'It was a mistake coming here. A big mistake. God, I hate this place!'

I lit a cigarette. 'What about Helen?'

'I can't very well leave her with you, can I? She'll be happy with me. She'll have a stable life. You can see her whenever you're in a condition to. She's your daughter.'

'That's mighty charitable of you.'

'Please don't make it worse, Manas.'

'Christ, Zelda, you know she'll be better off in Australia. She'll at least have some bloody future. What does this country have to offer her, other than a skin complex?'

'I'm not going to Australia. And that means Helen isn't either. Don't make a scene out of this, okay?'

I drew on the cigarette and coughed. I put my head in my hands.

'Oh, God, Zelda … please don't go.'

Zelda's eyes grew harder. 'Damn you, Manas! You broke a promise!'

'One mistake and you walk out. You were looking for any excuse, weren't you?'

Zelda laughed bitterly. 'One mistake! The final straw, rather! How long have we been together? Four years? And what have you got to show for it? Nothing but a wasted life. Wasted potential. Can't you see the hopelessness of it? Damn you, Manas!'

At that point it started raining again. Zelda opened the window and called, 'Helen! Come inside now! I don't want you catching a cold!' Helen came galloping up to the cottage. She burst into the room. 'Daddy!' she cried. 'Look what Mommy buyed me!'

'What Mommy bought me,' Zelda corrected.

Helen was holding a fluffy red elephant with a curled trunk. When she squeezed it, the trunk uncurled and made a trumpeting sound. I leaned over and kissed her cheek.

'It's beautiful, my baby.'

'I'm not a baby!'

'Daddy and Mommy are talking now, my girl' Zelda said. 'You must go and play in the room.'

'I want to play here! With you.'

'No, we're talking, darling,' Zelda said, firmly. 'Come, I'll find something for you to do.'

'Will you read me a story, Mommy?'

'No story now, my girl. Mommy wants to talk to Daddy.'

'But I want you to read a story!'

'Off you go, my girl,' I said. 'Mommy wants to give Daddy a talking to.'

I received a black glare from Zelda as she led Helen off to the bedroom. I got up and went through to the kitchen and made some coffee. The reality of it hadn't fully dawned on me yet. When I came back, Zelda was sitting next to the fire, warming her hands. She was staring into space, lost in thought. I placed her coffee on the floor next to her feet. She didn't touch it. I put my hand on her shoulder and kissed her cheek. It was like kiss-ing stone.

I sat down again. 'Come on, let's not make hasty decisions. Give Australia a chance. Things will work out there, I know.'

Her mouth twisted. 'Hasty decisions? Hasty decisions! This ... oh, what's the bloody use talking to you! You're just giving me the shits.'

'We've been through a lot together, Zelda. Why throw it away now?'

'Throw it away? Me? Jesus, you've got a bloody nerve! I hate the way you blame everyone else.'

'I'm only trying to be placatory.'

'Placatory? What sort of fucking word is that? I'd rather you were honest.'

'Do you have to swear?'

'I've got the shits, Manas. In case you haven't realised.'

'Being a fishwife doesn't become you, Zelda.'

'It's time you started to stomach things you don't like.'

I lit another cigarette. My head almost burst as I coughed. I longed for a drink to dull my persistent hangover. My mind refused to register. Ja, disaster was stalking me like an angry spider and all I could think of was drink.

'I suppose I should just get up and go,' Zelda said. 'But I want you to tell me something first. Was there ever a time when we meant more to you than screwing yourself up? Tell me.'

'You mean everything to me.'

'Everything? Don't insult my intelligence.'

I held up my hands. 'Ag, Zelda, you won't accept anything I say, so why ask me?'

'I want to know. Were we worth so little?'

'It's got nothing to do with worth.'

'It's got everything to do with worth! Everything! That's why I'm leaving. Helen and I are not worth enough to you.'

'Okay, you've obviously made up your mind about that. So what now? Is it back to being an ordinary white person, Zelda?'

'You know with Helen I can never be an ordinary white person.'

'Is it back to hearth and home? Into the Sutton fold? Kith and kin, with our little piccanin?'

'Don't make me hate you, Manas.'

I went over and put more wood on the fire. I stared at the flames, knowing everything was slipping from my grasp.

'Please don't leave me, Zelda. I need you. I need Helen.'

'I'm sorry, Manas. I have to be able to rely on someone. And it's obvious I can't rely on you. Can't you see that?'

'Come on. You can't leave me now.'

'It's too late!'

I rubbed the lines on my brow. I was sweating.

'Shit, you're so screwed up,' she went on, 'I think you just enjoy being miserable. No, don't shake your head. You enjoy letting life kick you around like a dog, don't you? You like being the victim. Are you listening to me, Manas?'

'Madam? Did you say something, madam?'

Zelda gave an exasperated cry. 'Please don't be stupid! I hate it when you do that!'

'Well, sometimes you come across like a white missus.'

'You've got a big chip on your shoulder, Manas.'

I stood at the window and stared out at the rain. Had I left things there and just let her go, maybe I could have entertained the hope that guilt would bring her back to me. But I could see John outside, leaning against the upturned boat. He'd rolled up his trouser leg and was rubbing the blue scars on his shin. Zelda had one weak spot and, God knows why, I went for it.

'It's him, isn't it? That bloody brother of yours. He's the cause of this.'

'Oh, don't start that again! John's done his best to keep out of your way. If anything, you're the one who's been making things difficult for him. All your clever, vicious remarks. I'm surprised he never clouted you.'

'You'd have liked that, wouldn't you?'

'No, but you've been asking for it.'

'Jesus, I can't win. You always take his side, don't you?'

'You just refuse to accept him. You refuse to even try.'

I laughed. 'Why the hell should I accept him?'

'Because he's my brother.'

143

'He's more than your brother.'

'That's right. He is more than my brother. He's my twin and I can't change that.'

'You can't change what he's done either. You expect me to accept that?'

It was as though with my demise I was compelled to scorch the earth.

'Don't start that, Manas! I swear, if you do ...' Zelda curbed what she was going to say and sat back, her eyes closed, her fingers pressed against her temples. And for the first time I saw John in her, in the way her nostrils flared with anger, and it filled me with hate. Not so much for the killer, but for the one she loves more.

'Don't deny it,' I said. 'You're doing this because you can't leave him.'

She made to get up. 'Fuck off, Manas. It's no use talking to you. I'm leaving.'

At that moment I knew I'd lost. And I hated her for my defeat. It was a stupid, irrational hatred, and it overwhelmed me. I pushed her back in her chair.

'Ja, there's no point in talking to me. I'm too bloody stupid to understand anything, hey? Too stupid to understand you're leaving me only because you can't let go of that sick bastard out there.'

'Get out of my way, please.'

But the words just kept coming, words I knew would push her to the edge.

'You can't let go of him, hey? So you find a convenient excuse to leave me. Stop drinking, Manas. Change your life, Manas. I am the truth and the light, Manas. Christ, I'm sick of it! The truth is you just can't let go of him, can you?'

Zelda shook her head. A muscle beneath her eye flickered. 'I don't believe I'm hearing this. Please don't make me hate you.'

I couldn't believe it either, but I kept on. 'I won't crawl after you begging forgiveness, Zelda. I won't give you the satisfaction.'

'Don't blame me or John or anyone else for what's gone wrong in your life, you ungrateful bastard! This is your fault! No one *else, okay? Now get out of my way!' Zelda got up and pushed me aside. 'I should've known better than to try to reason with you.'*

'Reason? Your idea of reason is to walk out the fucking door. Your idea of reason is to stay with that … that dirty killer who I'm supposed to accept as my own brother. Fuck him!'

Zelda's face went livid. She lashed out and struck my face.

'That's it, I'm finished with this whole bloody business!' She wiped away furious tears. 'You can rot, for all I care! You don't deserve any sympathy!'

'Sympathy? Fuck your sympathy! Save it for that murderer outside!'

Zelda struck me again in the face. I asked myself: Must I stand here and take it? Must I really stand here and allow this shrieking woman, this stranger, to strike me at will? I stood glaring at her, my body trembling.

Then we heard Helen crying and turned to see her standing there watching us, her eyes wide with horror. Even that didn't stop us.

'Fuck your sympathy!' I shouted again. 'Fuck your brother too!'

Zelda moved to strike me but I hit her first, flat-handed across the face. The blow stopped her short. She stood holding her cheek in shock, her glasses askew. I hit her again, harder, this time with my fist. The blow hit her on the edge of the eye, sending her glasses flying. Helen screamed. My senses were in shreds. I'd never hit anyone before in my life. Zelda began to weep loudly, violent, choking sobs that tore me apart. Still, I just stood there, refusing to give in, refusing to comfort her.

Then John burst in through the door. He paused momentarily, glancing around. With Zelda sobbing and holding her face, her glasses broken on the floor, it didn't take much to sum up the situation. He advanced on me, his dark eyes locked on mine.

'John … don't!' Zelda pleaded.

But that didn't stop him. He came on towards me, eyes flat and merciless, ready to break me into pieces. With one hand he lifted me by the throat to my toes. Paralysed by his strength and rage I watched him draw back his arm to strike.

145

It was Helen who saved me. With a thin wail of terror she ran over and clutched my leg. John hesitated. He looked down to see her clinging to my leg, wide-eyed and tearful, then let me go. Zelda ran over and picked her up. 'Oh, my baby!' she wept. 'Oh, I'm so sorry, my poor baby!'

John thrust his head forward aggressively. I thought he was going to give me the if-you-lay-a-finger-on-her-again routine, but he didn't. He just stood there staring at me, a naked contempt in his eyes. Right then, I wouldn't have given a damn if he'd killed me.

As they packed their things I sat in the bedroom with Helen, unable to believe what had happened. I avoided Zelda's eyes as tearfully, deliberately, she gathered her and Helen's clothes and crammed them into her suitcase. Never before had we screamed at each other like that, so furious and insane. Never before had we struck each other. It was crazy and we knew it had destroyed everything. As she packed I wondered how much Zelda could see without her glasses. Her one eye was badly swollen, almost closed. I sat there on the bed next to Helen, dazed by the unreality of it.

Helen was lying curled up in the blankets, fast asleep, drained by the terrible scene that, no doubt, had destroyed the flimsy foundations on which she'd built her trust. She looked so small and serene, her lips distorted against the pillow, breathing so lightly I could barely detect her chest rise and fall. My heart filled with pity for her. Sleep was her only protector. Like a tiny bird in the palm of darkness, she preferred the terrors of fantasy to those of reality. I longed to wrest her from the darkness, to take her in my arms, to show her I could protect her too. But as I watched her face I knew my limitations. When it came to protection, I could not compete with sleep. Ag, my kleintjie, I thought. You are just like your mother. You trust in sleep. Forgive me for what I am. Forgive me for my weaknesses, my child. You are all I have to connect me to the world, to humanity. With you, my misanthropy collapses into ashes, rebuilds itself, collapses again ...

And so they've gone. Across the lagoon, silver forests of rain scatter before the wind. The hills sag beneath the weight of clouds. Clouds ... clouds, let me fill my thoughts with clouds.

Let me force these things from my mind and think only of clouds. Let me close my eyes and think of clouds and God. Let me implore God to expel the darkness from my soul. I listen to the shudderings of this small home that has survived a hundred winters. I say to myself: Do not be afraid. Do not be overwhelmed. Consider the softness of water and time. Soft things that carve and erode.

*

Let me try again to take stock. How is it possible that two people once so close can be torn apart so violently? Are love and hate that entwined? The same thing in the end? And how were we once so close in the first place? For the answers I must go back to when Zelda's family rejected us, after John had delivered that surprise gift of a broken nose on our first meeting. As I recall, it was the end of winter and the spring buds of the poplar trees were bright green and the air had a crispness to it that was fresh and invigorating. The Eastern Cape was still in the grip of drought but for me there was the sense of newness and hope that good things would prevail.

Ja, a time of such desperate closeness; even now I feel my chest constrict as I think of it. A time when, in the aftermath of rejection, we flaunted our love with gay abandon as though to spurn the world. The fact that our love was wrong in the eyes of her family and illegal according to law became a strange aphrodisiac. Stubborn and obsessive, our defiance became attractive in itself, an insane rebellion against insanity. I discovered a hidden crazy streak in Zelda that carried with it an almost suicidal recklessness. She paraded our togetherness. During the day she'd insist on walking hand in hand around Grahamstown, occasionally kissing my cheek when others looked at us askance. Sometimes as we caroused around late at night she'd demand to make love in weird places. In her cramped Mini under the Drosdy Arch, or opposite the Law Courts. Among the baleful ghosts up at Fort Selwyn. Or, once, upstairs in the Masters' studios, on a chair pulled up in front of the window overlooking the police station. We were lucky never to attract anything more hostile than the odd expression of disgust, the way we carried on. But our stupid love-crazed defiance was not without consequence. To defy family and society was one thing, to defy nature quite another.

When Zelda's pregnancy tests proved positive, the enormity of having a child under our circumstances suddenly dawned on us. I have to hand it to Zelda for courage. Immediately, she came clean with her family. She drove down to Haslemere and made the announcement. It was a kind of either/or confrontation; either we could rely on their support, or not. All she got, aside from stunned, incredulous expressions of anger and shame – and the first tears she'd ever seen in her father's eyes – was the offer to pay for her to go overseas for an abortion. Neither of us could accept the idea of our love child being slaughtered as though it were the product of some sleazy fling in the hay. So Zelda came back, grimly determined that we would make it alone, come what may. The future looked pretty daunting. Where would we live? How would we live? Innocent, silly questions compounded by all the illegalities of South African law. The responsibilities that lay ahead weighed heavily upon us and we fretted over what our child might have to endure.

Zelda took the initiative. The wild behaviour stopped. She applied for and got an academic assistantship through the Fine Art Department, a minor teaching job that paid our rent with little to spare. Despite her father's wrath, her allowance had not been cut off so she stashed that away in a savings account, so we could afford the basics when the baby came.

And then I, too, had some timely good fortune. The English Department at Rhodes had been approached by the principal of a small, overcrowded school in Fingo Village called Phoenix. The principal, Mr Dlamini, urgently required a capable student to replace an English teacher who'd resigned suddenly. However, the township unrest proved a disincentive and no one volunteered. By chance, Professor Strachan got wind of this and (knowing our circumstances) suggested I apply. I went ahead and because black schools didn't require much by way of qualifications was accepted at once, after a perfunctory interview. Mr Dlamini was most courteous and accommodating; he bent over backwards to organise my timetable so I could continue with my university studies. In time I'd discover why Phoenix was not the Mecca of the teaching profession, but in the beginning I was filled with a sense of hope and purpose. Here was a chance to be independent, a chance to earn my living. To provide. So enthralled was I in this new role as wage earner, I wrote to Tak after my first salary cheque explaining my change of fortune and suggested he cut his support to only my university costs (a silly exuberance under the circumstances). Tak wrote back praising my initiative but insisting he would continue to provide a living allowance, as he'd promised my mother.

Given these new developments, the last thing we needed was any unnecessary trouble. After that visit from the cops a few months earlier I'd managed to convince myself I'd just been unlucky, that they'd just been nosing around because of Whitney. Still, the experience had shaken me and I thought it wise now to keep a low profile and not attract attention to myself. This is why I began to resent the worries the book posed for us. I came to see the book as a sword poised above my head, threatening to destroy everything. This anxiety was not without foundation. South Africa was not the place to be making subversive statements unless you meant it and were prepared to suffer the consequences.

The printed copies duly arrived in padded brown boxes from Patriotic Publishers in London. David was satisfied with the presentation: a simple white cover with the embossed title, *Black Bones*, above one of my pen-and-ink drawings, naturally depicting the screaming head of Woman. He was deaf to my misgivings; it became clear to me that David's only real interest in the book lay in his obsession with Whitney. The book was an act of devotion. He'd even dedicated it to her without my knowledge or consent.

Angry with myself for having become party to his obsession, I left the book in David's hands and hoped the whole sorry business would blow away eventually. He started off sensibly enough, placing copies with a few bookstores in Grahamstown and Port Elizabeth, but when only four sold in a month he abandoned this silly capitalistic enterprise, as he called it, and went around dispensing books like confetti. Ja, giving them away for nothing. Each ragged activist who pitched up at Stoneleigh was immediately foisted with a copy, regardless of whether he could read or not. I even saw David palm a copy off on one of the street beggars, who promptly used its pages to roll cigarettes with. In a single magnanimous splurge, he and Whitney gave away half the books free of charge at one of her campus meetings. (I tried not to notice the discarded copies in bins during the days that followed. Even Whitney's motley band of sycophants thought it stank!)

I had to hand it to David for persistence. Extracts of his poems and copies of my drawings managed to find their way into various student publications. He gave several readings on campus during meetings. He badgered the editor of *Grocott's Mail* to do a review. The editor, sensing he was treading on thin ice, roped in a local poet to do the dirty work, which he did with cruel forthrightness, to say the least. We were flayed alive, exposed for all to see, humiliated. Only one or two of the poems received some favourable comment, the rest were dismissed as 'childish revolutionary prattle'. My drawings were categorically dismissed as naive, vulgar or dishonest. I was accused of 'using cheap obscenity to obscure an ordinary talent'. David could not understand my dismay. 'What do you want, Manas?' he asked. 'To be accepted? It's the same *system of values* that made that prissy bastard write what he did that we're undermining! You don't want to support those values, do you?'

I did, to tell the truth.

The book brought with it only worry and fear. Any last vestige of faith I'd had in it disappeared. The intervening months had given me time to assess the poems and drawings more objectively and I realised, as Professor Strachan had warned me, that I'd been foolish to go through with it. Zelda remained supportive. Okay, the book's pretty much in-your-face, she said, but it needs to be to make its point. She attempted to allay my misgivings: 'Look at those German artists between the Wars, Manas. Grosz, Heartfield, Dix – they never pulled any punches, did they?' David was so pleased with this comparison he gave her a special autographed copy with a pressed veld flower stuck on the title page.

But despite Zelda's support, a sense of bitterness grew within me. It became clear that I'd placed myself at risk. And for what? For a bunch of stupid poems and drawings completely lacking in merit. My artful impressions of police and state were there for all to see and I feared the consequences. And I couldn't escape the fact that I'd compromised my integrity just to please David. Such was my bitterness, I began to exclude people from my paintings and revert to the safe confines of landscape. People, in whatever form, were just trouble, I thought.

Of course, my worst fears were confirmed when the book was banned. I'd hoped *Black Bones* would simply be buried and forgotten – it deserved to be forgotten. But no such luck. A copy happened to find its way into the gloomy chambers of the Publications Control Board and without much ado was pronounced undesirable. David and I received formal notification of the banning from the Board via the publishers in Britain. The fact that it was banned gave it more publicity than it was worth. The Eastern Cape newspapers, *The Herald*, *The Dispatch* and *Grocott's Mail*, all carried the story. GRAHAMSTOWN PROTEST BOOK BANNED, read one article. ANTI-APARTHEID POEMS PROVOKE BAN, read another. Not quite front-page stuff, but attracting, in my view, a great deal of unwanted attention.

But if I was nervous about this sudden splurge of publicity, David was overjoyed. How he revelled in the praise Whitney showered on him when *Black Bones* was banned. How they waltzed around campus arm in arm. She even let him join the secret meetings she held at night with the township activists. For David, the book had achieved its purpose. For my part, the unwanted attention soon showed itself in

151

different ways. With Professor Strachan, for instance, there was a distance between us, something I lamented deeply because I'd always valued his belief in me. I bore the humiliation of his silence ... that awful, embarrassed discomfort he now felt in my presence, and I in his. He didn't even mention the book. It seemed that in his eyes a compromise of integrity was an unacceptable perversion.

And the unwanted attention showed itself at the school too. I began teaching late in the year, just prior to exams. Because it was unsafe for whites to go into the townships Zelda used to drop me off at the bottom of Beaumont Street near Fingo Village on her way to the studio each morning, and I'd take a short walk to the school along the refuse-clogged stream where the women did their washing and past the beer hall that was surrounded by broken glass and empty beer cartons.

Phoenix was typical of so many township schools. A series of drab buildings with broken windows adjacent to a single playground without a solitary blade of grass growing on it. The buildings were covered in graffiti, a chaotic tangle of political slogans among which FREE MANDELA and VIVA ANC were most prominent. Litter and dust, and always a damn wind that picked up papers and dirt. There was a flag-pole outside the principal's office but for quite some time Mr Dlamini had ceased his patriotic ritual of raising the South African flag. It would always be cut down and burned by some unknown culprit.

So, for me, it was back to the tie-and-blazer brigade. No more Manas the bohemian (though I did keep the long hair). No, Mr Dlamini would not have people on his staff who looked like communists or drug addicts. Mr Dlamini, himself, alternated between two frayed navy blue suits. He also had a spectacular range of broad floral ties. A short, squat man with a big belly and a round, worried face, Mr Dlamini set the example. Always the first to arrive at school, always the last to leave. Sometimes he even slept at school so he could catch the graffiti painters, but they always outsmarted him.

In the beginning Mr Dlamini was always courteous

towards me, though he disapproved of my long hair (his own black dome remained meticulously shaved). Because of the stressful teaching conditions in the township, he had a high staff turnover, so I guess any teacher was valuable to him. He shook my hand each day, African style, and chatted idly about the dry weather, or clucked irritably about the latest bright new slogan on the walls. The communists teach them young, he would mutter. Mr Dlamini was a Zulu and proud of it. He espoused a strange mixture of educational psychology and tribal belief. And with his pride came a veiled measure of contempt for the Xhosas, among whom he lived and worked. I remember him once gesturing impatiently at a group of boys playing soccer on the playground. The trouble with these Xhosa kids, he said, is they have no discipline. They're not forced to undergo the old rituals, like circumcision, that turn them into men, and so instead they become tsotsis. Township trash, no good for anything.

And if, in the beginning, Mr Dlamini was always courteous towards me, the same could not be said of the children. Unfortunately, my teaching career began at a time when school unrest was worsening. I'd be greeted with sullen stares as I walked into the school grounds each day, books under my arm. The same stares would scan the teachers' faces as we gathered on the playground for assembly at eight o'clock. I soon came to realise the cause of this mute hostility. With all the trouble brewing in the township, the kids were a highly politicised force. They saw themselves as soldiers for the cause. They knew who the enemy was – the state. And what were schools and teachers other than instruments of the state? What else but agents of oppression?

In the classroom, the same stares, the same perfunctory behaviour, just going through the motions. Those blank, far-away looks. I'd stand at the blackboard in my new blazer and tie, trying to explain basic principles of grammar to inscrutable faces behind which lurked, no doubt, images of burning houses or bleeding people. I was an irrelevance in their lives, something to be despised. This contempt was never expressed openly; Mr Dlamini would not tolerate

153

insolence in his school, and was feared for his use of the cane. No, the contempt was always hidden behind a careless shrug of the shoulders as I laboured to win their confidence behind an occasional mysterious smile. At first I was filled with a sense of mission; I would help raise these poor wretched souls out of their squalor and misery … ja, through learning they would find freedom. But before long I was just going through the motions, like the kids. Before long I also resented the whole damn system, knowing from my own background that it was rooted in inequality. I asked myself, why should these kids be happy and contented when across the river they could see the fine schools for white children?

Despite my sympathy, the hostility persisted. It worked on my nerves and my self-esteem, and the days when I arrived at school with a hangover became more frequent.

But when the book was banned, and the news got around, the situation changed. Almost overnight the sullen looks changed to friendly, conspiratorial ones. Children would greet me with smiles as I walked down the corridors. In the classroom I was lured into passionate discussions about apartheid and the strife in the township. When dealing with such realities, the apathetic brains that would not put two written sentences of English together suddenly displayed remarkable agility and perception. Somehow the word got around among the kids that I was to be trusted, that I was on their side. And this impression must have been reinforced when the police arrived and took me away.

But that happened much later, after I'd been lulled into a state of complacency. Time went by and nothing terrible happened. The unwanted attention became a thing of the past. David and Whitney had dispensed with most of the copies and the whole business seemed over. Finished and klaar. I allowed myself to forget about it and to focus on the better things ahead.

*

Zelda decided against giving birth in the hospital because even in hospitals distinctions of colour are made. She said she would not go through the indignity of having her child born directly into the system, of her baby sucking the breast of apartheid. No, she would give birth at the house, in familiar surroundings. After several discreet enquiries we found a doctor and midwife who agreed to help with the delivery. And so I watched as Zelda changed like the seasons. I watched her belly swell, and felt the tiny movements inside. I saw her breasts grow large and her nipples become dark. I saw the brave resolve in her eyes as she prepared herself.

And now that she's gone, the memory seems so clear, so tangible. Even as she flies away, wings protruding from her cage, she remains, my denial the hallucinogen shaping the substance of her …

The moment comes. The perpetuation of ourselves through Helen. She lies on the bed amid antiseptic smells. It's early morning and the rising sun shines weakly through the windows. Outside, the sky is shot with magenta. Birds are singing in the trees. I listen to the voices of the doctor and the midwife. Their voices are firm and kind, reassuring. Zelda trembles with agony. The blood and bone we've made are splitting her within. The doctor comforts her with smiles and assurances. I comfort her. I rub her back. Tears stream down her cheeks as she fights to control her breathing. Outside, the world turns yellow. I watch her face, wondering what's going through her mind. It's not only the pain that makes her weep so. An aloneness has beset her. I'm there, but she's alone.

The blood-covered head of Helen appears. The sun flexes. Zelda heaves, the veins bulging at her temples, and Helen is pulled from her. The doctor exclaims happily, the midwife smiles with satisfaction. There's a lump in my throat as they allow me to sever the umbilical chord. Smiles against the yellowness of the day. I'm handed the red, bawling child. Terrified I might drop her, I hold Helen close with trembling hands. She shrieks through toothless gums. I place her at Zelda's breast. I kiss Zelda and she smiles. The doctor and

155

the nurse fuss around, a little embarrassed. I kiss Zelda again. Zelda has transcended the world of words. She is what men can never be. I can see it in her gentle smile as Helen sucks at her breast.

And my suspicion and fear of the world pales momentarily. I'm filled with new depth, a new humanity. I've witnessed a miracle, however common, and Helen is my messiah.

I go outside into the sharp winter air. I stand, dazed, joyful, aware of the painful contradictions in my life. Yes, everything is momentary, opposites leaning against each other, falling this way and that. I am condemned to opposites. A sudden vision of my father comes to me but I force him away. I walk down to the poplars along the river and stand in the winter sunlight, making promises never to be my father.

*

But the world of fact: While I was being blessed, others were being damned. The day Helen was born was momentous for less uplifting reasons. On that day President PW Botha declared a partial state of emergency to quell unrest in the country's trouble spots, which included Grahamstown. The big stick. The state of emergency gave the security forces almost unlimited powers. Powers to suppress, to ban, to silence. Powers to imprison, to kill. And so an era of unrestrained violence began, leaving many to contemplate what sort of future lay ahead. Anarchy? A wasteland?

On that day they also buried Matthew Goniwe. A month before, he and three companions had been found burnt and mutilated on the outskirts of Port Elizabeth where they'd attended a UDF meeting. The police denied any part in the murder of these men, known as the Cradock Four. Few believed the police.

And we were soon to be reminded of Helen's place in this world. Her birth certificate arrived from the Department of Home Affairs. Under 'Population Group' there was one word – Coloured. A single, dispassionate word that condemned her to a lifetime of inferiority.

156

But Helen kept the world of fact at bay, for the time being. We lived cocooned by her. For the first time in my life I knew what unconditional love meant. For the first time I realised how self-obsessed I'd been; even my mother's death had not tempered my inability to see things through the eyes of others. Now the sun rose and set for someone other than me.

There were other good things too. I had a large semi-abstract landscape selected for the Cape Town Triennial, the premier showcase for contemporary South African art. Zelda's submission, a group of five soldier figures, automatons with horned heads marching around in an aimless circle, was rejected; rumour had it the selectors found them too 'illustrative', which we took to mean too political. Certainly they were political. I'd watched as she pounded them into shape, at times whacking the clay with her fists. The violent technique, she said, was meant to be symbolic of the way the military processed ordinary men into stupid, obedient machines. Zelda was hurt by the rejection though she didn't say anything. She was happy for me and looked on my selection as a good omen. As the exhibition travelled around the main national centres, I was singled out for mention in reviews and TV documentaries. One of the venues, King George VI Art Gallery in Port Elizabeth, bought my painting for its permanent collection. I had gallery owners from Johannesburg and Cape Town offering to take me on when I finished university. For days I walked about with my head in the clouds. Ja, this did much to fill the chasm of self-doubt *Black Bones* had created within me. It didn't bother me that since the *Black Bones* fiasco I'd reverted entirely to conservative landscape painting, a capitulation for sure. And it did much to heal the rift between Professor Strachan and myself too. Shortly after the selection announcements were made, he came and shook my hand and gruffly said something about the prodigal returning.

The money I received from King George VI Art Gallery was more than five times my monthly wage as a teacher. Which wasn't saying much, when you consider the paltry wages of non-white teachers. I put most of the money in a savings account and with the remainder I had a ring made for Zelda, a simple silver band embedded with a polished piece of agate I'd found near the river where we often sat and talked. And I threw a party at the house that lasted two days. With the amount of booze that flowed, Whitney's glorious proletariat never knew what hit them.

Amid this, we heard that the Immorality laws had been repealed. It was legal for Zelda and me to love each other. We laughed at the absurdity of it. Ja, good things ...

And then Zelda's mother, Catherine, arrived one day at the house, unannounced. I came back from school to find her there, holding the baby and talking with Zelda. Helen's birth had caused much soul-searching in the Haslemere household and Catherine was the first to give in. Zelda's father and John still harboured grave resentments. How could Zelda have done this? What will the labour think when Zelda brings home her coloured lover and child? What will the other farmers think? We'll be the laughing stock of the whole community. Ja, Charles and John were unable to rise above their bigoted notions of station and status. Only Catherine succumbed to her love for Zelda, to her flesh and blood. She'd refused to accept Zelda's silence and had driven up from Haslemere alone.

Her intelligent blue eyes sized me up (lingering for a while on my hair) as I walked into the lounge. For my part, Catherine impressed me as a homely, well-groomed woman, who'd probably been slim in her youth but was now a little on the hefty side. Zelda introduced me formally and we shook hands. For a moment I thought perhaps I should kiss her – after all, were we not family now? But I desisted. You couldn't push your luck too far.

'It's nice to meet you, Manas,' Catherine said. 'We've heard so much about you. And please call me Catherine – none of this Mrs Sutton nonsense. I hope I'm not intruding by arriving like this.'

'Not at all, Catherine,' I replied.

Catherine glanced around at one of Zelda's horned soldiers against the wall. The corners of her mouth drooped a little.

'Goodness!' she exclaimed. 'That's so gruesome, Zelda!'

'Mother …' Zelda sighed.

'Really! There's so much ugliness in the world. I don't see why you must add to it.'

'I agree, absolutely,' I said ingratiatingly.

Zelda gave me a level stare. 'Oh yes? I can assure you Manas has also produced a few horrors in his time, Mother.'

'But I'm sure Manas would never expose little Helen to them, would you now, Manas?'

'Never, Catherine.'

Zelda laughed. 'Okay, if you two are going to gang up on me, I'll just leave you to discuss what sort of art I should be doing while I make some tea. By the way, Manas, my mother will be staying for a while, okay?'

'Fine by me,' I said, somewhat nonplussed.

So I sat in the lounge with Catherine, looking respectable in my blazer and tie, and told her all about my job at Phoenix and my course at the university. As I spoke I noticed her attention would shift now and then to Helen who lay sleeping on the couch next to her. I was glad she'd come, especially for Zelda's sake. Aside from Catherine's practical help with the baby, it would be a great load off Zelda's mind to have her parents' acceptance, for as we spoke Catherine made it clear that she'd come with her husband's blessing, albeit reluctant.

Then Helen woke and as Catherine fussed with her nappy I went through to the kitchen. Zelda was rummaging around for some biscuits. She found an old packet of shortbread and put some out on a plate.

'That'll have to do,' she said, picking up the tray.

I looked at this grand domestic achievement, consisting of stale OK Bazaars shortbread and tea in chipped mugs. Zelda caught the amused expression on my face. 'God, it's pathetic, I know. But my mother is just going to have to get used to it, I'm afraid.'

'Like a lot of other things.'

Zelda put the tray down and looked at me squarely.

'Manas, please don't get drunk while she's here, okay?'

159

It was the first time Zelda had ever confronted me about my drinking. I got very touchy.

'Well, we can't have the "boy" getting pissed now, can we?'

'Please don't be stupid. I'm just saying, Manas, don't get drunk. My mother won't like it. It'll ruin what chance we have to bridge the gap with my folks. I want them to like you, okay?'

'All right, I won't get drunk. On one condition.'

'What's that?'

'For God's sake, don't give your mother *Black Bones* to read.'

Zelda picked up the tray again. 'Okay, it's a deal, although I don't see why on earth you're so ashamed of your work. But remember, Manas, you're on your best behaviour. I don't need to tell you how important it is to create a good impression.'

I felt vaguely depressed. I could see the carefree days drying up. My bohemian Zelda was starting to toe the line.

Catherine stayed with us for a couple of weeks before returning to the farm – in time, she said, rolling her eyes, to prevent the males at Haslemere from going completely native. It was nice to see the way Zelda and Catherine got on together. Privately, Zelda told me it was the first time she'd ever been really close to her mother. There had always been too many differences between them before. And, indeed, they behaved much like good friends. On a few occasions I was left with Helen while they went off to watch a movie at Her Majesty's Theatre, and now and then they went off for a quiet drink at one of the hotels. Once they went on a shopping spree in Port Elizabeth and came back with Catherine's car overflowing with things we could never have afforded.

In the afternoons when I came back from school we sometimes went on walks around the farm, with Zelda carrying Helen on her back, African style, much to Catherine's amusement. Once we hired a cottage for a weekend at Kenton-on-Sea, but the time was spoiled when I was ordered to leave a whites-only beach by a council official. We came straight home after that.

The best times were spent down near the river where we picnicked under the poplars. It was peaceful down there, with the cattle and horses grazing nearby. The spring days were fresh and splendid. We were all getting along fine. I'd made a good impression on Catherine – always polite and respectful and I never touched a drop while she was there. I'm not naive enough to suggest that she would not have preferred things differently. Of course she'd have preferred to see Zelda with a nice down-to-earth white boy, preferably a wealthy farmer's son. But this was not to be and now she was making the best of a bad job, so to speak.

So she tried hard to get to know me. Down there under the trees next to the river she engaged me in long conversations. She talked about her university days in Grahamstown where, as a prominent judge's daughter (what else? – a good brain, a good behind, and a good bank balance), she met Zelda's father, and how little the town had changed since that time. And I told her all about my childhood, about Langebaan, about Nooitgedacht and my family. Catherine was fascinated. 'Goodness!' she'd say, peering at me over the rim of her glasses. 'I don't know how your poor mother coped, really I don't!' The thing I liked about Catherine was that, despite sometimes being condescending and patronising in her manner, she was always straight with me. Once, when Zelda had gone off sketching and we were alone, she opened her heart.

'I want to be perfectly honest with you, Manas,' she said. 'It probably seems utterly stupid and insulting to you, I'm sure, but this has been very hard for us as a family to accept, and I'm not sure whether my husband or my son, John, accept it yet – I don't think so.' Catherine shook her head, chuckling. 'You know, when I saw Zelda carrying the baby on her back, it reminded me of my children and how our Xhosa nanny used to carry them around. And I thought, my goodness, how times have changed! The point is that this turn of events has been hard to accept and sometimes it might show in what we say or do. As a judge's daughter, I'm not quite as conservative as my farmer husband and son. It's

161

not something I'll openly state in front of them but I do think
the whites in this country have been cruel and unfair. Instead
of allowing differences to blend, we, the whites, have stead-
fastly insisted on being separate – we've maintained the differences, made them part of our culture. Enforced them by
law. So the problem really lies with us. It's a result of our
upbringing, our European heritage which we don't want
destroyed. And if at times our hypocrisy shows, I ask you
please to ignore it. It's difficult to change suddenly. But my
husband and I have spoken long and hard about this. The
most important thing to us is Zelda's happiness and, of
course, little Helen's. I must say, all these silly, contrived differences really fall apart when it comes to Helen, don't they?
So all we ask of you, Manas, is that you love and care for our
daughter and see she comes to no harm. She has a head of her
own, that girl, and we have to accept that too, I suppose. But
it would break our hearts if she were to come to any harm.'

'I do love her, Catherine,' I said. 'And I'll look after her,
and Helen. I promise.'

Catherine smiled sadly. 'That's all we ask.'

Of course, Catherine was very good with Helen too. The
image of Catherine that comes most readily to mind is how
she clucked and fussed around the child like a broody hen.
Things went very well with her visit. She and Zelda were
closer than ever before and I stayed on the wagon, a paragon
of virtue. But it would be untrue to say it was all a bed of
roses. Catherine was clearly unimpressed with David and
Whitney. Nor was she charmed by the endless stream of ragtag activists who came stomping into the house at all hours.
Because of this constant coming and going the house was
always in a mess and Catherine detested slovenliness of any
description. David made a spectacle of himself on more than
one occasion by coming home drunk. Unfortunately, he was
inclined to be very foul-mouthed when drunk. Like the time
he started banging on Whitney's door at two in the morning,
yelling, 'What the fuck do I have to do, Whitney? Have I no
right to fuck? Am I a man who has no right to fuck? Well,
fuck you, Whitney!'

I cringed in my bed, hoping that Catherine had slept through it all. But, alas, I heard her voice in the passageway, berating David: 'For heaven's sake! Have you no consideration for anyone else in this house? People, *including a baby*, are trying to sleep! Stop this infernal racket at once, you stupid boy!' I heard David muttering as he stumbled off to his room.

And then there was one of Whitney's parties with some of her campus cronies, those bourgeois white liberals with one toe in the struggle. David got drunk and jealous; he thought everyone was screwing Whitney, except him. So he interrupted some heavy political debate with loud primal screams, as he called them – a sort of ululating Tarzan howl. And when Whitney told him to shut up, he started shouting at the astonished group, 'What right have you turds got to fuck? Hey? What right have you got to fuck?' Clearly, the issue of copulation entitlements was a matter of profound concern to David, but unfortunately he always seemed to express this concern with Catherine in earshot. He further raised her ire by vomiting outside her window one night.

And if Catherine found David hard to take, she found Whitney even worse. At least David, when he was sober, was remorseful and apologetic about his behaviour. That, in Catherine's eyes, was a tiny glimpse of decency and hope. But she drew the line with Whitney. Her ever-present glorious proletarians, with their sullen, hard faces and raised-fist greetings, seemed to test Catherine's new-found racial tolerance to the limit. And while Whitney was never as drunk or foul-mouthed as David, Catherine regarded her as far more threatening than David. David was merely a drunken nuisance – Whitney was dangerous.

'I don't know how you put up with it,' she said to us one day. 'That David needs psychiatric treatment! No, don't laugh, Zelda, he really does. And as far as Whitney's concerned, I don't trust her an inch. Not an inch. That girl's bad news, you mark my words. In fact, it surprises me you haven't all landed up in trouble already!'

'Oh, Mom …' Zelda scoffed.

'No, Zelda,' Catherine insisted. 'You mark my words. That Whitney spells trouble.'

More than once she urged us to move out but Zelda refused, accusing Catherine of overreacting. So in the end Catherine departed for Haslemere, leaving Zelda sad and miserable for days, and me with the memory of her fears.

*

Behind this, the terrible spiral: Grahamstown was a dreary mirror of a country going to pieces. The townships became a virtual war zone. The police were hard-pressed to cope with the upsurge of violence. Army reinforcements were called in. Now all white males between the ages of eighteen and fifty-five became liable for military call-up. Everyone from post office clerks to farmers. Only students escaped the net, for the time being.

For days, you could see smoke billowing from burning cars and buildings and helicopters buzzing across the sky. The army now maintained a permanent troop presence on the main road to King William's Town, which ran through the townships, to afford safe passage to travellers. Still, some people took to driving through with guns on their laps, determined not to fall prey to stones or petrol bombs. The violence became an awful tit-for-tat affair. The police used whatever means were necessary to restore order. Dogs and sjamboks. Tear gas, rubber bullets, live rounds. Arrests. Interrogations. At night, the comrades sought out police informers and meted out terrible vengeance. Each day, the grisly toll. Those with any foresight despaired for the future.

The anger became a tangible thing. You could feel it as you walked through the town. It was in the eyes of a farmer who roughly brushed aside a persistent beggar. It was in the faces of black youths as they sauntered across a road, ignoring the traffic – a sullen, careless contempt for everything the white man stood for. It was in the half-full belt of shotgun cartridges dangling from the opened doors of a police Casspir as it drove past.

From the snippets of the now regular telephone conversations and occasional visits, Zelda gathered from Catherine that John had been called up and was taking his duties in Midlands Commando very seriously. He'd even volunteered for extra courses and had been promoted to the rank of first lieutenant. Though secretly proud of John's soldierly aspirations, Charles, her father, complained that John was not spending enough time on the farm. I gathered Charles had no idea of the magnitude of the trouble. Even so, when he came into town he did so with a pump-action shotgun across his knees. Ja, he wouldn't put up with any kaffirs throwing stones at him, so he said.

'I don't know what the hell John's up to. He seems to be spending more time buggering around in the bloody army than on the farm. I mean, if he wants to play soldier then why doesn't he do it on the farm? We've got stock theft like you won't believe. Kaffirs just coming across the river and taking cattle as though every day's bloody Christmas!'

Charles said this to me the first time we met. After some prodding by Catherine, he'd consented to meet us at Stoneleigh one morning. The two of them arrived in the Landcruiser – of course, he had to make it a practical journey and get some dip mixture and fence wire while they were about it. Kill two birds with one stone, as he put it.

He stood there, one leg up on the front bumper of the Landcruiser, his eyes looking me up and down. Catherine and Zelda had gone inside but Charles seemed reluctant to enter our den of iniquity. Despite his age I could see so much of Zelda in him – the tallness, the sharp line of his jaw, the stern blue eyes – and I suddenly realised how hard it must have been for him to accept what Zelda had done. I guessed she must have been the apple of his eye.

'John needs to get his priorities straight,' he went on. 'Playing soldier doesn't pay the bills, you know.'

I couldn't have given a shit what John needed to do.

Catherine and Zelda came out onto the veranda. Catherine was carrying Helen. 'Come on, Charles,' she said. 'Come and see.'

Charles sighed and straightened up. Almost reluctantly, he crossed the yard to the veranda. I guess he knew he had no steel when it came to little girls.

'Isn't she beautiful?' Catherine said. 'She's just so gorgeous! Here, you hold her for a while.'

'Ah , Jesus, Cath,' Charles complained.

But he took Helen and looked down into her eyes. Helen gurgled happily because I think she saw Zelda in those stern blue eyes of his. And the most wonderful smile I've ever seen began to creep across Charles's face. Not a great beaming grin. Just a small change to his mouth and eyes that gave one a glimpse into his heart.

'Isn't she lovely, Charles?' Catherine clucked. 'Such an old-fashioned little tick!'

Charles raised his eyebrows, the smile still there. 'She's a happy little soul, by God.'

Catherine chuckled. 'Don't the two of them look a picture?'

'She likes her grandpa,' Zelda said.

Charles looked at Zelda. 'Christ, it'll take me awhile to get used to being called that.'

When they left he even shook my hand.

And so began the long thaw. Soon after, we received an invitation from Catherine to spend a long weekend at Haslemere. Zelda felt we should take advantage of such magnanimity while we could. She was particularly concerned about John who hadn't spoken to her in nearly a year. I could tell she yearned for his acceptance again. She was also anxious that John and I be reconciled as he'd refused to apologise for his attack on me.

But I was reluctant. Though Catherine had been very nice to us, I was still wary of her family, especially John. I couldn't bring myself to forgive him. My scarred nose was a reminder of that day he left me lying senseless and bleeding on the floor. I could think of nothing worse than being stuck on some damn farm for days on end while Zelda's illustrious family got used to my black face, and Helen's. Why on earth should I undergo this scrutiny? Who were they to sit in judgement over us?

'You go with Helen,' I said. 'I'll stay here.'

'Manas ...'

'Ag, Zelda, why put me through this?'

'Because it's important to me, Manas. It's important for you, too.'

So we went to Haslemere for the weekend. We drove down towards Bathurst and turned off to Martindale. After Martindale Zelda directed me along the Coombs road that took us over a ridge of hills, beyond which the Great Fish River valley dropped away in endless shades of blue. After a long dusty drive down the valley we came to the farm. As we crossed the cattle grid onto the farm I glanced at the Haslemere sign with the family crest on it and felt a sense of foreboding. It was like entering enemy territory. But I kept my opinions to myself as we drove along. The pastures were all dry and parched from the drought but the cattle were looking reasonably healthy. Charles had paid a fortune to bring in cattle feed, Zelda said. We drove up to the house on the crest of a hill, a fine old stone settler building set within extensive gardens that were also looking a little sad from lack of water. The house commanded a breathtaking view of the valley. I noticed an old stone tower with gun slits at one end of the house. It was in this tower that Zelda's intrepid ancestors had fought off the Xhosa raids. I also noticed the Mercedes parked in the garage and the peacocks roaming the brown lawns.

Zelda parked her Mini in front of the house and we got out. Two big Rhodesian ridgebacks came bounding over. When they saw me they started barking.

'Bonza! Jock! Shuddup!' Zelda hollered.

Catherine came out onto the veranda.

'Bonza! Jock! Go on, voetsek!' she shouted. 'Jacob!'

An old Xhosa gardener with white hair and beard materialised from behind a screen of tired-looking sweet peas. 'Missus?' he said.

'Jacob, tata lo inja,' Catherine ordered in her atrocious fanagalo.

Zelda laughed and repeated Catherine's instructions to

remove the dogs in perfect Xhosa. 'Judges' daughters weren't brought up like farm kids to know African languages like their own,' she said.

Jacob complied, grabbing the two dogs by their collars and dragging them off behind the house. He gave me a puzzled look, as if to say, isn't this what the dogs are trained to do? To chase off strange dark people?

Catherine came down the stairs and took Helen from Zelda.

'Goodness, she's looking well,' she said.

'Too well,' Zelda laughed. 'She wouldn't keep still the whole way here.'

Catherine sniffed. 'Phew! I think she needs a nappy change. Come inside. It's so hot and dusty outside. Just look at my poor garden. I'm afraid your father and John are out in the lands. But they'll be back soon. I'll get Gladys to make some tea.'

We went inside. Catherine called for Gladys and a maid appeared at the kitchen door.

'Make some tea, please,' Catherine instructed.

'Yes, missus,' Gladys, also an elderly Xhosa, said, giving me a sidelong glance.

'I've tried to prepare the servants for your arrival,' Catherine laughed. 'But as you can see, they're a little perplexed.'

'I can imagine I've upset the applecart somewhat,' I said.

Catherine seated me in the lounge. While she and Zelda changed Helen's nappy in the bathroom, I got up and perused the pictures on the walls. They were mostly old Eastern Cape landscapes, including a fine watercolour by Thomas Baines. There was a portrait bust of John by Zelda in the corner. I walked down the passage that was festooned with old school photographs of rugby, cricket and hockey teams. The Sutton males had all gone to St Andrews, of course, and the females to Diocesan School for Girls. I noticed Charles and John had played for the first team in both cricket and rugby. There were also photographs of Sutton men in army uniforms, going back to the Boer War. I went back to the lounge and looked again at Zelda's portrait bust of John. The likeness was indisputable, yet in a strange way I could hardly recognise him. Zelda had shown a side to John, a gentle, human dimension, that I've never seen. I didn't notice Catherine come up behind me.

'It's nice, isn't it?' she remarked. 'Just like him.'

I nodded. 'It's excellent. Zelda's amazing.'

'She did that a while ago, during her second year at Rhodes, I think. I really can't understand the work she's doing now. I can't fathom why she would want to see the dark side of life. It's so depressing, don't you think?'

I laughed. 'It depends how you look at it. I don't find it depressing at all. I think it's uplifting, actually.'

'Uplifting? Heavens! I don't see how pain and suffering can be uplifting! Why does Zelda do it, Manas? Why does she choose to show the dark side of life?'

'I don't know, Catherine. Maybe she feels guilty.'

'Guilty about what?'

'Guilty about not seeing the real world, Mom,' Zelda interjected. She was standing at the door, Helen at her hip. 'Guilty about having spent most of my life here on never-never land. Never any ugliness and never any unhappiness.'

'Seems a terribly *odd* thing to feel guilty about, Zelda,' Catherine said.

'Mother … oh, it's no use. You won't understand.'

'You know we've always done our best for you.'

'Mom …'

I could see this was not going to be an easy weekend.

Gladys entered with the tea and placed the tray down on the table. We sat for an hour or so and talked amicably about everyday things. And then Charles and John arrived back. We heard the Landcruiser pull up and the doors slamming. They came stomping through into the lounge, both covered in dust and grease. I stood up. Charles kissed Zelda and shook my hand.

'Hello,' he said, 'How was the drive?'

'Dusty,' Zelda said.

Charles laughed grimly. 'Bloody drought! Christ, everything's turning to dust.'

'Language, Charles …' Catherine chided.

Charles turned to John who had remained silently at the door. 'John, you know Manas. Come on, shake hands.'

John came over, his face expressionless. He knew me all right. I wondered what he was thinking as his eyes lingered on the scar across my nose. He put out his hand. I shook it and that was that.

Dinner that evening was a painful affair. Not that the food was hard to digest – no, the roast topside was done to perfection. It was John's silence that made it uncomfortable. He sat throughout the meal without saying a word. At least Catherine attempted to keep a lighthearted conversation going and Charles tried to be jovial by plying everyone with wine. But I could see John's stony silence was working on Zelda's nerves. I almost heaved a sigh of relief when the meal was finished and we all went outside to the veranda.

We sat on chairs and looked out at the darkness. The crickets were singing. The two Rhodesian ridgebacks sidled up and lay on the steps next to John. One kept growling at me and Charles reached over and smacked its nose. Zelda kept glancing over at John, an anger building in her eyes. Catherine was rocking Helen in her arms.

'What a lovely evening,' she said. 'All those pretty stars.'

'Those pretty stars mean no rain,' Charles said.

'Don't be so pessimistic, Charles. The rain will come. I'm sure it will.'

'You don't know the cycles, Cath. I don't think the worst has hit us yet.'

'Have faith, Charles. There're others who are worse off.'

'You're right, Cath. I shouldn't complain. We're lucky to have river frontage. Unlike other farmers I can still irrigate, though the Fish's just a trickle these days.'

I thought I should say something. 'Zelda pointed out the boundaries of the farm to me as we drove in. It's a huge place.'

Charles smiled proudly. 'Actually, it's three farms, really. My family bought the two adjoining places during the last century.'

'Must be hard work running the place,' I said.

That set Charles off on a long, rambling account of how tough it was on the land. Instead of the cattle just grazing in the pastures he was now getting hay railed in from the Western Cape. He brooded about how long he would be able to afford it and reckoned that sooner or later he'd have to start selling off his herd for slaughter, if there was anything left with the amount of stock theft going on. And that brought John into the picture.

'Of course, it doesn't help now John's away half the time,' he said. 'The last thing I need right now is him sitting on his backside in the army.'

'You did exactly the same thing, Charles,' Catherine noted. 'Remember how you ran off to the war and left your poor father to manage the farm? Your father never complained, did he?'

'That was World War bloody Two, Cath. Not some township fracas. Christ, we've got kaffirs swarming across the river from the Ciskei stealing what few cattle I've got left, and John's away buggering around in the bloody army! Doing what, for God's sake? If he wants to play soldier let him do it here on Haslemere!'

'Mind your language, Charles!' Catherine huffed. 'We have a visitor, in case you've forgotten. I wish you wouldn't blaspheme so much.'

'And I wish you wouldn't call them kaffirs, Dad,' Zelda said. 'You know it's demeaning.'

Charles scoffed. 'Demeaning? What other word is there for those bloody thieves?'

'You'd also steal if you were hungry,' Zelda replied. She turned to John, the source of her disquiet. 'So, brother, how's the army? Sounds like a full-time occupation.'

John continued to stare out at the darkness.

Zelda waved her hand. 'Hello, John. I asked how the army was going. Talk to me, please!'

John shrugged. 'What's it to you, anyway?'

'I'm just asking, for crying out loud.'

'It's all right. Fine.'

'All right? Is that all?'

'What else do you want me to say?'

'I'm just interested to know what you think you're achieving. What you think the army can do to stop the inevitable.'

John glanced sharply at Zelda. 'The army's doing what has to be done. Don't you worry, Zed, nothing's inevitable. The situation's under control. Your terrorist ANC friends are getting a damn good hiding.'

'They're not terrorists. They're just trying to liberate their people,' Zelda said.

'Freedom fighters, hey? Bullshit. Murderous bloody cowards, that's what they are. I wish you could see some of their victims. Like some poor bastard burnt alive for being the cousin of a policeman. Left to bloat and stink in the street. You'd soon change your tune.'

'And what about the victims of the police?'

'Please, you two. Let's not have an argument,' Catherine interjected. 'Let's talk about something pleasant.'

'Healthy debate never harmed anyone, Mom,' Zelda said.

Catherine sighed. 'I'm sure Manas doesn't want to sit here listening to a silly squabble.'

Unfortunately, that was what I was going to get. Charles had had a glass too much wine to see where this was going. He added his two cents worth: 'Actually, I think it's a bit ridiculous them calling you up so often, John. I know there's been a bit of strife here and there, but surely to God! I mean, it's just about every second bloody week you're off to camp.'

John smiled. 'A bit of strife, hey? There's a state of emergency, Dad!'

'Okay, but you're doing more than your fair share. Every bloke I know just does his bit, but you volunteer for more! That's what I object to. As if we can afford you being away.'

'Someone has to protect us from the swart gevaar,' Zelda chipped in.

'Shut up, Zed. Bloody expert, aren't you?'

'Well, isn't that what it's all about? The communist onslaught?'

'Just shut up, okay?'

'Please, Zelda …' Catherine pleaded.

Zelda's eyes blazed. 'Oh, Mom, it's the only thing he responds to! Shit! How else do I get a word out of him? Am I supposed to go the whole weekend with him not speaking to me?'

'Please don't swear, Zelda.'

'But Mom, he just ignores me! I can't stand it! And all you want is a nice, pleasant conversation. We don't want to spoil the evening, do we?'

'No, I don't. But you obviously do.'

'I'd rather have an argument than have him ignore me!'

Catherine got up. She was close to tears.

'I'll put Helen to sleep,' she said. 'I think I'll be turning in, too.' She apologised to me for the family's bickering and added, wistfully, that it never used to be like this. I shrugged and smiled weakly.

'Don't go, Cath,' Charles said. But Catherine had made up her mind. She bade us goodnight and went inside with Helen.

'Hope you're satisfied, Zed,' John muttered.

'You're both to blame,' Charles said. 'There's no need to upset your mother like that.'

But Charles, too, would not let sleeping dogs lie. It wasn't long before he was back on the same track again, complaining that practically every bloke he knew in Albany District had been called up and that the country was bound to go broke at this rate. 'Hell, I'm surprised I haven't been called up,' he said.

'You're too old, Dad,' John said. 'The age limit is fifty-five.'

'Too old for what? To loaf around and drink beer? That's all you bastards in Midlands Commando do, don't you?'

John smiled. 'You're just upset you're missing out on the action, Dad.'

'What? Pulling a few kaffirs into line? Call that action? Come on!'

'It's a bit more serious than you think.'

'As far as I'm concerned township unrest is the job of the police, not the army. What's wrong with the bloody police?

173

Why can't they sort it out?'

'The police can't cope, Dad.'

Charles waved his hand dismissively. 'Bulldust, man! Kaffirs understand one thing and one thing only. Force. The police should stop pussyfooting around and use some real muscle, for Christ sake. Put a lid on it, once and for all.'

'It's not quite as simple as just using force. It's knowing who to use force against.'

'Well, I wouldn't be so bloody particular.'

Zelda stared at them, incredulous. 'They can use as much force as they like, but they'll never win. Don't you see? It's the will of the people. Anyone with half a brain can see the futility of fighting to preserve this cock-up of a system. You're fighting against your own people, John. People who have a legitimate cause, who simply want a square deal.'

'They're not my people,' John replied. 'And they want more than a square deal. They want everything.'

'And they're going to get it too, whether you like it or not. You can't win. You're standing against the will of the people, against the *majority*! Now's the time to negotiate, to share. Before you lose everything.'

I shifted in my chair, my discomfort due more to the depressing predictability of the arguments, from both sides, than the fact that I was a forgotten presence.

Charles gave a loud sigh. 'They should send the lot of you bloody university types to Russia or China, or some stink-hole like Cuba. Some place where you can get the wax out your ears and the sleep out your eyes. Let me tell you some-thing, Zelda, all this political nonsense has got nothing to do with the people, or any so-called majority. It's just a few bloody ANC terrorists intimidating everyone else. Rabble-rousers, that's all. Negotiate? Negotiate what?'

'To share the country, Dad. Before it's too late. What you say about the ANC is rubbish. They're the voice of the people, and you better believe it.'

'Jesus, girl, open your eyes. We saw the same thing in Rhodesia, and look at that country now. A total balls-up. Is that what you want, hey? It always amazes me how you bloody liberals fail to see what's really at stake. It's all about land and power, nothing else.'

'Exactly,' John agreed. 'And that's what we stand to lose, unless we fight. Simple as that.'

Zelda laughed. 'Oh, John! All you're fighting for is to prevent a small white minority being ruled by a black majority. It's unjust and it's undemocratic. Don't you see?'

'Don't be so naive, Zed. Sometimes you talk like you were born yesterday, I swear!'

'Naive? Who's being naive?'

'It's no use talking to you,' John said. 'A bloody art student, and you think you know it all, hey?'

'John, how can you blame black people for hating apartheid? What would you do if you were a black man?'

'I'm not a black man.'

'Well, you should try thinking like one. Then maybe you'd understand their position.'

'I'd need a lobotomy first.'

John and Charles burst out laughing.

'Ha. Ha. I suppose you think that's funny, John.'

'Sorry to see you've lost your sense of humour.'

Charles shook his head. 'Zelda … Zelda. You simply can't accept that there are fundamental differences – *evolutionary* differences – between us and the blacks, can you? You can't accept that we can never be one people, one nation. It's just not natural. It's simply an accident of history that we exist together.'

'Oh, Dad, it's so depressing to hear you talk like that. I really thought you had more sense. We're talking about poor, ordinary people who just want to be treated like human beings. This is about basic human rights …'

'Human rights – hell! I'm sorry if I lack the academic substance to which you've grown accustomed, my girl, but I happen to have lived just a little longer than you and I've seen Africa change for the worse. I look at every damn tinpot African state and all I see is chaos, where once under colonial rule there were viable economies and civilised systems. I've seen farmers, like us, who've lost their land, with no place to go. And nowhere, nowhere, do I see the things you talk about. Freedom and democracy. If there really was freedom and democracy in Africa then maybe I'd agree with you. Then maybe the whites here wouldn't be so intransigent.'

Zelda rolled her eyes. 'It's a bit unfair blaming Africans for the stupid foreign systems they inherited from the colonial past, don't you think? No one's denying Africa's a mess. But does that give us the right to treat people like slaves? The fact is you can't stop the inevitable. You're both going to have to accept there are other people in this country who have a right to freedom and self-determination. And that includes your own flesh and blood now, in case you haven't realised.'

Zelda's latter point seemed lost on Charles. 'You weak liberals will never face the facts, will you?' he said, tiredly. 'You'll never accept the hard truth about Africa. That the problem with Africa is the Africans. You always hide behind your stupid damn arguments about human rights. Do you know what black rule really means to us? It means one day a kaffir will just walk into this house and kick us out. That's the hard truth. End of story.'

Zelda looked at John. 'Oh, well, you've got the likes of John who're willing to die for your truth. Isn't that right, John?'

John's eyes were smouldering, but he said nothing.

Charles held up his hands. 'If John wants to spend his time in the army, that's his business. I've told him what I think, but he's old enough to make up his own mind.'

'After a lifetime of indoctrination,' Zelda replied.

'Christ, who's talking about indoctrination? It seems the commies at Rhodes have done a pretty good job on you!'

'Really, Dad, you're so bloody paranoid!'

Charles yawned and rubbed his eyes. 'Try looking at the real world for a change. Too many books, girl. You've got your head stuck way up in the clouds. Remember that old farming adage about the baboon in the tree? That the higher it climbs, the more of its arse you see?'

Zelda smiled mirthlessly. 'Very funny, Dad.'

Charles got up slowly. 'No, it's not funny. Make no mistake, I find nothing amusing about paying university fees to feed your silly delusions.' He yawned again. 'You'll have to excuse me. I'm off to bed. I'm afraid I haven't got the energy to argue politics all night.' He looked at me. 'Sorry the conversation wasn't more genial, Manas. Some of us have strong opinions.'

He went inside. John, Zelda and I sat in silence.

I feigned a yawn. ' I think I'll go to bed too.'

I kissed Zelda and went inside to the room Catherine had allocated to Zelda and me. Helen was sleeping peacefully in a cot between our separate beds. I watched her innocent face for a while before climbing into bed. Our room was within earshot of the veranda. Zelda and John were still outside. I heard a chair scrape on the stone floor.

'Don't go, John,' I heard Zelda say. 'Sorry I started talking politics tonight. I didn't mean to get anyone upset.'

'You've got a right to speak your mind,' John replied.

'I just hate it when you ignore me. I hate the way you've changed.'

'You're the one who's changed, Zed.'

'Stay for a while. Let's talk a bit. Not politics. I really wish we could talk nicely. Like we used to. Remember?'

'I'm tired.'

'You're angry, aren't you?'

'You could've saved your clever damn arguments, Zed. You know it irritates the shit out of the folks, not to mention me.'

'I brought up the army because I worry about you.'

'It's got nothing to do with you, Zed. Mind your own business! Sort out your own bloody problems before you start on mine!'

'Don't hate me, John.'

'I don't hate you. I hate what you've done. I hate how you've stuffed up your life like this.'

'You can't accept it, can you? Manas and Helen. You can't even try, for my sake. You make it sound like a tragedy. A crime. Is that how you think?'

'It's worse than a crime, Zed! It's a fucking betrayal!'

'Mom accepts it, and Dad's starting to.'

'Well, don't expect me to. Christ, when I saw that bastard kissing you just now…'

'Please don't talk like that!'

'What must I say? That's what he is. A black bastard. You know what we are. You and me. You know where you've come from – this house, this family! Did you ever think of that? And what's the next step now, Zed? What do you do? Where do you stay? In some bloody township with your black lover and your snot-nosed piccanin.'

Zelda began to cry. I lay there, mesmerised by the torment in their voices.

'Christ, Zed. Why? How could you?'

'I fell in love, that's all.'

'No, that's not all. You know it's not all.'

'Please don't hate me, John. Think of how close we were.'

'I think of that all the time, damn you!'

'Then accept what I've done. Please! Believe in me like you used to. Remember when we were kids how you and I were always best friends? More than best friends. When you laughed I laughed. When you cried I cried. Remember? You used to tell me there was no one more special than me in the whole world. Please believe in me like you used to. I need you to, John.'

John was silent.

'Please believe in me, John.'

'Get rid of that bastard Manas first.'

'Please believe in what I've done. Don't make me have to choose. Please, John …'

'Get rid of him, Zed. Get rid of him and your piccanin. Then I'll believe in you.'

Zelda's voice became angry. 'Damn you! How dare you bargain with my baby! Your own flesh and blood! Please don't give me ultimatums, John. Don't make me hate you.'

There was a long silence. Then I heard John give a choking sob. Startled, I sat up and looked out the window. John was standing there holding his face in his hands. Zelda got up and put her arms around him. He pulled her violently to him and kissed her hard on the lips. Then he pushed her away and ran off into the darkness. I heard the Landcruiser start up and drive off. In the still night air it took a long time to fade from earshot. That was the last we saw of him that weekend.

The rest of the time went by without any further drama, but it was tense all the same. Despite Catherine's heroic attempts at being bright and cheerful and making a fuss over Helen, the mood was hardly one of relaxed togetherness. We all felt John's absence but did not talk about it. Zelda couldn't manage a cheerful face and sat silently as Charles drove us around the farm, showing me the cattle and the ticks, the small trial herd of Angora goats, the irrigation pump and the dips, the chicory and pineapple crops and all the other frightfully interesting things that made life on Haslemere go round. Charles, while being warm and affectionate towards Helen, was ill at ease with me around. I'll give him his due. He tried but could not transcend himself, the white farmer. For him to communicate informally with me was, I imagined, virtually impossible since so much of his social repartee consisted of derogatory references to blacks – the sort of racist pub banter that is the white farmer's unofficial language. On the other hand I was aghast at what Zelda and I had done to this family. I found the sense of guilt suffocating and almost cheered when Zelda, Helen and I finally climbed into the Mini and got the hell out of there.

*

I grew accustomed to her silent, pensive moods. To the helpless moments when tears would fill her eyes at a sudden thought. To my own depletion as I wrestled with pity and loss, knowing something of her would always lie beyond my reach. And to my sense of alienation when the physical evidence of this came to hand. I found a letter in her studio one day, while she was out teaching. Something she couldn't finish:

179

My dearest brother John,

I don't know how many times I've tried to write this. Maybe you are wrestling with it too? While I would never wish such pain on anyone, I sometimes feel (sense) that you are. I have this image of you when we were small kids, how you used to inno-cently assume that we would be married one day – how Mom and Dad would laugh at the charm of your innocence, too kind to prick the bubble of your love. Sometimes I'm bewildered by what has been lost. How do I start to say how much I still love you? How do I explain that I regret what my actions have done but that I also do not regret my relationship with Manas or hav-ing our child? Oh, John, how do I convince you of the rightness of it? That we are all the same beneath our skins? I thought little Helen might have brought that message home to you, but you refuse to see it. Why so hostile, brother? I always thought that you, more than anyone, would understand. I worry about you. I worry about what this country is doing to you. How do I get you back? I can't bear losing you – it's like half of me dying. What must happen before I get you back?

So it ended. A letter without ending. My heart ached for her. How could anyone put such a strange and complex love into words? How could I, or even Helen, make up for the loss of it? There are some things beyond reach. I left the letter where I'd found it, feeling almost guilty that I was prying into her secret life – knowing she would always have a secret life.

I had to admire her toughness, though. Zelda would never back down from what she believed was right, not even for John. As much as his rejection broke her heart, she would not give in to any cruel ultimatums. And so John became an absence, a troublesome void in her life. For a while it seemed he wanted nothing more to do with us. Occasionally we saw him among the soldiers in the troop carriers that drew up outside the police station across from the Masters' studios. Ja, the tall one with lieutenant pips receiving deployment instructions from policemen in riot gear. The citizen force

180

unit he belonged to, Midlands Commando, was seeing an increasing amount of township duty. The quelling of unrest was generally the work of the riot police, but since the state of emergency was imposed the Commando's duties were expanded to include street patrols, guarding black council officials' homes and manning a gauntlet of troop carriers down the King William's Town road through the townships so traffic could pass by unhindered. Not exactly loafing around drinking beer, as Charles had suggested. No, the nervousness on the faces of John's brothers-in-arms, that banal assortment of men – municipal clerks, schoolteachers, motor mechanics, you name it – indicated they were antici-pating far less festive pursuits in the line of duty. Ons vir jou, Suid Afrika. For once I thanked God for the colour of my skin.

But that was all we saw of him. Just a glimpse every so often. A stranger in an army uniform, keeping his distance. Until one day we got back to Stoneleigh late in the after-noon, after taking Helen to the hospital for her measles injection. David and Whitney were still in town and the place had been left unlocked, as usual. Zelda was trying to calm a niggly Helen as we entered the house, when she sud-denly froze.

'What's wrong?' I asked.

She just stood there frowning, with Helen wriggling in her arms.

'What's it, Zelda?' I asked again.

'He's been here.'

I felt a bit spooked. 'John? How do you know?'

'I just know.'

She handed Helen to me and walked down the passage. She peered inside the lounge and dining room. Then she went through to our room. I followed hesitantly. I saw her go over to the slightly rumpled bed and pick up her pillow. She sniffed it and nodded. 'It's him. I can smell him.'

I said nothing, knowing there wasn't much I could say about what made John need to sneak into our house and lay his head on Zelda's pillow. That was all he'd done, it seemed.

Nothing else. It was some days later that Zelda asked me if I'd seen her copy of *Black Bones*, the one David had given her. She remembered leaving it on the lamp table next to the bed.

*

I kept abreast of my studies, though my lecturers all complained that my commitment had waned. They were right. My results for third-year Life Drawing and Painting were mediocre, to say the least, and I was just getting by in History of Art. Only Professor Strachan understood how fundamentally my life had changed.

I kept my studio at St Aidan's but went there only a few times a week instead of every day, as I did before. I was feeling burned out but vowed to get on top of things again the following year. Tak and Langebaan seemed a million miles away. Aside from the odd letter, there was little communication with him. I'd written to tell him I wouldn't be going home for Christmas, but never said why.

When the holidays came Catherine asked us to spend a week over Christmas at Haslemere. Being together for Christmas amounted to a tradition with the Suttons. But I convinced myself they still weren't really interested in having me around, so I told Zelda I wasn't about to subject myself to another sojourn in the home of guilty resentments and hidden torment. I told her to go if she wanted to. She chose to stay with me.

It wasn't my intention to play Zelda off against her parents; I just felt they must accept me, unambiguously, or reject me. Nothing in between. And there was another, more selfish reason why I was reluctant to go. David and Whitney were going away over Christmas and that meant we could have Stoneleigh to ourselves. More than anything I just wanted to be alone with Zelda and Helen. The way things had been going, a little peace and quiet would do us a world of good.

David had confided in me that he and Whitney were going up to Zambia over the holidays. Through the township activists, Whitney had established contact with the ANC and had made plans to meet in Lusaka, for what purpose, he didn't say. David had volunteered to go with her, and to his utter surprise she consented, on one condition. He would have to quit drinking. She could not afford to have her plans cocked up by a drunk, she told him.

David agreed to mend his ways. But before he did, he went on a mammoth binge that left him in the detoxification ward in Fort England Hospital. He emerged a week later, pale and resolute. Yes, for Whitney's sake, he would quit. There followed the most peaceful days we had as a group. The problem with David when he got drunk was he always caused a scene, he always got wild and unruly. Now we were spared those disruptions. A changed man, David was now a pleasure to have around and Zelda often commented on what a nice guy he was without booze. Ja, altogether a more sane and affable person for it, there was however a casualty – his poetry. He stopped writing. When I questioned him about it he just shrugged his shoulders and said there were more important things in life than poetry. I was amazed (and a little disconcerted) that he could relinquish it so easily.

Whitney's late-night meetings continued. Every night, there were furtive scurryings in the house. I'd begun to find the township activists something of a nuisance (you could always find one with his nose in the fridge) but I kept my feelings to myself and never asked what went on behind those closed doors. I didn't want to know, quite frankly.

And David and Whitney also started sleeping together. A strange turn of events indeed. What had changed Whitney's previously dismissive view of David was a complete mystery. The fact that he was sober? That he would be her right-hand man in Zambia? Had she finally succumbed to his persistent approaches? I don't know. I just remember David's rapturous expression as he emerged from her room after the first night. Ja, a man reborn. Comrade Eternal Smile. And I couldn't help but notice, too, that Whitney was a different kettle of fish. She was troubled. In her eyes there was a glimpse of failure, of disaster.

Such was the state of affairs in the house as the year drew

to an end. The only threat to the fragile harmony was my own drinking. I'm quick to talk of David's ravages, while my own persist. My only saving grace was I wasn't as wild and disruptive as David. Usually I'd lapse into a fairly docile idiotic state, which others, including Zelda, usually found amusing.

But I knew it was getting worse. Often I wondered why I was losing control, why a couple of social drinks were never enough to soothe the growing restlessness inside me. Perhaps it was the sense of inadequacy I felt in the company of Whitney's university friends, those smug intellectuals who'd arrive in their rags and feathers and sit around on the floor like peasants and smoke and drink and talk endlessly. Ill at ease, I'd pretend to lounge casually against the wall with Zelda. Sometimes Zelda breastfed Helen while she listened to the talk. She was always perfectly relaxed in such company, and that stirred a resentment in me. I drank to cope with it. I drank to cope with the bearded men and tired-looking women with hairy armpits who sat around me, exhaling plumes of smoke and clever sentences. I drank because it loosened my tongue. It made me compete. And so my contributions to the conversations came in the form of sarcastic diatribes that everyone found funny, when they weren't too insulting.

Those feelings of inadequacy that had plagued me when I first arrived in Grahamstown returned like a slow, insidious disease. I was out of my social depth, living with Zelda. I knew I could never achieve the pseudo-bohemian panache of Whitney's university friends (which, deep inside, I desired). And my confidence was further eroded by the awful sense of futility that now accompanied my teaching. I was never a good teacher by any stretch of the imagination. It didn't take long for that initial idealistic fervour to wane. It didn't take long for me to grow tired of achieving nothing with the kids, except those long political discussions that now seemed so pointless, so negative. Being the banned artist, I was never victimised (unlike the poor Afrikaans teacher who had her car tyres regularly slashed) but I nevertheless grew weary of the undisciplined kids at Phoenix. I'm no missionary. I couldn't give without receiving in return, and I was getting nothing back at Phoenix except my paltry salary. The political tensions in the township had created an impossibly negative situation. A nationwide campaign of disruption sanctioned by the ANC saw schools being targeted as instruments of apartheid. Consequently, no amount of appeasement or punishment could change the attitudes of these children.

My absenteeism became an issue. Mr Dlamini tolerated it for a while before he started asking questions: 'A staff member who I shall not name,' Mr Dlamini would say in his roundabout way, 'told me he could smell liquor on your breath. Is this true, Mr Smith? Do you drink?' And I would answer, my eyes evading his, 'One or two, sir, now and again.' Mr Dlamini knew my problem, however. He, too, could smell it on my breath. But he had bigger things on his mind than an alcoholic staff member, though I was threatened with the sack on a few occasions.

As the tensions in the township increased, so did the general discontent at Phoenix. Mr Dlamini began to lose his grip and at times his behaviour might have been laughable, were it not so pathetic. For instance, he ran out of the government-issue green paint he used to cover up the graffiti on the walls. Desperately he began to use any paint he could lay his hands on – white, black, vermilion, indigo, turquoise, even gold and silver. The school began to shimmer. Mr Dlamini was losing his mind. Every morning at assembly he would rant and rave at the sullen children. Once, he broke down and wept. The children cheered and raised their fists.

There were a few arson attempts at the school. Despite police investigations no one was brought to book. But there was no doubt in Mr Dlamini's mind who was responsible – ja, the kids themselves, the wayward Xhosa youth, the tsotsis. He began sleeping on a mattress on the floor of his office at night, determined to catch the culprits in the act.

But getting back my state of affairs. A person's disintegration can sometimes be inevitable regardless of how much his life has been enhanced. So it was with me. Despite the good things in my life I was haunted by a sense of foreboding. Nothing seemed solid or certain. I had nothing to offer Zelda and Helen. What could I be if I was not to be a teacher? What other title could I possibly attach to myself? Artist perhaps? But what did being an artist really amount to? What did being an artist mean in a country where people's hearts had dried up like carcasses in the veld, where our true culture was the shrivelled flower of cruelty and hate? What was I amidst this?

Perhaps it was all of this that made me drink. Perhaps there were other reasons. David once offered the poetic theory that artists drink because they bleed when they create. A nice romantic idea, but, of course, it's all crap. The trouble is, people like me always search for reasons while ignoring the fact. And that's why I wanted to be alone with Zelda and Helen that Christmas. To get my bearings again.

*

We took David and Whitney to the airport in Port Elizabeth and saw them off on a plane to Johannesburg, where they would catch a connecting flight to Lusaka. We drove David's car because Zelda's Mini would have been too small for all of us. While in Port Elizabeth we went looking for another car. We'd finally had enough of cramming ourselves and Helen into the Mini, along with all the other junk artists cart around with them. I'd saved some money from my teaching and the university had recently bought one of Zelda's sculptures for its collection, so we could afford something inexpensive. We went around to a few used-car dealers. Those jaunty white salesmen kept giving us funny sidelong glances but kept their comments to themselves (one can always turn a blind eye to immorality if there's money in it). Eventually we decided on an old Ford Cortina station wagon, a little rusty under the doors, but the engine looked sound.

I followed Zelda back to Grahamstown. The station wagon rattled a bit at the back and the wheel alignment was out but our judgement has since proved to be correct; the car was solid and reliable and has stood us in good stead.

The lull before the storm. That's how that time was together, just the three of us. For once, nothing interfered. My drinking tapered off because Whitney and her flock were not there to test my sense of worth and, of course, Phoenix was closed for the holidays. I'd passed my exams, not as well as the year before, but it was something to buoy my spirits at least. Zelda was supposed to have completed her Masters Degree, but because of our circumstances had chosen to carry it through the following year.

It was a good time together, a gentle interlude, and I was glad we'd not gone to Haslemere. We allowed each day to pass without thinking of the next. Zelda did some work on her thesis which she'd tentatively titled *Images of Denial: Art against Apartheid, 1950-1985* – basically a survey of South African protest art aimed at exposing forms of political censorship.

I pushed art to the back of my mind. I spent my time decorating the house for Christmas and playing with Helen. When Zelda wasn't working we went on walks and swam in the river. We talked about everything. I confided my fears in Zelda. I told her Whitney's activities scared me, that sooner or later there'd be trouble and we should think of moving. But Zelda was adamant. She said as we both had just one more year at university, there was no point in moving now. Besides, where could we go? Finding another sheltered haven like Stoneleigh would be difficult. No, it would be best to stay in the house for the time being. Reluctantly, I agreed. So we talked about the future. What should we do with our lives once our studies were finished? What would South Africa have in store for us? For the first time I suggested we emigrate. I'd come to believe it was the only real solution to our problems. But Zelda was sceptical.

'Where would we go?' she asked.

I shrugged. 'I don't know. Any place.'

'You can't just go anywhere, Manas. Who'd have us?'

'Canada. Australia. What about Australia?'

I could see the idea did not sit well with her.

'Think of it, Zelda. We'd have a future – Helen would have

187

a future. I'm sick of this damn country. I just want to be somewhere where I don't have to worry about where I'm allowed to live and what bloody colour my child's been classified.'

Zelda shook her head. 'Leaving? Shit, the thought's never entered my head. No, Manas, I'm not ready to give up on this place yet. Things are coming right. I know it's slow, but it's happening. Petty apartheid's falling away. It's not illegal for us to be together, remember? And the government's making noises about releasing Mandela. There's still hope.'

'Ag, token gestures, that's all! Shifting the chairs while the bloody ship sinks. Botha says Mandela can only go free if he renounces violence. Mandela says he'll never accept terms dictated by the government. So, what's really changed, Zelda? South Africa's still a police state. They're still throwing half the nation into jail!'

A furrow of irritation formed on Zelda's brow. 'Please, I really can't think about this. It's too soon. There're so many things you haven't considered. It's all right for you. You don't have any family.'

'I just want to live in a normal world. Leaving's our only chance. This place is bloody insane.'

'It's only the government that's insane,' Zelda replied. 'And the government won't last. Apartheid won't last. But I don't want to talk about leaving my family. Not now, at Christmas.'

Having planted the seed, I hoped it would germinate.

Christmas Day was sunny with a cool ocean breeze, making the tree tops sway gently. Helen woke us early with her usual shrill protestations. I changed her nappy and Zelda fed her. Then we went through to the lounge and opened our few presents under the Christmas tree. Helen gazed blankly at the tree with its twinkling lights. She received the toys we foisted on her with a slightly bemused air, electing eventually to apply several coats of spit and snot to some brightly coloured wooden blocks (a present from Catherine and Charles). Zelda was pleased with the book on Rodin from me, and I was thrilled with the one on Fred Williams, the

Australian landscape painter (an omen?) from her. We kissed long and tenderly. Then we had a light breakfast and by the time we'd cleaned up, Helen had fallen asleep, so we left her in the lounge next to the Christmas tree and went back to the bedroom.

The presence remains. Her aura persists ...

As Zelda undresses, I stand naked at the window, gazing out at the sun-kissed countryside. I'm simply happy and contented. Nothing more, nothing less. Zelda's soft white hands curl beneath my arms. Her fingers tremble as they knead my flesh. Her face rests in the crook of my neck and shoulder. She kisses my neck.

'What are you thinking?' she asks.

'I'm not thinking. I'm just happy.'

'Tell me what happiness is.'

'I'd have to think to do that.'

She chuckles gently and presses herself against me. I feel her soft breasts against my back and her pubic hair against my buttocks, the very touch of her skin arousing me

'Think then,' she says. 'Tell me what happiness is.'

'I can't think and be happy at the same time. So don't ask.'

Her hands slide down to my erect penis which she strokes gently with her finger tips. My penis throbs. I turn and embrace her, amused at the vacant, sleepy expression in her eyes now that her glasses have been removed.

'You won't think for me, Manas?'

'No.'

She laughs. 'Then show me what happiness is.'

I smile, searching the depths in her eyes. I kiss her gently. I rub my hands down her flanks. She shivers and pushes her mouth hard against mine, and we collapse on the bed, hunting for the exquisite pain. Her legs around me we writhe and heave, shiny with sweat, searching, searching, lingering ...

Yes, she persists. I cannot let her go.

In the afternoon we took our time over dinner – turkey and Christmas pudding done to the best of our ability, which isn't saying much. How we laughed at my ungainly carving, and how we battled through the rubbery pudding! But we got quite mellow on champagne, mellow enough for Zelda to want to phone her folks. She put the call through and spoke first to Catherine, then her father. She came back to the table, her eyes brimming with tears.

'I miss them,' she said.

I put my hand on her arm.

'Mom and Dad send their regards. Mom says it's been pretty quiet there, for a change. She sounded so ... so downcast. John didn't go home either.'

'Look, Zelda, I'm sorry ...'

'Please don't say that, Manas, because I'm not. At least, I am sorry for them but not for us. I'm happy here with you and Helen. It's best we stayed. But I do miss them, even so. Can you understand that?'

'Yes,' I said.

And I felt mellow enough to phone Tak. He sounded glad to hear from me and kept me talking for a long while about mundane matters. I felt a great sadness for him. There was an empty joviality in his voice and I thought of him there in the Groothuis, alone with himself, alone with painful memories.

After we'd eaten, we went down to our favourite spot under the poplars next to the river. We sat and talked and watched Helen playing on the blanket. I wished the day would never end. But the sun went down behind the hills and the land was thrown into muted purple.

'God, this country's so beautiful,' Zelda said. 'No wonder they're fighting so cruelly for it.'

The lull before the storm ...

*

We fetched David and Whitney from the airport in Port Elizabeth after their stay in Zambia. On the way back to Grahamstown we asked them how things had gone. Whitney chatted endlessly about what an interesting place Lusaka was (poor but free) and how nicely they'd been treated by everyone. Lots of trivial gossip, but nothing specific. When David started being more specific she quickly silenced him, saying she didn't want to seem unsociable but there were some things they couldn't discuss. Business was business.

They were back in our lives and things returned more or less to what they were: the continual presence of Whitney's glorious proletariat and her campus cronies, the bullshit revolutionary hype, and David's futile struggle to win her love. For a while he continued to stay sober but when he came to realise that Whitney's feelings for him had cooled since their return, he quickly slipped back into his old habits.

One night in my studio at St Aidan's he and I resumed our previous drinking partnership. Since nothing serious had come of it, my anger over the *Black Bones* debacle had long since receded. We polished off a few litres of Tassenberg and David started getting morose and bitter about his relationship with Whitney. In the haze of my memory I recall him, glass of Tassies in one hand, cigarette in the other, swaying as he spoke. A lost soul.

'I don't understand it,' he said. 'Remember how she was before we went to Lusaka? Christ, every night I got laid like it was the end of the bloody world. I was in fucking paradise, man!' David shook his head. 'And in Lusaka the same story. Everything was hunky-dory. We shared the same hotel room … shared the same fucking bed. I tell you, Manas, I was on cloud nine, man! We did everything together. She wouldn't let me out of her sight. But now we're back … boom! She turns off the fucking taps.'

'Maybe you should back off,' I said. 'Whitney doesn't like being crowded.'

'Bullshit. You wouldn't say that if you'd seen her in Lusaka. She was all over me, man. Wouldn't let me out of her sight. What's her case, Manas?'

'She's a nutcase, you idiot. When are you going to learn?'

'Seriously, why's she fucking me around?'

'I don't know. Maybe she was scared.'

'Scared?'

'Ja, scared of playing with the big boys.'

'You mean she slept with me because she was scared? What kind of fucking motivation is that, hey?'

191

'I said maybe. I don't know. Who can figure out bloody Whitney?'

David sighed emptily.

'You're wasting your time with her, David. You should know that by now. Face it, she's a dead loss.'

David's eyes grew moist. 'Ah, fuck it, man, I love her. I'll do anything for her.'

'That's the wine talking, David.'

'In vino veritas. In wine there's truth.'

'In wine there's also bullshit. Lots of it.'

'I don't care what you say, Manas. I fucking love her, okay?'

'You shouldn't. She's not worth it.'

'I can't help it, man. It's not something I can control.'

We drank in silence for a while. David nodded his head as he mulled something over.

'You're right, you know,' he said eventually.

'Right about what?'

'About Whitney. She was scared. Not that anyone else could tell. The meetings we had with the ANC were kind of low-key. Just a few comrades dropping in at the hotel every day, so they could sus us out. I tell you, those guys must've thought Whitney was Miss fucking anti-apartheid-Joan-of-Arc in person, the way she carried on. Forward the struggle, amandla, and all that crap. But I could see she was scared shitless.'

'Who wouldn't be? She's playing with fire.'

'I've just never seen her like that. Scared. Didn't think that was why she was fucking me, though.'

'You're playing with fire too, you fool.'

'I don't care. She's worth it.'

'Worth it? Christ, David, Whitney's going to get you in deep shit one day. I wish you'd stop this ridiculous infatuation. It's pathetic!'

But David wasn't listening. 'Ah, what the hell. I can't help it, man.'

'You need a bloody shrink, David.'

David laughed. 'I know. But, please, don't shit on me, okay? Just be my friend. Let's get pissed and talk about something else, okay?'

'Whatever you want, David,' I said.

Life was never dull now that David was back to his old ways. He fought Whitney's rejection by inviting self-destruction. He dropped out of university, after failing his supplementary exams, which meant he'd failed his final year a second time. It was just as well. I don't think he would have been tolerated much longer. To many in the English Department, he'd become insufferable. He was argumentative and obnoxious. He'd appeared before disciplinary committees, once for calling a lecturer 'a pen-pushing parasite who didn't know real poetry from her arsehole'. Then he was caught driving under the influence and was fined and had his license suspended for six months. It didn't help that he called the cop who stopped him a 'Nazi bonehead'.

Then there were newcomers to the house. Three men we hadn't seen before. Unlike the township activists, they were quiet and unobtrusive, usually arriving after dark and being immediately whisked behind closed doors by Whitney. The three men were introduced to Zelda and me as comrades Peter, Elias and Johnson. It wasn't hard to guess they were ANC operatives, Umkhonto we Sizwe – terrorists in the eyes of the police. At first we fretted about what their presence might bring. I dreaded the thought of a police raid. My mind was filled with the news of recent security-force attacks on ANC bases in neighbouring countries, raids that left a lot of people dead. But we soon got used to them coming and going. In fact, they weren't there very often; frequently Whitney went off with them for days at a time, which made them worth the worry in my eyes. In the end we even got to like them. They were always polite and friendly, of different ilk to the embittered activists whose loitering presence I found irritating. Peter, in particular, had a soft spot for Helen. He used to pick her up and rub his chin on her belly and make her laugh, and sometimes dress her up like an African maiden with beads. Zelda thought them intelligent, courageous men, and if I look beyond my innate suspicion towards men of violence, I guess they were.

But although the comrades tried to be unobtrusive, they

193

hadn't reckoned on David. David managed to be sober for most of their meetings but occasionally he'd pitch up drunk and Whitney wouldn't allow him to take part. This would send him into a fury and he'd bang on the door and start his no-right-to-fuck routine. The comrades' restraint was commendable but one night David became so abusive that one of them, Johnson, came out and gave him a black eye. More than once Whitney expressed her regret in having involved David, but it was too late. He wouldn't take a back seat now.

Zelda and I did not pry. The meetings, the intrigue, David and Whitney's absurd one-sided relationship. We took the naive view that none of it was our business. So we turned a blind eye to it and as the weeks went by we were too busy to take much notice anyway. Zelda with her thesis, me with my final-year studies, both of us with our teaching. And, of course, taking care of Helen. It was enough just keeping our own boat on an even keel.

We felt curiously detached from what was going on in the world of fact. In March the government lifted the partial state of emergency. The violence continued. So, in June, a full nationwide state of emergency was declared. The final resort of a desperate regime. Within weeks thousands were arrested and imprisoned. The strife intensified. Violence and death became normality for so many. We lived apart from this, coping with banal day-to-day things.

The long thaw with Charles continued. Our visits to Haslemere became quite frequent and were without incident. John still refused to have anything to do with us. If we were coming to Haslemere he'd make sure he had other plans, either some army commitment or pursuing a tentative new romance with a farmer's daughter from nearby Fort Brown, who (according to Catherine), looked a lot like Zelda. There were no further clandestine visits to Stoneleigh.

After my mediocre performance the previous year I tried to get stuck into my final-year studies which were more focused on my painting major. Aside from Theory of Art I had no written subjects to worry about. I opted to do a course in etching to broaden my skills but withdrew when it became too time-consuming. Campus life hadn't changed, but every-thing was different for me. The university was no longer the centre of my universe. Zelda and I seldom took part in any campus activities. I felt more a visitor now, attending what I had to, then leaving. But I spent as much time as I could at St Aidan's. Despite my waning productivity, the studio was a reassuring place to be, filled as it was with work accumu-lated over my time at Rhodes.

Zelda finished her thesis and submitted it to her super-visor for assessment. To her surprise (she'd never given her-self much credit for academic aptitude) her supervisor was satisfied with it and suggested only a few minor changes. Zelda complied and had the final manuscript typed, copied and bound, relieved that the more onerous component of the Masters Degree was behind her. She'd managed to book the Monument Gallery (a venue much in demand) for her final assessment exhibition at the end of the year. Buoyed by this prospect, she spent as much time as she could in her studio, putting the finishing touches to her sculptures.

*

The winter lingered and went, and in its place came the world of fact. It started with my studio. I arrived at St Aidan's one Sunday afternoon to find the downstairs entrance door ajar. I thought this was strange; the place was usually deserted on Sundays and all the students who had studios knew to keep the entrance locked because theft was so rife in the town. As I climbed the stairs I could see my studio door was broken off its hinges. Someone had defecated on the entrance floor. And when I looked inside I felt sick with fear.

To make an unoriginal comparison, my studio resembled the aftermath of a cyclone. Except a cyclone could never have been so systematic. Everything was trashed. The few bits of furniture and equipment – tables, chairs, easel – were smashed to pieces. Drawers tipped out onto the floor, brushes, tubes of paint, charcoal sticks and crayons broken and strewn everywhere. My few cherished books lying in pools of paint and ink. Worst of all, my canvases and sketchbooks torn to shreds and trampled in amongst the debris on the floor. I stood in the doorway in a state of shock, looking at the complete devastation of nearly four years' work. It was common in Grahamstown for burglaries to be malicious, where thieves not only stole but vandalised too. But nothing had been stolen and anyone could see this was no ordinary burglary. Even without the slogans (*Oppas ANC/UDF varke! Die boere is hier om te bly!*) daubed on the walls. The culprits had even been so brazen as to leave brightly coloured patterns of their fingerprints on the walls.

Not knowing who else to turn to I went to Professor Strachan's house in Henry Street nearby and told him what happened, after rousing him from his afternoon nap. He came to the studio at once and flew into a fury when he saw the destruction. As he ranted and raved, I sank down on my haunches in a corner, close to tears. The world suddenly seemed like a cage. Vaguely I heard Professor Strachan's futile invective. Then he simmered down and sat on the floor next to me. He craned his head to catch my downcast eyes. He put his hand on my shoulder. 'Don't worry, Manas,' he said. 'I'll fix it so this won't affect your year mark, not that it's much consolation. But don't let it get to you, boy. You must not let it defeat you!' I just stared at the floor emptily.

Professor Strachan called the police. They duly came and sauntered around the studio, poker-faced. They took a statement and left. I knew nothing would be done.

I never went back to St Aidan's.

Next, the police came for me at school. It was during the tea break and I was in the staffroom, nursing a foul hangover and trying to avoid any conversation with my colleagues, lest they smell the alcohol on my breath. It was all I could do to keep my hand from shaking as I drank my tea. Through the window I saw the yellow Ford turn in at the gate and drive up past the playing children. It stopped outside the principal's office and I saw the two plainclothes cops, Jan and Boetie, climb out. Surreptitiously I placed my teacup down and left the staffroom. On the way to my classroom I saw Mr Dlamini talking to them outside his office. I went into my classroom and closed the door, my heart racing with fear. I sat with my head in my hands, praying it had nothing to do with me.

But a few minutes later there was a knock on the door. I got up and opened it, and, alas, there they were. Jan, Boetie and Mr Dlamini. At least there was no dog this time.

Mr Dlamini was looking apologetic and officious at the same time.

'Mr Smith,' he said, nervously, 'these two gentlemen would like a word with you.'

'What about?' I asked.

'You'll find out,' Jan said. 'Come with us.'

In full view of the children on the playground I was escorted to the yellow Ford. And as they pushed me into the car, the kids gathered around and began to jeer and chant. Boetie, who was sitting on the back seat next to me, stuck his head out of the window and shouted, 'Fuck off, kaffir shit!'

This caused an even greater commotion. As we drove off I looked out and saw a black sea of small raised fists. And, incredibly, I raised my own. Ja, my sense of self-preservation completely deserted me! Fidel Castro himself. Raucous cheers for the departing martyr. Defiant young faces running alongside the car. Boetie grabbed my fist and yanked down my arm. Scrawny creature that he was, I was surprised by his strength. 'You'll pay for that, vuilgoed,' he said matter-of-factly.

Jan drove out onto the main road but instead of heading into town, as I expected, he drove north towards King William's Town. We travelled along in silence for about fifteen minutes, then Jan pulled off onto a dirt road and after we'd gone a few kilometres into the bush, he stopped. It was hot and silent in the car. Jan and Boetie wound their windows down, and the sound of birds in the bushes outside broke the silence.

Jan turned in his seat and eyed me for a long time. The liquor component in his breath must have been as strong as mine. I kept my gaze lowered.

'So, Mr Smith, we meet again,' Jan said. 'Last time you were just a poor coloured boy looking for work, not so?'

'Looking for work up a tree!' Brains Trust Boetie joked.

They both laughed. I said nothing. Boetie was looking at me with a smirk spread across his face. Then he held up his finger as though he'd just remembered something. He groped around on the floor and picked up a short dog whip made of plaited hide, the kind farmers use. He twirled the end through his fingers.

'That was a nice little display back there at the school,' Jan went on. 'Black power salute, hey? Very good. Quite a hero, hey?'

'What do you want with me?' I asked. 'I've done nothing wrong.'

Boetie flicked me on the leg with the whip. Though his movement was restricted by the confines of the car, he still managed a good swipe.

'What do you want with me, baas?' he corrected. 'Have you lost your bloody manners?'

'What do you want with me, baas?'

Jan shook his head. 'You don't ask questions here, jong. You just fucking listen and answer, you hear me?'

Another flick on the leg.

'Yes, baas.'

Jan reached over and opened the glove compartment. I felt my heart sink as he took out a copy of *Black Bones*. He paged through it casually. 'What are you trying to prove, Smith?' he asked eventually.

I couldn't answer. Another flick on the leg.

'If you're looking for trouble, jong, we can give you more than enough. That I promise you.'

'I'm not looking for trouble, baas.'

'Then why do you write this shit?'

'I didn't write it. I did the drawings.'

Another flick.

'Baas,' I added.

'Same fucking thing!' Jan shouted. 'Don't get clever with me! What are you up to, Smith? Why do you do rubbish like this?'

'I don't know, baas.'

'You don't know? Well, let's have a look and maybe you'll remember.' He turned a few pages, then pointed at a drawing of a policeman masturbating in front of a burning township, his penis the shape of a gun. 'Explain this to me, Smith. Maybe I'm a bit stupid, but I get the impression you don't like the police. Don't you like the police, Smith?'

'I like the police, baas.'

'Then explain this picture to me, if you like the police. I want to know what it means.'

'It doesn't mean anything, baas. I wasn't serious when I did it.'

'Oh, so you think you can just draw things like this? Fuck what it means. Fuck what the police think it means.'

'No, baas.'

'No? Then you know it's wrong but you still do it?'

'No, baas. I didn't mean to cause offence.'

'Didn't mean to cause offence? Then what did you mean to cause, Smith? Happiness?'

'No, baas. I didn't mean to cause anything.'

'Don't fucking lie to me! You knew exactly what you were doing! Just like your friend, whatsisname – Harris.' Jan turned a few pages. 'Let's look at some of his shit. Hey, what about this? *... and so the fuckheads in blue, riding astride their corrupted Bible, bring death to the innocents ...* Fuckheads, Smith? Corrupted Bible? Oh yes, and this is a good bit: *... and when the beast of apartheid pulls its head out its arse, what shall be left? A fuckhead legacy ...* Explain this to me, Mr Smith.'

Another flick, this time on my balls. I tried to cover my groin with my hands but Boetie knocked them away and gave me another swipe for good measure.

'Explain these words of wisdom, Smith?' Jan asked again. 'I'm just a stupid policeman. I can't work it out.'

'Please, baas ...'

'There must be a good reason behind this. I mean, you don't just say these things without a good reason, not so?'

'No, baas. There was no reason.'

'No reason, hey?'

'No reason, baas. We were just stupid.'

Another flick on the balls. I began to squirm.

Jan affected surprise. 'Ag, but you're a teacher, man. How can a teacher be stupid? Come on, teach me the meaning of this book.'

Another flick.

'Come on, Mr Teacher. You're not as bloody stupid as you look.'

'Please, baas … I was very stupid. I didn't know what I was doing. Please!'

'You see, Smith, when I read shit like this I think, fuck it, this must be the ANC talking. Am I right? Are you a member of the ANC?'

'No, baas.'

'Are you sure, Mr Teacher?'

Another flick. I could hardly breathe, the pain was so bad.

'No, baas … I mean, yes, baas. I'm sure.'

'Quite sure?'

'Yes, I'm sure, baas.'

Another flick. I began to writhe.

'Please!' I begged.

'Please what?' Boetie asked.

Another flick. I began to cry.

'Please stop hurting me … baas!'

'Ag, shame,' Jan said. 'The teacher is crying, like a little baby. What's the matter, Smith? Things getting too rough for you? Is the game getting too rough?'

Boetie closed one eye and took aim.

'Please, baas …'

Another flick. I screamed.

Jan shook the book in my face. 'You must think very carefully before you play games with us, Smith. You're playing with fire, you hear me?'

'Yes, baas.'

Another flick. I screamed again.

'Have you had enough, Mr Smith?'

'Yes, baas. I've had enough.'

Another flick. This time I wailed.

'Please baas! I've had enough, baas!'

But Boetie went on with me writhing and wailing until Jan held up his hand. 'Okay, Boetie. Mr Smith says he's had enough.'

'I think he wants some more,' Boetie said.

'Please, baas! I've had enough!'

Jan jabbed his finger at the book. 'Well, we've had enough too. Enough of you clever bastards who think you can just write what the hell you like. Understand? Now, I want you to apologise. Apologise to the South African Police.'

'I'm sorry, baas.'

'No, no, that's not good enough, jong. You can do better than that.'

'Baas?'

Jan opened the book to the first page and handed it to me. 'Right, you can apologise for every page. Come on, spit!'

I hesitated.

'Spit!' Jan shouted. Boetie laughed, shaking his head.

I spat.

'Come on, every page!'

I spat and spat, until it began to run off the book onto my lap. I spat until I could spit no more.

'Please, baas.' I pleaded. 'My mouth is dry.'

Jan's eyes widened in mock astonishment. 'Your mouth is dry? Well, why didn't you say so sooner? I'm a reasonable man. What I have, I share. Come on, maak oop.'

'Baas?'

'Open your mouth, you fucking baboon.'

I opened my mouth. Jan cleared his throat and spat into mine.

'Now, go on, Smith. Spit!'

And so I went on, with Jan and Boetie spitting into my mouth (occasionally missing and getting me in the face) and me spitting at the book, again and again, until every page was done. Boetie was beside himself with laughter. When I was finished Jan reached over and opened the door. 'You can keep that book as a memento, Smith,' he said. 'Now get your dirty arse out of here! Move it!'

I climbed out, clutching the sodden book in one hand and my burning crotch in the other. I prayed that was the end of it but then Jan and Boetie got out too. Jan ordered me to turn around and walk into the bush. In a state of abject fear I walked, listening to their footsteps behind me. A short distance from the road I was told to stop and turn around.

'This is a good spot,' Jan said. 'Okay, Smith. We're finished playing games. Get a move on. Dig.'

'Baas?'

'I said dig. I'll tell you when to stop.'

So I began scraping at the hard dry soil with my bare hands, shaking with fear. While I dug, Jan and Boetie sat in the shade of a nearby tree and watched. Boetie, the arselicker, got up on two occasions to mark my measurements out on the ground in case I'd missed the point of the exercise.

The ground was hard and progress was slow. After an hour or so I'd made a hole the length of my body, about a foot deep. Jan and Boetie got up and inspected my handiwork. There were comments about my soft girl's hands. I was made to stand in the hole, facing them. I must have been a pathetic sight in my new blazer stained with sweat and soil. I could hardly stand, my legs were shaking so. Blood was dripping from my broken nails.

Jan came forward and stood a few metres from me. He pulled out his service revolver from under his safari suit and pointed it at my head. Terror surged through me. I remember thinking, stupidly, that this was the first time I'd seen a firearm actually being used. That I was to be its arbitrary victim was too much to bear. I fell to my knees and began to plead.

'Please, baas, I beg of you ...'

Jan shook his head. 'Too late, Smith. This is what happens when you fuck around with the police. We don't play games, jong.'

'Please, spare my life ...'

'Christ, you black bastards are all the same. No fucking shame. You all grovel like dogs, hey? Can't even die standing up like a man!'

'Spare my life, please …'

'Why should I spare your life? Why? Give me one good reason.'

'Please, I beg of you …'

'You see? You can't even find one good reason to stay alive. Your life is worth fuck all, Smith. Nothing. Just food for the worms.'

He pulled back the hammer. I put my hands in front of my face in a ridiculous defensive gesture and closed my eyes. This is where it ends, I thought. A shabby death in a shallow grave. One of the many who simply disappear. I thought of my mother and Helen. They seemed to be the same person in my head.

It was like someone cracked a whip next to my ear. I jumped with fright, then felt myself waver and fall forward onto my hands. There was the smell of cordite. Almost absently I heard myself gasping for breath. Then I heard them laughing. I opened my eyes. Jan was still pointing the gun at me.

'Must be losing my edge,' he said. 'Usually get them first shot.'

Without warning he took another shot, this time past my other ear. I cowered on my hands and knees, listening to the report echoing through the bush. Jan fired two more shots into the ground in front of me, spattering dirt in my face. I continued to cower and gasp for air. Boetie was laughing hysterically. Then Jan slowly put the revolver back in its holster.

'Hell, I like watching a man shit himself,' he chuckled.

On my hands and knees I watched them walk back to the car, Boetie still giggling. They got in and Jan started the engine and spun the car around in a U-turn. He gave me a thumbs-up sign, then drove off.

I got shakily to my feet and watched them go. Far off, to the south there were clouds gathering along the horizon and I could hear the distant crackle of thunder. The book was lying on the ground close by. Sobbing uncontrollably, I picked it up and threw it violently into the grave, my grave, and buried it. Then, amid the sound of singing birds, I started walking.

I never told anyone about this. Not even Zelda, though she questioned the state of my clothes and hands. I told her I slipped down an embankment trying to take a short cut home after school ('You weren't drinking, were you?' was all she said). But especially not David and Whitney. I could not have taken any looks of pity or outrage on their faces. My humiliation was an insidious, irrational thing. I could not bring myself to confide my fear and shame in white people, whatever their persuasion. Should I have warned David? Perhaps I might have overcome my inability to confide my humiliation, or the fact that I blamed David for my ordeal, had I thought it necessary to warn him. I like to think so. But I knew it wasn't necessary. David was not the target. And he wasn't the only one to blame. In fact, he was an innocent compared to the one who was. I knew this without a shadow of doubt.

And while I never talked about it, it stayed with me. Even now, it hangs on to me with tireless jaws. At night I'd wake sweating, tormented by impotent hate and humiliation. I'd clasp my head, unable to rid myself of the spectre of Boetie and his whip. Of them spitting into my mouth. Of myself kneeling in my grave. And, like a growing cancer, the memory of the pressed flower that fell out of *Black Bones* when Jan opened it.

*

My moral cowardice tormented me too. I despaired at my collapse of purpose. I resented myself for my lack of defiance – that I didn't use my little weapon of art to fight back. But art seemed so futile and pathetic against the tactics of humiliation and brutality. For the first time I understood and sympathised with those who would use violence to overthrow evil. You must fight fire with fire. Real fire, not the timid little flames of art.

The relentless momentum: Devoid of purpose, I lost interest

in my studies. Professor Strachan had to keep chasing me up about my Theory assignments. And while I was told the destruction of my work would not affect my year mark, my efforts in studio classes ebbed to the point where I was just going through the motions. Zelda surmised it was all because of my studio. She couldn't accept this abject surrender and for the first time we began to argue. Being negative is not the way to respond to this, she said. Perhaps if I'd told her about my little excursion with the police, and who was behind it, she might have understood, but I didn't. I couldn't contemplate what such a revelation might cause. I knew she was right, though. Nothing good would come of giving up. But it was not something I had control over.

And my situation at Phoenix was becoming increasingly desperate. It became a weekly ritual that I'd be hauled over the coals by Mr Dlamini, usually for absenteeism. Looking tired and dishevelled from his sleepless nights lying in wait for arsonists, he'd wag his finger at me, saying, 'I need good teachers, Mr Smith, and I need people who can turn the tide – people with commitment.' No doubt, he'd looked for a replacement, but people with commitment were hard to come by.

But aside from being absent or hung over I was also reading the signs, and they were not encouraging. Unlike Mr Dlamini, who spent his days painting over graffiti (without reading what it said), I could see no positive purpose to Phoenix, not in the present political climate at any rate. The children had begun to boycott classes regularly and while the staff sat twiddling their thumbs and Mr Dlamini raved on and on about the stupidity of it all, no one really believed in solutions. Solutions fell into the category of dreams. We lived with the demoralising realities of failure, of the inevitable collapse of an untenable system. Ja, we had no wish to teach the unteachable. But, of course, there was much hypocritical hand-wringing about incomplete syllabi and children being forced to repeat. It was all a fine dramatic rendition and I confess to being one of the chief actors. Few of us would stare truth in the face. Few of us would openly acknowledge that until the country was put right, the situation in black schools would remain untenable. We all knew that if the boycotts continued the government would start closing schools, but we preferred not to think of it. We just clung to the system like sad leeches, drawing our meagre pay, knowing that unless a miracle happened a time would come when it would end. But few of us had any idea it would end so suddenly.

It happened the night Zelda and I were invited to dinner at Professor Strachan's house. It was the first time we'd been asked to his place. While Professor Strachan led a fairly exuberant existence on campus, he liked to keep his home life private – hence our visit was something of a privilege. We met his wife, Jean, for the first time, a lively, scatterbrained woman who immediately held Zelda captive with a torrent of chatter. Unlike her obstreperous husband, Jean was thoroughly old-fashioned, her head crammed with home-grown remedies and recipes. She kept poor Zelda pinned down with talk about babies, cooking and garden plants (just down Zelda's alley!) as they put Helen to sleep in one of the spare bedrooms. Every so often, Professor Strachan and I would receive a helpless sidelong glance from Zelda, the sort one might expect from a flood victim.

'Jean was a copper miner's daughter,' Professor Strachan whispered to me under his breath, by way of explaining it all.

Jean's virtual capture of Zelda left Professor Strachan and I alone to talk. We sat in the lounge, a huge cluttered room filled with an odd potpourri of things – a wild profusion of African masks, drums and spears, and somewhat demure watercolour landscapes and portraits on the walls. It seemed Professor Strachan's feral extravagance and Jean's ordinariness were engaged in an eternal struggle for supremacy.

We were a little ill at ease at first but mellowed after a few drinks. Professor Strachan started talking about his days in Northern Rhodesia, when he used to ride out on horseback into the bush for days on end delivering post to far-flung communities.

'The best days of my life,' he said. 'I'm not joking! God, being a postman was the most meaningful thing I ever did. I was a kind of lifeline to all those folk stuck out in the bush. Never had so much free booze in my life!'

I laughed. 'So how did you make the transition from postman to professor?'

'That's a long story, Manas. You see, I used to dabble in painting in those days. You know, landscapes, sunsets, charging elephants, that sort of stuff. Basically kitsch. I was pretty good at it, I suppose, because I sold a lot of it. Once or twice a year I'd exhibit in Jo'burg and eventually I was making a lot more money than I did as a postman. So I stopped being a postman and after I married Jean we moved to Jo'burg, where I decided to study art at Wits. I suppose like all amateur painters I wanted to be recognised as a 'real' artist. I wanted the credentials of training. And, of course, my art changed. From kitsch to crappy outdated cubism. Never realised it was the same bloody thing! I had some shows around the country and did pretty well. Then I applied for a job here at Rhodes and got it. I kept on producing crappy cubist landscapes which, despite being fifty years behind Picasso and Braque, were eventually considered a major breakthrough in South African art. And so I became recognised. Then I stopped painting and became a professor. That's about it, in a nutshell.'

'But why did you stop, Prof? You used to joke about being colour-blind. Was that why?'

He smiled. 'Well, actually it had nothing to do with that. I've never been seriously colour-blind. My paintings were monochromatic anyway.'

'So what made you stop, then?'

Professor Strachan sighed. 'You see, I discovered a terrible thing, Manas. I discovered that painting cubist landscapes was utterly meaningless. I realised that the rubbish I used to paint as a postman, those bloody awful baobabs against the sunset, was infinitely more meaningful and pleasurable than the pseudo-modern crap I'd turned to. Becoming a 'real' artist killed my love for painting. So I stopped and turned to books. I began doing higher degrees in Art History and Philosophy. And before I knew it I was stomping through the hallowed halls of learning with all sorts of silly titles after my name, the old days of riding through the bush just a distant memory.'

'Don't you ever paint now, Prof?'

'No. In fact, I got rid of all my work. I even burned some of it. That's why you don't see anything of mine on these walls.'

He laughed and took a big slurp of his whiskey.

'It's a shame you stopped, Prof.'

'One could say the same about you. I hear you've virtually thrown in the towel.'

I avoided his eyes, unable to reply.

'Our stories are very different, Manas. But some things are the same. I allowed my disillusionment to destroy my sense of purpose. And I regret it very deeply.'

There was a long silence, then he laughed irrelevantly. 'That's why I asked you around tonight. I hate seeing what's happening to you. Your heart's not in your work any more, and it reminds me of a jackass who stopped painting long ago when he shouldn't have. I know it's been tough with those brainless bastards wrecking your studio like that. But don't let it destroy your sense of purpose! Don't give up, boy.'

'I understand what you're saying, Prof. Zelda tells me the same thing every day. But it's not something I can control … Art just seems so stupid, so bloody irrelevant!'

'But it's not, Manas. That's the point, damn it! Doing art in this fuck-up of a country is one of the few things left that's positive and constructive. You *must* keep working! You must persevere, come what may. You have the ability. Believe in yourself. For God's sake, don't throw it all away!'

There was another long, deliberate silence. Professor Strachan took a hefty swig of whisky. He laughed. 'Hell, I had no idea how I'd broach the subject, but it seems a little whisky around the epiglottis has done the trick. But, seriously, don't give up, Manas. Believe in yourself, okay?'

'I appreciate you talking to me, Prof.'

Professor Strachan eyed my empty glass with horror. 'For God's sake, fill that bloody glass of yours! And while you're about it, you can do mine too.'

As I was pouring the drinks, Zelda and Jean came through. Jean immediately appropriated the conversation and we spent a fascinating half-hour listening to the intricacies of planting Virginia creepers. How strange it was that she was so steeped in the ways of her race and generation and yet not at all perturbed by having me, a coloured man, to dinner. I remember thinking what a marvellous couple they were – both colour-blind.

After drinks, we went through to the dining room for supper. Jean brought on a curry that would have made a hardened Hindu sweat. She waffled on about the medicinal qualities of eastern spices (I gathered she was something of a homeopath) as Zelda and I sweated our way through the meal. Desert consisted, thank God, of simple ice cream and fruit salad that adequately performed the task of dousing the inferno in my mouth.

After dinner we had an Irish coffee in the lounge and then I, the very picture of alcoholic temperance, said we should be going as I had school the next day. Professor Strachan (who, I'd noticed, had given his coffee an extra dose of whisky) looked gloomy. 'I suppose we all have to earn a living, don't we all?' he slurred.

Zelda fetched Helen and we went outside to the car. The night sky was being cleaved by the spotlight on Gunfire Hill. You couldn't see the townships from Professor Strachan's house but we could hear a commotion coming from across that way, shouting and dogs barking, sirens.

'Looks like the natives are restless tonight,' Professor Strachan said morosely.

'I really don't know why people can't do things peacefully, really I don't,' Jean said.

We said goodbye and drove off. Zelda was cradling Helen in her arms and singing softly to her. Then as we drove down Beaufort Street, she exclaimed, 'My God, Manas, look!'

I was already looking. Across the stream in Fingo Village, the school was burning. I stopped the car and we sat and watched the flames leaping into the sky.

'Oh, Manas …' Zelda said.

I just sat there shaking my head, thinking this was one Phoenix that would not rise from its ashes ...

The next day I picked my way through the charred, smoking buildings with the other teachers. Out on the playground, the kids stood huddled in groups, watching us. We searched through the ruins for anything – books, personal effects – that might have survived. But nothing had survived. Everything had been burnt to a cinder, including Mr Dlamini whose remains were found by firemen in the gutted shell of his office.

*

A piece among pieces ...

One day we took Helen to the circus. We should have known even that wouldn't be straightforward. Helen and I were refused entry because we were non-whites. We were told to come back on the non-white day. The man in the ticket office was one of the clowns, sitting there in a dirty vest with his hairy white arms leaning on the counter, red nose, droopy white mouth and all. He had the gall to tell Zelda she could go in. Zelda told him to get stuffed.

We weren't the only angry ones. A crowd of blacks began to gather around the perimeter of the circus encampment. They started jeering at the white families walking around inside the enclosure. A few stones were thrown and the police were called. They arrived with their dogs and guns and sjamboks and formed a cordon around the circus. We stood outside with the ragged throngs and watched the white people nervously going about their pleasure.

There was a journalist taking photographs of this bizarre scene. He turned to us and gestured at the line of cops. The end is nigh, he said, shaking his head.

Ja, pieces of a broken town ...

*

A few weeks after the school had burned down I was notified that my services as teacher were no longer required. This did not rest easy with me. Despite my poor performance, the brief period of employment had been important to me, if only to provide the illusory notion that I was independent and was doing something worthwhile with my life. Of course, Tak had never stopped providing a basic living allowance – we'd become used to this extra bit of money each month, to the extent that it no longer seemed 'extra'. Without my salary things would seem a bit tight, but there was still some money from my Triennial sale left over and I figured with Zelda's small teaching income and the allowance she received from Charles we'd make ends meet. But Zelda was not so restrained when it came to matters of money. I burned with embarrassment when she asked Charles to make up the shortfall. Charles immediately complied by increasing Zelda's allowance to the tune of my previous salary. Nothing to him.

Not that Zelda intended sponging off Charles indefinitely. She started checking the newspapers for teaching posts and applied for an Art History position at Michaelis School of Art in Cape Town. She didn't like the idea of teaching history but felt she should apply anyway, as art posts were scarce. She sent an extract of her thesis along with her application, and to her surprise was short-listed for an interview. I was left with Helen when she flew down to Cape Town. She phoned me after the interview, astonished she'd got the job.

'Incredible,' she said. 'I wasn't the best qualified, but they liked my thesis. The Head of Department's an expert on protest art, and I think that's what swung it in my favour – that, and the fact that the other applicants must've been real bums. So I guess I'm lucky.'

'Don't talk yourself down,' I said. 'They chose the best person.'

'I've got mixed feelings about it. I'd rather teach sculpture, but it's a start. A foot in the door. I want to make something of our lives.'

'I know. I'm glad for you.'

'We'll make it together, Manas. We'll finish university and make it together, okay?'

'Okay, Zelda,' I said, not with the same confidence.

When she got back, we threw a party at Stoneleigh to celebrate. Practically the entire Art Department turned up as well as most of Whitney's proletariat. Professor Strachan gave a fine inebriated speech and David tore a ligament in his knee doing a Russian dance. The three ANC comrades, Peter, Elias and Johnson, were there too, standing inconspicuously to one side, amused at the antics of the revellers. They left early. I remember Whitney deep in heavy conversations, breathing plumes of smoke in people's faces, and David hobbling around after her like a lost dog. I remember Professor Strachan bumping his head when he tripped down some stairs. Then I got myself in a stupor and don't remember much more.

But behind this, when I dared contemplate what lurked inside me, I sensed a parting of ways. I envied Zelda's optimism and deplored my inability to transcend the dreary truths of logic. For her, the future now appeared filled with promise. Getting the job in Cape Town had done wonders for her self-esteem. Ja, things were slotting into place, while I struggled against an insidious pessimism. I tried to maintain a belief in the future, that once the year was over and I had my degree there would be better prospects. But I worried about the future. What really lay ahead of us in South Africa? What did the future hold for Helen? Anyone who was prepared to open their eyes could see the political situation was out of control. Each day there was bitter fighting around the country. Internecine killing in the townships, massacres in the homelands. Bombs in nightclubs, bombs in supermarkets. You didn't have to have cops trash your studio or force you to dig your own grave to know things were falling apart. Why invest in the future when the future was a bleak place? In South Africa at any rate.

The idea of leaving the country was the only thing I could get positive about. I became convinced that if we were to have any future together we'd have to emigrate. Or try, at least. It seemed the only sensible option, at least until things in South Africa changed. Of course, it wasn't easy persuading Zelda. I was not insensitive to her position, to the importance of her family and, now, the prospect of a good job. Nevertheless, I implored her to look at the big picture and not to let these things cloud her judgement. I offered the sweetener that it wouldn't have to be forever, just until the situation improved. Zelda remained opposed to the idea but eventually agreed to go through the application process. For Helen's sake, she told me. She'd make a final decision if and when our applications were approved. I guess she thought no country would accept a couple of unestablished artists. So I phoned the Australian embassy in Pretoria and asked them to send the application forms. The forms duly arrived. We completed them, applying under the Independents Category, and sent them back. I knew our chances were slim, but it was something of a comfort to know at least we'd tried. A letter came back informing us the process could take many months – understandable, considering the exodus of South Africans to Australia.

At this time I also suggested getting married. I thought it might help our applications (to be frank, it was also a symptom of insecurity). Zelda's response was to kiss me and shake her head. No, she said. Not yet. She didn't want to enter into holy matrimony with apartheid. Until the system fully acknowledged her right to love a coloured man, she wouldn't consider tying the knot. Zelda's moral stances were always more lofty than mine.

Such was our state of affairs; my side of the ledger weighted by negatives. But our fates weren't the only ones in question. Late one night, as Zelda and I lay talking in bed, there was a knock on the door.

'Who is it?' Zelda called.

'Me, David.'

The door opened and David stood there looking at us with a strange expression – scared, yet defiant. At first, I thought he was drunk, but he wasn't.

'What's the matter, David?' Zelda asked.

213

David raised his hands and dropped them.

'Ja, what's up?' I joked. 'Come to read us a bedtime story?'

David gave a strained smile. 'You're both good friends. The best friends I've got, both of you. I just want to tell you that. Whatever happens, I want you to know that, okay?'

'Spill the beans, brother' I said. 'What shit are you in now?'

'I'm not in any shit. Sometimes you've just got to tell people what they mean to you, that's all. Both of you mean a lot to me. I hope things work out okay for you.'

'Come on, David. You can talk to us,' Zelda said.

He sat on the end of the bed and was silent for a while. Then he looked up at us and said, 'Whitney'll kill me if she finds out I talked to you. But I know I can trust you guys. I'm going to Zambia with Whitney. To join the ANC.'

'Oh, Jesus!' I exclaimed. 'Get a brain, man! You're crazy to let Whitney do this to you!'

David held up his hand. 'I know how you feel about her. But this is my decision. I'm going nowhere in life. This is a chance to do something right.'

'Oh, David, David ...' Zelda pleaded. 'If I didn't know you so well I'd kiss you for being brave. But you're doing it for all the wrong reasons. You don't join the ANC because it's therapeutic, or because you're in love. Please don't go, David.'

'I'm going, Zelda. Call me a fool if you like, but I'm going. It's only a matter of time before the fucking army tracks me down anyway, now that I've dropped out of varsity. The way I see it, it's a choice between dodging petrol bombs in some bloody township or doing something worthwhile.'

I sighed. 'You are a fool. And I suppose it's no use pleading with you, hey?'

He shrugged and shook his head.

'Shit, you're something else,' I said. 'When are you leaving?'

'I'm flying to Jo'burg tonight. I'll catch the early plane to Lusaka tomorrow. Whitney said she'll join me there in a couple of days. She's got some loose ends to tie up here first. She reckons it's best to split up. Looks less suspicious.'

'But what about your things?' Zelda asked. 'What about your car? You can't just go like this, David.'

214

'Throw my stuff away, or give it to the beggars in town. I don't care. It doesn't amount to much anyway. As for the car, I've given it to the ANC guys. Johnson's picking it up from me at the airport. I shouldn't be telling you this. Whitney'd kill me if she knew.'

'Fuck Whitney,' I said.

David gave me a wry smile and got up. 'I better go. I don't know when I'll see you guys again. I just came to tell you what you mean to me.'

He kissed Zelda and shook my hand, African style.

'Look after yourself, David,' I said.

Then he turned and went out, closing the door behind him.

Zelda looked at me and shrugged. 'Shit, he's a weird bastard. I hope he knows what he's doing.'

'David never knows what he's doing,' I said.

Then we heard David's footsteps on the wooden floorboards as he went outside. We heard his car start up and drive off towards town.

We had a similar farewell from Whitney a couple of days later, though not quite as informative. She breezily dismissed our questions with vague answers laced with her usual rhetoric. She kissed Zelda goodbye and gave me a nicotine-stained handshake, African style. Then she stomped off out of Stoneleigh leaving only the smell of her cigarette smoke.

*

The end of an era. A couple of weeks later our landlord pitched up unexpectedly early one morning to tell us we had to move out because they were going to demolish the house to make way for a bypass. A stout man of florid complexion, Mr Gaites seemed genuinely apologetic, though there was a distinct hint of incredulity in his eyes as he came to terms with the sight of Helen on Zelda's hip and me still in my pyjamas. To his credit, he made no issue of it. He wasn't happy about the bypass carving up his farm, he said, but had no say in the matter. He told us it was to solve the problem

215

of the main road to King William's Town going through the townships. If they spent the millions for the bypass on upgrading facilities in the townships, Zelda said, maybe it wouldn't be so dangerous driving through them. That seemed to be a point Mr Gaites hadn't considered. We had a month to move out.

With the loss of Stoneleigh, and with the end of year fast approaching, there was no other option but to move temporarily to Haslemere. Charles and Catherine agreed to put us up. They had recently built a guest cottage a short distance from the house and offered it for our use. We borrowed one of the farm trucks and picked up our belongings from Stoneleigh. Zelda wept as we drove away. I was beset with the morbid realisation that the place where we'd consummated our love, the place where Helen was born, was about to be erased from existence. We didn't talk the whole way back to Haslemere.

The cottage had everything we needed – two small bedrooms and a lounge overlooking the valley. The kitchen was fitted with all the mod cons, though we had most of our evening meals over at the house. Catherine even insisted on sending the maids over in the mornings to make breakfast and clean up. I found the unfamiliar experience of having servants scurrying around me uncomfortable, to say the least.

Zelda and I tried to focus on finishing our studies. We drove to Grahamstown only when we needed to, about three days a week. Aside from finalising arrangements for her exhibition at the Monument, Zelda had only a couple of first-year classes to teach. I had my studio classes and lectures to attend. But as far as my studies were concerned, I was coasting, waiting for this empty time to end. The only thing I looked forward to was correspondence from the Australian Embassy. Since I'd sent in our forms, we'd complied with routine requirements from the Embassy. Birth certificates, qualifications, medical examinations, police clearance certificates, and so on. I poured over books on Australia. I annoyed Embassy officials, already inundated with anxious South

Africans wanting to leave, by constantly phoning to find out how our applications were progressing. Zelda, who'd had more time to consider the hard sense of leaving and, thankfully, had become more positive about it, cautioned me against getting my hopes up too high. The chances are we'll get knocked back, she said. Save some faith for staying.

Charles nearly flipped when he heard. He was one of those staunch South Africans who saw leaving the country as a form of treason. Zelda left me to field his derision: 'Joining the chicken run, eh? Australia? Flies, gum trees and giant hopping rats – that's Australia for you! Full of convicts and drunk Abos. What d'you want to go to bloody Australia for?' Alone, I defended Australia's good name.

Generally, though, I was beginning to get on quite well with Charles. Now that we were staying on Haslemere, we kept no alcohol in the cottage. My consumption was limited to a couple of beers at the house in the evenings or a glass of wine at table, so there was never any danger of me going overboard. We'd sit with Charles and Catherine out on the veranda and watch the sunsets. Charles, after one or two under the belt, began to relax in my presence and he'd tell me about how things were on the farm in the old days. How, for instance, they never had to lock up the house when they went away. Now, of course, things were different. If you didn't chain something down it was gone in the morning. He even took an interest in my background. When I told him about Tak paying for my education, he laughed and said, 'Jesus, for an Afrikaner farmer he must be an exception to the bloody rule in those parts. Can't imagine the boere are exactly liberal around Langebaan! Not Mandela fans, I'll bet!'

'About as liberal as you Eastern Cape boere,' I replied, which drew a laugh.

For a month there was no sign of John. According to Charles he'd been living a pretty rootless existence between the army and his girlfriend from Fort Brown. When it came to the subject of John I sensed an uneasiness in Charles and Catherine, as though they were expecting the unexpected. Zelda, too, seemed to anxiously await his arrival. I noticed how she'd sometimes pause and glance down the road, expecting, I suppose, to see him come driving along. Needless to say, I took his absence as a blessing.

But then one evening he arrived. We were sitting out on the veranda, having our usual drinks before dinner, when his Landcruiser pulled up. Dressed in army fatigues, he gave us all a cursory greeting as he came up the stairs. He exchanged some small talk with his parents, then stomped into the house, had a bite to eat in the kitchen and went to bed. The next day he resumed his farm duties as if nothing was amiss. Catherine said this was typical.

Once again, the atmosphere on Haslemere became unbearably tense. Though John was an old hand at hiding his emotions I could see my presence on Haslemere was a thorn in his side. Every so often, at the dinner table (when he'd deign to eat with us) or if he joined us for drinks out on the veranda, I caught him staring at me. That look of contempt was too much for me to bear. I felt like exposing him then and there, letting Zelda and her parents know what a piece of work he was, but I didn't. Instead, I started making excuses not to go to the house in the evenings.

I wasn't the only thorn in his side. Charles's attitude towards him had changed. The old veiled pride behind his criticisms of John's army commitments had been replaced by frustration and anger. Now he was fed up with John's unreliability, the way he came and went as he pleased, the way he just disappeared for weeks on end. The bickering between them was most unpleasant. Charles implored John to settle down, to spend more time on the farm. 'Get your bloody act together,' he said. 'You can't run your life like a bywoner.'

John brushed off his demands. 'If you don't like the way I run my life, I'll go – no problem,' he told Charles. Charles was forced to accept there was no answer, save throwing him off the farm.

And with growing dismay I watched as Zelda resumed her forlorn quest to reclaim him. John brushed off these advances with the same spite. At night I'd wake to hear her crying next to me. I'd try to comfort her, steeped in the knowledge that as long as we were together any hope she had of restoring their bond was futile. Ja, not an easy knowledge to live with.

I waited for the inevitable encounter, and it came soon enough. It became my habit to take long walks in the evening, just another excuse to get away from the tense atmosphere in the house. One evening, as I was walking down near the river I saw John's Landcruiser heading in my direction. I waited resignedly on the side of the road. He pulled up and got out. Eyes fixed on mine, he advanced on me. I stood my ground.

He stopped a few feet from me. 'Avoiding the happy family gatherings, are you, Manas? Too complicated for your liking, hey? Now that you've fucked everything up.'

I was sick of his bullshit. 'Don't blame me,' I replied. 'You're the one who's fucked everything up.'

He stood there glaring at me, rubbing his fist in the palm of his hand. Big deal.

'What? Are you going to hit me again, John? Don't think you can intimidate me. It's not going to work.'

He shook his head. 'No idea, hey? Completely oblivious to what you've done.'

'What have I done, John? Tell me.'

'You've turned everything to shit. Everything was okay in this family until you dragged your black arse into our lives.'

'Everything was okay until you started acting like a moron.'

His nostrils flared. 'Don't push me, Manas. I swear, one of these days I'll put a bullet through your head, just like that.' He snapped his fingers.

I sighed. 'Spare me the he-man heroics, John.'

'Don't underestimate me, Manas. You've fucked up Zelda's life but I won't let you destroy her. I swear to God …'

'The only thing that'll destroy her are the things you stand for.'

'I'm talking, damn you! Don't bloody interrupt me!'

'Oh, I see. I must behave like one of your servants. Okay, John. Talk. Tell me how I've fucked up Zelda's life. I'll be interested to know.'

'You bloody well know why.'

'Why? Because I'm a coloured, hey? Is that it?'

He stood there at a loss for words.

I shook my head. 'John, this is all because of my skin. Nothing else. That's your problem, not mine. It's a disease called racism. And until you overcome this disease, you and I have very little to talk about. So if you'll excuse me, I'd like to get on with my walk.'

I made to go but he blocked my path. His dark eyes bored into mine. 'Don't stray too far on your own. It's a big farm. You might get lost. Things happen, you know.'

I affected a patient nonchalance. Then he stepped aside. Behind me I heard him say, 'You better watch your back, Manas. Don't underestimate me. I swear to God ...'

I turned to face him again. 'I don't underestimate you. I *know*, John! I'm not stupid. I know what you did. Your dirty little arrangements with the police. Ja, give the coloured bastard a hard time and maybe he'll run away. Fine friends you have, hey? Bastards, just like you. No, I don't underestimate you, John. I know exactly what you're capable of.'

He was rattled. 'What are you talking about?'

I scoffed. 'Ag, please! Don't give me that crap! I knew you were a snake, John, but I never thought you'd stoop so damn low. What do you think Zelda would do if I told her, hey? You think she'd be grovelling around trying to get you back? You think she'd still choose you above the father of her child?'

'I don't know what the fuck you're talking about.'

'Just like you to deny it, hey? I'm not blind, John. It all fits together. I thought you were big enough to fight your own battles. Obviously not. The only reason I haven't told Zelda is because, unlike you, I respect her feelings. Because it would destroy her, knowing what a treacherous bastard you really are.'

John shook his head. 'You're fucking deranged, that's your trouble. Tell her what you like. I couldn't give a shit.'

'Yes, you do give a shit, John. Otherwise you wouldn't stoop so low.'

'You've got a screw loose, Manas. I should put you out of your misery. Shoot you like a mad dog.'

I smiled. 'Such a hero, hey? A credit to your family.'

John glared at me. 'You're asking for it. I swear, one of these days I'll blow your brains out, for sure.'

'You sure you've got the guts to do it?'

There was a flimsy look of defeat in his eyes. I couldn't resist giving my baser nature some free rein. 'John, I think you're a gutless coward. And let me tell you something else. There's another serious disease you suffer from. It's called ingrown cock. If you don't do something about it, you might just fuck yourself to death.'

That set him off. He lunged at me, then stopped short. He screamed something unintelligible in my face. I affected a patient nonchalance again. He whirled around and kicked the side of his Landcruiser. I pursed my lips and shook my head. He pointed his finger at me, trying to voice his rage, but couldn't. After several other contortions he jumped into the Landcruiser and sped off, showering me with dust.

I walked back to the cottage feeling good for the first time in a long while.

A few days later he left to do another stint in the army, much to my relief. But every so often I thought back to his face during this confrontation, and saw again what was in his eyes. That awful, desperate hate. A hate born of what? Only of love for the one, Zelda, who was closest to him. Ja, a pure umbilical hatred born of love. And it came to me with dismal finality that he was so fundamentally part of the ruptured equation of Zelda and me.

Those last days went by in slow succession. I found the long drive to Grahamstown tedious, and my commitments at Rhodes had become a chore. The place that had transformed me now seemed dull and unappealing, soured by bad memories. I did my exams in an indifferent mood. I knew I'd passed, but only just, my original aim of walking away with distinctions forgotten. On the other hand, Zelda's assessment exhibition at the Monument was a triumph. She passed *cum laude*; the external examiner thought it was the best Masters show he'd seen from Rhodes in many years. There were rave reviews in the *Herald* and *Dispatch*. For the benefit of invited senior academics, Professor Strachan gave a slightly pedantic speech at the packed opening, asserting Zelda's sculpture to be a profound example of 'postmodern political narrative'. Charles had dusted off a rumpled suit for the occasion, about as big a gesture of respect as one could expect from a farmer. He and Catherine seemed impressed by all the people, and also astonished so much of the work sold. In fact, the show was practically a sell-out. Zelda was sorry to part with her sculptures (her children, as she indulgently called them) but was also glad they'd struck a chord in people. She was delighted when the King George VI Gallery in Port Elizabeth bought the group of soldiers for their permanent collection – sweet justice indeed after her Triennial rejection. She also gave some pieces away to people like Professor Strachan. In the end there were just three torsos from the angel series left. She gave one to her parents, and kept the other two for ourselves.

When the exhibition ended we used one of the farm trucks to clear out her studio. Once that was done we were finished with Grahamstown.

*

Christmas at Haslemere was a quiet affair. Only Helen seemed imbued with a truly festive spirit. She tore open her presents with great zeal, more intrigued by the wrapping paper than anything else. John was away, doing his bit in the army. There'd been more strife in the townships and his company spent their Christmas in camp on standby. Rumour had it he'd broken up with his Fort Brown girlfriend; no doubt she'd become fed up with playing second fiddle to the army. Catherine and Charles gave me an expensive watch as a gift. I forgot to phone Tak.

A few days after New Year we departed for Cape Town. As a start to her working life (and, no doubt, an enticement not to leave the country) Charles had offered to buy Zelda a small place to stay. We hunted around and eventually Zelda chose a two-bedroomed flat with an enclosed balcony in Sea Point overlooking Table Bay and Robben Island. The flat was convenient because I could gain access to it from the fire escape without being noticed by the neighbours.

At the first opportunity I went back to Langebaan. I went alone, partly because I didn't know how Tak would react to my new circumstances and partly because I simply needed to be alone, to be with what was mine, at least in memory. I cleared away the bush around the cottage and swept the sand away from the doors. I got rid of a bees' nest in the chimney. I visited my mother's grave. If Tak was offended by my long absence he showed no sign of it. He seemed elated when I showed him my final-year results and offered to pay for me to travel up to Grahamstown to attend the graduation ceremony, which I declined. He also offered to pay for the teaching course I was considering doing through the University of Cape Town. For the sake of your mother, you must find a proper job, he said, never one to believe an artist can make a decent living. I couldn't bring myself to tell him about Zelda and Helen. The thought of explaining every-thing exhausted me emotionally. I felt I didn't know Tak well enough to talk about such intimate things. What would he say? Would he accept Zelda and Helen? Would he allow them the same unlimited access to the cottage as me? The truth was the barrier between master and servant that for-bade frank intimacy was still there.

Back in Cape Town I duly enrolled in the teaching course and began attending lectures. Zelda began teaching at Michaelis. She appeared to enjoy it though it was heavy going in the beginning. Each night she sat up until late researching her lectures and arranging slides in carousels. She was frustrated by the fact that she had no time or space to continue with her sculpture, but vowed to resume her studio work as soon as circumstances allowed. The only mute reminder of her former brilliance were the two torsos left over from her Masters exhibition that now stood together in the corner of the lounge. Using the flat's enclosed balcony as a studio I tried to get back into my painting. I contacted one of the gallery owners who'd approached me back in Grahamstown, when my work was on the Triennial, and organised an exhibition for November. I thought it would be an incentive, but it wasn't. I just couldn't exorcise the sense of futility that filled me whenever I picked up a brush.

For a while we tried to socialise, trying to reconnect with the world we once found so exhilarating. We attended exhibition openings and the odd party thrown by Zelda's Michaelis colleagues. Zelda seemed to slip back into the spirit quite easily. The old sarongs and beads got a second life, along with some hippy stuff she festooned herself with from Greenmarket Square. I made an effort to be part of it but soon tired of the art crowd. The affectations, the silly egos – sadly I realised what consummate conformists we artists really are.

Meanwhile we sent off our newly-acquired qualifications to the Australian Embassy. Things were dragging on with our applications. Such were the delays, we had to undergo medical examinations and get police clearances again because the previous ones had expired. I received a kind letter from Professor Strachan who urged me to persist with my painting and to stay in contact. He reminded me that I had it in me to succeed as a painter. I wrote back, telling him I was working hard.

We also got an unexpected phone call from David's father, Aubrey Harris, who was trying to locate David. I told him what we knew. There was stunned silence from Aubrey. He finally muttered 'Jesus God', left a number where we could contact him if we heard from David, and hung up. I didn't think much more of it.

Of course, my drunken stupidity continued in Cape Town. This time it had nothing to do with being a bleeding artist, or any such romantic notion; it was simply a growing shadow. Zelda began to criticise my behaviour, especially if I made a fool of myself at exhibition openings or if I got drunk in front of Helen. Ja, a growing shadow …

And so the months went by as though hidden in a fog. Like me, the country stumbled along. I paid little attention to the worsening strife in the townships or the violent rift

between the ANC and Inkatha. I missed the polished per-
formances of the new clowns in parliament – Allan Hen-
drickse's clashes with PW Botha and his much-publicised
swim at a whites-only beach in Port Elizabeth; Amichand
Rajbansi's outraged responses to accusations of impropriety.
Botha called an election for whites in May. The fact that there
was a big swing to the right and that the Conservative Party
ousted the Progressive Federal Party as official opposition
merely served to reinforce my belief that South Africa was
doomed.

In November Govan Mbeki, one of the original ANC
group sentenced to life imprisonment with Nelson Mandela
in 1964, was released from prison to tumultuous welcome by
the black community. This was a move by the government to
appease growing international hostility. But Mbeki's popu-
larity soon unnerved the powers that be and he was restricted
under the emergency regulations, compounding South
Africa's bad image. The powers that be had a knack for turning positive initiatives into disasters. I followed Mbeki's fortunes (the big picture) while trying to come to terms with the
abject failure of my exhibition (the little picture, to use a lame
pun). I'd managed to scrape a few works together, mainly
Langebaan scenes. Big skies and low horizons – semi-abstract
kitsch, to be honest. Hardly anyone turned up for the opening. Out of a total of twenty-four paintings only three sold,
which didn't even cover my framing expenses. The gallery
owner made polite sounds about the work but I could tell she
wasn't impressed by the way I'd regressed since Grahamstown. I think it was only out of loyalty that Zelda hung a few
of the pictures in the flat. The newspapers didn't think it
merited a review, good or bad.

How I passed the teaching course, I can't say. Not that my
subjects were difficult. No, just boring. I missed lectures and
performed at a mediocre level in my pracs. There was some
argument as to whether I should be allowed to pass, given
my bad attendance record, but in the end I was pushed
through. The irony didn't escape me. On paper, my credentials were looking good. A degree, a teaching diploma and

some teaching experience. An attractive proposition? Ja, well, looks can deceive, not so? I checked the education gazette for vacant art-teaching positions in coloured schools around Cape Town but there were none. I inquired if there were any part-time positions at the University of the Western Cape but there was nothing there either. The only thing going was an English post in a school in the black township of Guguletu but considering the virtual war in the Western Cape townships and Crossroads squatter camp in recent years I didn't bother applying as the last thing I needed was another Phoenix. So Zelda and I decided she would support me while I waited for suitable work. Meanwhile I'd continue to paint. And I'd look after Helen during the day.

Zelda went home for Christmas without me. I went to Langebaan to lick my wounds, the failure of my exhibition like a knife in my side. In front of Tak I feigned a sense of purpose. He was pleased to see I was now fully qualified with a bright future ahead of me. When he queried where I'd be staying in Cape Town and how I'd make ends meet, I fobbed him off by saying I'd be staying with friends and would get by with part-time menial work. Tak seemed to think that was being independent and resourceful. I had a braai with him on Christmas Day. We reminisced about the old days and how my fortunes had changed. Your mother was right, he said. You've elevated yourself, Manas. Out of Tak's view, I resorted to some heavy bouts of solitary drinking.

I went back to Cape Town when Zelda returned from Haslemere. For a while I worked hard at my painting. Increasingly I resorted to complete abstraction, with few promising results. My paintings lacked substance, they had nothing to say. Just stupid paint. With dismal finality I realised the extent to which my art had become an escape from reality. So when Zelda went back to work at Michaelis I spent most of my time with Helen. It was a good excuse not to paint. I read to her. We played games. We watched the children's cartoons on TV. I let her scribble with crayons in my sketchbooks, not minding if she destroyed old drawings.

Sometimes we'd catch a double-decker bus down past Camps Bay, just for the ride. Or we'd go into the city and walk up to the Gardens where we'd feed the cheeky squirrels. Or we'd collect shells and pebbles on the beach. The days went by like this and I didn't mind not doing anything productive myself. Ja, I liked being with Helen. She never asked difficult questions.

Then out of the blue the Australian Embassy called, asking us to attend an interview at the Consulate in Cape Town. While I cavorted around ecstatically, Zelda received the news with some reserve; since starting her job at Michaelis I'd noticed her enthusiasm about the subject of Australia had waned somewhat. Still, she wasn't about to derail everything at this late stage, so when the interview day came we spruced ourselves up and went along to the Consulate in Adderley Street. The interview seemed a perfunctory affair, more a final face-to-face check that we were who we said we were. The Australian official was cheerful and considerate, and seemed very taken with Helen. We were asked simple questions, such as where we intended to live and what we intended to do. He gave us six months to move to Australia. We shook hands and that was that. As I came out of his office I nearly kissed the portrait of Queen Elizabeth in the entrance foyer. And as we drove back to the flat I was a sure-fire contender for the happiest man on earth, while Zelda was in a state of shock and grew tearful at the thought of leaving, now that it had become a reality.

It took some effort to convince Zelda again of the wisdom of leaving. I pointed to the upsurge of vigilante violence in Cape Town's townships. I pointed to the peace marches broken up by police. I asked: What kind of world will we inherit from this? Why squander the chance for freedom? I rested my case when one of her colleagues who lived in Somerset West and had to drive past Nyanga and Khayelitsha townships on the way to work had his car pelted with rocks and narrowly escaped being killed. Eventually she gave in and phoned her parents to tell them of our plans and, not surprisingly, they too went into a state of shock. In a show of

227

generosity Charles offered to pay our fares. With a heavy heart, Zelda accepted his offer. With an equally heavy heart, she handed in her resignation at Michaelis; she would finish work at the end of June. She decided not to sell the flat. She would rent it out as a form of income. I thought it was a foolish idea, that it would be best to make a clean break. But I didn't press the issue – this was not the time to be getting into arguments. Our passports arrived from the Consulate with the vital Australian Permanent Resident stamps. I went to a travel agent and booked our flights. I paid mine out of the money I had left over from the Triennial sale. I didn't want to be beholden to Charles.

Once our affairs were in order we waited for our departure date to arrive. It was a strange time; we seemed suspended between countries, neither one thing nor another. Just waiting. It was my intention to go to Langebaan one last time and explain everything to Tak. Charles and Catherine were planning to come down to see us for a few weeks; we'd also planned, once Zelda finished work, to go back to Haslemere for a final visit. But none of this would eventuate.

*

As we waited in our strange limbo between countries, John's moment of truth came. The first we heard of it was when Charles phoned at three in the morning, the day of their intended departure to Cape Town. Zelda had been restless and fretful that night and was awake when the phone rang. She was stricken as she listened. She wept so uncontrollably afterwards she could hardly tell me what had happened. Not that I had long to wait to hear the full story. That day all the newspapers in the country were divulging the terrible details beneath such descriptive headlines as SLAUGHTER OF THE INNOCENTS or GRAHAMSTOWN BLOODBATH – LATEST.

I read the stories, scarcely believing them, scarcely believing I knew the man being held responsible for the deaths of thirty-two civilians and countless others maimed and injured. I shook my head. I tried to comfort Zelda but she was inconsolable.

From what I could gather the facts were as follows: John had been in command of one of the troop carriers stationed out on the main road through the townships. It had been a long, tense night. Rioting had been breaking out like wildfire. One minute up near Makana's Kop, the next down in Fingo Village. John and his men watched and waited as the spotlight from Gunfire Hill raked over the smoke-shrouded hovels and streets. They were expecting trouble but hardly of the magnitude in which it came.

Then John received an order to render assistance to a police patrol vehicle that had come under attack in Fingo Village. He set off immediately. Along the way the troop carrier failed to negotiate a corner into one of the multitude of unlit streets and overturned in a ditch, pinning John and two others underneath. John lay there in agony, his leg trapped beneath the wheel. The other two men under the vehicle were dying, their cries terrible in the darkness. The remaining soldiers, though hurt and shaken, tried to free them, to no avail. All they could do was wait for help. But help came too late.

In the darkness they heard the mob approaching. Soon the overturned vehicle was surrounded. John ordered his men into firing positions around the vehicle. For what seemed an eternity they listened to the moans and death rattles of the two men under the troop carrier. The people heard them too and they began to dance and cheer. One man mimicked an orchestra conductor – the sounds of death and suffering music to his ears.

Then, as John stated under oath in the inquiry, the crowd became more aggressive. A stone struck the side of the troop carrier. More stones landed around them. The soldiers became jumpy. Some of them begged to open fire. John ordered a warning shot, above the crowd. The shot rang out. The crowd disintegrated. Some panicked and bolted. Others milled around. A few shouted defiantly. And then in the confusion John thought he saw a flame. Just a quick flash out the corner of his eye. A struck match it might have been. Somebody lighting a petrol bomb, perhaps. John also smelled the ruptured fuel tank and he imagined his own fate trapped beneath the burning vehicle. In his mind were the dreadful charred corpses, the victims of petrol bombs or necklaces, that were the common aftermath of township violence. He panicked and ordered his men to shoot. The men needed no second bidding. The night erupted with gunfire. John himself emptied his magazine, shooting blindly at the mass of people.

And then (now I surmise), through the pain and the panic, he saw himself. For the first time he saw himself in others, not of his kind. He saw himself in the men and women who dropped like sacks of meat, in the children who whimpered where they lay. And he screamed at his men to stop but they were beset with a wild madness that only hatred and fear begets, and only when there was nothing more to shoot did the firing cease. And when they stopped the dead and wounded lay everywhere.

Of course, there was an international outcry. There were demands from presidents and prime ministers that the perpetrators of the 'Grahamstown Massacre', as it became known, be brought to book. Trading partners threatened boycotts unless there were answers. All the band aid reforms of the South African government went out the window. As an embarrassed response, the government ordered a full public inquiry into the incident led by a prominent Supreme Court judge, Justice Benjamin Haig.

Zelda said she had to be with John in his time of need and left immediately for Haslemere, taking Helen with her. I decided against going with her, as I thought my presence might exacerbate things. So I followed the details of the inquiry, alone in the flat, faced with the disturbing realisation that John's predicament elicited mostly sympathy from me. I hated what he'd done. I was appalled at the magnitude of suffering and death. But I also knew he was no monster. He was simply one of his kind. One of many misled young fools who believed in the system and sacrificed their souls for it. I thought it a cruel fate indeed that he should be reminded so savagely that we are all brothers and sisters beneath the skin.

Once, while Zelda was away, I got very drunk. It happened late one afternoon in the city. As I walked along the avenue of oak trees through the Gardens, I looked at the people sitting on the benches, and the swift clouds through the bare branches of the trees, and I felt empty and defeated. The air, as I recall, was cold as twilight approached; it was winter – a time in Cape Town when strength is important if you feel alone. But that afternoon my strength drained, suddenly, inexplicably. And I had to get drunk. So I bought a demijohn of wine and found myself sitting on a bench in the Gardens, looking up at the statue of General Smuts which had been the subject of much controversy in the past. The statue was neither heroic nor of meticulous detail; hence it had clashed with the public's expectations of what a statue should be. The more I drank the more I found myself wondering what on earth all the fuss had been about. As statues went, it was certainly better than most. It reminded me vaguely of Zelda's sculpture, of the quick, expressive way she modelled, her economy of means. I swigged more wine (the bottle disguised in a plastic bag) and found myself laughing at the ridiculous behaviour of people. How stupid and blind they were to the deeper things in life! The statue was indeed a fine piece of work, far superior to the dreary traditional ones. Ja, all those pigeon-shit giants that glare in all directions over the city. I began offering aesthetic critiques to passersby. Those people looked at me with strange, scared expressions, shaking their heads as they avoided me. Concerned at their lack of interest in cultural issues, I drained the bottle. How those last drops burned against the cold emptiness in my heart, how they replenished my lost strength! Standing on the bench I began a rousing speech about politics and art to strangers. As the last rays of sunlight faded on Smuts's bronze features I raved on and on, my ragged voice dominating the birds and traffic. And as I interrupted my oration to relieve myself on the flowers, a policeman suddenly appeared. With my leaking penis jammed in my fly, I was hauled off to the police station where I spent the night in jail. The next day I was charged with being drunk and disorderly. I had enough money on me to pay the admission of guilt fine.

As I caught the bus back to Zelda's flat I was overcome by a terrible despair. I caught a glimpse of death's shadow, and I knew I could not go on like that. If I did I would only end up in the gutter or the grave. I was filled with a fear of the meaninglessness of being. That we have as much purpose as the ants we crush beneath our feet.

My father, the hero of a dozen fishing harbours, winks …

The Haig Inquiry went on for weeks. As the details emerged and soldiers and civilians alike gave their versions of the tragedy, a nerve was touched in white South African society. Ordinary white people wrote emotional letters to the newspapers, expressing their sorrow and anger that things had come to this. They argued on radio and television. They seemed to realise that John represented them all, that it could have happened to anyone who believed so much in the system. The hideous guilt that was his to bear really belonged to them all.

Finally the Haig Inquiry found that while excessive and unnecessary deadly force had been used, John and his men had acted under extreme duress and provocation and, consequently, were cleared of any criminal negligence or intent. Needless to say, there were many who were not satisfied with this finding. In the eyes of many, John was a murderer set free.

Zelda came back to Cape Town with him. She'd persuaded her parents that he needed a break, a complete change of scenery. There had been some argument about this but she got her way. Of course, in my state it was the very last thing I needed. But I made no issue of it. I knew that in this desperate time Zelda's allegiance had shifted. That I was no match against John if it came to decisions.

John was an unshaven, dishevelled wreck. So was I after weeks alone. I shall not forget that look of disappointment on Zelda's face when she saw my condition. That was when she suggested we come out to Langebaan, where John and I could get away from everything, where we could heal. Where only one of us would finally have her.

*

The sky aches with winter. Clouds like black dogs bound overhead. Fine threads of rain, infinitely miserable in their loveliness, whisper across the lagoon that has risen with the tide. So much is held in the grasp of winds. The cottage shudders with each wild gust. Eerie moments of vulnerability, of smallness. A boat goes by, lurching through the swells. Ja, the frayed strands of life.

How often have I gazed out of this window upon this bleak place of sand and water and wondered if it held my salvation. As a child I used to watch the craggy hills across the lagoon changing colour as the sun set behind them, and ask myself if it were possible to exist away from Langebaan with only memories to substantiate my past. And always such thoughts brought about an acute sense of longing, as though a separation had already taken place.

We exist in the fear of separation …

And so this is my time for parting. The facts are clear. I know I must go to Australia. I know I must cut South Africa from me like a surgeon cuts away cancer. There are no other options; nothing can change what has happened. Zelda has made her decision. I can't go back to her now. And I can't stay here either, living off Tak's charity. Ja, the facts are clear. My story is simply the equation of memories. Now, if anything, the purging of my past must blow me out into the world like a mote of dust. It's time to change my history. To rebuild myself in a distant place.

The last thing you lose when you lose everything is fear. To lose fear is to lose despair. In this there's a strange freedom. But this freedom does not bring with it a loss of accountability. I don't callously absolve myself of what I've done to Zelda and Helen. There's much that must be repaired, much that must be restored. No, the loss of fear simply means I must go forward. Alone. I must go on without hiding under Zelda's wing or being led by Helen's tiny hand around my finger. I mourn for the loss of them. I don't know if redeeming myself to them is within my grasp. Time will tell. I mourn also for the loss of my country. But its redemption belongs to the variables of fate, to things beyond my control.

And so I confront the future, the lone product of my memories. I embrace the old cliché. Today is the first day of the rest of my life. I must rebuild. I must regain my sense of purpose. I must seek courage to face the depth and substance of life. I must seek goodness. One day at a time. I must look beyond the failures. That's right, it's not how one falls that matters, it's how one gets up again.

I massage the lines on my forehead. I inspect the problems foretold by my palms. I close my eyes and for the last time think back, way back, before the world beckoned. Small patches of sunlight. I see myself sitting with my mother on the beach waiting for the boats to come in. The sun is nice and warm. I prod my toe into a pile of reeking weed that has washed up on the shore. It is spring. The dunes are aflame with colour. Terns are plunging into the water from high. A pink flamingo feather floats by in the breeze. Small waves splash on the beach. Bees and flies are buzzing. The sounds make me drowsy, and I curl up against the warm bulk of my mother. The boats drift in smelling of snoek ...

PURPOSE

I arrived in Cape Town on Saturday two weeks ago, after a marathon flight from Melbourne. Zelda was late to meet me at the airport so I bought a newspaper and waited in the arrivals lounge. The newspaper was full of gloomy economic predictions and crime. I read that Robert McBride, the nightclub bomber-turned-foreign-affairs official, was languishing in a Maputo jail on suspicion of gunrunning and no one seemed all that keen to get him out. There was also a story about an off-duty cop who shot dead three car thieves in Durban. The way it was written, such violence seemed run-of-the-mill.

Zelda arrived, looking flustered as she came running across to meet me. She apologised for being late, blaming the traffic. We embraced and kissed. I was surprised to see her eyes brimming with tears.

'You look okay, Manas,' she said in her frank way, holding me at arm's length. 'Not exactly athletic, but not the seedy oaf I used to know either.'

I said she looked okay too. Actually, she'd aged a bit and looked tired and gaunt, but I was never blessed with the gift of frankness. I complimented her on her trendy oval spectacles with red rims, which were an improvement on her old tortoiseshell ones.

I still had the newspaper's pessimistic forecasts in mind as we drove to Zelda's flat in Sea Point. But looking around the economic slump it had referred to seemed hardly credible; there were buildings going up everywhere and trucks and company cars were racing past us on the freeway. Hardly the signs of an ailing economy.

'I thought the New South Africa was going to the dogs,' I said. 'Looks pretty healthy to me. Just look at this place.'

I pointed at a massive construction site called Century City, teeming with workers. Zelda took a while to answer.

'There are problems, Manas. Big problems. No one's denying that. What you're looking at are islands of affluence in a
sea of poverty. And the sea's rising. Economically, we're in
the shit. The rand's worth nothing these days. The gap
between the rich and poor is getting wider. Crime's on the
increase. But, still, this country's a bloody miracle, considering what it used to be. Absolutely no question about that.'

'If it's a miracle then how come the newspapers say everyone with brains or money is leaving?'

Zelda shrugged. 'Okay, some people are leaving, for whatever reason. The crime, no job prospects for their kids, education standards. If that's their choice, good luck to them. But
the country's not going to fall apart because a few decide to
jump ship. Give the rest of us some bloody credit. There're a
hell of a lot of South Africans left who're determined to make
the miracle work.'

'Good to see you still believe in miracles.'

'Problems are there to be solved. You forget what this place
used to be like. You've always been a sceptic, Manas. The
minute you realised what was going on in this country you
gave up on it.'

'Ja, and I suppose South Africa's got no use for sceptics.'

'Sceptics don't contribute anything. Only people with hope
and idealism do.'

'I'd have thought that with all your brains and money
you'd at least have paid me a visit in Australia.'

Zelda gave me a level stare. 'What makes you think I've
got money?'

'Surely your old man bankrolled you with a little Sutton
inheritance when he sold the farm?'

'Get real. My folks got nothing for Haslemere. You can
hardly give those farms on the Fish River away these days.'

'But surely the Sutton clan rallied to keep the old place?'

Zelda scoffed. 'As it turned out, the Suttons are pragma-
tists when it comes to money. Just like everyone else in this
country. Family history meant nothing. None of the family
wanted the place once they'd done the sums. In the end, Dad
sold it for a song to one of his neighbours. Enough to buy a

mouldy little cottage in Wales with a few acres and a couple of cows. That and enough to pay for Helen's schooling.'

I watched her profile as she spoke – that fine nose and straight jaw, those thoughtful blue eyes that never suffered fools easily, other than me. I affected a posh accent. 'Diocesan School for Girls. I thought you were against private schools.'

'I was. But it's become more a necessity than a privilege these days if you want your child to have a proper education. Besides, my folks insisted. You know how they were. St Andrews or DSG for the Suttons, nothing less. God knows, I couldn't pay for it.'

'Helen's not only a Sutton.'

'I know, Manas. But at least they took her into the fold. They didn't reject her.'

'How are your folks? Wales must be a change from the Eastern Cape.'

'From what I can gather, they're pretty bloody miserable.'

I shook my head. 'Christ, who'd ever have thought they'd leave, the way your old man used to talk? Remember how he carried on when we decided to go.'

'They went because of John. John changed everything. They couldn't stand living in this country anymore.'

We were silent for a while. I debated whether I should ask about John, and decided against it.

'How's your drinking?' Zelda asked. 'Have you really given up?'

I nodded. 'Ja, on the straight and narrow. Nearly six years now.'

Zelda smiled. 'Shit, you've even picked up a bit of an Aussie twang.'

'What? You mean I've lost my perfect South African accent? How tragic.'

That drew a laugh. A bumper sticker on a car in front of us drew another. It read, *Fuck the Rhino, what about the White Ou?*

It was around noon when we got to her flat. Her TV was still on, with the Comrades Marathon on live. Looking around I noticed none of her old sculptures, nor any of my paintings for that matter; only a few woodcuts of township scenes by African artists and a small watercolour landscape by Helen which, for her age, showed promise. I asked Zelda about the two sculptures she'd kept from her Masters' exhibition and she told me she'd sold them because they depressed her. I phoned Tak's lawyers and we arranged to meet at ten o'clock on Monday morning. While Zelda went out to get some pizza for lunch I sat and watched TV. Some Russian had beaten Comrades hero Bruce Fordyce's record. Russians were prominent among the gold and silver medallists. It struck me as incredible that the Comrades Marathon had become more or less a contest between South Africa and Russia. Some of the country's past prime ministers must be rolling in their graves. My head began to swim. I had a shower and collapsed on a bed in Helen's room. I wasn't too tired to notice one of my drawings on the wall above the bed. The one of the beggar woman, my first gift to Zelda. Then I fell into a dreamless sleep, waking only once to see Zelda's silhouette in the doorway, watching me. I could hear the TV in the background. I thought it was another dream where I'd wake in Australia feeling lonely and depressed.

I felt listless all Sunday. In an attempt to perk me up Zelda drove me around the Peninsula, to no avail. She also drove across the Cape Flats past Nyanga and Khayelitsha townships to Sir Lowry's Pass, pointing out the growth of squatter settlements. The way things are going, she said, some day Cape Town will look like Rio. I was reminded that Sundays in South Africa are usually depressing. What was really bothering me was Helen.

How does a father explain a ten-year absence to his daughter? There was no denying that Australia, on the face of it, had been good for me. It had offered me a place to rebuild. A place to earn my keep, first as an art teacher in a small school in Bairnsdale, Victoria, and then as a landscape painter of somewhat clinical bent and mostly limited appeal. In the beginning I hoped that once her anger subsided Zelda would relent and follow me to Australia, but she didn't. Not even at the height of the violence in 1993, when thousands were killed in political bloodletting, did she give any hint of wanting to leave. Not even after John's suicide. And so the onus was really on me to go back, but the years went by and I never did for the simple reason that I feared going back. As a refugee from myself I knew I could not return until I'd overcome my demons. It took me all of four years to kick my alcohol dependency, a battle I never wish to repeat. I was also too poor. I was not a teacher blessed with much patience or insight into the psychology of Australian youth, and consequently found the children at the school in Bairnsdale too rude and irksome. Teaching became a torment, my only solace being the weekends and holidays that were spent trying to capture the minute detail of the Gippsland landscape on paper or canvas. Heartened (and perhaps deluded) by a few sales through a local gallery, I gave up teaching after just three terms to paint full time, condemning myself to some very lean years where it was a struggle just to pay the rent. It was only a year or so ago that my circumstances began to improve, when one of the Melbourne galleries took me on and I started making a name for myself. And then a letter arrived from Tak's lawyers telling me he'd passed away, along with a Qantas ticket to South Africa, one way.

While such excuses might explain my absence to myself, or even to Zelda, when it came to Helen they have an empty ring to them. The fact was the years had gone by and I'd not been there for her.

When I told Zelda I was anxious to see Helen she said we should wait; Helen was busy with her midyear exams and who knows what my presence might do to her concentration. 'You've been away ten years,' she said. 'Waiting a few days longer won't kill either of you.' So back at Zelda's flat I phoned Helen at her boarding school in Grahamstown and told her that Zelda and I would be travelling up to fetch her the following week when the schools broke up. I didn't talk for long. Helen's voice sounded strained and choked and I guessed she was close to tears.

I soon realised Zelda's income is not exactly comfortable. Aside from the small two-bedroom flat which her father bought when she finished university, she has nothing to her name – to be frank, the ancient Volkswagon Kombi she drives around in is more a liability than an asset. Since I left for Australia, her employment has been sporadic. She's had a few stints teaching art theory and sculpture part time at various art schools. She told me she's been too busy scratching around for work to do any sculpture herself. Besides, she can't afford studio space. Currently she works as a freelance art critic for the *Cape Times*, which doesn't pay much but doesn't tie her down either. So she was at my beck and call, as she magnanimously put it.

On Monday morning she drove me to the lawyer's offices in the city. All the way we talked about everything. Helen, Australia, Tak's will … everything except John. I was so engrossed in our conversation I nearly missed the white man in a suit, begging at some traffic lights. A cardboard placard around his neck read, NO JOB. FAMILY TO FEED. PLEASE HELP. In the old days black or coloured beggars were plentiful but the only white ones you saw were the occasional tramps, boemelaars, never a well-groomed man in a suit.

We arrived fifteen minutes late for my meeting. I'd noticed tardiness had become something of a habit with Zelda. She parked the car in Long Street outside Groenewald & Jooste, Prokureurs, and browsed in a bookstore while I went upstairs. I needn't have worried about being late since I was kept waiting a further twenty minutes before Groenewald, the senior partner, a short bespectacled Afrikaner, called me into his office. His secretary brought in some tea and we talked informally for a while. It was strange (and nice) to speak Afrikaans again after all these years.

Groenewald read me the will and explained that in order to die debt free Tak had sold off most of his land to pay his creditors and estate duty, as well as to compensate the two coloured families, the Arendses and Witboois, still living on the farm. A small strip of twelve hectares stretching from the road to the shore, including my family's home, was all that remained in his possession when he died. This piece of land had been left to me. Groenewald informed me that the Parks

Board had bought up the rest of the farm and was in the process of adding it to the existing West Coast National Park. The Park, in effect, surrounded my land. The Groothuis would be used as an information centre and accommodation for the rangers. He told me that Tak wanted his ashes scattered in the lagoon. I signed the necessary papers, took Tak's ashes and left.

Talking of ashes, it's almost unheard of for Afrikaner farmers of Tak's generation to be cremated, especially given the fact that there is a consecrated graveyard on the farm where all his family lie buried. Afrikaners like the notion of a place for their kind, even in death. But that was Tak for you. A man who felt he belonged nowhere …

I spent the afternoon buying a few odds and ends at a nearby grocery store for our stay at Langebaan. That evening Zelda and I walked along the promenade watching the cold Atlantic swells surge through the kelp beds. Far off on the horizon, a few lights twinkled on Robben Island. I looked up at Lion's Head and at Zelda's pensive profile, and felt good to be back.

*

We left Sea Point early the next morning. It was a brisk winter's day with a few showers that cleared as we neared Langebaan. The journey seemed to pass quickly since I was so engrossed in the passing countryside, the miles of dune scrub and fynbos that was so familiar to my eye. We arrived at the cottage around midmorning and spent most of the day clearing the encroaching scrub and sand away from the building and cleaning and airing the dank interior that had not been opened since I left.

When we'd finished with the cottage I left Zelda to relax and walked up the road to the cemetery on the hill where my family lies buried. I stood at the foot of my mother's grave and paid my respects, my head bowed, remembering what she'd meant to me. The presence of my father's grave next to hers didn't annoy me as it used to. In fact I felt a grudging affection for him, incorrigible scoundrel that he was. I was glad he was there to keep her company.

In the evening I built a fire outside and braaied some fish. Zelda watched me as I poured her a white wine. I contrived a certain nonchalance as I swirled it around and sniffed it, affecting a discerning air as if quality had always been a prerequisite with me. She laughed, shaking her head. We sat and watched the sun going down over the hills across the lagoon.

'Was it hard to give up?' she asked.

'Drinking? In the beginning it was. It got easier when it finally penetrated my thick skull there was no other option.'

'I'm glad you've given up.'

'So am I.'

'So, what's it like to be home?'

'You mean here, at Langebaan?'

Zelda nodded.

'I don't know. It's strange. I'm still coming to terms with owning this place. It's what I always wanted, I suppose. I don't know how I feel, quite frankly.'

Zelda laughed. 'Do you know how much this land's worth? You've landed with your bum in the butter, Manas.'

'I know.'

'I'm glad it turned out this way, Manas. Tak was very good.'

I looked down at my hands guiltily. 'Ja, Tak was more than good.'

'Are you going to stay?'

'God, another hard question. I don't know, Zelda. It depends ...'

'You're not seriously thinking of going back to Australia, are you? Now you're the landed gentry?'

'I don't know. Logic tells me I should go back. I was just starting to do okay with my painting. On the other hand, Tak's changed things a bit. There's Helen too.'

Zelda gazed up at the first stars. 'There's plenty of time to decide.'

It was cold so I put my arm around her shoulders. I asked if she minded. She shook her head. It was strange being with her again. Despite her warmth (those tears I saw in her eyes at the airport) I sensed a certain wariness in her. I knew I was under scrutiny. Time had passed and we'd both changed. Or, at least, Zelda needed to know I'd changed. I had no right to expect any lingering affections. Still, I felt a cautious elation. I'd been surprised by her warmth. I'd expected some hostility, not the quick intimacy we shared from the moment we embraced and kissed at the airport. Platonic, yes, and vaguely forgiving. Something I could live with. Ja, I thought, I live in hope.

After we'd eaten, I took the urn containing Tak's ashes and waded out into the shallows in front of the cottage. Zelda watched me from the shore. There was a half-moon and the tide was going out. When I was waist deep I paused to think of the old man who had changed my life so completely. An old Afrikaner misunderstood by many, including me. Now in death he had given me what I'd asked for. Thank you, Oubaas, I whispered into the wind. Forgive me for squandering your affection. I kissed the urn and said a small prayer, asking God to bless Tak's soul. Then I scattered the ashes into the receding tide and threw the urn out into the deeper water. Shivering in the cold water, I closed my eyes and stood there for a while, imagining Tak exhaling the breath from his lungs and sinking slowly to the lagoon bed, lying there, eyes closed, listening amidst the silent watery flow for my mother's voice. Then I turned and waded back, filled with a sudden sense of grief.

Later, while Zelda slept in what used to be my mother's room, I sat at the kitchen table and read through some newspaper articles she'd saved for me. They concerned David and Whitney. Disturbing stuff indeed. I read how Whitney, while in Zambia, had been exposed as a police spy – this had happened not long after I left South Africa. Yes, a captain in the Special Branch, no less. It turned out the sole purpose of her campus activities in Grahamstown had been to infiltrate the ANC. David had been branded a spy too, by association. They ended up in separate prison camps in Angola. While the articles provided no detail as to Whitney's ordeal, I could hardly bear to read the horrors David endured. Torture and torment that broke his bones and spirit. Left for two months in a pit covered by sheets of corrugated iron in searing summer temperatures. Living in his own shit, existing off scraps thrown to him by guards. His father, Aubrey Harris, fought tirelessly to have him released. When no one across the political spectrum appeared to show the slightest interest in David, the ANC eventually conceded he was person of no consequence and let him go. David underwent a long period of physical and psychological rehabilitation. Apparently, he now lives in Edinburgh. The photographs of him in hospital were almost unrecognisable. He looked gaunt and old, his eyes dull and dejected. His hair had fallen out. Poor David. What a price to pay for foolish love. The South African government secured Whitney's release a year after David's by exchanging some ANC prisoners. One could only surmise what she'd been through, since she refused to discuss her ordeal with the press. There was one photograph of her being escorted through an airport terminal. You couldn't tell much from it. Dark glasses. Taking a drag on a cigarette through rotten teeth.

The articles simply confirmed what I already knew. Zelda had written to tell me of these developments while I was in Australia. I remember feeling relieved to be so far away from the place that could generate such brutal consequences for misplaced loyalties. But I was also overcome by doubt as to who was behind my encounters with the police in Grahamstown. That it might not have been John became another source of guilt.

I sat at the table thinking of them, of that time in Grahamstown. The only positive thing I could glean from the saga of David and Whitney was the vague satisfaction that my dislike for Whitney had at least been based on something. But that all seemed so distant, another world. No longer worth unravelling.

*

The strange thing was, there at Langebaan, I dreamed of Australia. My dreams glowed with the dusty greens and ochres of Gippsland and the subtle silver reflections of clouded skies on the lakes. Mostly they were sweet dreams of a safe and tranquil place, but sometimes they were imbued with an eerie nostalgia, where the forests and fields began to writhe beneath the winds, the roaring of the trees so loud I woke breathless to the gentle sounds of the lagoon – the lapping of small waves on the beach below the cottage and that almost imperceptible sighing as the tide ebbed – feeling confused and disoriented. I think for some travellers the soul is slow to follow.

We spent just over a week at the cottage. The weather, fortunately, was fine, if a little windy in the afternoons. We went on a couple of drives around to Geelbek and Church-haven and further afield to Saldanha and Pater Noster. We did a few walks, once taking a whole day to climb the bare windswept summit of Constable Hill across the lagoon. We also climbed the granite hill that used to be on the farm's northern boundary, now almost abutting Langebaan's spreading residential area. There's a stone cottage on top of this hill where, during my childhood, the lonely Xhosa shepherd Moses stayed. The one who was evicted under the pass laws. The cottage now stands more derelict than it became after Moses left, just a stone shell. It seemed to say so much about the past.

Zelda tried a bit of sketching, small watercolour and wax-resist studies for sculptures that, no doubt, would never see the light of day. I felt no inclination to do any painting myself. I simply took pleasure in Zelda's company while I had it, not thinking too much of what might lie ahead. Quite unlike the last time we were there – that awful winter where it rained so incessantly.

In fact, we didn't talk much about art, despite the fact that we both make a living out of it, one way or another. Once or twice I asked her what was in fashion these days in South Africa, and she told me that while the overseas market has welcomed the return of South African art with open arms, the art itself has been pretty dreary, that it's been flogging the dead horse of apartheid too long – that, or subordinating itself too slavishly to the conceptual installation trends of America and Europe. I found all of that pretty predictable and not of much interest. Zelda didn't show much interest in my Australian endeavours either. I'd brought along some photographs of my better paintings. She glanced at them, nodding her head. They're nice, was all she said.

I knew why we didn't want to talk about art. It might get too close to the bone as to why neither of us had fulfilled our real potential. Zelda had been worn down by life's realities – raising a child, making ends meet, dealing with tragedy. With me, it evoked the memory of a massive collapse of courage and faith. It went back to our time in Grahamstown where we lived and breathed a wonderfully idealistic but naive and futile art. I get depressed if I think about it too much. That's why I view art these days with such disdain. I know paintings are just trinkets for the rich. That is all I provide these days – trinkets for wealthy city folk burdened by a sentimental affection for the bush. I know artists are but fleas on this world.

So mostly we talked about ourselves, or rather we answered questions about ourselves. One day the subject of other partners came up. Zelda told me she'd had relationships with half a dozen men since I left, one of which lasted a couple of years. She added she wasn't seeing anyone at the moment. I came clean too, sort of. In Australia I'd allowed myself two difficult relationships which failed because both women thought they'd find something deep in my reclusiveness – the depth they found could be measured exactly by the shallowness of the landscape paintings I churned out for my keep, not quite kitsch but within the vicinity. The hysterical behaviour of these women when things fell apart made me question the emotional cost of sexual relationships. After that I kept my distance from women, except for an occasional fling in a Melbourne brothel, which suited me because there were no strings attached. Then I got worried about the emptiness that drives men to whores and stopped going to the brothel. I told her about the two women, but didn't tell her about the whores. With the whores I figured we were about even, if you can tally up such things. Not that either of us had any obligation to each other.

They say a sense of belonging comes down to place and people. But for all the familiarity I felt for Langebaan, something was missing. I sensed the umbilical cord between heart and place had been cut; the special intimacy I'd once known for this place was no longer special. And as far as people were concerned I felt strangely disconnected. I was happy just to keep to ourselves there in the cottage. There was no desperate urge to mingle with my people, the coloureds, again. Sure, the familiarity was nice. The language (that unique earthy banter) and mannerisms. But I could not define myself as one of them. I'd lost the need (if I ever had one) to be defined as belonging to a 'people'. I sensed this was a loss, but was not concerned by it. The plaasvolk who used to stay on the farm, the Arendses and the Witboois, had all moved into what used to be the coloured township, north of the village. Considering the ill-will they felt towards me and my mother I didn't bother looking them up, but I did bump into Abram Witbooi one day who was manning one of the boom gates to the Park. He was looking old and bitter and didn't offer much by way of conversation, except to say, ja, so gaan die wêreld, Manas, so goes the world. I guess he said that out of resentment and didn't take much notice of it. But after seeing Abram I felt my old demons queuing up to introduce themselves again. I felt the inordinate complexity of my previous life begin to reassert itself, the constant moral quagmire of the past and the endless fretting for an unknown future. I confess, the thought of getting drunk crossed my mind. The past was a burden I had no wish to carry again.

I walked the perimeter of my twelve hectares a few times, trying to get used to the idea of ownership, but not succeeding entirely. I thought perhaps I should fence it off to make the entity of my possession more emphatic but realised there was no time or need for that. The property was uniquely situated, surrounded as it is by Parks Board land; it would be best to allow whatever animals they reintroduce to roam freely.

The ownership of land is a curious thing. Just after I'd signed the will papers, Tak's lawyer, Groenewald, assumed a conspiratorial air, leaning close as he spoke. Reeking of pipe tobacco, he told me how valuable the land was. Langebaan real estate is sky high, he said. Just go and look at Langebaan village. You'll see all the fancy mansions the rich Capetonians have built. They all want a piece of it. The whole town's changed – nothing like you knew as a kid. Your land's worth a fortune, Mr Smith. I'm prepared to pay you a fair price if you're interested.

It was true, of course. Langebaan was experiencing a real-estate boom. In fact, it had started back in the seventies where I'd already seen the village beginning to change character from a random cluster of old fishing cottages, beach shacks and a weathered Victorian hotel to a resort town complete with tarred roads and expensive holiday mansions, many completely out of keeping with their surroundings. The old hotel became the most spectacular example of this incongruity, undergoing so many eclectic architectural transformations that in the end probably any nation on earth might have felt at home in it, except West Coast South Africans. Now the whole place seemed to have gone that way. There was little to remind me of the old village, not even the grotesque hotel, and it disturbed me that it didn't seem to matter, and that I didn't feel much one way or the other about Groenewald's proposition.

While it was nice to know that as long as the Parks Board was my neighbour the land adjoining my property would remain unspoilt, I nevertheless felt curiously detached from my only earthly possession. More important to me was Zelda's presence and the knowledge that we were comfortable with each other, not given to forced or unnecessary talk or gesture. I liked to think it was just like old times, but, of course, it wasn't. Perhaps we were just older and wiser. I often thought about the last time we were there. It seemed difficult to believe we were at each other's throats so, considering the easy give and take between Zelda and me now. Only once did I bring up the subject of John, if indirectly, one evening as we walked along the shore. We'd been talking about Tak.

'How was Tak after I left?' I asked.

'Do you want me to be honest, or assuage your guilt?'

'When have you ever assuaged my guilt?'

'I've always assuaged your guilt. But to answer your question: Helen and I used to visit him once a month, more or less. I don't know why. I hardly knew him, really. I felt sorry for him, I suppose. I couldn't stand to see his loneliness. If you want to know the truth, he felt pretty let down that you left.'

I shook my head. 'Let down? Jesus, the old hypocrite. What did he expect? What did he think was left for me here? What future was there? What was there worth staying for?'

Zelda looked at me, not bothering to answer.

'I'm sorry. I didn't mean it that way.'

'Stop saying you're sorry.'

'I am sorry. I'm sorry I was away so long.'

'You don't have to explain anything to me, Manas. It was your life. You did what you thought was best.'

'Ja, but I should've stayed for you.'

'Not for me. For Helen, maybe.'

'Okay, I meant for Helen.'

'But you didn't. That's what really upset Tak. He could take the fact that you left South Africa. Tak was never one of those blood-and-soil Afrikaners. I never heard a bad word from him about your leaving the country. He could even take the fact that you never wrote to him. He knew you never gave a damn about him. But he could never come to terms with the fact that you left Helen, your own flesh and blood. I think he saw your mother in her. She became very dear to him. When I had my breakdown, guess who cared for Helen? Not my folks. Like me, they were busy falling apart because of John.'

'Tak. I know.'

'Yes, Tak. He took her in and looked after her. Spoiled her rotten. And when I told him I was sending her to boarding

251

school he fretted and cried like it was his own child. But I had no choice. She'd already missed a year of school because of me.'

I sighed. 'I'm just sorry I wasn't there when she needed me most. I'm sorry so much time has gone by. But you know I had to go. You accept that, don't you?'

'Yes, I don't blame you. You did what you had to do. But it was hard on Helen. I tried to explain everything to her but she's struggled to understand it. Manas, you can't change what happened. It's done. Think about how you're going to make it right. You're back. That's a start.'

'I'm still amazed Tak gave me the land.'

'I think he always intended to. He was waiting for you to trust him.'

'That was fine for him, to play games of trust. Having a right to land is something you whites always took for granted.'

'Not any more.'

'Shit, this country is so bloody complex.'

'Of course it's complex. But I don't want to live anywhere else.'

'Has Helen been given a choice in the matter?'

A furrow of irritation appeared on Zelda's brow. She raised her arms and dropped them. I changed the subject.

'Are you okay now?'

'What do you mean?'

'I mean since ...'

'Since John died?' She tried to make light of it. 'Oh, I'm okay, I suppose. Back to normal, more or less – probably less! They say less is more! Shit, what am I saying?'

I took her hand. 'I'm sorry it happened, Zelda. I really am. I'm sorry I wasn't here to be with you ...'

'I know, Manas. I don't blame you.'

'I feel so bloody guilty though.'

'Don't feel guilty. I'm glad you weren't here to see me fall apart. There's nothing you could've done, anyway. When you lose a twin it's like half of you dies. I know it sounds a cliché, but it's true.'

'I can't begin to imagine it.'

She withdrew her hand and slowed her step.

'Manas, please. I can't talk about him. Everyone says I should. Part of the healing process. God, I've been to psychologists and everything, but it doesn't help. I just can't talk about him. With you or anyone, okay?'

'I'm sorry.'

'Stop saying you're sorry, for Christ sake! I hate it when you bloody apologise all the time. Look ahead, Manas. The past is dead. Gone!'

She smiled bitterly and kissed me lightly. I didn't bring John up again.

*

Tak was the one who told me about John, in one of the many letters I received from him in Australia. One might have thought that with such awful news this time, at least, I might have replied, but I didn't. Tak said it happened after John had been called to testify in another commission of inquiry into the events surrounding the Grahamstown Massacre. Although John had been exonerated by the Haig Inquiry back in the eighties, various pressure groups had never accepted that outcome and had lobbied relentlessly to have the case reopened. With the change of government in 1994 it was decided, in the interests of reconciliation, to look into the terrible event again. It proved too much for John. He first tried to kill himself on the farm, locking himself in one of the sheds and slashing his wrists. By chance, Charles happened to notice the dogs nosing around the shed and scratching at the door. He and some workers broke in and got to John just in time. He was rushed to Settlers' Hospital in Grahamstown. Charles and Catherine kept vigil while he recovered. Zelda meanwhile raced up from Cape Town to be at his side. He seemed composed enough when she arrived, enough to make them all think he was over the worst. They were all taken in by that most difficult of deceptions to recognise – the cheerfulness of the truly suicidal. Zelda would never forgive herself for not seeing it; she believed that she, his twin, should have had the intuition to sense the finality in his despair. But she didn't, and nor did her parents. He managed to convince everyone, doctors and psychologist included, that he was no longer a danger to himself. After a week of always having at least one of them at his bedside around the clock, Zelda and her folks decided it was okay to leave him alone for the night while they caught up on some sleep at a hotel in town. In the early hours of the morning he managed to sneak down a fire escape and hang himself by an electrical cord from a tree in the hospital grounds.

One might forever ask why he chose to leave his loved ones with such an image of him in death. But that was John for you – resolute, savage. The awfulness of it made all the reasons why I once hated him seem so small and petty. It even left me with a strange sense of loss.

So when I probed about John it was not the detail of his suicide that I was after. As far as that was concerned I knew all I wanted to know. No, what I was after was the hidden extent of Zelda's pain. But that was something she would not share. It was all she had left of him.

*

We decided to leave for Grahamstown a day earlier than planned. I was keen to take a longer drive up through Prince Albert in the Karoo and link up with the Garden Route at George. We set off before daybreak, first back to Cape Town to collect a rental car (Zelda's old Kombi was certainly not up to the long journey) and so that Zelda could pick up some clean clothes at her flat, then north up past Paarl and on towards Du Toit's Kloof.

It was raining as I drove and the mountains were obscured by clouds. I felt a mixed elation as we sped through the winelands. It occurred to me that everything in my life seemed shackled to distance, even such elusive absolutes as freedom. I knew this journey to the heart of my child was simply the unfinished conclusion of the one I began when I left South Africa. Of course, the circumstances were different. I had changed. The country had changed. I prayed these were good omens.

It was good to see the familiar countryside of the Western Cape and Boland again. A touch of Europe in the vineyards and pastures, in the towering mountains and brackish rivers. Once through Du Toit's Kloof the clouds began to clear, revealing some snow up on the high slopes. The splendour of the mountains near Worcester lit by dramatic shafts of sunlight was breathtaking, a landscape so un-African yet uniquely South African. A landscape so unchanged to my eye, except for the growth of squatter settlements around the towns.

Once past Touwsrivier the vegetation thinned into sparse Karoo scrub. In the distance the Witteberge formed a long southern rampart against the Cape rain. To the north the Karoo stretched on forever in subtle gradations of water-colour browns and hazy greys that belied its stony aridity. Beyond Laingsburg we turned off the main road and drove east, reaching Prince Albert around noon. We bought some takeaways for lunch, stretched our legs with a short amble through the quaint town, then pushed on. Small clouds were casting eerie moving shadows on the mountainsides as we zigzagged our way over the Swartberg Pass. The massive convulsions of rock were so impressive that we stopped for a while to take in the immensity of it. The vastness seemed to frighten Zelda. As we drove on to Oudtshoorn, she became increasingly pensive and troubled. I asked if she was okay.

She smiled. 'I'm sorry, Manas. I go through phases. Sometimes everything just seems too big to cope with. I haven't been back to Haslemere since my folks left. It's going to be painful. I don't know how I'll handle it.'

'I'm sure you'll be okay.'

Zelda put her hand on my arm. 'It's nice being with you again, Manas.'

We drove on in silence. We linked up with the Garden Route at George and went on to the Wilderness. Zelda insisted that we stop over at a hotel near the beach, where, she wistfully told me, her family had spent many holidays during her childhood. We booked in and spent the late afternoon walking along the beach. There was a strong swell pounding the shore, making a deafening noise. Zelda seemed unable to shake off a pervading sadness. When we got back to the hotel she told me she needed to be alone and went off to her room. I began to imagine my presence had something to do with her mood.

Zelda would not join me for dinner, so I ate alone. There was only a handful of people in the dining room when I went downstairs. I ordered the catch-of-the-day, a grilled galjoen. Feeling he had time on his hands, the manager spent a while chatting with me. He seemed an ambitious young man, full of confidence and swagger, keen to prove himself in the world. He sang the New South Africa's praises continually. When he heard I was back from Australia, he reprimanded me half-jokingly. 'Australia? That bloody place! Full of flies and convicts! Man, how could you leave South Africa? The best country on earth. The best people. And, ja, the best rugby. You watch us clean up the Wallabies this year!'

Realising, eventually, his jovial repartee amounted to one-way traffic, he gave me a firm handshake and moved off to attend to the other guests. I finished my meal, fretting about Zelda. Then I went upstairs and knocked on her door. There was no answer, but the door was unlocked so I went in. She was lying face down on the bed. I felt a terrible helplessness when she turned to look at me, her eyes red and swollen. I went over and sat awkwardly next to her. I put my hand on her shoulder.

'Is there anything I can do?' I asked. 'I hope I haven't offended you.'

She didn't respond.

'Say something, Zelda. Please tell me what I can do.'

'There's nothing you can do. You haven't offended me.'

'Do you want me to go?'

She shook her head. 'No. Please lie here with me.'

We lay there silently. Outside we could hear the surf crashing. Then I kissed her cheek and said what I'd been waiting a long time to say.

'Remember that last argument we had? Before you left me?'

She nodded.

'I'm sorry I hit you. Truly.'

Zelda turned over to face me. 'You're what?'

'Sorry I hit you. It's the worst thing I've ever done. I can never forgive myself.'

She sighed. 'Oh, that! Jesus, don't tell me you're still cut up by that. I hit you too, remember? I asked for it. It's past, Manas. Water under the bridge.'

'It was unforgivable. Nobody asks for that.'

'Shit,' she scoffed, 'you're not exactly a violent psychopath, you know. More a nerd, to be honest.'

'Thanks.'

Zelda chuckled and took my hand. 'It's past, Manas! We'd both reached the end of our tether. We were both screwed up. I don't even think about it anymore! I think about Helen. And I think about Helen's father and the time he has to make up to her.'

'And what about the time I have to make up to you?'

'You don't owe me anything. It takes two to tango. I'm as much to blame for everything.'

'You've always been too generous, Zelda.'

Zelda looked me in the eye. 'Generosity's got nothing to do with it.'

We were silent for a while, then I kissed her and asked, 'Still friends?'

She smiled. 'I'll always be your friend, Manas. Nothing will change that.'

I kissed her again, long and tenderly. We lay talking, knowing we were more than friends. Then I went back to my room. As the giant waves pounded the long beach in front of the hotel I lay awake thinking of her. I could still smell her perfume. I fell asleep aching with yearning and desire. Zelda was an angel come down to earth. No longer a sacred thing of virtue.

During the night I woke half a dozen times, not knowing if it was the roar of the surf outside or my fear of losing them, now that I had them so close, that disturbed me. I found myself obsessed with the question of place and belonging. Knowing how much Zelda needed the physicality of place to ward off loss, I probed myself for a sense of belonging. Why did my home at Langebaan mean so little? What had I forfeited by losing my sense of place and community? The inner distance I'd so carefully cultivated in Australia to cope with loss seemed suddenly strange and threatening.

I thought of Tak and my mother. I had banished the period when they were together to the most arid and desolate region of my heart, a place where memory barely survives. Was it because my memory of this time had no substance that its physical place, Langebaan, had no further relevance? Did the suppression of memory diminish me? I feared that it did; there was an absence of humanity in it, a denial of belonging but no sense of loss. Did the fact that I did not banish Zelda and Helen to the same desolate region of the heart offer grounds for hope? And if I failed to convince Zelda and Helen that I was worth keeping in their lives, to what part of my heart must I banish the memory of them so that I, Manas, could survive the finality of loss?

So many questions and no answers. Ja, the story of my life.

*

After a fitful sleep I managed to rouse Zelda early and we were on the road by 5.30. We made good time, stopping only once for petrol and a bite to eat at Humansdorp. We got to Grahamstown around noon. The place was packed with visitors there for the annual Arts Festival. We stopped first at the Settlers Monument to stretch our legs and look at the view. The Monument itself looked like a bazaar, festooned as it was with posters and banners advertising the various Festival shows. From Fort Selwyn adjacent to the Monument we looked out over the town that had changed our lives so completely. The university and Settler homes and shops down below, the great spire of the Anglican cathedral at the end of High Street, and the townships stretching up to Makana's

Kop in the distance. It was blowing a gale where we stood. Zelda soon went back to the car because she was cold, leaving me to ponder how little the place had changed. From a distance, at least.

We drove down through the town, past the Festival throngs and beggars waving cars into parking spots, down Somerset Street past the Drostdy Arch and Rhodes Art School. We turned into New Street and went along to where the old Masters' studios used to be. But now the double-storey building was a private dwelling, renovated almost beyond recognition – no longer the slightly rundown, turpentine-reeking sanctuary we remembered. The police station across the road was gone too – not a trace left of that dreary place that had been our stark reminder of South Africa's disintegration. Bulldozed from view, but not from mind. We drove past St Aidan's. It too had changed; the dilapidated old school was now a fancy hotel.

We bought boerewors rolls for lunch and strolled down High Street looking at the hawkers' wares as we ate. We watched a busker do a pretty inane performance. Then we looked for some accommodation for the night. We should have known better. With the influx of visitors everything was taken, so Zelda phoned an estate agent in Kenton and booked a cottage for the weekend. Zelda said we might not make it there before dark, so the agent said we could pick up the keys from his house and gave the address.

I was hoping for a chance to see Helen but Zelda persuaded me not to turn our reunion into an anticlimax.

'You have no sense of occasion, Manas! She's expecting you tomorrow. A fleeting glimpse of you now will just upset her.'

'Upset her?'

Zelda rolled her eyes. 'Yes, Manas. Upset her. Be dependable for once. You've been away ten years. This is a big moment for her. Don't spoil it by being your usual unpredictable self.'

That made no sense to me, but I placed my trust in Zelda's intuition. I had to admit, I wasn't fully prepared for it myself.

So we decided instead to front up to what she had to do and go down to the farm. We filled up with petrol and drove out of town along the Port Alfred road. For old time's sake we stopped off at the King William's Town bypass where Stoneleigh used to be. The place where the house once stood was now just an excavation. Of course, this came as no surprise. Still, it bothered me to see the huge scar where the house had been, to see how emphatically it had been gouged from the earth.

We went on down towards Bathurst and turned off along the dirt road to Martindale. The road was atrocious, forcing me to slow down to a crawl. We passed the dilapidated railway siding of Martindale, then took the Coombs turn-off, driving north into the sun, a plume of dust billowing behind the car. The pastures were looking dry, though most of the dams were full from good summer rains. We passed a few run-down homesteads with no sign of a living soul around. When I pointed them out to Zelda, she said, 'It's tough being a farmer in South Africa these days. People in rural areas like this live under constant threat. I'm not exaggerating. Hundreds have been killed in the past few years.'

I was amazed. 'That's news we never got in Australia. Are the killings political?'

Zelda shook her head. 'I suppose some are, but mostly it's just plain banditry.'

'Jesus, I had no idea it was that bad.'

'A lot of farmers have walked off the land because of it. I don't know how the ones left here along the Fish River stick it out when they're so vulnerable to attack. It makes me feel relieved my folks got out in time.'

'What's happened to the farm since?'

'The neighbour who bought us out just uses the land for grazing. Not that he got a bargain, considering the amount of stock theft going on. It was bad enough when my folks were here. Remember how my dad used to complain? It used to drive him insane.'

'Ja, I remember. I used to think it was a bit of a joke. A kind of sweet justice.'

'I did too. I never realised the old man was fighting a losing battle. They all are, the ones who're left.'

'Why do they persevere?'

'Settler spirit, I suppose.'

I shook my head and scoffed. 'Settler spirit! You bloody jingo, Zelda!'

'Give them some bloody credit, Manas. They're a pretty resilient bunch. You can't deny that.'

'Resilient? Crazy, maybe.'

Zelda laughed. 'Crazy and resilient. That about sums up the Eastern Cape farmer!'

'If the neighbour's only using Haslemere for grazing, what's happened to the house?'

'I don't know. I hear it's gone to ruin. We'll find out soon enough.'

We climbed a steep, winding pass and crested a ridge that dropped suddenly down into the Great Fish River valley. As we descended the vegetation changed to low thorn scrub and aloes. A warthog family foraging along the roadside scurried away into the bush at our approach, squealing loudly. We passed a few more dilapidated homesteads. Aside from the noise of our car, there was an eerie stillness which, to tell the truth, made me nervous. Since we'd turned off the main road we hadn't seen another vehicle. We, too, were silent, Zelda pensively gazing across at the river which had always been, for so many white South Africans, the symbolic dividing line between black and white Africa.

The signpost at the farm turn-off that had the Sutton family crest and the name *Haslemere* was gone. Zelda shrugged her shoulders philosophically but I could see that proud old Sutton stoicism faltering in her, so I hesitated for a while before crossing the cattle grid onto the farm. We drove along the winding road, now much in need of repair, to the north-facing slope where the house stood overlooking the river. I parked on what used to be the front lawn, now a bare patch of dirt. As we got out the spooky stillness seemed to descend like a weight on us. The only signs of life were a few mud huts miles across the river and some cattle grazing on a far pasture. Two turtle doves flew off from the ruined house as we approached. I was so jumpy the sudden clatter of their wings nearly made me shit myself.

No doubt, Zelda's worst fears were realised. The once extensive gardens had been consumed by the surrounding bush, the stone rockeries and birdbaths drab reminders of their former splendour. The house had been stripped of literally everything that could be removed and carried away. Only the stone block shell remained; it had been reduced to an empty relic, like the adjoining tower with gun slits built in the last century. Now bougainvillea creepers had taken over, enveloping the exterior, making us stoop to enter the building. We walked through the rooms that had once rung to the sounds of six generations of the Sutton family. Zelda didn't speak as she contemplated each desolate space, emitting only a sigh now and then. When we came to the kitchen she sat down on the dirty stone floor. I could see she was fighting back tears.

'Oh, God, Manas,' she sighed.

I sat down next to her. She looked up at the sky through the creepers and laughed bitterly. 'Well, it's certainly *different*, as my mother would say.'

I smiled lamely. She raised her hands and dropped them.

'God, what *would* my mother say!'

Her voice faltered. Helplessly, I felt the rout of her life.

'Shit, Manas, this is so hard. I suppose I should've expected it. But there's nothing left. Nothing! It's all gone.'

I had no words to offer.

'I can't bear it. Life seems so bloody abstract. So damn transient and futile. I can't even feel them. It's as if my family never existed, as if my whole life here was just a dream.'

She wiped her eyes. 'I suppose that's life, hey? Nothing's certain. People come and go like nomads. Leaving only memories. The trouble is I can't live off memories. Memories have no substance. I need people. I need my family. I'm lost without them.'

I put my arm around her.

'Say something, Manas. Make it easier, please.'

I floundered, then said, 'I know it's painful, Zelda. I know you still grieve for John. But think of what you still have. You still have your family. Your parents. You still have Helen. It's not the end of the world. A few days ago you told me to look ahead. To stop dwelling in the past. I think you should do the same.'

'I know. I keep telling myself that. It just scares me that everything we were, everything we amounted to, can be wiped off the face of the earth. Just like that. Why do we have hearts, Manas? Just to feel pain? What's the bloody purpose?'

'Don't be bitter, Zelda. Think of Helen. Think of what you still have.'

Zelda looked up at the cracked walls of the house.

'I'm not bitter, Manas. I have no right to be bitter. I suppose I'm just scared of life. I suppose I wish everything would go back to what it was, so John could be alive. You're right, I still grieve for him. I can't let go. Even now I almost expect him to suddenly appear. To come and tell me this is all a bad dream. Some cruel joke. I just wish the pain would stop.'

'It will. One day.'

'That's what everyone says. The stupid shrinks I went to all said it'll pass, it's part of the grieving process. Process! God, how I hated them for their textbook understanding of loss! It's not quantifiable, Manas. You can't measure loss.'

'Think of what you still have, Zelda.'

She shook her head. 'I can't breathe in here, Manas. Let's go.'

We got up and made our way outside. We walked past torn-down sheds and the guest cottage where we'd once stayed, now derelict. I followed Zelda to the crest of the hill behind the house where a tall stone marker stood. Beneath this simple granite obelisk, in the earth that had formed him, lay John's remains. A bronze plaque on the stone read:

In Loving Memory
John William Sutton
1961 – 1994
Rest Forever in Peace

Zelda knelt down on her haunches next to the stone. She touched the earth and closed her eyes.

'Do you want me to leave you alone?' I asked.

She nodded. 'Just for a while, Manas. Don't go far, please.'

I walked off down the hill to a rocky outcrop and sat shivering in the late afternoon sunshine. I could see Zelda's kneeling figure near the stone. I could see the ruined homestead and beyond, in layers of fading blue, the river valley stretching out as far as the eye could see. In the stillness I made my own peace with John. The small sounds of doves and beetles seemed to sharpen the stillness. The sun had gone down when she called me. I returned to the grave and stood next to her. She took my hand.

'It's nice up here,' she said. 'Really nice and peaceful.' She ran her hand over the plaque. 'I feel I can almost let go. I feel he's at peace. Truly at peace. Do you believe in an afterlife, Manas?'

I shrugged. 'I don't know. I try to, I suppose.'

Zelda smiled. 'Sceptics never quite make the final hurdle, hey?'

'No. We can only stumble along behind those with hope and idealism.'

She laughed, emptily. 'You haven't lost your old sarcastic flair.'

'I wasn't being entirely sarcastic.'

'I'm sorry. I shouldn't tease you, Manas. I don't have any answers either. I also struggle to believe. For a sceptic, there's a lot more substance in your life than mine right now.'

'Depends what you mean by substance.'

We stood at the stone for a while longer. Then Zelda said, 'Thanks for coming here with me, Manas. It was important. I had to come.'

'I know.'

'I don't think I could've come on my own.'

'I'll bring you back whenever you want.'

'Do you promise?'

'I promise, Zelda.'

'You better not let me down.'

'When have I ever let you down?'

She kissed me and laughed. 'You prodigal misfit!'

We drove back in silence. It was dark by the time we got to Kenton. We picked up the key from the estate agent who directed us down to the cottage next to the river. Zelda unpacked some things for Helen in the bedroom across the passage from ours. We washed and went looking for a place to eat. I called Helen from a public phone near the shops. I said we'd fetch her tomorrow after school. I couldn't help saying I loved her. It made her cry. I didn't know if that was good or bad. She said Zelda had explained everything to her. I didn't know if that was good or bad either. We had dinner at a pub. Zelda's mood seemed cheerful as we ate. She joked about my abstinence, saying I'd drunk up more than my life's quota years ago. But I knew she was hiding a lingering sadness. I asked if she was okay. She smiled and said, 'Let's not complicate things tonight, Manas.'

When we got back to the cottage we sat in the lounge and talked a bit. I was tired and anxious about seeing Helen. When I got up to go to bed Zelda put her arms around me and pulled me close. 'Sleep with me tonight,' she said. 'I need you.' And so we made love in an aura of sadness, in the shadow of transience and futility. We explored our bodies like the places of our past. Zelda clung to me with a desperation that scared me, and it was only when she fell asleep that she let go. I lay awake, dazed by the sweetness and pain. I reached out under the blankets and caressed Zelda's naked form. I followed the curve of her spine, I slid my fingers over her hips, entranced by her nearness. I kissed the nape of her neck, thanking God for her and for Helen. And I was bereft of my former cynicism, convinced again of miracles. And it came to me that we all break and bleed. It is the suffering that makes us accountable to each other. It is the suffering by which we measure our love …

*

And so my day of reckoning has arrived. The point at which flesh and blood intersects again and where hope is the only thing I can cling to. And here, at the end of this journey that will bleed into another, I find myself hesitant with words. I have no profound message to give, no lesson to teach, except to say that inner distance is no cure for loss. Inner distance is our way of surviving loss, but it is no cure. The journey that lies ahead, across that distance, to the heart of my child now fills me with the true magnitude of what might or might not be regained. If nothing else, I understand this.

I was up early this morning, before daybreak. There was a full moon shining over the sea. Small clouds were racing across the sky, heralding another windy day. I sat outside on the veranda and drank a cup of coffee. There was a stillness about the moon that was deeply alluring. Distant and serene, it seemed to gently mock the small clouds racing to and fro around the world. I wondered if my Khoi ancestors worshipped the moon for its stillness.

We left for Grahamstown after breakfast so that Zelda could take in a few exhibitions. 'Might as well write a review while I'm here,' she said. So we spent the morning doing the rounds. Needless to say my attention wasn't on art. I vaguely recall the expressive technique of Nhlanhla Xaba, the Young Artist of the Year, whose work was on show up at the Monument. Zelda went from painting to painting, writing down notes. 'Nice work,' she said, 'but I can already hear gloomy accusations of affirmative-action prejudice from certain quarters.' I also vaguely recall the paintings and drawings at Rhodes Art School by one of the lecturers (one of what seems to have been a clean sweep of teaching staff since our days there). Pretty frank depictions of naked girls and boys that had been the subject of much recent controversy. The media were calling it the 'child porn' exhibition. Again, Zelda walked around writing notes and shaking her head. 'This stuff is valid – what are those boneheads talking about!' she exclaimed. I can't say I had much of an opinion. I just remember thinking: Is this what it takes to make a splash these days?

As I say, my thoughts have not been on art. An incessant wind blows as we wait in the car beneath the jacarandas across the road from the school. By my watch, the kids should have been out ten minutes ago. Well, Zelda did say it was pointless getting here early.

Twice I've walked up and down the street, hands in pockets, kicking at leaves swirling in the wind. Zelda has been reading the newspaper, fuming over the 'child porn' debate which, once again, is front-page news. When I got back to the car, she said, 'For God's sake, calm down, Manas. You're making me nervous.'

'Easy for you to say, Zelda.'

'Oh, Manas. I know what this means to you. But just … just don't go overboard, okay? You don't want to scare her off. You don't want her to think you're some kind of psycho nutcase or something! Come on, get in the car and calm down.'

So now I sit next to her, eyes closed, breathing deeply, listening to her go on.

'Can you believe it, Manas? The Deputy Minister of Home Affairs, no less, is talking about prosecuting the artist. About banning the exhibition. God, we're still in the Dark Ages! Nobody's learnt to distinguish. I mean, nobody in their right mind condones pornography, least of all child pornography, but did you honestly think that work was pornographic?'

'I couldn't give a shit what it was, Zelda! This is not the time or place to be talking about child pornography!'

Zelda sighs and shakes her head. 'It's ridiculous! I give up. When a bloody politician who hasn't even *seen* an exhibition wants to *prosecute* an artist on *hearsay* … Jesus! The whole thing's moronic! Don't they understand it's the artist's bloody job to explore the limits of experience? To explore life for meaning? Not just paint pretty pictures. If that means taking on the tough issues, like sexuality, even *child* sexuality, that's part of it, for Christ sake! I mean, just because a painting shows a vagina or a penis, does that mean it's pornography? Does it?'

'Zelda, I don't want to talk about pornography. Especially not child pornography.'

'But it's not child pornography! That's the point!'

I am about to say to hell with art and artists, that I couldn't give a damn if artists took all their crappy, arrogant, pea-brained notions of exploring life for the benefit of humanity (as if humanity will perish without the shit of life being shoved in its face) and stuck it where it belonged. But, thankfully, no such outburst is necessary. The girls have started filtering out to their parents' cars. I get out and wait. I watch while other kids kiss their parents. I watch them throw suitcases in the boots of expensive cars and drive off.

Then I see her coming through the gates, dressed smartly in her green uniform and carrying a small suitcase, one of the few dark faces among the throng of girls. She walks with a complex-ridden awkwardness, one slightly plump adolescent girl among others, eyes downcast beneath the brim of her straw boater. One of her friends calls her name and she looks up, smiles, and waves goodbye. Then she glances up and down the street. Now she sees me and pauses across the road, and in this moment, in her shy, beautiful face, in the nervous, searching look in her eyes, I see my purpose.